382

POST STORIES OF 1941

POST STORIES
OF 1941

WESLEY WINANS STOUT, *Editor*

Associate Editors:

A. W. NEALL, E. N. BRANDT, RICHARD THRUELSEN,
MARTIN SOMMERS, STUART ROSE, ALAN R. JACKSON

W. THORNTON MARTIN, *Art Editor*

L. B. KRITCHER, *Associate Art Editor*

BOSTON

LITTLE, BROWN AND COMPANY

1942

CONTENTS

POST STORIES OF 1941

AFTERNOON OFF

By Glenn Allan

Boysi scuffed his towel over the last dinner plate, stacked it with the others and paused, head bent toward the swinging door. There was no sound from the front of the house. Moving with an air of suppressed excitement, he opened the vegetable bin, scraped aside a layer of potatoes and drew out an oblong package. Even in his haste he was careful to wind the string in a loop, to fold the wrapping paper, but his hands trembled as he fondled the contents — a pair of unbelievably pointed shoes of patent leather.

"Sister, bar the do'!" His feet beat a pattern of delight on the kitchen floor. "Sharp like a needle and big as a boat, new shoes, don't you never lead me wrong."

Tenderly, Boysi set his treasures on the window sill above the sink. He frowned. This was a no-good window; the frosted panes could not be looked through and they let in such feeble light that the beautiful shoes scarcely glistened. Strictly no good, this window.

He filled a kettle and turned on the stove by clicking all the switches until the place where he held his hand grew warm. There he set the kettle and turned off most of the unused switches. The refrigerator yielded celery, olives and the remains of the dinner chicken. Boysi considered defrosting the box, but one of the trays could still be pried loose with the bread knife, so he reconsidered and started making the salad for supper.

"Herbert!"

Boysi stiffened. No one called him Herbert except the madam and the police recorder. Judge Yeaton was unlikely to be prowling around on a Sunday afternoon, so this had to be the madam. He cast a worried glance about the kitchen and bent to his task.

"Her-bert, why don't you answer me?"

Boysi treated this as the rhetorical question which repetition had made it.

"Where is the cleaning fluid?" Mrs. Oates paused in the door. She was a pretty little woman, but with the harried, faintly defensive manner of a woman in an otherwise masculine household. "Did you give the boys something for their picnic supper?"

"Kah-ka-ka!" laughed Boysi heartily. "Them boys strip' my kitchen like a plague of locus'es. Cake and p'loney and all the breakfast eggs. I had to wrastle Junior to the flo' for this very same chicken."

Mrs. Oates shook benzine on a cloth and dabbed at the mass of pink satin over her arm. "How on earth did this hideous stain get on my bedspread?"

"Well, what do you know!" Boysi cried with vast astonishment. "That must of happened the time Larry's dawg was sniffin' around the p'fooms on your dressin' table."

"Herbert! I don't want you to call baby by that ugly name. Call him Laurence, if you must. Furthermore, the dog isn't allowed in the house."

"Ten p'licemans couldn't keep 'at dawg in the yard. He just sifts in th'u the cracks. That li'l' old greasy spot come when I run over to coax him from the p'foom bottles. Nat'ly, I had to drop the boss' boots I was polishin'." He cast about for a diversion and spied the kettle on the stove. "I'm fixin' to set a wine jelly. Boss sure does fancy a wine jelly with a smidge o' rum in the whiff' cream."

Mrs. Oates sniffed. "I ordered strawberries. Herbert, you didn't let the boys take the berries? You know that they always give baby an awful rash."

Boysi glowered. "What kind of baby? Ol' Larry is goin' on for ten years old."

"Remind me to speak to the butcher," Mrs. Oates said coldly. "That chicken today was very tough."

"It didn't eat so meller, for a fact," Boysi agreed. "That was Junior's old rooster. Junior been plaguin' me for 'most a year to buy 'at old rooster out the housekeepin' money."

He shelled eggs and set them, quartered, around his salad; sprinkled capers. He did these things mechanically and with one eye over his shoulder, for the madam was definitely conjuring up a task. This was one time Boysi wanted no extra work. This was a second Sunday; this was his afternoon off.

"Herbert! Whose shoes are these?"

Women certainly do ask the silliest questions. Boysi made a little swirl of mayonnaise, topped it with a peeled white grape and stepped back. "Lovely," he crooned. "Stric'ly a lovely sallit."

"I dislike capers," Mrs. Oates objected.

"You do?" cried Boysi in vast astonishment. "Well, you just shovel 'em off on the boss' plate. Boss sure do love them pickled li'l' buckshots."

Mrs. Oates sighed. "I declare I don't know why I put up with all this. A person might think I didn't count in my own home. Capers for Mr. Oates, the housekeeping money for Junior's ancient rooster, strawberries for ba—for Laurence. . . . Herbert, stop that noise and let me remember what I wanted you to do this afternoon."

Boysi redoubled his clatter with pans and spoons as he measured port wine, orange juice and sugar. He sprinkled gelatin over cold water and plunged into a closet for the rum bottle.

"Just this once," begged Mrs. Oates, "can't we have vanilla in the cream? You know that rum disagrees with me."

"Boss can't abide p'nilla," said Boysi firmly.

Mrs. Oates pushed open the screen door and hung her bedspread to dry in the shade. As she repassed the icebox, Boysi held his breath; there was a sort of gamy odor that he hadn't been able to locate.

"Why hasn't the lawn been mowed?" demanded the madam. "And I distinctly remember telling you to make ice cream for dinner. It's no use begging again for an electric churn; the boys would have it in pieces within a week. One of these days, young man, I am going to lose all patience with you."

She paused, but Boysi knew better than to offer rebuttal. He cocked his head and the madam stamped her foot.

"Don't try that on! Every time I start scolding, you pretend to hear the telephone. Another thing, when you empty ash trays, do not do so behind the greens in the fireplaces. I bought an expensive garbage pail —— "

"I don't like 'at bucket," moaned Boysi, snatching at a straw. "Ol' bucket bites me."

Mrs. Oates tottered.

"Ol' lid bites me. Look." Boysi held out a massive paw, across the back of which was a deep bruise.

"Oh! But I have told you to keep your foot on the pedal. Like this." The madam pressed the treadle, and the cover rose majestically. She lifted her foot and the lid fell with a heavy clang.

Boysi shuddered. "I likes the kind of bucket you can stric'ly th'ow things at. Like when I sep'rates eggs for uh angel cake. Twelve eggs and I got to make twelve long trips over there. Ever' time I chunks in a shell I got to duck, else I'll lose me a finger —— "

His voice trailed away in stricken horror, for the madam had trod on the pedal again. This time the lid did not slam shut. With flushed face and panting breath, the madam prodded through the refuse with the handle of a dish mop. She made a birdlike grab and turned. Boysi backed away, holding the mold of jelly against his chest. The mixture was hot and he was forced to juggle it from hand to hand, blowing on his fingers, but he feared parting from even such meager protection.

"Oh, dear!" wailed Mrs. Oates. "My gorgeous crystal vase!"

Boysi's deprecatory laugh ended in a cough that almost strangled him. "Shucks, ma'am, there wasn't no more give to that vase than a li'l' old soapy bubble. I no more than breshed against it wit' my broom handle —— "

The madam's stony eyes drove him into silence. She turned back to the garbage pail and tenderly laid her treasure to rest. As she straightened, all the horrid disappointments of the day came trooping through her remembrance. The violated bedspread, the uneatable chicken, the fireplace littered with rubbish. "Herbert!" The unmowed lawn, the flavor of rum, the outrageous food that would surely sicken the boys. Mentally, she laid out the castor oil, the

water bottles and her second-best kimono. "Herbert!" The strawberries; preposterous to say that baby was growing up, when he was
only nine. Then she knew that her younger son, like his brother, had
passed beyond that period of helpless dependence and was not far, if
not already there, from the barrier males build for their mutual profit
and against all women. She felt dreadfully alone.

"Herbert," she said, and her throat was choked with sobs, "I cannot go on like this; I simply won't go on. I must have a woman in
the kitchen. Herbert, hang up your apron and go. I will mail a
check for the month's wages."

Boysi set the jelly on the floor and stepped over it. "Ma'am, you
know I didn't mean to break 'at li'l' old dish. Anybody could have
uh accident wit' a broom handle. I have that kind of uh accident all
the time." He drew a deep breath. "I tell you what, ma'am; you
take it out my wages. You go ahead and do that." He paused, and
then his voice rose in shrill incredulity, "You mean I is truly fired?
Why, I nat'ly can't get fired today! I — I got reasons to need my
job!"

"I won't listen!" Mrs. Oates' voice soared to the rim of hysteria.
"Don't you dare go to Mr. Oates, either! He has saved you before,
but this time I have reached the end of my tether! . . . Don't flap
your ears, Herbert! Don't!"

"May I die uh unsanctified sinner," moaned Boysi, "if the telefoam
ain't ree'ly ringin'. But wait —— "

The door closed. Had it not been a swinging door, it would have
slammed.

Boysi's eyes puckered, his mouth opened in a howl of dismay,
"Ma'am, you stric'ly can't fire me today! You can't do such a thing!
Why — why, today I'm gettin' married!"

Mr. Oates was a simple man and his pleasures were simple, chief-
est of them a Sunday afternoon spent in a state of complete inertia.
He dropped his paper to the terrace floor, dislodged the cat from his
chest and adjusted his chair to the position marked Full Recline.
The radio was tuned until the orchestra was no more than a bleat of

brasses, an occasional whimper from the string section, and with a sigh of content he glanced at the sun, calculating that he had two hours before lowering the awning or moving his chair. Even that remote necessity made him frown.

The sun had not shifted an inch before he stiffened in dismay at a too-familiar sound within the house. A chair scraped, heels bit quick little steps from the floor and the screen door slammed.

"Guess who telephoned?" demanded Mrs. Oates. Mr. Oates tried to put into a groan all his boundless disinterest, but his wife hurried on, "You would never guess. Just passing through, but of course I asked them to supper and overnight. The guest room is ready. Or is it? I meant to tell Herbert to clean the woodwork. Oh, dear, this would have to be Sunday, with everything closed. John, don't you suppose Mr. Carmody would open his store? I simply must have some squabs. Mushrooms. I want cream and some of that quick-freeze asparagus and raspberries. John, do you hear what I say?"

"No," mumbled Mr. Oates.

"You just wake up at once, John Oates. After all, I cannot cope single-handed. Not all the time. What's the good of you and Mr. Carmody being lodge brothers if he is no use at a time like this? Call him up and give the cry of distress, or whatever it is."

"Laura!" cried Mr. Oates in horror. He sat up, brushing imaginary crumbs from his lap. "I will thank you not to discuss matters of which you don't know the meaning — of! The idea! What do you think a lodge —— Well, it most certainly is not."

"You boys in men's clothing," laughed Mrs. Oates lightly. Her frown returned. "Do you know anybody in that new grocery on Braley Street?"

Mr. Oates said huffily that his factory made furniture; he did not cater to the grocery trade. He knew nobody who would sell mushrooms on a Sunday afternoon and, furthermore, he cared less than a great deal for mushrooms.

Still furthermore, he was trying to sl—— to enjoy a symphony orchestra. He suggested that Mrs. Oates take a nice, refreshing nap.

"Sh!" said Mrs. Oates absently. "I am trying to remember what I have on hand. I'll run out and check with Herbert."

"Boysi's long gone," grunted her husband.

"Gone? He can't be. Herbert never leaves without a word with me."

"Probably didn't care to interrupt your telephoning. Told me, instead. Isn't this his afternoon off?"

"But he always stays on in emergencies. He is supposed to do that."

"Hmph! Seems to me you generally concoct an emergency on Boysi's day off."

"You are not amusing. Herbert gets every other Sunday off."

Mr. Oates eyed her curiously. "I wonder if you know just when Boysi got off last? Two weeks ago he stayed to stake chrysanthemums. Two weeks before that you asked the Phelpses to tea. Before that —— "

"Perfectly absurd!" cried Mrs. Oates, her color rising. "I — I don't believe it. In any case, it doesn't matter to Herbert. It isn't as though he had a family to visit. Staying on here keeps him out of mischief."

"A typically feminine argument," growled her husband. He filled his pipe deliberately and suddenly pointed it at Mrs. Oates. "I chanced to probe Boysi just now, and I was astonished. Boysi hasn't had a full afternoon in five months."

"That can't be true," faltered Mrs. Oates. "He should have reminded me. Herbert is like the rest of you — you men in this house. You expect me to remember everything and to be infallible as a machine. Well, I am not a machine. Herbert never complained. I will say that for him; he was most obliging."

"Was obliging?" repeated Mr. Oates.

Mrs. Oates dabbled at her lips. "I discharged Herbert after dinner today. He provoked me until I simply could not cope any longer." She glanced at her husband's shocked face and went on rapidly, "My lovely spread, my strawberries —— John, do you know what Herbert did? He smashed my gorgeous crystal vase!"

"You fired Boysi?" shouted Mr. Oates. "Because he broke a silly little —— Laura, are you feeling well? Hadn't you better take a tonic?" He mopped his brow with stiff, angry gestures. "I never heard of such folly in my life. Boysi is the best servant we ever had. The kids are crazy about him."

"I want a woman cook, for a change!" wailed Mrs. Oates. "Then you will see real service in this house."

"Hmph, hmph!" went Mr. Oates in a peevish humor. "I thank you to remember that I sold furniture in every state in the South. Always on expense account and stopping at the best hotels. I guess I know service, and Boysi suits me fine."

"Herbert is trifling and wouldn't lift a hand to help us. He is stupid and never uses his head. Also, he sweeps dust under the rugs."

Mr. Oates pointed out that Boysi was the first cook who did not strain all the goodness from the fruit juices. "You can forget this nonsense," he finished peremptorily. "I like Boysi; I depend on him a lot. He washes the car and mows the lawn."

"Not always. He had the impudence to tell me that the lawn mower has vanished."

Mr. Oates glared. "Ed Carmody borrowed it Friday. I could have told you, had you asked." He paused and stared at his wife almost with pity. "So you fired Boysi without a word to me? And today, of all days."

"Why not today? He broke my crystal —— "

"Because Boysi is getting married. Because he has been trying to get married for months, but each Sunday you 'faced an emergency' and the bridegroom could not be spared."

"You are making that up," panted Mrs. Oates. "John, you are acting like a spoiled child. I have troubles of my own, plenty of troubles. Capers on the salad, shoes on the window sill and, now, the Meltons inviting themselves to supper."

"Do you mean Sam Melton? You're crazy. Sam lives in New York. I had a big order from him last week."

Mrs. Oates sighed. "Listen, dear, and try to understand. Mr. and Mrs. Melton are on an auto trip. They telephoned from downtown. They gushed over Southern hospitality and surprise visits being so jolly — there's the story. My story. But of course your precious

Herbert means more than your factory's biggest customer. Herbert is getting married, so the Meltons can feed on — on husks. Mr. Melton is just a millionaire. They are just the people who entertained us so elaborately when we went to the World's Fair."

Mr. Oates swung his fat legs over the side of the couch and sat up. "I've got it," he said presently. "We'll take them into town for dinner."

"Splendid! I have just had an earful of the Meltons' weariness with hotel food."

Mr. Oates padded across the terrace and back. "You'll have to scrape up a meal somehow. You aren't absolutely helpless, are you?" He snapped his fingers. "Boysi probably fixed something for our supper."

"Chicken salad and a mold of jelly. The Meltons will think they are at the Ducky-Wucky Tea Room. Get the car, John, and go after Herbert. Tell him I will pay for the extra work."

Mr. Oates lit his pipe and hurled the match into the shrubbery. "Boysi will dearly love favoring us after being booted off the place. Well, I shan't ask him. It wouldn't be right. That kid has been stopped from getting married by us. Every penny of his savings has gone into furniture. His girl is getting fed up with these delays. Boysi says she told him either to show up this afternoon or not bother to call around again. I'll not interfere." He reached over, patted his wife's shoulders. "Now, Laura, you are upsetting yourself over nothing. Surely you can manage a little supper for two friends."

Mrs. Oates blew her nose. "Perhaps you never noticed that Mrs. Melton keeps a butler and three maids?"

"What of it? I bet she never tasted decent fried chicken. That's the stuff to give them; fry up a couple of chickens —— What's the matter? Can't you even fry a chicken?"

Mrs. Oates swallowed uneasily. "Are Junior's hens in the back yard the proper sort for frying? Suppose you run out and kill a pair."

"Who, me? I never killed a chicken in my life. Well, think of something else. My gosh, I thought all women knew how to cook."

"I suppose you thought it comes natural. Like long hair and a bust measure. I was brought up by an aunt with a liking for restaurants. I taught school and boarded until I married you."

"Pity I wasn't a poor man," laughed Mr. Oates with heavy sarcasm. "You would have had to learn to cook."

Mrs. Oates drew a deep breath. "Had you been a poor man, perhaps I wouldn't have married you."

"Is that so?"

"Yes, that's so!"

Angry silence flooded the terrace, hurt pride and bewilderment. Mr. Oates recovered first and laughed again with even less humor. "It has taken fifteen years of married life to bring matters to the surface."

"Believe me, John Oates, the years have s-seemed just as long to me. If you want to call quits, I am ready. I am capable of supporting myself and — and the boys. F-fortunately, I have an education."

"College never taught you to get along with people," the man growled. He shook his head, as though to clear it, and stretched out a placating hand. "Laura —— "

"Don't touch me! You cannot lose your temper and then make peace so quickly! . . . What people can't I get along with?"

"Ah, Laura."

"What people, John Oates?"

"If you must know, I was thinking of poor little Boysi, chased off the place on his wedding day. I was thinking of me and the kids, our comfort sacrificed for the sake of an absurd vase that a decent goldfish wouldn't inhabit."

"That finishes it! I am taking the boys to my aunt tonight. Entertain your precious Meltons at the hotel. Take them to — to Jericho, for all I care."

Mr. Oates leaped from his chair, his round face puckered in alarm. "Laura, you aren't serious. You can't do a thing like this. No matter how much you — you dislike me, there's our futures to consider.

The Meltons are very strait-laced people. Promise you'll stay at least until after they have gone."

Mrs. Oates put away her handkerchief. "On one condition."

"Anything. I will do whatever you say."

"Then get the car and go after Herbert."

"No," said Mr. Oates stubbornly. "I won't do that."

"Then I shall pack my bag. Immediately. . . . Oh, Lord, there's a car at the gate!"

Mr. Oates moved the garden hose, his paint cans and three barrows of rubbish from the other half of the garage and, after a great deal of shouting and gesturing, managed to get Sam Melton's big sedan under cover. He ducked irritably as the other joined him in the driveway and attempted a friendly slap on the shoulders.

"A lovely drive, John. You and Mrs. Oates certainly live in Nature's bountiful lap. City dwellers like Mrs. Melton and myself ought to make these impromptu trips more often. Smell that air. Bracing! I warn you, it's given me an appetite like a two-year-old."

Mr. Oates smiled weakly. He said in a placating voice, "Laura, wouldn't you like to show Mrs. Melton through the garden?"

"I am afraid there's no time. After all, I am the kitchen staff to-night." Her laugh was not very successful. "I warn you all that we shall eat entirely from cans."

"I am not worrying," chuckled Mrs. Melton. She was an ample person who looked as though a poor meal would really worry her. "I know the reputation of you Southern women as cooks. I wager you have thousands of old recipes tucked away."

"Mint!" cried Melton suddenly and plunged across a bed of petunias. "I never saw it growing before. Isn't it wonderful? . . . John, you must make some juleps. I bet they will be juleps to remember. The heart of the Old South, and juleps are definitely called for."

"John is very proud of his juleps." Mrs. Oates smiled. "His poker crowd keep Herbert busy —— " She broke off and swallowed.

"John," she said anxiously, "I suppose you can make juleps?"

"Eh? Oh, certainly. Nothing to juleps." He, too, swallowed. "I tell you, Sam, juleps take a long time. An awful long time. May have to give you a rain check on the juleps. But there's some Scotch, I think. . . . Laura, have we any soda?"

"You must ask Herb— Perhaps the drugstore will send some over." She turned to Mrs. Melton. "Such an inconvenience, living in a suburb. No proper stores open on Sunday, and the servants we get! I leave it to your imagination. . . . What did you say, John?"

"It doesn't bear repeating! . . . Sam, suppose you and I shake up a few drinks, and then we will run into town for dinner."

"I wouldn't dream of it," gushed Mrs. Melton. "The sight of a hotel menu turns me positively green. I think I shall just slip into something loose, the better to enjoy our little dinner here." She stroked Mrs. Oates' cheek. "Now, don't go to a great deal of trouble, dear. Just give us whatever you usually have when friends drop in. I should offer to help, but I feel sure you don't want me prying around your kitchen. I might steal some of your wonderful recipes."

"Yes, wonderful!" muttered Mrs. Oates, and cast a look of desperation toward her husband. . . . "John, I don't suppose you would care to help?"

Mr. Oates paused. He said uneasily, "Sam, wouldn't you like a couple of he-man steaks sent out from the hotel? Nice, thick steaks with —— "

"I can eat steaks anywhere," Melton grunted. "What I look forward to is something particular to this section. . . . Do you get bouillabaisse here, Mrs. Oates, or is that farther south?"

"I wouldn't know, Mr. Melton. What color can does it come in?"

"Ha-ha!" Melton shook a roguish finger. He followed the path around the house and stumbled over his host, transfixed in his steps. "What's the matter, man?"

"The awning," mumbled Mr. Oates. "I certainly never lowered it."

"Makes a mighty cool retreat, old boy. And what's this?"

"Oh-h!" cried Mrs. Melton, and clapped her hands in girlish affectation. "You naughty, naughty people. Frightening Sam and me with your starvation stories, and all the time —— "

A figure in immaculate white jacket emerged from the house. The figure set down a tray that was silver and frost and the cool fragrance of mint. The figure came forward and took Mrs. Melton's wrap, bowed to Mr. Melton.

"Rest your hat, suh? It's a stric'ly fine day for juleps befo' dinner."

Mr. Oates put on his bathrobe and went into the dressing room for the late news broadcast. On the table was a glass of fruit juice, richly thick, flanked by his favorite salt wafers; the tobacco jar was full and the pipe rack bristled with long, competent matches. Sighing pleasurably, he sank into his chair and flicked the radio switch.

He did not glance up as his wife entered, but said diffidently, "Are the Meltons tucked away?"

She made no reply; simply bowed her head and started toward the bedroom. Midway, she turned and crossed back to make a totally unnecessary adjustment of the draperies. This brought her very close to Mr. Oates, but she ignored him, kept her back toward him. He sat rigid, and then, suddenly grinning, reached out and pulled her to the arm of his chair.

"Stop," she whispered hoarsely, but made no struggle and presently lay quietly against his shoulder. "There's the telephone."

"Let it ring. Didn't I hear the boys come in?"

She nodded. "There isn't a sign of rash on baby from the strawberries. Perhaps he is growing out of —— " She broke off, swallowing hard. Then she said, firmly accenting the name, "Larry's chest is almost as well developed as Junior's, though there's three years' difference." She rubbed her cheek against Mr. Oates' shoulder. "They looked so scrubbed and so — so dependable after their bathes. With all the Meltons' money, I don't envy them a single butler."

Mr. Oates sipped his drink, wiped his mouth neatly and kissed his wife's ear. "Seven butlers couldn't match that dinner we had to-night. Or run a house better than ours. . . . Come in, Boysi; we were just admiring your cooking."

"Yassuh? That swimp bisque like to gone wrong. I was ironin' me out a clean jacket and it come within a lick of reachin' a boil."

Mrs. Oates sat up, tucking in the ends of her hair. "The chicken pilau scored with the Meltons. Where did you get hold of things on Sunday?"

Boysi hung Mr. Oates' freshly pressed suit over a chair and returned to his place at the door. "Fella I know cleans sto' for Mr. Carmody and I figgered he'd have a key."

"Look," cut in Mr. Oates. "It was lucky for us you came back this afternoon. How did that happen?"

"I forgot something," Boysi muttered. "The madam had my mind so lathered I went off without my jab-toed shoes." He moved self-consciously, and light glistened on patent leather. "I hadn't no business in the gues' room, but I needed me a shoehorn, and that's how come I see the comp'ny's satchels. I knew right off a little dab of sallit and wine jelly wouldn't do for this kind of comp'ny. From the size of their clothes, I figgered they was stric'ly big feeders."

Mr. Oates prodded his wife with a rude elbow. "That's the boy you said never used his head." His chuckle died a-borning and he cleared his throat diffidently. "Did — did you get married this afternoon?"

"Nossuh," said Boysi tonelessly. "I didn't get married."

There was a long silence. Mr. Oates struck a match to his pipe and found he had forgotten to fill it. "We'll set that right!" he cried loudly. "Next Sunday, by golly, you can have the whole day off! How's that, huh? Your gal won't mind waiting another week, will she?"

"That gal, suh?" Boysi raised his eyes. They were expressionless. "Fella I know just telefoam' me. That gal done got married."

Mr. Oates coughed shatteringly and took off his spectacles. "What about the furniture you bought?"

"They had to sell 'at furniture for travelin' money. Fella got a job in Al'bama or some sich furrin place." His shining toe sketched an idle pattern on the rug, slowly scuffed it out. "I don't believe I was ree'ly in a swivet to get married. I didn't act'ly need my jab-toed shoes to stand befo' the preacher; no law says you got to have new shoes. The closer I got to the church the mo' I figgered what I was givin' up to marry 'at gal. I kept slowin' down and slowin' down. Like a streak of lightnin' it come over me 'bout my shoes on the window sill." He slowly raised his eyes. "Boss," he said simply, "I wouldn't of been happy with 'at gal. I don't believe 'at gal loved me any stric'ly too much."

"Everything turns out for the best," gulped Mrs. Oates. "Herbert, I have decided to raise you two dollars a week."

Boysi evaded her eyes. He said vaguely, "That No'thern lady offered me big money to work for her."

"What?" shrilled Mrs. Oates in outrage. "The idea! People ought to be jailed for stealing cooks! I've a mind to wake up those Meltons and —— "

"Calm down," commanded her husband. . . . "Boysi, how did this occur?"

"It was when the lady come out for the corn-puddin' ressypee. She kept sayin' how lucky y'all was and did I have a happy life with y'all. I told her I didn't work here no more. I said the madam done fire me. She forbid me goin' to the boss, so I must be stric'ly fired."

"Absurd!" said Mrs. Oates weakly.

"Yassum? That's what I figgered." He paused. "The lady said y'all got a right nice li'l' kitchen, but hers is two times as big."

"The way that woman eats she needs a big kitchen."

"She's got uh ee-lectric dishwasher."

Before this magnificence Mrs. Oates quailed. "I never knew you minded washing dishes."

"Shucks, I like it. Dishwater feels good on the hands. But there's a thing out yonder I ree'ly don't like." His voice faltered, but he bore on swiftly. "When I'm standin' by the sink I gets downright lonesome on account I can't see th'u the window. Ma'am and boss, that's a stric'ly no-good window."

"Why, I had the panes frosted on purpose!" cried Mrs. Oates in astonishment. "They give you so much more privacy! There is nothing to see from the kitchen."

"I guess you never was jailed," returned Boysi politely. "Else you wouldn't crave too much priv'cy. There's plenty to see out that window. There's Junior's chicken yard, the gyarden patch, the garridge —— Why, if that wasn't a stric'ly no-good window, I could see ever' delivery boy all the way up the block."

"I think we can change the window," Mr. Oates grunted. "Any more blackmail?"

Boysi ventured a fleeting grin. "You sound like Jedge Yeaton readin' me out in p'lice court. Herbert Wash'ton. Black. Male. Ten dollars and cos'."

"Oh, dear," sighed Mrs. Oates. "Now that you aren't saving for furniture, the dice games and courts will take all your money again."

"No, ma'am!" cried Boysi fervently. "I got me the savin' habit for good, but I ain't buyin' no more furniture. No more jab-toed shoes, neither; they look good, but they pyure bites my feets. Whilst I was ironin' the boss' pants I figgered what I'd save t'ards gettin'."

Mr. Oates laughed. "I can't imagine a thing that some smart woman couldn't take away from you."

Boysi grinned. "Boss, how long you reckon I got to save befo' ever' toof in my head is stric'ly solid gold?"

LET THERE BE HONOUR

By *Kay Boyle*

IT WAS one night in March that the first group of Foreign Legionaries came into the military canteen; there were five or six of them in
khaki, with their heads under their beaked caps still shaved. They
strolled in from the station platform casually enough, but as soon as
they set foot inside the door their eyes began seeking for what they'd
been told she would be like. They'd heard it first in Damascus, and
the second time on the cattle train going to Beirut, and the last time
they'd heard it was on the ship coming back to what had once been
France. It was just as explicit as if the details of the story had been
typed indelibly out. Only it was never written out; it merely went
like this from ear to ear, and the men who heard it believed it because
they wanted to believe in something; by this time they had to believe
in something or else there wasn't any sense in giving the salute or
wearing the uniform any more.

They believed every word of it; they believed that once you got to
this city, either by boat, or by train, or on a bicycle, or on foot, all you
did was to walk to its railway terminus and get past the gendarmes
at the gates — and some of them even believed that the gendarmes
closed their eyes, for what were they but Frenchmen, with their con-
traband hope in it too? And there you crossed the station to the left-
hand platform and you walked into the canteen, and when you got
near enough to her, to that one girl behind the counter — not to the
lady at the cash desk or any of the boys helping, but to that particular
one — you said the first word of the ritual to her; you said, "Honour"
to her, and she would answer, "Honour Higgins." The story had it
that she was a Lady, that her name was actually Lady Honour Higgins, and then she would say, "Did you want coffee?" and you would
answer, "I've come a long way for it, and I'm willing to go farther."

They believed all this; all those weeks or months or merely days it took them to get there, they believed in this, but when they had got inside the door the terrible moment of misgiving came. Perhaps, after all, it was hoax or lie or legend, and perhaps this had nothing to do with the way to do it in the end. So the Foreign Legionaries paused that night in March as other men had paused after stepping just inside the canteen room, and then the big blond man who had taken the lead began making his way through the crowded tables to her. He was taller and stronger than any other man in the room, and he elbowed his way past the others, kicking aside the knapsacks in the aisles when they stood in his way. Men were collected two deep at the *zinc,* drinking their coffee and looking at her, and he made his way past them as well, with the other Legionaries following behind. Once there before her, he stopped short and took off his cap — before the girl with light, longish hair with a blue veil over it (perhaps the same color as her eyes if he could have seen them by day) and the red cross on the white band on her forehead the same red as her lipstick (or as nearly as he could tell in the equivocal light).

She was pouring coffee for two recruits, but the Legionary had waited too many weeks already, and his patience was at an end. He wet his lips, and he leaned forward and said the one word to her. He said, "Honour," pronouncing the single word as well as any Englishman might have, and then he waited, his eyes on her. The girl had glanced at him once, but now that he spoke, she gave no sign of having heard. She had asked the recruit how old he was, or where his father had fought the last war, and she waited for the answer while the blond Legionary's eyes and the eyes of the others with him did not leave her face.

Once the recruit had answered, she looked at the Legionary again, at the decorations on his left breast pocket and at the width of his shoulders, and she said, "Honour Higgins," but nothing had altered in her. It was in the men's faces that the change had come. "Did you want coffee?" she said as she wiped the *zinc* dry.

"We've come a long way for it," the blond man said, still speaking the flawless English to her. "We're willing to go farther."

"All of you?" said Lady Higgins.

"Yes, all of us," said the Legionary, and Lady Higgins turned and took six cups from the stack drying on the wood and set them on the counter one by one.

So that was, after all, the way the thing began. Madame Pichot working there with her at the cash desk knew that much of the machinations of it, but what happened afterward was never spoken of. Lady Higgins made her own dates and kept them, and the next afternoon the blond Legionary went alone out to her little house on the sea. She didn't have a veil on her hair. She was wearing slacks, light gray like the shirt, and she was smoking by the fire. When he was shown in by the Frenchwoman in *espadrilles,* she stood up for a moment and gave him her hand.

"You're a very good imitation of an Englishman," she said.

He said he was Viennese, smiling the bright white smile a little too much on his sunburned face. He looked even bigger here in his khaki in the fisherman's low-ceilinged plaster room.

"I was educated in England," he said.

"What are they doing with the Legion?" she asked. She offered him a cigarette from where she sat by the fire.

"They're sending a lot of us back to Austria," he said.

She sat looking at him a moment as he ate and drank the tea; the hair on his head was just beginning to grow in, and the skull that bent to the cup had a heavy, naked, almost Prussian look.

"And you don't want to go back to Austria?" she said.

He said he had been a Heimwehr, and then he cleared his throat. "I don't fancy the idea of facing a firing squad one early morning over there," he said. He took another sandwich of synthetic anchovy paste spread thin on zwieback and gulped it down with tea. "They say Vichy's handing us over in exchange for potatoes," he said. "We're a commodity; we're not men any more," and he went on saying: "But those of us who went to see you last night, we want to make the break."

Lady Higgins sat by the fire, smoking, with her ankles out of the gray slacks stretched and crossed. They were almost as slender as her wrists, and she saw his eyes were on them. The firelight moved on his face, laying quick, uneasy shadows there, and the thought came, not for the first time or even the second, but this time almost with conviction to her. She could hear the sound of it as clearly as if a voice were saying it aloud: "Sometime you may make the mistake, Honour Higgins. Sometime you may fatally mislay judgment's quality."

It was about half an hour later when they walked out through the sea-burned cactus and palms to the sandy road that he himself said it aloud. He had to be in barracks by seven, and she came this far with him and repeated the last things to him in the sea-washed dark.

She had said, "So I wish you good luck," and then he said the thing she had been thinking.

"I should think you'd be afraid of one thing," he said in a low voice, and because he stood so near to her, she said, "Not of men, anyway, my friend. Only that they may not be heroes in the end."

There were a few stars out, very big and bright through the palms' papery leaves, and she took a step away from him and waited there.

"I mean, someday you may make a mistake," he said. "Someday someone who isn't an Austrian or who isn't whatever he says he is may walk in and say, 'Honour' to you, and then it will be all over. Someday it's going to be somebody else, and then the gentlemen in gray will get you up one morning before sunrise too."

"That's just a chance I happen to be taking," said Lady Higgins, and without warning, the Legionary took her in his arms and kissed her mouth.

When she could say it, Lady Higgins said, "That isn't such a good imitation of an Englishman." She took out her handkerchief and smeared it hard across her lips, rubbing the feel of it and the violence and the memory out. "Now, just get out," she said savagely, and the Legionary or whatever he was turned and went down the road.

II

That was in March, and in April the thing that really mattered happened. About two o'clock one morning the Englishman walked in. He was not too tall and not too young, and his hair was a little blond at the temples, as if the sun had done it, and he came right over to the counter and leaned his arms on the *zinc*.

He was wearing a darkish jacket that must have belonged to someone else before him, and blue workman's trousers, still quite new. His nose was short, and his upper lip was longish, and his eyes were casual but steady.

"Hello, Honour," he said, saying it wrong from the beginning. He didn't look at anyone or anything else in the room, but leaned there on the counter.

"Honour Higgins," she said, without a trace of anything in her voice. He pushed the beret on the back of his head, and as he did it she saw with something like tenderness the small-knuckled, boyish hand. It might have been hand of brother or cousin out of its glove for a moment and on the snaffle rein at home, or lifted to slap a horse's shoulder, or just lying will-less on English paddock grass. "Did you want coffee?" she asked. Either he was English or else marvelously cast in the role, and then she heard him miss his cue.

"I don't know. It's pretty foul stuff these days," he said. He leaned there, his fingers cupping his elbows where the sleeve lining showed, looking not intently, perhaps even without so much as expectation at her.

"If you'll show your military papers at the cash desk and get your ticket, I can serve you," Lady Higgins said. The others had always been simple enough — lost foreigners asking a direction, and their faces lighting like children's when you spoke the words they knew. But this one had put the rigmarole aside, and even when she pointed out Madame Pichot at the cash desk to him, he made no move to go. "You're the first we've seen come through," she said, countryman saying it to countryman, and she wiped the *zinc* off. "Did they give you a bad time getting down?"

"I forget," said the Englishman. "Ran into a few prisons sort of thing," he said, and without any drama in it, he added, "I've been six months on the way."

Lady Higgins had set the clean thick cup down in readiness before him, and now she spooned the sugar out, but whether or not he got anything to eat or drink seemed of no interest to him at all. He simply wanted to lean there telling her, in bits and pieces, this thing which might sum up one man's history in the end. There were lines at the corners of his eyes, and lines on each side of his mouth, and his cheeks were a little hollow, but he hadn't a word to say about hunger or cold or any kind of pain.

"Good old organization," he was saying, and he said that in a German prison camp at least you knew where you were. "I take off my hat to organization," he said, and Lady Higgins said, "You've still got it on."

He reached up when she said this and took his beret off and put it in his jacket pocket, and Lady Higgins liked the way he moved his head and hands.

"That's for the French look of the thing," he said about the beret. "The French lock you up," he went on with the story, "and then they forget you're in prison and they give you a bottle of wine by mistake or shoot a game of billiards with you. All that leads to confusion."

"They're not such an easy lot outside," said Lady Higgins about the French. "You'll have trouble getting past them."

"I've had trouble before," said the Englishman. "When I skipped the jerry camp, the French locked me up for six weeks for swimming without a bathing suit. I didn't do it out of choice, because it was nearly Christmas. It was just one way of getting across the line."

"If you'll get your ticket at the cash desk," Lady Higgins began again, and she added, "I'm sorry. It's regulations."

"Good old regulations," said the Englishman, and he turned and looked for Madame Pichot. When he saw her, he turned and walked the length of the counter to where she sat.

Lady Higgins stood there, her eyes on him, watching him go, watching the part-casual, part-arrogant English-gentleman walk as he crossed the boards, watching him pause there at the cash desk and fish rather vaguely in his pockets for his military papers, as if it were of no importance where they were or if they were actually on him, and finding them where he didn't expect them to be. She didn't hear the wash boys talking behind her, or the train whistles crying outside in the dark, but stood there simply watching him as if, after the months of exile, she could never see enough of her country's blood and bone. It was only when he turned around again that she saw his face was harder and more bitter than any man's under thirty had the right to be.

"The second time it was because I didn't have a license plate on my bicycle," he said, leaning on the counter again. He took a swallow of what nobody called coffee any more. "I should have traveled by night, but 'mad dogs and Englishmen go out in the midday sun,' " he said. "I'd been locked up so long I thought once I got over the line, all I had to say was, 'Look here, I'm English. Bad luck, Dunkirk and all that, what?' and then we'd sit down and have a drink together. But it didn't work out like that. 'So you're English sort of thing, are you, my lad?' they'd say, and then the fun'd begin."

"How funny was it?" asked Lady Higgins, and the Englishman looked at her.

"Not very funny," he said.

It was just beginning to be dawn now, and the little coast omnibus was rattling into shape outside. The repatriated wounded had begun packing the remains of their food up and folding their bits of paper carefully away. The Englishman heard the movement behind him, and he stopped what he was saying. "I'd better clear out with them," he said, but Lady Higgins shook her head.

"They aren't going out," she said. "They're taking another train. They're going home."

And the Englishman said, with no perceptible interest in it, "That's where I want to go."

He had seen the scrap of bread somehow left forgotten on the table when he turned his head, and now that they had gone he took the two steps to retrieve it and laid it on the *zinc*.

"Jerry bread," he said; "you can tell by the color of it." There it lay between them, whiter than any bread she'd seen in months. She told him the wounded were back from Germany, and brought provisions with them. "It's nearly the same as we used to have in Munich on a summer night between the acts of Lohengrin," the Englishman said. He stood looking at the bit of bread as though it were a dove of peace come quietly to rest there. "Lady Higgins, my dear, there's something rather odd about the whole show," he said, and then, as if continuing the same sentence and without looking up, he said, "How do I get across?"

It was Madame Pichot who brought the matter of his papers up; she said they looked too authentic to be true. She said this to Lady Higgins at half past four in the morning when she came past the cash desk to get more sugar from the reserve. Madame Pichot leaned forward from her chair and touched Lady Higgins' arm and whispered it through her teeth, so that no one standing near might overhear. She said she liked the look of the young man, and the way he spoke, but she didn't like his papers.

"I've never seen anything so complete on a military fugitive," she whispered, and the light glinted on her glasses as she brought her face closer to Lady Higgins' face.

"He comes from Mousehole," said Lady Higgins. She stood there, wondering, with the empty sugar tin hanging from her hand. "He's absolutely all right."

"How do you know?" asked Madame Pichot.

"I was born and bred with them," said Lady Higgins. "I've hunted with them, was brought up with them, married one, even," she said a little grimly.

"What about Lord Haw Haw?" whispered Madame Pichot through the steel-white light of dawn.

"But his people —— " Lady Higgins began, and then, without warning, the Foreign Legionary interrupted her. He might just as

well have been there, big and blond and smiling in the flesh, aping to
perfection the English tongue. "Someday you may make a mistake, a bad mistake," said the phantom Legionary to her, and Lady
Higgins felt the blood run suddenly cold through her heart. "Someday somebody may walk in and say 'Honour' to you, who has no
sense of honor," the Austrian said, and because of all that hung on
the doubt, she let him go on. "You can't get away with it forever,
you know," he said, and then Lady Higgins brushed the two of
them — the Frenchwoman at the cash desk and the memory of the
Austrian — impatiently aside.

"I ought to know my job by this time," she said, and she went to
the door of the reserve and savagely pulled it open and savagely
jerked on the light. "Mousehole and Noel Coward," she said, but
the thing was spreading like poison in her as she filled up the empty
tin. When she came out, her eyes fled down the room at once, and
he was there still; his feet in the ancient tennis shoes crossed, and his
shoulders hunched, and his arms in the worn sleeves folded on the
zinc.

At six there were three trains in, and Lady Higgins served the
recruits who walked into the canteen and slung their knapsacks
down.

At a quarter past six the Englishman said, "I ought to be clearing
out now." He dropped the end of his cigarette on the floor and put
his heel on it. "I wish there were someplace where we could sit
down for five minutes together," he said, but his eyes were asking
her nothing at all.

The gendarmes were busy at the gates, checking the papers of those
going out, so she took the Englishman across the tracks and up on
the other platform and into the Buffet de la Gare. The place was
big, and perhaps not more than a dozen people seated at the marble-
topped tables, with their bags beside them and their faces weary from
the distance they had come. At the farthest end, in the shadows
still, was a swinging door, the top half of it mottled glass, and lettered
across it, HOTEL DE LA GARE ET DE L'UNIVERS, elegantly, in gold. The
Englishman ordered white wine because she said she wanted that,

and then he looked around him. When he saw the swinging door half lost in the dark, his eyes stopped moving.

"So that's the way I might go out?" he said.

"You might," said Lady Higgins. She took out her cigarette case and took one from it. "I should think it might save you from showing your papers to the lads outside," she said. She didn't add that over a hundred men had come into the Buffet with her and gone out that way, some by night and some by day, and none with papers on them. The Englishman struck a match and they both waited in silence until the sulphur perished from the air. "You picked it very quickly," she said. She sat there looking steadily at him.

"I had to find it," he said. "I didn't see any other way."

The waiter had put the bottle and glasses down, and the Englishman poured the wine out, a little in his own glass first, and then hers full before he filled his own.

"So if it's poisoned, you'll die too," said Lady Higgins. "I think that's how the whole thing began."

"It's better than the version about the cork," he said. He lifted his glass and took a swallow of wine. "So I just walk out there," he said. "And then what do I do?"

Even though she didn't say anything then, he still seemed to believe she was eventually going to say it. But she talked instead about the way they had of growing the wine here, with the vineyards tilted up among the seacoast's stones, and about the legends.

She said, "Maybe you could add to the German legends," watching him a little narrowly. "There's the one about changing water into petrol," she said, sitting there smoking and drinking her wine. "It's like the Indian rope trick. I mean, you never meet the person who's actually seen it. But still you hear it everywhere, over and over. And the one about the man-eating crematoriums."

"There's one about every lift boy in every newspaper building in Paris wearing a *feldgrau* uniform under his mufti," the Englishman said. He offered her his packet of Bleues across the table.

"And the tiresome one about the correct German officer," said Lady

Higgins, taking a cigarette from the paper in his hand, "who gives his table to two Frenchwomen in a restaurant, and then turns and announces to all the Frenchmen still seated in the room that he is giving them a lesson in French gallantry."

"And the one about Lady Honour Higgins," the Englishman said in a quiet voice. "I believed in that one," he said, and he held the flame to her cigarette and watched her suck the smoke in. "I still believe in it." He didn't touch his wine now, and he hadn't taken a cigarette. "Look," he said, in the same quiet voice. "Is there a Lord Higgins somewhere?"

Lady Higgins sat still for a moment, saying nothing, her eyes not on his face any more, but on the familiar, narrow-wristed, cousinly or brotherly hand.

"There was," she said in a little while. "He brought down fifteen of them before they got him. He was one of those 'pilots lost.'" She sat looking into the clear light color of the wine. "He was pretty good while he lasted," she said, and as if to stop the sound of it she looked straight up into his face. "How do you expect to get over?" she said.

"I know how the country lies pretty well," said the Englishman. He was asking absolutely nothing of her; it might have been that he had never expected anything at all. "It'll go off all right," he said, and she sat on the other side, watching him. "Maybe we could drink one drink to Lord Higgins before I go," he said, and nothing happened to her face.

They touched glasses without looking at each other, and he didn't say much more. After a moment he stood up and laid the pieces of money down, and he took the beret out of his jacket pocket and put it on for the French look of the thing, and he said, "My name's Dorset — Chris Dorset. I'll send you a post card if I get through."

After that he crossed the buffet with his rather casual, rather arrogant walk, and went out by the elegantly lettered door, and the mottled glass swung into place behind him. Now that he was gone, Lady Higgins sat there at the table for what must have been a certain length of time, not knowing why she sat there like any traveler in any station waiting in blank, speechless listlessness for time to pass, or for a train to come, or for the name of a destination to be called aloud through the amplifiers in the four corners of the hall. She didn't know what sense there could be in sitting there facing his empty glass and his empty chair, and yet she could not bring herself to get up and go. It must have been the wine, she thought; the wine, or else the very face and features of home denied, which had left her sitting hopelessly and helplessly there. She watched the black iron arm of the big clock above the entrance to the platforms jerk slowly from one minute to another, and she thought, *He didn't have anyone to tell him how to do it before, and he made it. He got on all right alone before,* but it was her own tears that stopped her. She felt them running, hot and senseless, down her face.

"Oh, damn you," she said. "Whoever you are, damn you for coming," and she could hear the sound of his voice in her ears still. She dried her cheeks savagely, and blew her nose, and painted on her lipstick. It was just past seven when she got back into the canteen. There were four recruits drinking coffee and eating sandwiches at the counter, and a dozen or more asleep on the benches. Beyond them, the wash boys were making fresh coffee and stacking the clean cups. There was an hour still to go.

III

The secret police had nothing in common with the gendarmes. They wore plain clothes and the look in their eyes was different, and usually they weren't Meridional men. They'd come into the canteen in shifts, two at a time, at any time of night, for coffee, and when they came to the counter the French would shut their mouths. Madame Pichot would give them a grim-lipped smile from behind the cash desk, and Lady Higgins would put clean cups and saucers out and set the sugar extravagantly before them. They liked standing there talking to her, talking about anything to her — the weather, or the food situation, or the last small country to have folded, or about

England. But whatever they talked about may have been the excuse to stand there looking at the unfading color of her eyes and mouth and hair.

"When are you going to write that letter home and tell them to let a few boats through?" one or the other might say to her, holding the synthetic bread and the meat they called "chopped dog" in his hand. "Down in Brazil they're dumping coffee into the sea because they don't like it any more. I saw the pictures of it."

"There'd be bloody revolution if they showed them here," the other one might say, and then he'd offer a cigarette to Lady Higgins.

"This is the last night of sugar," she said to them one night. "You'd better help yourselves while you can. You'll have to bring your own with you, the way you do everywhere else. It's a bit thick for the soldiers coming through."

"You drop a line to Churchill and tell him that," said the secret police. "You tell him we don't like the way he's running this blockade." He'd hold the flame with a certain careful gallantry for her, his shirt cuff and his hand and his nails soiled from the station's grime and from the lack of soap, and he'd say, "He'd listen to you. Even an Englishman might turn almost human if you talked to him."

Because they said almost everything in front of her there, one night toward the end of April they said something else.

"Did you see that Englishman they brought in last week?" one of them said, and the other one shook his head and picked up his cup from the zinc and drank.

"Have you got your bread tickets, gentlemen?" Lady Higgins asked, and she knew her voice was as steady as her hand. "Fifty grams each," she said, and she brought the stork-billed scissors out.

"They picked him up near Fontac," the first one went on. "Military age, trying to cross the frontier. When they brought him in, I asked him why he hadn't saved his skin with the rest of them at Dunkirk. 'Took you some time to make up your mind to skip,' I said to him," and the two secret police laughed.

"So what will they do with him?" asked Lady Higgins. She cut the green bread coupons steadily off. The first one shrugged and felt for his sugar in the pocket of his coat, and when he had it he undid the bit of paper there was around it and dropped the one lump in his cup.

"Some day the *préfectures* of this country are going to be reorganized and, like everything else, they need it," he said. "Good old organization," said Chris Dorset's voice from somewhere out of the long lonely corridors of memory, and the secret police stirred the liquid with his spoon. "Absolutely fresh-roasted coffee being dumped in the sea," he murmured, and then he thought of the Englishman again. "Unfortunately, being English isn't a crime yet in the unoccupied zone, so they don't know what to do with him." He had his mouth open to say more, but suddenly he put his cup down and he didn't say it. The station's siren had begun to blow.

The call began in the station yard, it seemed. It jumped the rails and fled to every corner of the canteen room. "Lights out, lights out!" the voices bawled, and above the sound of them the siren cried out in anguish to the night. Madame Pichot had gone at once to the switches and brought them smartly down, and instantly the benches, tables, the sleeping recruits, the police with their hats on, were jerked into obscurity.

"They'll never learn to stay home, the English won't," was the last thing Lady Higgins heard the police say as they started across the blotted-out room. She could hear them colliding with the tables and the benches and the still sleeping men, but cursing only the English and the roar of their bombers passing overhead.

They came in waves, and at intervals, and the siren's wail soared higher, almost beyond human hearing, in wild inhuman pursuit. It assumed an uncanny presence in the nothingness, no longer a signal of warning, but a tall, bereaved woman standing wringing her hands in grief and crying for the dead. Lady Higgins felt the cold of it on her flesh and she shivered a little. Then she felt her way down the counter to the cash desk and asked Madame Pichot where the candles were.

"That's just it," said Madame Pichot through the dark. "We melted them down for soap last month."

Lady Higgins leaned on the counter near Madame Pichot, unseeing and unseen, and listened to the English passing. As soon as one throbbing wave of sound had almost ceased, another rose behind it, swelling and boiling hard over them a moment, and then rippling evenly away.

"There're a lot of them tonight," Lady Higgins said, and waiting there it seemed that the dark was alive with their faces, tough little grim-lipped English pilots' faces, flying high and fast. *In another half hour they'll be crossing the big mountains,* she thought; *they'll pass Mont Blanc and the glaciers in starlight and cross Geneva's quiet, neutral lake and leave Switzerland behind.* And then she said something aloud to Madame Pichot about Chris Dorset.

"The flics picked up an Englishman at Fontac last week," she said. "I suppose that clears him."

"Except that he didn't get the information they want," Madame Pichot whispered. "They'll have to get him back here to try again."

"So you think he'll come back," said Lady Higgins, and the thought of it stirred her a little. "It's been just about three weeks," she said, and she closed her eyes. They might have been falling asleep there in the darkness, their voices murmuring while the bombers droned with the siren's wail toward sleep's or silence's extinction. "Whatever he was, he was very convincing," said Lady Higgins softly. "He played the part very well. He was much better than the old English colonel that sat on the park bench with the tropical bronzed skin and the clipped military mustache."

"But still you went up and spoke to him," murmured Madame Pichot severely. The sound of planes was growing fainter in the night.

"I said 'my goodness, my Guinness' to him," said Lady Higgins, and Madame Pichot yawned beside her and asked her what that meant.

"*Mon Dieu, mon demi,*" said the man's voice without warning from the other side, and Lady Higgins jerked her head and held tightly to the counter in the swinging dark. He must have been there, just within hand's reach, had perhaps been standing a long time there with the beret on the back of his head and his jacket out at the elbows and the blue workman's trousers still looking new. "Or even *Sainte Thérèse, ma bière anglaise,*" he said. "This could go on forever. You might have told me about it before."

"Hello," said Lady Higgins, as if he were anyone at all.

"I came back to tell you I muffed it," the Englishman said. He said it casually and not very loud, and Madame Pichot laid her hand on Lady Higgins' arm. "I'm out on parole," he said. "I'm a free man since an hour ago. That makes my thirteenth jail," he said. "Maybe it'll change my luck," and Madame Pichot's fingers still pressed in warning. There he stood on the other side in the darkness, and Lady Higgins knew there was no possible small talk to exchange with him. There was only the one thing to say.

"Madame Pichot doesn't like the look of your papers," she said. "They haven't been through as much as you have."

"They're new," said the Englishman. "I bought them from a jerry about six weeks ago. You can buy everything from a jerry except his uniform," he said, and he added that he was in a good position now, better than he had ever been before. "They're getting me a *carte d'identité* and a *permis de séjour* at the *préfecture,*" he said. "They've done it for so long for the English — ever since Warwick probably — that they don't know what else to do."

"So you're staying here then?" said Lady Higgins, and she said it rather bitterly. "So why have you come back to the canteen?" she said, and her voice was as cold as stone.

"I wanted to ask you about the address," the Englishman said. "I thought if I sent you the post card here, it might look a bit on the queer side to them."

Lady Higgins wanted to put out her hand and touch him and start laughing aloud over nothing, as you could with brother or cousin or anyone like him at home. She said, "I live out on the sea," and she told him the town's name and the house's name, with the sense of pride and triumph rising in her. "That's where my people write to me," she said, and even now Madame Pichot tried to keep her from going on. "Just send it to me there," she said.

It was then that Madame Pichot said she was going to switch the lights on, now that the all-clear signal had begun to blow.

"Not before he gets out," said Lady Higgins, and she linked her arm through the Frenchwoman's arm and held her where she was. "Good luck, Dorset," said Lady Higgins. "You'd better go."

He said, "Good night, Lady Higgins," and then he said, "Look, you'll be coming back to England, won't you? I mean, if I get through this show, you might like coming down to Mousehole. It's quite a country," he said, and then he didn't say any more.

The voice seemed simply to be wiped away, and then Madame Pichot crossed to the switches, and with the lights' return a little breath of "ah" went around the room. The recruits were on the benches still, and the boys had begun clearing the cups and saucers off the *zinc*, but the Englishman and the sound of him were no longer there.

IV

The next interval was a shorter one; it was only three nights later that the secret police walked in and went straight to where Lady Higgins was. The weather was getting warm and their hats looked too tight on their heads, and their shirts and their hands and waistcoats more soiled than ever in the heat. The story was this: that the Englishman who had been caught trying to get over the frontier had been let out on parole.

"He promised to be good, so they let him out, that's what the *préfecture* did," the first secret police started telling it. "Here we are, sweating ourselves to the bone to keep anything queer-looking from passing the gates out there, and what do they do but let an Englishman of military age out on parole. Someday," he said, "they're going to see things as they are and they're going to put every gendarme in this country under arrest."

"So what?" said Lady Higgins.

"So of course he walks out on them," the first one said, and Lady Higgins remarked that it didn't sound much like an Englishman.

"Not like an Englishman?" said the secret police in a high, baffled voice. He seized a chopped-dog sandwich off the wire tray. "Not like a what? Not like a —— "

"Don't say it," said the second one. "Don't waste your breath on it. The dice are cast."

"Wait," said the first one, his cheek big with bread or whatever went by that name now. Lady Higgins asked for his tickets, and he took out his ration card and slapped it down on the *zinc*. "Just wait," he said. He didn't even watch how many coupons she cut away. "That Englishman simply walked in past the row of gendarmes out there and took a train," he said bitterly. "Nobody knows when he did it, but that's what he did. It was only when he didn't report next morning that the *préfecture* woke up and telephoned Fontac and Pertinau to keep an eye out for him. So, when he got off at Pertinau, they were there to meet him with their guns loaded and even a pair of bracelets for him. They telephoned up here to the *préfecture* to ask what they should do with him, and the *préfecture* said to bring him back," said the secret police, his voice soaring again with the absolute fabulousness of it. "They couldn't trust Pertinau with him. They were better equipped for the really big criminal types up here!" Lady Higgins watched him bring his open hand down hard on the *zinc*. "And every word of this is true," the secret police was saying in actual pain. "I talked to the gendarmes who brought him back from Pertinau. They were five hours in the train with him, and they spent it playing cards and drinking *pinard*. I asked them if they knew their prisoner was an Englishman and, if so, what in the name of God they were doing playing —— "

"Don't waste your breath on it," said the second one.

"So they brought this Englishman back from Pertinau," said the first one. "That was this afternoon." And suddenly it all got beyond him again, and he stood there, a big fat man in a brown suit, looking as if he were going to cry. "They took him up the three flights of stairs to the captain's office, and the captain got up and shook hands with the prisoner when they brought him in."

"The captain told him the place had been lonely without him," the second one said, and the first secret police leaned his head on his hand and groaned aloud.

"The gendarmes had a train back to Pertinau that evening — that's this evening — " the first one went on, "and there didn't seem to be any reason to hang around. A fellow'd broken his parole, and they'd brought him back, and so they thought they might as well go home. They'd seen a lot of handshaking going on, and anyway they had five hours of drinking behind them, so there was nothing for it but they must shake hands with the Englishman too. Oh, it must have been wonderful!" said the secret police in agony. "And now, just listen to this: The prisoner said, 'Wait a minute and I'll go down the first flight with you. It's no trouble at all. It's right on the way to my cell.' And after five hours of *pinard* and all the handshaking, this sounded all right to everybody there. How the captain was filling in his time just at that moment, nobody knows. He was probably putting the champagne on ice in preparation for the evening game of cards. So the gendarmes' story is that they said good-by to the prisoner on the second-floor landing and told him how much they'd enjoyed the day with him and hoped they'd get together soon again, and the Englishman said he'd accompany them down the next flight." He stopped talking for a moment, and with one hand he shoved the cup impatiently aside. "So the man they've just brought back under heavy guard walks down the three flights of stairs with them and straight out the door. That's how he did it," he said. "That's how he walked out on them a second time."

"That's one up for the English," said Lady Higgins, smoking.

"Not yet," said the secret police, "because we're out to get him. We're going to reorganize this city's police system if it means crossing the Channel to do it."

"Good old organization," said Chris Dorset's voice from a long way away.

It went on all that night for Lady Higgins in blame and bitterness and fury, and when she went home to fall asleep in her own bed in the morning, the dream of failure, outraged, violent, implacable, was there. *So you let them down,* the voice of conscience repeated in the

room; *you let down brothers, cousins, the dead and the living, the*
pilots' faces, and whatever country is. You let him go off through
the uncertainty of that again, the first time and the second, and now
the third, out of suspicion or doubt or fear.

It went on all day as she slept, and toward evening as she dressed
she kept saying: "Perhaps it isn't too late, perhaps he'll remember the
name of the town and the name of the house, and come."   Out of all
the possible ways to his destination, perhaps he might still come by
this one, but she couldn't see it happening that way.   She tried pic-
turing him on the port, or walking into the hotel bar, or climbing the
rocks by moonlight, but she could not see the Englishman anywhere
in it.   So that when she actually did see him, she didn't believe it any
more.   She had just begun walking up the sloping lane toward home,
and frogs were calling out deeply and sorrowfully in the orchard
reservoirs.   It was past dusk, and the light was going fast now, when
the Englishman came walking down between the cypress and the
olive trees.

He said, "Hello," and he looked at her for a moment.   "It's the first
time I've seen you without a veil," he said.

"It's madness for you to go about like this," she said, not listening
to him.

"I was looking for you," he said, and they started together up the
road.

"You'll have to get out tonight," she said.   Ahead of them was the
line of the cliff, purely and wondrously defined against the fading
sky.   And as they walked she began telling it to him, speaking in a
low, unhurried voice as they climbed up the road between the lizard-
infested walls.   "You see, it can't be the question of a frontier any
more," she said.   "There's been too much of that and they're watching for it.   You follow down the coast," she said, pronouncing the
names and the possibilities with dogged exactitude for him, repeating parts of it for clarity, keeping nothing back.   "You cross that
cliff," she said, just as she had told all the others who had done it before him.   "You do it by night.   There's a good path and the stars
are out and you won't have any trouble.   It's the fourth town after

you've passed the cliff that is your town, and there you walk up the Rue Principale to the Bar de la Marine." She told him the name of the man who sat behind the counter all day and slept above the *bistro* at night, and she said, "He'll have the papers for you, and he'll give you the sailing date, and he'll see you through. You'll wait where he tells you to, and until Casablanca you won't be Chris Dorset any more; you'll be Louis Blanc or Jean Dupont or whatever the papers will say you are, and on the boat you'll work like one of the crew. The French identification is the only one you'll have with you. Don't try to take your other papers, because that sort of thing has been the end of other men. You're Louis Blanc or Jean Dupont and you've never heard of the English until you get to the Rue du Sphinx in Casablanca," she said, and she repeated the number to him, and told him whom to ask for there. "You can talk to him as you've talked to me, and he'll get you through to Lisbon." It was only when she had finished talking that she knew he had scarcely heard it, that she would have to say it all over again in a little while to him, because he had probably not even been trying to listen to what she said. "I should have told you all this a month ago," she went on saying, and her voice had altered as she walked up the lane beside him in the growing dark. "I don't know why I had to have so many proofs from you. Perhaps because I couldn't believe I'd ever meet anyone again who was everything I wanted him to be."

"But look," he said quietly, "I always thought all this was what you call the legend. I mean, after I saw you I believed that the first part was true, that you were English and that you were there and that you were so beautiful that men never stopped trying to get there just to look at your face. But as for the rest of it, I thought I only embarrassed you when I asked the ways and means. I thought it was pretty rotten of me to go on insisting you tell me something that you yourself didn't know." They were far from any house now, mounting through the dark maquis; the stars were out, and the sea moved hollowly and distantly on the shore. "So it wasn't for that I wanted to go on seeing you," he said, and Lady Higgins knew this must come to an end.

"Now it's the war," she said, "but next year when I go down to Mousehole, I'll remind you where the conversation was when we left off."

But whatever Lady Higgins said, however she explained it time after time in the slack hours of the night, Madame Pichot would have none of it. She knew what he was; she had known it from the game of come-and-go he played, and the state of the papers on him, and even when the post card came from England it did not change her mind.

It was sent from London, and Lady Higgins brought it into the canteen to show it to Madame Pichot behind the cash desk. It had taken more than a month to come, and it said, "Let there be Honour," without making any attempt to take the grandiloquence away.

ANGEL-FACE

By Jean C. Becket

On my way home I did not see a single human being. Everybody in Winsett was eating supper. Ted Dugan's dog knew me, but dogs are smart, and I did not think a human being would know me, not right off. You cannot feel so different without it showing. You cannot have such a wonderful thing happen to you and still look the same.

I felt old and sad, like after the measles. It was awful to think that just about everybody in Winsett was Damned. Mr. Mudge said —— Well, I will show you later what I mean.

Just then Ben Orr came out of the post office. I said, "Ben, I am Honesty Blake. Do you know me?"

He said, was I crazy? I said no, but didn't I look different? And he said, "You look all right. Someday you will be a fine-looking woman."

Just then a car drove up where we were standing by Washington's Oak. Our Oak is spang in the middle of the road, with a fence around it and the plaque telling how "George Washington, the Father of his Country, Stopped to Rest in the Shade of this Ancient Oak on his Way to Boston." I read it out loud to the people. They had an Oregon license. Ben keeps track each summer of all the license plates that come to look at our tree.

I am sorry for people that cannot live in a famous place like Winsett, with a landmark like Washington's Oak that people come to look at from all over. My father says we are a dead town and nothing has happened in Winsett since Washington stopped here, and we have been resting on our Oak ever since. You are supposed to laugh when he says it, because it is a joke. But I do not laugh. He says we are just basking in past glory and we will never make the front page

again. My father is smart, but he does not know everything, because we did make it again. You will see.

Besides, why would Mr. Pope come all the way from Utah to write
his book about the Revolution in Winsett, if we are not famous?
Mr. Pope is very smart. He used to teach History. He offered his
head to father in the name of Science, when he dies, but father said
no. My father is not a polite man.

Mr. Pope does not look smart. He is bald and he does not have
enough chin, but father says it is what is inside a man's head that
counts, not what is on the outside, like Robert Taylor.

Father has not got enough hair to cover all his head any more
now, so he puts something on at night. Mother says she hopes he
will be bald as an egg soon, so she will not have to smell that awful
smell much longer.

Well, I left the post office. I passed the Sampsons' house, where
father was called out the night before on account of Mrs. Sampson
had eaten something. Then comes Mr. Coyle's house. He is the
plumber, and father says it is lucky he got shingles, because we have
had a lot of trouble with the laundry tubs lately, and the bills will
just about break even.

Mrs. Judson's Antiques sign was creaking in the wind. A long
time ago Mr. Judson drank poison, but nobody knows except our
family. Father pretended it was his heart, on account of Mrs. Judson. There was a new ad on the side of her barn. A girl and a man
in the Navy, smiling like everything.

That reminded me of Elsie Clyde, that was going to be married
the next day to the ensign from Boston. I thought of how father
said if Elsie had not gone to study in Boston, she would be marrying
my cousin Frank, like everybody expected. Frank lives with us since
his mother died.

All through high school Elsie and Frank were in love, and they
kept right on after, but then Elsie went away and met this uniform,
and father says all women are fools for a uniform.

Elsie's father is Judge Clyde. He takes the collection in church
and he makes the speech to the seniors at commencement. Every-

body is crazy about him, but he is not strong. He is all the time having these attacks. He could not give the prizes this year on account of being sick. I won the posture prize.

I noticed the mailbox was full in front of Mr. Brooks' house. He is the minister. I read a post card from Harold. He is in the draft, and he is a scream. The Brookses do not mind if I read it.

Then I passed the Webbs' house. Any day now Mrs. Webb was going to have a baby. It is queer how people are so selfish. Our family never goes away for summer vacation like other people, because ladies are all the time having babies.

This summer I have had seventeen post cards, and I thought if Mary Lee sent me one from Boston, which is all the distance she has gone to, I should die. Mother says if I am so set on going away I should have picked a different father. You would not believe what things she says. Because how can a tiny baby pick out her father? I said, "That is silly, mother." And she looked at father and said, "George, why are all our children so grim?" Just the same, it makes a girl very ignorant never to go anywhere.

It was late, but I stopped a second in front of Schuyler's Fine Furniture Mart to look at the dressing table with skirts. I thought, *Mother says already I cannot have it for Christmas. I guess I can never have it, but there is no harm looking at it.*

Father was late for supper too. He was eating soup, and mother and Steve and Frank were on the veal cutlet. We are always on different courses in our family. Mrs. Curtis brought in my soup.

Mrs. Curtis is a very lovely lady, and she would not have to work at all, only for having all her eggs in one basket, father says — and railroads at that. She tripped on Steve's football, and three peas rolled onto the rug. That made our dog, named Red, get up and walk around between our legs under the table till he found them.

But he kept on smelling under there, so mother said, "Can't you count? You ate three and that's all there were. Lie down." Then she said, "George, where did you get that tie? I put it in a Bundle for Britain."

And father said, "I took it out again. . . . What's for dessert?"

Steve was back just three days from camp, with a duffel bag full of dirty clothes and things, and he had to go away to his prep school Monday — two weeks early for football practice. He is the captain of the team. He thinks it will be all his fault if they do not win every game. To hear him, you would think there is nothing in the world important except football. Not a war or anything. He practices passing with Jim Clyde all day, and even after supper.

The telephone rang, and father answered. Our telephone has a long cord that stretches from the sideboard to father's place at the table.

Steve took one of mother's hands and looked at it. He said, "You should never have had children — anybody with such small hands. That's why I can't pass better. Hands too small to get a decent grip on the ball."

Mother said how thoughtless of her, and she apologized.

Father said he could not hear the telephone. So I got up and turned off Lowell Thomas.

Father said, "All right, then; keep on with the drops. Good-by. . . . That woman is a pure neurotic. She is strong as a horse and will live to be one hundred and five, but she is not satisfied unless she is taking something. Those drops are nothing but —— "

And mother said, "Little pitchers, George."

So father looked at me and said, "Nonsense, Martha; this sort of thing goes right over her head. . . . Why do you buy such tough meat?"

Well, nobody noticed I was different till mother started to give me a second helping of chocolate pie. I said, "No, thank you."

Mother said, did Mr. Pope give me a double-decker ice-cream cone on the way to the lime quarry this afternoon? And I said, no, he did not.

"George," mother said, "Honesty is coming down with mumps."

Everybody looked at me then, except father. Whenever we begin to talk about feeling sick or having a pain or a cut or anything, he starts to read the paper.

Mother looked at Steve in a funny way and said maybe he would not be able to go to early football practice after all. "Quarantine."

Well, Steve jumped up so fast his chair tipped over. He looked sort of fierce. Then he began to yell about how he was not going to have the whole footbool season spoiled and be a failure, all on account of a bird-brained moron like me.

Mrs. Curtis came to see what happened, and then Jackie, my little brother that is in bed with a cold, was hanging over the banister in his pajamas. He said, was it a bomb, and mother said it would be a bomb if he did not get back to bed pretty quick, because she was coming up and spank him. Mother is very old-fashioned about children.

Steve stamped out of the dining room.

So I waited till everything was quiet, except for Jackie making his siren noise upstairs, and I told them.

I told them how I never did get to the quarry to look for fossils with Mr. Pope that afternoon. We started out, but we stopped to look at a dead snake in the road, that he said was rare, and while I walked back a ways to look at a turtle, Mr. Pope got in the car and drove off without me. I was not surprised, because he is always doing things like that. Like Mrs. Curtis says, he has so many big things on his mind, he cannot bother with little things.

Father said, "The man's half-witted."

I said, "You better not say that in front of Mrs. Curtis." I did not see her coming in with the water.

Father asked, "Why not?"

I said, "Because she is in love with him."

Mrs. Curtis almost dropped the pitcher.

Mother said, "Honesty! The idea!"

Everybody was red in the face except father. He is the same color all the time. Mrs. Curtis made a beeline for the kitchen, and mother said, "Look out for the telephone cord!" But it was too late. Mrs. Curtis ran into it, and the telephone started ringing right there on the floor.

It was Miss Lucas. We all groaned, because she always talks forever, and father's supper gets cold. But he sneaks in bites while she talks.

When he hung up he said, "Why does no one have a common cold any more? Why must it be grippe, or flu, or pneumonia? Why must every sore throat have a fancy name? And if you stuff yourself like that Sampson woman and get disgustingly fat — why, that's glands. . . . Lie down, Red. . . . Now Miss Lucas is insulted when I say she's got lumbago. Says it's her sacroiliac. Well, I say, damn her sacroiliac!"

I said, "Father, do you want to burn in Hell?"

He kind of blinked. He said, "Not particularly. Why?"

"Because it is wicked to say 'damn' or —— "

"Honesty!" mother said.

"Mr. Mudge said so," I told her.

Mother kind of gasped. "George," she said, "Honesty's been out to one of those horrible revival meetings at Fox Hollow!"

I said, "It was not horrible, mother. It was beautiful."

Then I told them how I was walking home after Mr. Pope forgot me, and passing Fox Hollow Ball Park I noticed a lot of people. So I thought I would go and watch a game. But nothing happened. Nobody even warming up. Then all of a sudden everybody stood up and began to clap, and a car drove right out on the diamond, and a man stood up in back and held up his arms. He was *praying,* right out in front of all those people. His voice made you shiver. It would be high and low, and then he would stretch up his hands and tremble all over. And the lady next to me began to cry, and the man on the other side, he kept shouting "Amen!" but I did not jump so bad after the second time he did it.

Mother said, "George, it is sacrilege. That man is an old humbug. He rants and raves and scares the farmers' wives out of their wits with fire and brimstone, and then he takes their money. He is a pious old fraud, and he makes a mockery of religion. I tell you, George, he ought to be arrested!"

"Who?" father said.

Mother sighed. She is always sighing like that, but I do not think she is sad.

I told them I was late for supper because I was almost the last to be saved.   When I came up on the platform thing they had, Mr. Mudge sort of wiped his eyes and gulped like he was crying.   I told how he rested his two hands on top of my head, and his voice got like the organ in church, and he said, "What have we here, my fellow sinners? A blue-eyed angel from heaven? Surely this little lamb is as pure as —— "

Father said, "As the driven snow."

Sometimes father is wonderful, because that is exactly what Mr. Mudge did say.

Then Mr. Mudge said, "And yet, brothers and sisters, if this innocent and beautiful child hungers after" — some word I can't remember — "how much greater is our need!"   And some of the ladies sobbed and blew their noses.

Well, he made me tell my name, and he said it was the most wonderful name he ever heard.   And I said I hated it, and it came from an old primitive ancestor, and mother interrupted to say "Puritan."

Mr. Mudge asked, did I know what a glorious mission I had in life, with a name like that?   Always to tell the truth and be worthy of my name.   So I promised to always tell the truth forever and ever amen.

Father said, "I would not do that, Honesty, if I were you."

"George!" mother said.

And father said, "She could make trouble.   Look at her, with those eyes on the ceiling.   She is a throwback to her primitive ancestor. You cannot monkey with a thing like the truth.   It is dangerous, like a gun that is loaded, or a strong drink.   You cannot take it straight."

So I said, "Mr. Mudge says everybody would be happier if they did not pretend all the time.   And people should live frank, open lives, and tell the truth, and not hide things."

The telephone rang again, and father took up the receiver and kept right on talking to mother, and saying, "She will carry it too far, Martha."   So I do not know what the people on the other end thought.   It was Mr. Webb.   Father said, "Pains every twenty minutes.   That's fine."   Then he hung up.

For the first time we noticed how Frank was not eating anything.

"Frank," mother said, "you *must* eat something!"

Well, you would think she had insulted him. He got up and threw his napkin on his chair. Only it floated, because we are using paper ones to save the wash. And then Frank was running upstairs three at a time to his bedroom. He slammed the door, and then we heard him locking it.

Mother looked at father and sighed again. She said, "George, I thank heaven I am an old woman of forty. I simply could not bear to suffer like Frank, or worry like Steve. Do you realize that Frank is dying a slow, horrible death right here before our eyes because Elsie is marrying that ensign tomorrow? Now Honesty has got religion, and she will take it hard, like the way she took whooping cough. George, it is too much."

Father said, "Look at that dog drooling on the rug. And she knows we never feed her at the table." So he gave Red the soggy part of his piecrust. Then he had to answer the telephone. He said he would go to the Clydes'. He shook his head at mother. "The judge is at it again. One too many. He won't be fit to give his own daughter away tomorrow. Someday people are going to smell a rat, you know, Martha. They won't swallow this sort of thing forever. Besides, I am running out of alibis." He drank down his coffee. "And I am sick of all this subterfuge."

I said, "What is subterfuge?"

And father said, "It is pretending to be something you are not. . . . I will answer the bell, Mrs. Curtis; it is probably for me."

So he came back to say somebody had fallen down the cellar stairs, and she would not let anybody touch her till he got there, so he would have to go, and she weighed two hundred pounds. And mother said not to forget the Webb baby.

Then mother and I were alone. I asked her about what a wedding is like, because I had never been to one except in the movies, and here I was going to be a Flower Girl in one tomorrow. I would not admit it to anybody but mother, but I did not know exactly what "engaged" was, even, so she told me.

She told how one night she was walking down the street with father in Boston, after a concert. And all of a sudden they stopped, and father said how much he loved her, and she said so did she love him, and then they kissed each other, right under a lamppost, and they were engaged.

"Someday we are going to put up a little plaque on that lamppost," she said.

"Like the one on Washington's Oak?" I said.

And she said, "Exactly."

Well, I went out and sat on the swing, and who should be there on the porch but Mrs. Curtis, instead of doing the dishes. She was very excited.

She said, "Shame on you, Honesty! Promise me never to speak that way to any living soul again!"

"What way?" I said. She kept fanning her face with her apron. "You mean about you being in love with Mr. Pope?" She looked all round, like they do in the movies if they have shot somebody. I said, "I cannot promise a thing like that, because Mr. Mudge says love is beautiful, and the more of it in the world the happier people will be. And it is a girl's duty to tell the truth." Then she heard something and ran inside quick.

So I sat and swung in the swing alone. I felt sad, like in church. If you live in a doctor's family you cannot help finding out things. I mean, you think somebody is a lady because she is very polite on the outside, and then one day maybe your father keeps her waiting, and she gets mad, and from the way she talks on the telephone you find out she is not a lady at all.

Then take Mr. and Mrs. Price. They had a big party for being married twenty-five years, and everybody said they were the happiest couple in Winsett. But father had to go there the night before the party, and Mrs. Price could not wear her new dress without sleeves because of the bruises on her arm. She was trying to stop Mr. Price from hurting their new spaniel that is not housebroken yet. But on the outside Mr. Price is the loveliest man.

I got to thinking of school opening in two weeks, and everybody telling what they did and what they saw — except me. I had just sat here all summer. Last year when school opened I made up a lot of things about where I went, and Miss Ewing, even, believed me. But this year I couldn't do it — on account of Mr. Mudge.

Then who should be passing but Elsie Clyde. I called her, and she came and sat on the swing with me. She is red-haired and pretty, but she looked kind of queer. You see, Elsie promised I could be Flower Girl long ago, when everybody expected she would marry Frank. I thought it might not be loyal to Frank to keep on being Flower Girl when he was not in the wedding, but I could not help it. I told her I could hardly wait for the wedding tomorrow.

She said, "How's Frank?"

I said, "He is dying a slow, horrible death right before our eyes." She sort of screamed. "It is true," I told her. "Mother said so. When does the ensign from Boston get here."

She said she would rather not talk about tomorrow, but did I know if Frank was coming to the wedding?

I said, "Of course not. He will go up the creek in his boat, or he will lock himself in his room, like he did at supper. Steve says he would shoot himself, only he cannot find a gun."

Elsie was saying how Frank was her best friend, but he did not love her. That was only a schoolboy crush. She said he told her so last night.

I said, "If Frank told you he did not love you, he will roast in Hell." And I explained about Mr. Mudge, and how it is important not to tell lies.

Then we started looking at the pictures in the old yearbook Frank had been brooding over, mother said. They showed when Elsie was Class Secretary and Frank was Class Treasurer, and when Elsie was head of Student Council. There was one of them sitting next to each other in the Cercle Français, and one of Frank standing behind Elsie in the Dramatic Club, with Frank looking scared to death.

She stood up quick, and I said, "What's the matter? Does it make you sick to swing?"

And she said, "No, it is just old times and memories." So I saw she was crying.

Just then Frank came out. He was so mad I was scared. He

grabbed my arm. He said, "You little devil, what are you doing to her?"

I said it was wicked to swear, and he said something so bad I did not think he knew the word, as he is a nice boy — not tough like my brother, Steve.

Elsie tried to tell him it was the yearbook, but she could not talk. She sort of choked and ran down the steps, and Frank after her.

Now, I am not nosy, but I had to see Mr. Pope, so I could not help following them round the corner. They were walking together, very fast.

Mr. Pope was sitting on the porch where he boards. It always takes him a minute to remember who you are. I sat down and he said, "Well, well, Prudence; how are you this fine afternoon?"

I said it was night, almost, and my name was Honesty, and I had to see him about a matter of Life and Death.

He said, "Well, well, some fine day you and I must go out to the quarry and hunt for fossils. . . . Life and death, eh?"

"Yes," I said. "Mrs. Curtis is so much in love with you she cannot keep her mind on her cooking. The piecrust was awful."

He did not get red like Steve. He got purple. He said, "Are you certain of this, Prudence? I have always admired Mrs. Curtis enormously, but I did not dare to hope that —— " Then he stopped.

I said, "She is always sticking up for you when father says you are not all there, and she says you do dopey things because you are so smart."

Well, he sat and rocked very fast, and his lips kept moving, but he did not say anything. I guess he forgot I was there, because he jumped like everything when I said, "Look! There's Elsie and Frank passing."

They did not see us. They were just looking at each other all the time.

Mr. Pope said, "Yes, young love is beautiful. But real love, like wine, is sweeter in an old cask. Let us hope they will be happy."

"That is Frank," I said. "The ensign from Boston that she is going to marry cannot come till tomorrow."

He said, "You are mistaken, my dear. Those are lovers, if I ever saw them. And a handsome couple they will make at the altar."

I told him how it ought to be Frank, but Elsie had to marry this uniform tomorrow. And I reminded him he was invited to the wedding.

All of a sudden he got excited. He said it was a crime against love, and such a thing belonged to the Middle Ages. And who did Judge Clyde think he was, to force his only child into marriage with some rich old man?

I said I did not think he was so very old. Not over twenty-five. But Mr. Pope was walking up and down the porch in a stew, and not even listening. He said females were still sold in certain parts of China, but this was America! And something ought to be done!

He was so excited I thought I had better go, so I did, and he went right on talking, anyhow. Around the corner I saw Frank and Elsie again. They were walking very slow. Then they stopped under the lamppost. It made me think of mother and father in Boston, when they got engaged.

Then, all of sudden, it happened! Frank was putting his arms round Elsie and they were kissing!

Well, I did look lovely, if I do say it. Father bumped me on the stairs, and said "Oh, excuse me," thinking I was a friend of mine. I went to the church once, but it was too early. They were still putting up the awning. I had my rose petals in a paper bag, so strewed a few for practice. They were going to give me a fancy basket for them later. I ate lunch standing up, on account of my dress.

The second time I met some ladies on the way. Miss Cooper said, "Why, Honesty, I hardly know you with your hair out of braids. You look sweet. Where is mother?"

I told her she was letting Mrs. Curtis come instead of her, seeing Mrs. Curtis was so crazy about weddings. And mother was trying to get Steve's clothes ready for school.

Miss Cooper said didn't it break mother's heart to lose her little boy. Children grew up so fast and went away to school.

I said, "Look, Miss Cooper, you do not know Steve. If he stayed home one more day, mother would go bats. We could not stand it."

And she said, "Oh."

Then Mrs. Coyle asked if father wasn't coming, and I told her how the pains had stopped, and he was still waiting round for the old Webb baby. She sighed, and said how a doctor's life was just one long service to humanity. And they all sighed.

I said, "How is Josephine, Mrs. Coyle?"

She said, "Fine, Honesty. Quite a big girl now."

So I said, "Yes, I know. Father was saying if you would pay for Josephine, and Mrs. Lee would pay for Alec that is in nursery school already, we could put in a new bathroom upstairs."

Then, all of a sudden, Miss Cooper and I were alone. I guess Mrs. Coyle was mad, but it is God's own truth about Josephine.

Some more people came up and talked. The ladies had their hair curled up all the same, right out of Sue Orr's Beauty Salon. Mother says Sue does not have enough imagination.

Miss Cooper said, "I don't know what I would do without your dear father, Honesty. I am so high-strung and nervous."

I said, "Father says you are strong as a horse, and will live to be a hundred and five. But some people are not satisfied unless they are taking something."

Mr. Sampson began to cough like anything, and then we went up the steps of the church. A lot of people were standing round. I saw Mr. Levering, but not Mrs. Levering. I am polite, so I went up to him and said I was sorry Mrs. Levering did not feel like coming, but she would be all right after the baby came. Mr. Levering sort of swayed and began to swallow fast, and people crowded round him, and I explained how I heard father telling Mrs. Levering on the telephone just this morning that she would stop being sick after the third month, like I always hear him when people are having babies. But then they were taking Mr. Levering outside. I think he went home and did not stay for the wedding. So maybe I should not have said anything, only I cannot see the harm in telling the truth.

For a while I talked to my friend, Petey Judson. He had one of father's nice, neat dressings on the back of his neck where he is always getting things. Mrs. Judson says it is acid in his system. Father says it is dirt on his neck.

Then I heard somebody say what a shame Judge Clyde was too sick to give Elsie away, and somebody said did I know what it was this time?

I did not say anything at first, and pretty soon I could just see Mr. Mudge's shiny eyes, so I said, "It is called One-Too-Many, and father says someday people are going to smell a rat."

Everybody looked at me. At first nobody said a word, and then everybody started talking at once. A friend of Frank's whistled.

Mr. Price took my hand and we went away from the crowd. He said what did I have in that paper bag? And I said, rose petals to strew. He said, "Are you sure it is not another cat to let out?"

I said, "Mr. Price, you know I would not bring a cat to church."

And he said, "Wouldn't you, my little angel-face? I am not so sure." He hummed something. Then he said, "That was quite a bomb you dropped in the vestry just now. But bombs or rose petals, they are all one to you."

Then cars came up, and it was Elsie in her white dress, and somebody stepped on her veil.

A Bridesmaid said, "Honesty! We have been looking all over for you. You should not be here." Then she gave me a basket for my rose petals, and somebody pushed me and, in a minute, there I was walking down the aisle.

The church was so pretty I almost cried. I forgot to strew my rose petals, after saving them all summer. Ferns round the altar, candles, and white ribbon tied on the pews. Lots of people I did not know at first, they were so dressed up.

The sun shone through the big stained-glass window and made Mrs. Judson look green and Mr. Coyle purple. It is the window that Judge Clyde put there in memory of his mother. Father says he can just remember her, and she had a mustache, and she wore a wig on account of she was bald as an eagle, and she used to throw medicine bottles and things when she was mad.

Sometimes I wish I did not know so much. It is a lovely window, and I would like to look at it and feel all holy inside, but I cannot do it.

Well, before I knew it, Elsie was standing beside the ensign from Boston, and Mr. Brooks was talking. The more I looked at the ensign from Boston, the more I thought about Frank. All of a sudden I remembered last night, with Frank and Elsie kissing under the lamppost like mother and father.

It was like a flash of lightning inside your head. I could not breathe, even. Everybody knows you cannot marry one man if you are engaged to somebody else. There is a word for it that I have forgotten. It would be worse than subterfuge. They might even put Elsie in jail! I knew I had to do something, but I did not know how to start.

And then I heard Mr. Brooks say if anybody knew a reason or something why they should not get married, to say so now or forever keep still. So I said, "I know!" It came out pretty loud, but it was a good thing, because even in the back pews they heard me, so Mr. Brooks could not pretend he didn't, like he started to.

The best man told me to shut up. And Mr. Brooks sort of smiled at me, but like a fish.

I said, "She cannot marry him because she is engaged to Frank." Well, the best man grabbed me, but I kept my knees stiff, and I said, "She got engaged last night. I was there."

The best man started to pull me towards the side door, so I bit him. And I really bit him, because he does not know that I bite, like Steve knows.

Mr. Brooks said it was very irregular, and he kept mopping his head, even on top. Then Elsie started to cry, but she could not find her hankie.

And then Mr. Pope came walking down the aisle. He said, "If your ritual is not an empty mockery, you will listen to this little child."

Well, for a minute there was not a sound in the whole church.

Only the squeak that Grandpa Sampson's box thing makes. He is deaf.

All of a sudden he said right out loud, "Why don't they speak up? I can't hear a dang word!"

Everybody began to talk, so Mr. Brooks put up his arms, high, like Mr. Mudge, with his fingers shaking, and he said, "Let us all pray."

We closed our eyes and bowed our heads, but I saw something white by the side door, and when he said "Amen" Elsie was gone.

The next morning everything happened so fast you would not believe it. First father opened some letters by his plate at breakfast, and he said, "Good Lord, Martha, here are three checks I never expected to see. What on earth's struck everybody?"

I said, "Then is Josephine Coyle paid for now?"

But mother was pointing at something in the paper. She passed it to father and almost knocked over the asters. "They've got it in the paper! Read it, George!"

It said Elsie ran away and eloped with Frank, which is an awful lie, because when we found them up the creek in Frank's boat at suppertime eating egg sandwiches, they said that they would not get married till next spring.

"Well," I said, "we are on the front page again, father, and you said we never would be. But of course, we are famouser for the ancient Oak where the Father of Our Country rested."

Father did not say anything, and mother did not look at me at all.

I was going out when mother said, "Honesty, you are not to go off the porch — do you hear? — not off the porch."

"There is some mistake," I said. Then I remembered Steve was in their room talking before they were out of bed, so I said, "If Steve says I have done anything, he will descend into Hell and be Damned, like Mr. Mudge said, because it is a wicked lie."

And father looked at me. He said, "Now I know why the Spartans exposed their female infants to the elements. . . . Go away."

Petey Judson was out on the porch, and he asked me to go to the movies. Then two more friends came up. And Mr. Lee said, how was I feeling, and wasn't it a lovely day? Other people came up the walk, and everybody was very nice to me, all of a sudden.

Mr. Price stopped by, and said didn't I want to walk with him a ways? Well, you have to be polite to a man like Mr. Price, so, of course, I walked downtown with him. A lot of people said hello, and Mr. Price said, "My, but you are a popular young lady, aren't you, angel-face?" He said wouldn't I like a little present, and I thought and then I said I would love a manicure with red on my nails.

We went into Sue Orr's Beauty Salon. But she said if she did it, father would skin her alive, so I had two hot-fudge sundaes with marshmallow sauce instead.

Then there was Steve, driving our car, though he is not old enough for a license, and could be in jail, and he grabbed me by the straps of my green jumper dress right where they cross in back, and he pulled me into the car, as if I was about six years old.

When we got home he told mother everybody was trying to get on my right side, and bribing me, because nobody was sure how much I knew, or what I might make up, and did she realize those sundaes were exactly the same as hush money, like in the movies?

And he said he never thought he would live to see a blackmailer in his own family.

They were going upstairs, and I did not hear the rest, because a big truck was backing up in front of our house. Two men carried in this big thing and dumped it in our hall. You will not believe it, but it was my dressing table with skirts — right out of the store window. And there was a card on it that said, "To Honesty, from Frank. Thanks a million."

Then mother said, "You can help me pack. Come along upstairs now."

I did not see why Steve could not pack his stuff himself, but I came up. And there she was — packing *my* things!

Well, I just could not get over it. Here I was, all of a sudden going away to visit my uncle, on a train, and I never knew it till this minute.

I said, "Here I have been dying to go away all summer, and now at the very end we have to be in a big rush. It is funny."

Mother said, yes, it was very funny.

So I said, "I wish you had told me sooner, so I could look forward all summer."

"We did not know," she said. "Just today father and I decided this would be a good time for you to be away a little while. It will be nice to have a change before school opens."

At first I could not say anything much. I just sat on the bed and thought how wonderful everything was. Then I knew.

"Mother," I said, "it is like a reward!" She said to hand her my toothbrush. "It is a reward," I said, "for always telling the truth."

Mother was hunting for something in the bottom of a drawer, and her face got all red. At last she said it was not a reward at all. There were lots of times when it was better just to keep quiet and not tell the truth. I was so surprised my mouth fell open, and then she was answering the telephone.

It was the nurse from the Webbs' at last, so father took the car and there we were without any car to get to the Junction.

Mrs. Curtis was standing in the doorway. She said she was certain Mr. Pope would be glad to drive us in his car, and if mother did not like to ask him, she would.

So in a little while we were on the way, all in the front seat — mother, me, and then Mr. Pope. It is an old car, with the top down, but he drives it very fast in the town and very slow out where the traffic is light. Father says he is a menace on the roads.

He had to go slow round the fence at Washington's Oak. I said, "Washington rested here." I said it just from habit, I guess.

He clucked his tongue. He said, "Amazing how such a legend has been allowed to stand all these years!"

Well, I could feel mother draw up tight beside me, like she does when she is insulted. She said, "Legend?"

He said, "I fear Washington was never within ten miles of Winsett."

Mother said, "Look at the plaque and everything. It must be true."

Mr. Pope sighed. "In the work I am writing it takes just three paragraphs to prove, beyond a shadow of doubt, that this is just one more of New England's pretty fables. . . . Well, well, you will be missing your train."

I was cold all over. I grabbed his arm, and we almost hit another car. I said, "Mr. Pope! You would not TELL!"

Mother looked at me. She said, "But if it's the truth, Honesty?"

Well, I just could not believe my own mother would say such a thing — seeing it was our Oak. I thought how everybody would just about die of shame, and they would have to take down the plaque, and the licenses would stop coming from all over, and I just could not bear it. Mr. Pope was patting my knee and saying not to cry, and then we got to the Junction. Mr. Pope kept saying all the time that it was a scholar's religion to tell the truth and not hide it.

I said, "Mr. Pope, if you tell, I will never speak to you again." He was saying something, but we could not hear, as the train came in that minute. And before I knew it I was up those stairs and inside, and mother was telling me again how my uncle would come for me, but I was not listening.

Then mother and Mr. Pope were standing under the window that was open, and Mr. Pope started to say something. The train began to move, so he had to walk along with it.

He said, "Prudence, my dear, if you feel so strongly about it, I will strike it out."

He had to run then, to keep up, and he kept shouting that he would strike out the whole page, and not tell a single human soul.

I waved and waved, and they got smaller and smaller, and then I sat right down on a lady's purse. But she did not mind. And I said, "Men are wonderful, aren't they?"

And she said she was glad I thought so.

MONARCH THE BUM

By George Agnew Chamberlain

MONARCH BOOM, named after prosperity the way mothers name their babies after the current President, was foaled late in the bumper year of 1928. The rules of the ancient Trotting and Pacing Association decree that every colt becomes a yearling on the first of January next following the day of his birth, consequently the Monarch, classed as a two-year-old at the age of fifteen months, got off to a bad start. This fact seems to have depressed him throughout his long career. He is still very much alive, thank God, but he has always been a melancholy horse, big, awkward, lanky in the legs, short in the barrel and with a hammer head a shade too heavy for his longish neck. However, fortune smiled on him wanly in two ways: he was a plugger by nature, and at the calendar age of five he drifted into the possession of Biggo Trumpet.

Between that time and the racing season of 1940 he became known on every minor trotting circuit in the country as Monarch the Bum, and this is how it happened. Mr. Trumpet, who was made out of whipcord and wire as to body, clothes and mind, looked tall and wasn't, looked meek and wasn't, looked dumb and had a brain as quick as a weasel's jaws. His specialty was either finding soft spots or making them and, owing to his genius, the ungainly stallion went around reaping in small stakes as steadily as a combine bags wheat. Since Biggo was owner, manager, trainer and driver of his one-horse string, expenses could be pared to the bone, and as a result the Bum established the record set forth below.

For seven years he supported Mr. and Mrs. Trumpet and their two sons; the elder of whom, Charles, he put through college and law school. At the advanced age of ten he provided a handsome funeral for Mrs. Trumpet and enabled Biggo to employ a permanent swipe — a swipe being a groom, handler, horse nurse or handy man. Incidentally, the Monarch paid for a powerful roadster of so ancient a vintage it had a dickey instead of a rumble. Also he raked in the price for the contraption it towed — a box stall on wheels so awesome it had to be seen to be believed. In addition, he was the source of Biggo's safety wad — forty-five dollars tucked into a grimy empty ointment jar and never used except to make a night jump away from disaster. Finally — and this must have been a bitter pill for the old warrior — he supplied the cash for the purchase of his destined successor, a saucy young filly registered as Molly Q.

On the last day in June of the year that made the Monarch a twelve-year-old, Beech Tree Park was drowsy with well-being, pleasant odors and ruin. Time was when it had been the scene of many a historic meet, but ever since the banks had foreclosed on the property, the park had been sliding downhill into disreputable beauty. Beside the great gate, too rotted to close, stood the house of Samuel Biggers, the caretaker. He was a good-natured man who, for a couple of dollars, and often for nothing at all, would let an outfit bed down while laying over between racing dates. None of the hundred stables was in good repair, the track was overgrown, and its rail more down than up, but the horses could be worked on sod, the grass inside the oval was belly-high and there was such peace as only sherry-glass elms, domed maples and a spreading beech can bring to the soul of man and beast.

With Windsor, the scene of the Fourth of July battle for cash and honor, only a few miles and four days away, the harness-horse fraternity had been drifting into the park like pigeons to their cote. Bill Davis, the horseshoer, would have none of the tumble-down blacksmith shop. He had set up his tent and portable forge under the great beech, and at this sunset hour when the nags were munching grain and man's stew was still in the pot, he was holding court, as is the custom of his trade the world over. Owners, trainers, drivers and swipes were lounging around; everybody from Mr. Biggers and his twelve-year-old daughter to Crocodile Ben, a darky with the widest mouth in Christendom.

Bill Davis sat on a nail keg with a newspaper spread across his knees. "Well, folks," he said, "I see here how Old Man Pap Biggo Trumpet won a first for hisself down to Hanover yistidday."

"Will that Monarch the Bum never die?" murmured a jealous trainer.

"If he'd won it with the Bum," said Bill, "that wouldn't be news. It says here how he done it with a brown filly named Molly Q. by Happy Frolic out of Nancy Prank."

"What line is that?" scoffed the trainer. "Bingen, I'll bet. So old Monarch the Bum is dead at last."

"No, sir, he ain't," said Bill, "because it says here how he took third money in the same race."

Instantly everybody tensed with interest. "If that's so," boomed Crocodile Ben, "who druv him?"

"G. Trumpet, driver," read Bill.

G. Trumpet had them all stopped until little Jessie Biggers sprang to her feet. She had a heartshaped face and big eyes set at a flaring angle from her trembling chin. In sneakers, socks and an abbreviated play suit that left displayed an astonishing stretch of gangling legs, she looked as wobbly as a new-dropped calf.

"G. stands for Geoffrey," she gasped, "and that means Stump."

"Stump!" jeered several voices at once.

"Why, honey," said Bill, "that Stump couldn't drive no hoss except to a jog cart; he's only fo'teen. Besides, he ain't much taller'n you are and for his feet to reach the stirrups of a bike they'd have to build a bridge. Perhaps it was that wo'thless swipe, Bundle, took Stump's name."

"Bundle's almost blind," said Jessie, still breathless with excitement; "he can't see further'n a cat can spit."

"Well, anyways," said Bill, "I can see fur enough to reckon Biggo Trumpet has pulled another fast one. Minds me of the time up to York when all the boys was milling around the hotel lobby, figurin' whether to start for Bridgeton. Biggo come bustin' in, rams hisself in the telephone booth and slams the door without noticin' how it jams on his coattail. He puts through a long-distance call to the sports editor of the Salem Standard and Jerseyman, and all on us hears him say, 'Al, what entries they got over to Bridgeton? No! What? Andover Farms, eh? Golden State too? Ted Thomas up behind Blodget Black? You sure, Al? Thomas the Great?' Then the old man kind o' chokes with rage, an' he says, 'That ain't no race meetin', Al; it's a free exhibition with the drivers holdin' the sucker's bag.' He come out black as a thunderhead, steals a chair when somebody stood up to spit, pulls his cap down to his chin and goes to sleep."

"Is that a story?" asked Jess, too young to stand the silence.

"No," said Bill, "but the rest on it is. While Biggo set there sleepin', Ma Trumpet and her boys, with Monarch the Bum in his trailer hutch, was eatin' up the road to Bridgeton. Biggo went down in the mornin' by train and his phony phone call netted him four hundred dollars as easy as holdin' your mouth open under a persimmon tree."

When the laugh had died down, somebody asked, "How fur you make it from here to Hanover, Bill?"

"You're worried already," said Bill, "an' you got a right to be. I make it all of four hundred miles, but I'm betting Pap Biggo Trumpet will pull in here afore nooning tomorrer."

Crocodile's cellar-door jaw opened, quivered and spoke. "There's him now," he announced, "comin' tru de gate."

The strangest thing about Biggo's outfit was that no matter how often seen, every fresh manifestation left the observer appalled, but this time the innovation of housing for two horses instead of one froze the group around the forge into the staring immobility of waxworks. First came the powerful roadster with the old man and his younger son under its patched canvas top. Next came the dickey, stuffed with Bundle and the bedrolls. Next a link of strip iron that looked as if it would break any minute, but that hadn't broken in five years. Then came the marvel of marvels, a sort of hutch on wheels, with a penthouse to protect the protruding heads of the horses and drip rain on Bundle. The hutch was roofed and had a hinged back wall that could be let down for a runway. Wired to the axle of the trailer were the shafts of two sulkies — bikes to the cognoscenti — one piled on top of the other to save its delicate pneumatic tires.

This startling motorcade, or road serpent, coasted to a halt under the broad beech and Biggo Trumpet climbed out. Because space was scarce, he wore all his driving gear — mud goggles pushed heavenward over a visored cap, a pepper-and-salt three days' beard, coat, jumper, black silk shirt and whipcord driving pants with straps under his insteps. His eyes were so deeply set under furry eyebrows you couldn't tell whether they were gray or black and, as a matter of fact, they took turns being one or the other, according to mood. There was no doubt about his hair; it showed gray when he pushed back his cap to give his sweating head a good scratch.

"What kep' you so long, Pap?" asked Bill.

"Stopping at Bantam to give the old hoss a drink of pond water," said Biggo solemnly. "Somehow a swig o' pond water seems to do him more good than ary two-dollar bottle of leg wash."

Stump, since yesterday the only fourteen-year-old boy on record to have driven in a standard meet, stepped down from the roadster. As to clothes, he was a replica of his father, and he wouldn't have looked so short if he hadn't been so square. Belligerent eyes stared out of a freckled face and dared the world to deny he was a driver. Jessie ran to him, stopped in awe and rubbed one instep against her other calf.

"Stump," she whispered, "did you sure enough drive in a race?"

"Sure," said Stump, "I druv all right."

"Did they have to build a bridge to the stirrups?"

"Shucks," he said, "come have a look." He led her around to the rear where Bundle already had freed the lashings on the sulkies. The one on top was brand new, the other was old and scarred. He pointed to its freshest wounds where the steel hoops of the stirrups had been unscrewed from the shafts and moved all the way back. "I can reach 'em fine," he said, "but it most splits me in two."

She looked at him adoringly, because a driver is a driver whatever his age or height. Impulsively she pulled out a crumpled package and offered him a lemon drop, her only available tribute. He took it because Jess was Jess, but as soon as she wasn't looking he spit it out and substituted a chaw of picnic twist. He and Bundle separated the bikes and rolled them into shelter. They let down the runway and slid out the tack trunk. The Monarch backed sedately down the incline, but the filly had to be turned and led.

When the horses were stabled in the two least leaky of the remaining vacant stalls, Bundle stayed to care for them while Stump went back to the group around the forge.

Crocodile Ben raised on one elbow. "Haw, haw, haw!" he brayed. "How's G. Trumpet?"

Stump flicked his chaw into his cheek and squirted a jet that splashed the darky's bare foot. "You still a swipe, ain't you, Croc?" he asked unsmilingly.

The darky stared up at him and his big jaw wobbled uncertainly. "I sho is, Mr. Stump," he said humbly. "This here shine ain't nothin' but a swipe, an' never will be."

"Set down, Stump," said Bill, the horseshoer. "I hear how you druv a right good race down to Hanover. Seein' how late it is, I'd be pleased if you and your pap would have supper with me."

The crowd took the hint, not suddenly but with a languid spacing that made each departure seem a melting away rather than a break. Mr. Biggers had to take Jessie's hand, because she was trying to walk with her head swiveled around like an owl's, her big eyes fixed on the blur of Stump's form.

"Daddy," she said, hurt, yet with awe in her voice, "Stump was chawin'."

"Don't let that worry you none," said Mr. Biggers comfortingly. "He don't like tobacky any more'n I do, and shouldn't wonder he won't never chaw agin. He's just showing how he's a driver now."

Bill ladled out food on tin plates and poured boiled coffee into pannikins. The long twilight faded and from all about came the glow of half a dozen mess fires and the twinkle of swaying lanterns. A heavy fragrance permeated the air, the delectable aroma of horse.

"Biggo," said Bill, "that's a likely filly you picked on. Does Q. stand for Question?"

Biggo mashed natural leaf in his palm and crammed it into his pipe before he answered. "Not rightly," he muttered.

"Why don't you tell Bill the truth?" said Stump. "Molly Q. is a hedgerow filly. The old man slipped the Monarch through a fence and a year later he come back and bought the puzzle foal off'n the farmer for next to nothin'.""

Bill laughed. "Saved a winter's keep, some money and a peck of trouble."

"Molly Q. ain't my trouble," said Biggo sullenly; "this here Stump is my trouble. He's pig iron to whip and pig-headed to reason with. I look ahead and plan to fix me a filly can put him through college the way the Monarch did his brother, and what does he say?"

"What do you say, Stump?" asked Bill.

"I say I don't need no college nor law school nuther to learn me to sell insurance."

"Is that what Charles is doing now?" asked Bill.

"Yes, sir," admitted Biggo; "he had to start somethin' somehow."

"Well," said Bill, "it's nice work while your friends last."

Stump rose. "I'm going to bed in alongside the Monarch."

The two men watched his stocky form stalk toward the stables. "I shouldn't wonder that lad has a lot of foresight," murmured Bill.

"Foresight or hindsight," muttered Biggo, "I promised his ma I'd put him through college like we done Charles, and I'm a-gonna do it if I have to prod him with a whip spur till his behind shows blood."

With the Windsor race meet only four days away, everybody was plenty busy reading entries and jockeying around for a soft spot. Knowing Biggo Trumpet would smell it out if there was one, interest naturally centered on Molly Q. Since Biggo permitted no one but himself to work her, apparently he intended to drive her, and many were the railbirds out to clock her speed. But the old man was too canny for them. He never let her go a mile all out, and the one time he did a half it was split in two by a marker instead of being from post to post.

Bill, the horseshoer, was not numbered among the snipers, and spent all his spare time watching his friend of many years, Monarch the Bum. The old horse was never haltered. After his workout he would stand while Bundle ran the foam off him with a scraper and rubbed him down and Stump wrapped his legs. After his toilet was complete he quit being a horse and became a huge ungainly dog. Wherever Stump went, he followed him around so close it looked as if he was going to bite the patch off the seat of Stump's everyday pants. If Stump stopped or sat down, the horse would graze, but the minute Stump moved, he would fall in behind again, just like a dog.

On the afternoon of the second day Bill saw smoke rising from the abandoned blacksmith shop in the distance and strolled over to find out who was poaching on his preserves. To his surprise, he discovered a fresh fire in the forge, but no interloper. Just as he was about to leave, Stump strolled in, followed as usual by the lumbering Monarch. Stump fished a green wisp from under his jumper and fed it to the horse.

"Dawggone!" exclaimed Bill. "That's the fust time I ever seen a hoss eat mint."

Stump stared at him gravely. "It's on account of his third owner being Colonel Rumpmeir, of Lexington," he said. "The colonel was poor and he seen how the Monarch was outgrowin' the only sulky the colonel had. So to stunt him he started feedin' him mint juleps out of a old ten-pound lard can. It shorted the Monarch lengthwise, but not up and down, and he ain't never forgot the smell of mint."

"Dawggone!" breathed Bill, looking in vain for the trace of a smile on the boy's face. "Say, son, what is it you want? Because for that yarn you can have anything I got."

Stump sank on his heels, laid a hand on one of the Monarch's big forefeet and looked up eagerly. "I want him shod here with clips for four-ounce toe weights, Bill, and only you and me to know about it. That's why I got the fire goin' in the old forge."

"You figurin' to double-cross your old man, Stump?" asked Bill, after a pause.

"Yes, I am," said Stump promptly. He rose, reached his arm over the Monarch's drooping neck and hugged his big head. "I'm figurin' to double-cross him so he can see his left ear with his right eye."

"Wal, sir, I passed my word," drawled Bill, "so they ain't much else I can do but keep it.   You bring the Bum in here tomorrow morning when all the others is out on the track and I'll fix him up.   You want the toe weights on or off?"

"Off," said Stump.   "I'll want 'em in my pocket, Bill, and when you see my jumper quit saggin' over to Windsor, you'd better get your bettin' done."

"Sure, sure," said Bill, "that's the way to talk."

Jess Biggers had been keeping in the background for three reasons: Because she knew enough to stay out of the way when men were busy, because she detested boys who chawed tobacco, and finally because she was twelve.   Twelve is an ungainly age for a girl, and she knows it; if she is going to be shy only once between the day of her birth and the date of her death, it will be while she is twelve.   Nevertheless, when Stump was on his way to the blacksmith shop the next morning, all he had to do to bring her to his side was to beckon with his head.   "What's been the matter with you?" he asked.

"Nuthin'," she said, examining his mouth for traces of tobacco, and finding none.

Stump looked her over critically.   "You're nigh as funny as a late yearling," he began ominously; and then went on, "But I know fillies, Jess, and you're hung together right.   By the time your legs quit wobbling and your flesh gets set, I wouldn't be surprised you'd be the best-looking girl anywheres in the whole country."

Tears of gratitude rushed to her eyes, but she knew better than to let them fall.   "Oh, Stump!" she breathed.

"You want to help me?" he asked.

"Of course.   Anything you say, Stump."

"The Monarch's wearing a halter this morning, and that's so you can hold him for Bill while I do somethin' else.   And don't say nothin' to anybody about what Bill does to him, Jess; not to your dad nor nobody."

"I won't."

"You goin' to Windsor tomorrow?"

"Yes.   I begged and dad promised."

"I'll need you there too," said Stump, frowning mysteriously.
"What for?"
"Never mind.   You just be around when I want you."

While she stayed in the shop, hanging to the Monarch's halter and with her cheek pressed to his velvet muzzle, Stump hurried back to the stables.   At this hour they were deserted, Bundle and all the rest of the riffraff hugging the rail to watch the drivers give their prospects a final workout.   Stump unlocked the Trumpet tack trunk and hunted through the bottles of leg wash, body wash, liniment, Old Man Candy's Remedy, grain alcohol and Danbury's Colic Cure, until he came upon a smeared and opaque jar that had once contained Maxa Wonder Mixture.   He unscrewed the top and extracted Biggo's forty-five-dollar safety wad.   No qualm of conscience troubled him; the Monarch had won that money a hundred times over, and as for himself, Biggo had conveniently forgotten to give him his driver's percentage or suggest a wage.

All the way to Windsor the next day Biggo talked a steady streak, and here is a sample: "Son, while we're rattlin' along so's nobody can hear nothin', not even Bundle, I'm goin' to tell ye ag'in how we're goin' to win this here race.   We're entered in the two-ten and the two-twenty trots.   The two-ten comes first on the card and guarantees a thousand-dollar purse to the winner; the other's only a measly four hundred.   Naturally, the boys think I ain't so crazy as to take a green filly into no two-ten events, but you and me is the only ones knows all about Molly Q.   She's by Monarch Boom out of a country Morgan mare, and she'll keep right on hammering her four little hoofs until her harness rots from sweat.   So while the boys is figurin' we're laying off for the two-twenty, you be ready to go and step out for the two-ten.   We don't know what places we've drawed, and it don't matter.   When we git the 'Go' you carry the Monarch out of the ruck for all that's in him, and you and me knows it's plenty.   If you and him can't trot all these fancy jugheads off their feet by the halfway mark, you're never going to be no driver and the Monarch ain't no hoss."

For the first time Stump broke in, his eyes smarting with tears.

"He's the greatest hoss ever lived," he declared thickly. "He's fed you and me and buried ma and wasted half his winnings on educatin' Charles."

"There you go!" barked Biggo irascibly. "Who'm I working for, you ongrateful little sawed-off? You do like I say or I'll hire another driver and warm your hide to boot. But don't forget this last bit. Once you've shook off the bunch, you ease down, open up and let me through. Now quit your whumpering, 'cause if the Monarch seen you cry, I swan, he'd cry too."

Arrived at the track, they were allotted the humblest quarters in the Forty Horse Barn, and it was easy to keep out of everybody's way. Jess gave her father the slip and did a sort of hop, skip and jump over the sulky shafts down the long line of stables until she came to the last and worst.

"Hello, Stump."

He appeared not to hear her, but presently beckoned her inside the Monarch's stall, out of sight and hearing of Bundle and his father. He took out the safety wad and peeled off thirty dollars while she stared. "You know any of the bookies?" he asked.

"I know Mr. Brussy."

"No, no, that's the auction pool. The auction sells tickets to win the race whether it's two heats or four. What I mean is the handbook guys with a blackboard showing the odds on each heat separate."

"Mr. Trout comes to the house a lot."

"Fine," said Stump. "He's fair and he's honest. Now, Jess, here's somethin' nobody else knows, not yit. We're going out for the two-ten trot, and that's the next race. You take this." He cut down the thirty dollars to twenty and then to ten. "Don't you never let on where you got the money, but as soon as the odds go up, you bet this sawbuck with Mr. Trout on Monarch Boom to win the heat."

Stump's driving pants and the mud goggles pushed back on his broad forehead looked very businesslike, but there was a glassiness in his eyes and a white line around his mouth that frightened Jess.

"Stump, ain't you feeling well?"

"You bet I'm feeling well. You get outa here, or the first thing you know you'll be missing the best odds."

Etiquette decrees that a driver arrive at the track in the following manner: With his swipe leading the horse, he himself walks behind the sulky, his short whip at the slant and the long reins draped over one arm. Having passed the gate, he swings a leg, lands in the seat of the bike, plants his feet in the stirrups, takes his handholds and nods. The swipe hooks the checkrein, steps away, and the driver proceeds to warm up his entry, sometimes trotting half the round of the track before coming back to score.

Stump, being his own swipe, climbed into the sulky at the stable and drove from there. The Monarch stepped out briskly, telegraphing back along the reins to his young master not to worry. But Stump was worrying all right; his throat was clogged with a big lump and he found he couldn't spit. When he reached the track, two things happened — a great laugh went up and the Monarch took charge. In no time the laughter was tempered with admiration. Not a boy but envied this fourteen-year-old with legs so short he looked as if he was doing the splits; not a man but wished his own youngster or even himself could handle a big horse with such cheeky confidence. Molly Q. had drawn third place from the pole, and the Monarch seventh, with two more horses in the second tier. It was an awkward field to handle, and the trotters scored five times before the starter lost his patience.

"For shame, gentlemen!" he shouted. "I warn you, gentlemen! Take a lesson from the youngest among you, Mr. Geoffrey Trumpet, who has had his horse in position every time."

"He means the old Bum rammed Stump into position!" yelled a railbird, but before a laugh could reward him the horses were off.

It was a ragged start, such a start as invariably follows a warning, but Stump was lucky. Like all the others, thanks to the Monarch, he whirled two paces short of the mark he had been using, and the wise old horse beat the starter's "Go" by half a length and crossed the line trotting all out. Nobody worried about his lead, least of all the drivers. Stump, even to his father, was only a boy showing off. Against the old hands up behind such horses as Lily Put, Doremus Cub and Outlander, he couldn't hold the lead with a motor bike, let alone a sulky. Biggo was also lucky. Because he stuck to his plan to lay in behind, he avoided a tangle between the three hottest entries, and in the backstretch sidled out of the ruck to find nothing ahead but the Monarch.

The old horse was pulling him so hard he didn't have to worry about what was behind. He tightened his grip on the handholds and for the first time called on the filly for speed. She had it and gave it, but to his amazement the gap between him and the bike ahead failed to close. He set himself to drive, though still so far from home it was against his better judgment, and only at the bend before the stretch did he draw close enough to yell: "Hi, Stump, ease up! Hi-yah, Stump, you hear me? Stump, ye little pot o' meat, let me get to you or I'll whale the livin' lights —— "

Take a pencil and do a little figuring, but first measure off forty-four feet. A trotter traveling at a two-minute clip covers forty-four feet per second. This is a fact never absorbed by the crowd and often forgotten by the most experienced driver. On this occasion, so great was its foreshortening power that when Stump swept into the straight-away his mind was still in the backstretch, and the screaming grand-stand with a long-legged girl jumping up and down like a jack-in-the-box on stilts became a dream, but a glorious dream. Just as he would have done had the hallucination been real, he spread his arms as wide as his legs, held the reins high and carried the Monarch under the wire a winner by a length.

The old horse turned of himself just short of the quarter mark and came jogging back in time for Stump to hear the loud-speaker blare: "Ladies and gentlemen! Winner of the first heat of the two-ten trot, Number Seven, Monarch Boom, in two minutes eight and one quarter seconds. Second, Number One, Lily Put. Third, Number Three, Molly Q."

Stump waited to hear no more, since he had a special interest in getting to the stables ahead of his father. By the time Biggo got there, fingering his driving whip nervously, Stump was holding a pitchfork in one hand and scraping down the Monarch with the other. He stared at the short whip, Biggo stared at the two-pronged fork.

"Did you hear me yell at you to ease up?" demanded Biggo.

"I heered a faint calling somewheres behind," said Stump, then his eyes flared with fight. "Say, what did you want I should do, pull the race under the judges' noses and git me barred? Or was you figurin' I ought to jump out, pick up the Monarch and carry him back where you and his jughead daughter could lick him?"

Biggo turned purple, but before he could answer the cohorts arrived — worshiping boys, admiring fathers, one little girl on the edge of the crowd, and Crocodile Ben, shouldering through to offer Stump his services as swipe, handler, nurse and guide, free gratis for nothing.

As the Crocodile went to work on the Monarch he began to sing, feeling around a bit for a while at the start, then letting her go:

> *"Jonah, Jonah!*
> *Some folks say no whale swallered Jonah,*
> *But I seen Jonah swaller a whale."*

The thirty minutes between heats passed all too swiftly for Jess, and not until Stump, with Crocodile at the Monarch's head, started for the track could she get within whispering distance.

"Stump, I got it. Mr. Trout wanted to give it to dad, but dad said it was none of his business and to give it to me. Stump, it's such a lot, what'll I do?"

"Nothin'," said Stump, staring straight ahead. "See you later."

Biggo drew up alongside. "I'm asking no favors this time, you, Stump," he said. "Do anything you're a mind to, because the day I can't beat any ongrateful, freckly-faced, fourteen-year-old five-gallon tub of a swol-headed boy I'm ready to eat hay and bray."

That's the way all the other weathered drivers felt, and they proceeded to prove they were right. The Monarch in an outside position was one thing, but his win put him on the pole and made him their meat. They came down for a clean start and stole the rail before

Stump knew the race was on. The heels of the horses ahead battered him with an incredible barrage. Clots of mud from the damp
track, mixed with pebbles, rained on his goggles and stung his cheeks.
Half blinded, he would glimpse an opening and make for it, but when
he got there the gap had closed. With startling suddenness the fusil-
lade ceased and he knocked up his goggles to see what had happened. Lily Put, Outlander and Doremus Cub, followed by Molly
Q., were taking the curve into the homestretch. He stared, fas-
cinated, at his father as the old man laid the filly on her side as if she
were a yacht and shot downhill to steal the pole.

He straightened her as he hit it, and his frenzied voice floated back
in a terrific crescendo, "Take 'em, Molly! Lay your belly down!
Oh, Molly-olly-olly-olly! Hi-yah! Hi-yah! Yah! Yah! Yah!"

So engrossed was Stump in that masterpiece of driving, he all but
got the red flag that excluded the horses behind him from further
participation in the two-ten trot. Having escaped that disgrace, he
loafed along slow enough to hear the result: Molly Q., first; Outlander, second; Lily Put, third; Doremus Cub and Monarch Boom
also ran. He kept round the right way of the track to the stables
and found Jess waiting for him.

"Oh, Stump, I'm so glad you've come Here, take it. Three hundred and ten dollars. You count it, Stump. Dad said make you
count it."

Stump added the odd ten dollars to the thirty-five still in his pocket,
hurried over to the tack trunk and packed the safety wad back
where it belonged. Then, while Crocodile went to work on the
Monarch, he pushed Jess into the deepest corner of the stall, pressed
the three hundred dollars back into her hand and closed her fingers
around it.

"Listen, kid," he said, "if you're skeered take your daddy with you,
but you git out there quick and bet every cent of this on Monarch
Boom to win."

She looked at him, her face as white and drawn as his own. "Race
or heat?"

He could have kissed her for that question, so deep in horse lore it would have done credit to Biggo himself. "Yes, sir," he said, "you're right. If I come in second to a Cub first, I could still win the race. So that means the odds for the Monarch to win the heat will be longer."

"Oh, Stump," begged Jess, "don't do it, please don't. Three hundred dollars is an awful lot o' money."

Somehow, it was the wrong thing to say. Stump's chin stuck out and his eyes hardened. "Sure," he said, "and the Monarch's an awful lot of horse. You git like I told you and bet on the heat. All of it on the nose, mind you."

Jess went straight to Mr. Trout and read his board:

	WIN	PLACE	SHOW
Lily Put	4	2	0
Molly Q.	10	8	4
Monarch Boom . .	30	15	5

That's as far as she got; never mind about Doremus Cub and Outlander.

"Mr. Trout, please, I'd like a hundred dollars on Monarch Boom to win."

"Eh?" said Mr. Trout. "Jessie, you'd better run to your mother and get her to feel your head. You ain't well."

She ran to her father instead, and was a little puzzled to find him quite willing to help her. She didn't have to argue at all, and with his assistance placed fifty dollars with Mr. Trout at thirty to one, sixty with Mr. Burney at the same odds, forty with Mr. Welles at twenty-five to one and a hundred with Mr. Fargo at twenty to one. That covered the bookies Mr. Biggers was willing to trust, and he took her into the auction tent. Sitting on her father's shoulder, and amid much good-natured kidding from everybody who knew Stump and herself, she bid in fifty dollars' worth of tickets on the Monarch to win at an average of twenty to one.

"Jessie," said Mr. Biggers as he led her out from the crowded tent, "I'm glad that's over and mighty glad you've said good-by to every cent of the three hundred. The odds on the board never lie. Mr.

Trumpet is driving a green filly, so he's discounted under Lily Put in spite of his win. As for Stump, just like the board says, even with a better hoss he wouldn't have no more chance than a puppy against a bunch of tigers. But I'm glad you've put up every cent because it's goin' to teach you kids from the start that money don't grow on trees."

"I don't care what happens," said Jessie in a weak voice. "Stump told me to do it and I did it. I love Stump."

"Sure," said Mr. Biggers, giving her hand an encouraging squeeze, "and you go right on loving him. Stump's a fine boy, and the best thing about him is he can take what he's surely going to get."

When Crocodile was through with cooling the Monarch, Stump led him into the stable and rolled the door shut. He reached his arms around the old warrior's neck, pulled down his head and laid his cheek against his silky nose.

"Monarch," he whispered, "you got to listen, and listen hard. If you win this one heat, Monarch, you won't ever have to race again, only loaf and eat sugar all your born days. And I'm here to help you. I got a present for you, something you never wore before. It's going to take heart to throw them out, but that's what you got, Monarch, more heart than a white-oak tree." He dropped on his knees, fumbled in his pockets, brought out the toe weights and slipped them home. "Don't you worry about them flyin' off," he said to the horse. "Bill done a good job, and the harder you pound, the tighter they'll git."

"Mr. Stump," brayed Crocodile from outside, "they's calling the third heat of the two-ten trot!"

Before they could get the Monarch hitched and ready, the four other horses left in the race had stepped out on the track, warmed up and whirled into position.

"We're waiting for Mr. G. Trumpet!" megaphoned the starter.

"Aw, heck," yelled a driver, "we're goin' to wait for him all the way, ain't we? Let's go!"

The Monarch plodded through the gate with Crocodile at his head, and though Stump had to scramble awkwardly to reach the seat of the bike, this time nobody laughed. Crocodile snapped the checkrein home and stood away. The old horse started down the track, but when Stump tried to turn him, he gave his head a shake and kept on. He knew his rights; let the other horses fuss and their drivers holler. These things on his toes felt funny. They certainly weren't meant to make him stumble, so what were they for? He turned of his own accord, and as he trotted briskly back he found out. So that was the answer — lift your forefeet a little higher, just a little higher, and you feel that magic pull, something heavy yanking you out and on. The rest of the horses were waiting and watching, and matched his pace going back for the score. The five sulkies whirled and hit the start to the thunder of twenty pounding hoofs.

"Go!"

This was it, this was the race. A great lump was in Stump's throat, choking him. He had betrayed the Monarch; in that hurricane start he had let the veteran drivers show him up for the sawed-off punk he was. Then a message came quivering through the reins, up his arms and into his brain along the oldest telegraph line known to man. The Monarch was talking to him, shouting at him, yelling: "Hold me up, boy, because I'm going to go!"

Stump took a wrap on the reins and lent the big horse his steadying weight. The Monarch lifted his forefeet higher, trying them out. Then just a little higher, and the hoofs that had pounded through two hundred miles of battle discovered a world beyond, that half inch of stride that thunders on the gates of the Valhalla of the two-minute trotter and bids them open to another hero of the track. He flung out his forefeet boldly, and for every yard the bunch at his withers traveled he gained an inch. He was on the outside, but what of it? All he needed now was heart, and heart was what he had. Whirling wheels no longer troubled his vision, only sweat was in his nostrils, horse sweat like his own.

Thus came true the dream of every spectator — five trotters fanning around the bend into the homestretch as even as a fanning windshield wiper. This time Stump knew where he was, knew it in the clarity of a blazing light that made the wire ahead as big as a cable. He threw away his whip, wrapped the reins on his forearms, wrapped them again and stood up. Never before had any driver pulled that stunt, all his weight in the stirrups, with only enough pressure on the bit to hold his balance and head the Monarch true.

"Hi-yah!" he yelled with all the sobbing passion in his heart. "Take 'em, Monarch, take 'em!"

With no weight in the sulky, the old horse had to surge to keep his feet. Sweat loosened his hide and oiled his joints until Stump straddled rippling flesh and rode a rushing river. The great horse widened his belly like a flying squirrel and laid it to the ground. Out of the corner of his eye he caught the scarlet gleam of one nostril, then of another, then of a third. Three horses were down and out, fading into the ruck, and that left only one. But that lone contender was Molly Q.

"Monarch," sobbed Stump, "it's that hedgerow gal, your own murdering daughter! Take her!"

The Monarch knew what to do and when to do it — at the wire he stretched out his long neck and won by a nose. Stump forgot who he was, where he was and what he was doing. The first thing he saw when the Monarch brought him back was Crocodile Ben in the middle of the track, stamping his own straw hat into powder. His eyes bulged, his fingers snapped, his feet stamped and his jaws clanged as he sang:

> *"From the outside!*
> *Oh, me! Oh, my!*
> *Jonah! Jonah!*
> *Some folks say no whale swallered Jonah,*
> *But I seen Jonah swaller a whale."*

It took the loud-speaker to overpower him: "Ladies and gentlemen! You have just witnessed an event that will live in memory as long as trotters trot. You have seen the youngest driver in a major event on this or any other track drive a twelve-year-old horse to a new record. The winner of heat and race, Monarch Boom! Time: two minutes, one and one half seconds! Will the driver, Mr. Geoffrey Trumpet, kindly proceed to the judges' stand to receive purse and cup?"

When Stump fell off the bike into his father's arms he was crying. Biggo held him tight, hiding the boy's face. "Hush, you, Stump," he said. "Fer that one race you're a driver till the day you die. Start your laughing now, son, because tonight you and all the rest of the folks is going to watch me eating hay and listen to me bray."

Stump licked the tears from the corners of his mouth and looked up into Biggo's face. "Will you promise never to race the Monarch again?"

"Sure, son," said Biggo, "I'll promise anything you say. From now on, you don't even have to go to college."

Mr. Biggers, dragging Jessie along, shouldered the crowd aside. He was feeling pretty cheap and his face was grave with wondering how he was ever going to reinstate himself as a worthy guide to the young. "Shouldn't wonder someday he'd found a college, Biggo," he said, "and hire you and me for janitors. . . . Stump, what you want Jess should do with your winnings?"

"How much is they?" asked Stump.

"Seven thousand, three hundred dollars, not counting the stake or your share of the purse."

Biggo's jaw dropped an inch and stayed dropped, but Stump's eyes only locked with Jessie's. "You keep it, Mr. Biggers," he said. "Someday Jess and me is going to need it."

HELEN, THY BEAUTY IS TO ME—

By John Fante

WHEN love came to Julio Sal, he was not prepared. Julio Sal, Filipino boy, forty cents an hour, Tokyo Fish Company, Wilmington. Her name was Helen, she wore a smooth red dress and she worked at the Angels' Ballroom, in Los Angeles. Five feet, four inches was the height of Julio Sal, but when that Helen's golden head lay on his shoulder, strength and grandeur filled his body. A dream shaped itself in his Malay brain. She sensed it too. She always sensed that sort of thing in the Filipino customers. A gallant flame possessed them, and they bought more tickets. The dances were ten cents apiece; she got half of it.

Towering over the golden hair, Julio Sal saw half a hundred of his countrymen gazing after him, watching the serpentine undulations beneath the red dress, watching the fast-diminishing roll of tickets in Helen's left hand. The dances were one minute long. Somewhere behind the four-piece colored band, a bell clanged the end of each number. Since ten o'clock Julio Sal had danced continuously.

Now it was almost midnight. Already he had spent twelve dollars. Forty cents remained in his pocket. It meant four more minutes with the golden hair, and it meant his fare back to the canneries.

The bell clanged, the dance ended, another dance began. In the best alligator style, Julio jittered the dream toward the glass ticket box. Her hand over his shoulder tore a stub from the string and dropped it into the slot.

"Only one left," the girl panted as Julio bounced her in the corner. It was her first word in an hour. Sweat oozed from the dark face of Julio Sal. Again he gazed across the floor at the group of his countrymen.

Ten of them strained against the railing, each clutching a fat roll of tickets, ready to rush upon the golden girl the moment Julio's last ticket disappeared inside the glass box. Despair clutched the heart of Julio Sal. Resolution showed in his brown eyes.

"I get some more," he said.

The bell clanged, the dance ended, another dance began. There was a smile on the girl's white, hot face as she dropped the last ticket into the slot. This time it was a waltz, a breathing spell. Julio Sal nodded to the ticket man, who made his way through the couples, coins jingling in his money apron. Dismay seeped into the faces of the Penoys pressed against the rail. Julio's fingers dug into his watch pocket. Surprised widened the blue eyes of Helen when she saw forty cents — nickel, dime and quarter — pinched between Julio Sal's thumb and forefinger.

"Four tickets," said Julio Sal.

The ticket vender rolled a cigar through his teeth. "Only four?"

"Please."

The bell clanged, the dance ended, another dance began. Out of the corner of his eye Julio Sal saw the dismay leave the faces of his little brown brothers. Their smiles mocked him. They had waited so long; they would gladly wait another four dances. The bell clanged, the dance ended, another dance began; again the bell clanged.

"Helen," said Julio Sal. "Helen, I love you, Helen."

"That's nice," she said, because all the Filipinos loved Helen, because all the Filipinos managed to say it when they got down to their last two or three.

"I write you letter," said Julio Sal.

"Please do." Because she always said that; because letters meant that they would be coming back on payday. "Please write."

"You write me too?"

But the bell clanged, the dance ended and he had no more tickets. She slipped from his arms. The wicker gate opened and he was lost in an avalanche of little brown men fighting for the golden girl. Smiling weakly, he stood at the rail and watched her settle her child's face against the chest of Johnny Dellarosa, label machine, Van Camp's, San Pedro. A wave of tenderness suffocated Julio Sal. A small white doll — that was his Helen. The blissful future revealed itself in a reverie that shut out the boogy-woogy and the clanging bell — she was frying his bacon and eggs in a blue-tinted kitchen like in the movie pitch, and he came grinning from the bedroom in a green robe with a yellow sash, like in the movie pitch. "Ah, Helen," he was saying to her, "you are most wonderful cook in whole California. Pretty soon we take boat back to Luzon to meet my mamma and papa."

The reverie endured through twenty-five clangs of the bell before he remembered that his pockets were empty and that it was eighteen miles to Wilmington.

On his way out, buttoning his square-cut, shoulder-padded, tight overcoat, Julio Sal paused before a huge photograph of the Angels' Ballroom Staff; forty beautiful girls, forty. She was there, his Helen, her lovely face and slim-hipped figure third from the left, front row.

"Helen, Helen, I love you."

He descended the stairs to Main Street, saw the fog flowing north like a white river. Julio Sal, well-dressed Filipino boy — black serge suit, hand-tailored overcoat, black patent-leather shoes, snappy, short-brimmed hat. Breasting the white river, he walked south on Main Street. Eighteen miles to the harbor. Good. It had been worth while. He breathed fog and cigarette smoke and smiled for his love. Mamma, this is Helen; papa, this is Helen, my wife. The dream held. He couldn't marry her in California. The law said no. They would go to Reno. Or Tijuana. Or Seattle. Work a while up north. Then home to the Philippines. Mamma, this is Helen. Papa, this is Helen.

Eighteen miles to Wilmington.

II

He arrived at six o'clock, his patent-leather shoes in ruins. Behind the cannery, in the duplexes, the five Japanese families were already up, lights from their windows a dull gold in the deep fog.

He smelled the fertilizer vats, the tar, the oil, the copra, the bananas and oranges, the bilge, the old rope, the decaying anchovies, the lumber, the rubber, the salt — the vast bouquet of the harbor. This, too, was part of the dream. While working here at this spot, I met my love — I, Julio Sal.

Like one barefoot, he walked down the long veranda of the flat, salt-blackened building. They were single apartments set like cell blocks — one door, one window; one door, one window. A board creaked beneath his step, a baby wakened and cried. Babies, ah, babies. A little girl, he hoped, with the face and eyes of Mamma Helen.

He lived in the last apartment; he and Silvio Lazada, Pacito Celestino, Manuel Bartolome, Delfin Denisio, Vivente Macario, Johnny Andrino and Fred Bunda — all young men who had come to America as boys in the late 20's.

They were asleep now, the cramped room reeking with the odor of fish, bodies, burned rice and salt air. Bunda, Lazada and Celestino were in the wall bed; Andrino lay on the davenport; Bartolome, Macario and Denisio on the floor. Good boys. Loyal countrymen; though he had been gone all night, none had taken his bed in the bathtub.

On tiptoe he made his way over the sleepers to the bathroom. Through the gray fog-swept light he saw that someone was in the bathtub after all. The sleeper lay deep in blankets, old linen and soiled clothing, his head under the water spouts, his feet on the tub incline. Julio Sal bent down and smiled; it was Antonio Repollo. He had not seen Antonio in two years, not since the Seattle and Alaska canneries. Julio Sal whistled with pleasure. Now his letter-writing problem was solved. Antonio Repollo was a graduate of the University of Washington; he could write beautiful letters. Antonio Repollo was not only a university graduate, he also wrote poetry for El Grafico in Manila.

Julio Sal bent over and shook him awake.

"Antonio, my friend. Welcome."

Repollo turned over, a laundry bag in his arms.

"Antonio, is me. Julio Sal. I have girl."

"Is American?" asked Repollo.

"Is blonde," said Julio Sal. "Is wonderful."

"Is bad," said Antonio.

"No," said Julio Sal. "Is good, very good."

"Is very bad," said Repollo. "Is worst thing possible."

"No," said Julio Sal. "Is best thing possible."

He slipped into his greasy dungarees, found a clean shirt behind the kitchen door, and put that on too. It was Vivente Macario's turn to cook breakfast. Since 1926, at the asparagus fields, the celery fields, the canneries from Alaska to San Diego, Vivente Macario always prepared the same breakfast when his turn came — warmed-over rice, three cans of sardines stolen from the cannery, a hunk of bread and tea. They sat around the knife-scarred breakfast nook and ate quietly over a table whose surface was a mass of initials and dates of the hundreds of Filipino cannery workers who had come and gone throughout the years.

His brown face glowing from cold water, Antonio Repollo came into the kitchen. The poet, the college man. He was here, in their house, and they were honored; had even provided him with a bath-tub in which to sleep. They made a place for him at the table, watched his long beautiful fingers remove sardines from the can.

"Julio Sal," he said, "what is the name of the woman?"

"Is Helen."

"Helen? No more? No Anderson, no Smith, Brown?"

"No more. Helen, all the same. Helen."

"He has girl," explained Repollo. "Name of Helen. He wish to marry this girl. American girl."

"No good," said Fred Bunda.

"Crazy," said Delfin Denisio.

"Too much trouble" — Johnny Andrino.

"Helen?" Manuel Bartolome talking. "Is not same Helen for to work Angels' Ballroom, taxi dance?"

"Ya, ya," said Julio Sal. "She is him, all the same."

Bartolome sucked his big lips tight. "Is no good, this woman. Cannot be. For to marry, I try myself. She damn liar. You give money, she take. Give you nothing."

"No, no," smiled Julio Sal. "Is another Helen. This one, she is good. This one love. She like me. She say 'write letter.' This I am do tonight."

"Gnah," said Bartolome, coughing an evil memory from his mouth. "For why you believe that? Is applesauce. I am write letter, too — six times. She take my money, give nothing. She no love you, Julio Sal. She no marry Filipino. She take his money, but she no marry. Is not love. Is business."

The strong fist of Julio Sal whacked the table. "I make her love me. You wait. You see. Pretty soon, three months, cannery close down. I have money. We go for to get married. Reno, Seattle."

"Is bad," said Pacito Celestino.

"Crazy," said Vivente Macario.

"Is terrible," said Delfin Denisio. "Is awful."

"Is love," said Julio Sal. "Is wonderful!"

III

Said Julio Sal to Antonio Repollo, "You will write letter for me tonight, yes?"

Said Antonio Repollo, "No."

It was evening. The poet, Antonio Repollo, sat before his portable typewriter, line upon line of typescript rattling across the page. The fog had cleared. The moon showed big and yellow, rising over the American-Hawaiian docks.

"I am disappoint," said Julio Sal. "I write letter myself."

He asked for paper, and Repollo gave it to him. He asked for a fountain pen, and got that too. He sat across from the poet, his tongue making a bulge against his cheek. A half hour passed. Sweat broke out upon the brow of Julio Sal; the paper before him was white and untouched. Pleading eyes observed the dancing fingers of Antonio Repollo.

Said Julio Sal, pushing the paper away, "I cannot do. Is too hard to write."

Said Repollo, "You are a fool, Julio Sal. Sixteen years ago in

Hawaii I say to you: 'Go to school, Julio Sal. Learn to read English, learn to write English; it come in handy someday.' But no, you work in the pineapple, you make money, you play Chinee lottery, you shoot crap, you lose the cockfights. You have no time for American school. Me, I am different. I have big education. I am graduate, University of Washington. Maybe next year we go to Pasadena for the Rose Bowl."

"Maybe I write the Spanish."

"This Helen, she is Spanish?"

"No. She is American."

"What for you write Spanish?"

"I cannot write the English. I write the Spanish. Maybe she have Spanish friend."

"Fool, Julio Sal. Fool you are."

Julio felt tears stinging his eyes. "Is true, Antonio. I am make big mistake. You write for me letter. Next year I go for the school."

"I work hard for education. For write, I get paid. El Grafico, she pay me, for poetry, ten cents a word. For prose, one cents. First-class rates."

"I pay you, Antonio. Write beautiful letter. I pay you first-class rates. How much for this, Antonio?"

"For letter, prose composition, is one cents a word. Same rates I get, El Grafico."

Antonio rolled a clean sheet of paper under the platen and began to write. Julio Sal stood behind him and watched the letters dance across the white background.

"Good," said Julio. "Is wonderful. Write whole lots, Antonio. I pay one penny for the word."

The creative instinct in Antonio Repollo at once grew cold. He swung around and shook his hand under the fine nose of Julio Sal. "How do you know is good or bad? You cannot read the English good. How you know this?"

"She look good, Antonio. Look fine."

"I read to you," said Antonio. "I wish to give satisfaction all the time." As though harking to a distant foghorn, Julio Sal looked out the window and listened as Antonio read:

"Dear Miss Helen: The Immortal Bard has said, 'What's in a name?' I concur. And though I know not how you are yclept for a surname, it matters little. Oh, Miss Helen! Lugubrious is often the way of amour; profound its interpretations; powerful its judgments. Oh, bright Diana of the Dance! My love for you is like a muted trumpet sobbing among the brasses. Destiny has brought us together, and the aroma of devotion rises from your Humble Servant—"

Julio Sal shook his head. "Is no good, Antonio. Is terrible. Steenk."

"Is wonderful!" shouted Repollo. "Better than my stuff for El Grafico!"

Julio Sal sighed at the moon. "Antonio, you write, I talk. You put 'em down what I say."

A haughty shrug from Antonio. He lifted his palms. "As you wish, Julio. Same price for dictation. One cents a word."

Julio Sal was not listening. Both hands were cupped at his heart as the moonlight bathed his brown eyes. "Oh, lovely Helen!" He spoke in his native Tagalog. "Oh, wonderful moon girl! Thy beams have filled my soul with wild pleasure. Could I but kneel at thy feet in worship, the hem of thy red gown in these unworthy hands, I should die for joy. Many there are who are worthier than Julio Sal, but no man can say he loves you more. My wish and my hope is that you will become my bride. Back to the beloved motherland we will go, there to live forever beneath the coconut palms of beautiful Luzon. My wealthy father and mother shall welcome you to their plantation of fifteen thousand acres — rice, dates, pineapples and coconuts. Over it all you shall reign like a queen to the end of your days."

That was too much for Antonio Repollo. "You lie, Julio Sal. Your mamma and papa are peasants. They are poor people, Julio Sal. You betray them with such lies. You make them capitalist dogs. Caciques."

"You write," said Julio Sal. "I am pay one penny for the word. You write 'em down."

Repollo wrote it down, wrote three hundred and fifty-six words in all. They counted them together — three dollars and fifty-six cents. Expensive. But Antonio made no charge for punctuation marks, for "a" and "an," nor for the envelope, or for addressing it to Miss Helen, in care of the Angels' Ballroom, Los Angeles. Julio Sal was pleased with the cool, clean typescript and the boldness of his signature at the bottom, underscored three times, with a whirlwind flourish of curlicues.

"I pay," said Julio Sal, "come payday."

It came six days later, and Julio Sal paid thirteen dollars and eighty cents for that letter and three more. Even so, he managed to save another fifteen, for it had been a big week, with overtime. She did not answer his letters. But he could understand that; the life of a taxi dancer was not an easy one — to dance by night, to sleep by day, with never a moment to herself. All that was going to be changed someday. Pretty soon — after the tuna.

He saved his money. Was Betty Grable playing at The Harbor? All the little brown men loved Betty Grable; her autographed photograph hung over the kitchen sink; en masse they went to see her picture. All but Julio Sal. Seated on a piling at Dock 158, he smoked a cheap cigar and watched the stevedores load the President Hoover, bound for Hawaii and the Philippines. Came Madeleine Carroll, Virginia Bruce, Carole Lombard, Anita Louise — big favorites with the Penoys. But Julio Sal stayed home. There was the night Sixto Escobar fought Baby Pacito at the Hollywood Legion. And the night the bolo-punching Ceferino Garcia flattened Art Gonzales to the cries of "Boola, boola!" from his countrymen in the gallery. Where was Julio Sal? At home, saving his money.

IV

In September the tuna disappeared. And where does the tuna go, when he goes? No one can say. Overnight the roaring canneries shut down. No fish, no work. If wise, the Filipino boy had saved his money. Maybe he had three hundred, maybe five.

Home now? Back to Luzon and Ilocos Norte? No, not yet. Big money up north in the crops — lettuce, prunes, hops, olives, grapes, asparagus, walnuts, melons. Take rest, few days. Go to Los Angeles, see some girls, buy some clothes, chip in together and buy big car, ride down Hollywood Boulevard, maybe see Carole Lombard, maybe Anita Louise, can't tell. Then to the great agricultural centers of the north. Merced, Stockton, Salinas, Marysville, Woodland, Watsonville. Good-by to friends and fellow workers — to Celestino, Bartolome, Bunda, Denisio, Lazada, Macario. See you up north.

Said Antonio Repollo to Julio Sal that last day, "The prunes, she is good in Santa Clara County. You come with me?"

Said Julio Sal, "No. I go to Los Angeles for to get Helen. We go to Reno, maybe. For to get married."

Said Repollo, "You have letter then? She say yes?"

"No letter. Just the same, we get married."

"Maybe," said Repollo, not meaning it.

"No maybe. Is truth. You wait. You see. Pretty soon Mrs. Julio Sal, with ring."

"You have money, Julio Sal? Costa plenty for to have American wife."

"Three hundred fifty, I have."

"Is very small amount."

"Is plenty. I get some more in the crops."

Repollo took out his wallet. "I loan you twenty buck. After asparagus you pay me back."

"Is plenty, three hundred fifty."

Repollo held out a five-dollar bill. "This, for the wedding present. Some chocolate. Compliments, Antonio Repollo."

Mist welled up in the eyes of Julio Sal. He folded the greenback and wet his lips. "You are good Filipino, Repollo. Smart man. I tell Helen. Maybe someday I tell her you write letter on the machine — someday, maybe. *Gracias,* my friend."

"Is nothing," said Repollo. "For that I am A. B., University of Washington. Pretty soon we play Minnesota; we win maybe."

When he left the apartment that last time, a grip in each hand, his topcoat over his shoulder, he smelled sweet and clean, did Julio Sal, and he knew that, according to the pictures in Esquire, he was sartorially correct, even to the tan golf sweater that matched his light brown tie. There was one slight imperfection in his ensemble — his brown shoes. They had been half-soled.

It was forty minutes to town by way of the big red cars. At a quarter to one Julio Sal was on Hill Street. On the corner, there in the window, a pair of shoes caught his eye. They were light brown, a pock-marked pigskin, moccasin type, light soles, box toes. Fifteen dollars was the price beneath the velvet stand. Julio Sal bit his lips and tried to hold down his Spanish-Malay passion for bright leather. But it was a losing battle. Relishing his own weakness, he walked through the glass doors and stepped into a fragrant, cool world of leather and worsteds, silks and cashmere.

At two-thirty the new Julio Sal strutted up Hill Street with the grandeur of a bantam cock. The new shoes made him taller; the new gabardine slacks gave him a sense of long, virile steps; the new sport coat, belted and pleated in back, built him into a wedge-shaped athlete; the soft wool sweater scarcely existed, it was so soft, so tender. That new hat! Dark green, with a lighter band, high crown, short brim, pulled over one eye. At every window Julio Sal watched himself passing by, wished the folks back in Luzon could but see him passing by. The transformation had cost him a hundred and twenty-five. No matter.

Said Julio Sal to the handsome Filipino flashing past the shop windows, "Is better first to become engaged. Wait few months. Hops in Marysville. Asparagus in Stockton. Big money. After asparagus we get married."

The idea came to him suddenly, giving warmth to his conscience. But the coldness of guilt made him shudder. The first jewelry store in sight swallowed him up. An engagement ring. He was not happy when he walked into the hot street again, his purse thinner by seventy-five dollars. He felt himself falling to pieces with a suddenness that left him breathing through his mouth. Crossing to Pershing Square, he got no pleasure from his new clothes as he sat in the sun. A deep loneliness held him. What was the matter with Julio Sal? This Helen — not once had she answered his letter. He was a fool. Bartolome had warned him. But what was Filipino boy to do? For every Filipino girl in California there were twenty-two Filipino boys. The law made it so, and the law said Filipino boy could not marry white girl. What was Filipino boy to do? But Helen was different. Helen was taxi-dance girl. Working girl. Big difference. At once he felt better. He got up and walked toward Main Street, proud of his new clothes again.

v

First at the ticket window of the Angels' Ballroom that night was Julio Sal. It was a few minutes before seven. He bought a hundred tickets. On the stand, the four-piece colored band was tuning up. As yet, the girls had not come out of the dressing rooms. Julio Sal followed the wicker fence down to the bandstand, six feet from the dressing-room door. Then the band began to play the blatant hotcha wired down to a loud-speaker that spewed it in all directions out on the street.

By seven-fifteen the noise had lured five Filipinos, three Mexicans, two sailors and an Army private. The dressing-room door opened and the girls began to appear. Among the first was Helen.

Said Julio Sal, waving his tickets, "Hello."

"Be right with you," she said.

He watched her walk to the bandstand and say something to the trumpet player. She had changed in three months — changed a great deal. The memory he retained was of a girl in red. Tonight she wore a blue pleated chiffon that spilled lightly to her shoes. Something else — her hair. It had been a golden blond; now it was platinum. He had no time to decide whether or not he liked the changes, for now she was coming toward him.

"Hi. Wanna dance?"

"Helen, is me. Julio Sal."

The bell clanged and she did not hear him. Hurrying to the gate, he felt his legs trembling. She met him there, flowed into his arms professionally, yet like a warm wind. It was a waltz. She danced easily, methodically, with a freshness that made him feel she enjoyed it. But she did not remember him — he was sure of it. He was about to speak his own name when she looked up and smiled. It was friendly, but there was some peculiarity about it, an iciness in her blue eyes that made him suddenly conscious of his race, and he was glad she did not remember Julio Sal.

"You been here before?"

"First time," he said.

"Seems like I seen you someplace."

"No, no. First time here."

Gradually the place filled. They were mostly Filipinos. For an hour they danced, until he began to tire. Beyond the wicker fence were a bar and tables. He felt the pinch of his new shoes and longed to sit down. It made no difference. Dancing or sitting with her, the price was the same — ten cents a minute.

"I buy you a drink," he said.

They walked off the floor to the tables. Each was marked with a Reserved card. The waiter standing at the end of the bar dashed forward and yanked the card from the table where they sat. The bell clanged. The girl tore a ticket from the roll and stuffed it into a blue purse that matched her dress. Her small fingers tightened at his wrist.

"What's your name?"

"Tony," he said. "Is Tony Garcia."

"I like Tony. It's a swell name."

The waiter was tall, Kansas-like, tough, impersonal.

"Something to drink?" said Julio Sal. "What you like?"

She lowered her face, then looked up with blue, clean eyes. "Could I have something nice, Tony? Champagne?" She took his head in her hands, pulled it against her lips and whispered into his ear, "I get a percentage." He already knew that, but the touch of her lips, the warmth of her breath at his neck, the scent of her perfume, left him deliriously weak. The bell clanged and she tore away another ticket.

"Champagne," said Julio Sal.

"It's seven bucks," the waiter said.

"Seven?" Julio rubbed his jaw, felt soft, cool fingers under the table, squeezing his knee. He looked at the girl. Her face and eyes were downcast, her lips smiling impishly.

"Champagne."

They waited in silence. Four times the bell sounded and four times Helen's crimson nails tore at the thinning roll of tickets. The waiter came back with two glasses and a bottle on a tray. He gave Julio Sal a slip of paper.

"Nine?" said Julio Sal. "But you say seven."

"Cover charge."

"Is too much for to pay, only little bottle wine."

The waiter picked up the tray and started back to the bar.

Julio called to him. "I pay," he said.

After he paid, the cork popped. Julio lifted his glass, touched hers. "For you, the prettiest girl in whole California."

"You're sweet," she said, drinking.

Julio tested the wine with his teeth and tongue. Only fair. He had tasted better in San Jose, and for a third of the price. The bell clanged, the red nails nibbled, a new dance began. It was a waltz, Blue Hawaii.

Helen's eyes closed; she sighed and swayed to the music. "My favorite number. Dance with me, Tony."

They walked to the floor and she pressed herself hard against his body. The bell clanged as they reached the orchestra. She tore away another ticket and spoke to the trumpet player. The next three numbers were repeats of Blue Hawaii. Julio Sal was very pleased. She liked the music of the islands. She would like the music of the Philippines better.

She clung to his arm as they walked back to the table. The wine glasses were gone, the bottle of champagne was gone. Once more the table was marked Reserved. Julio Sal called the waiter.

"I thought you beat it," the waiter said.

"No, no. Only to dance a little bit."

"That's tough."

"But she was whole bottle. Only little bit, we drink."

"Sorry."

"Bring 'nother bottle," demanded Julio Sal.

They sat down, Helen holding the few remaining tickets like beads. "It's a shame," she said. "We hardly tasted it."

"No shame. We get more."

The waiter brought another bottle and two glasses. He handed Julio Sal another piece of paper, but Julio wouldn't accept it; he pushed it away, he shook his head. "I already pay. This one for nothing."

"Gotta pay."

"No. You cheat me. Nine dollars, not one drink."

The waiter leaned across the table and the waiter's thick hand clutched the throat of Julio Sal, pushed back his head. "I don't have to take that kind of talk from a Filipino. Take it or leave it."

Nausea flowed up and down the bones of Julio Sal — shame and helplessness. He smoothed back his ruffled hair and kept his wild eyes away from Helen, and when the bell clanged he was glad she busied herself tearing off another ticket.

The waiter cursed and walked away. Julio Sal panted and stared into his calloused hands. It wasn't the waiter and it wasn't the nine dollars, but why had she tricked him with three encores of Blue Hawaii? Julio Sal wanted to cry. Then there were cool fingers on the back of his hand, and he saw her sweet face.

"Forget it," she said. "I can do without, if I have to."

But Julio no longer cared, not even for himself.

"Waiter," he said.

That night Julio Sal drank five bottles of champagne, drank most of it himself, yet the bitterness within him remained dry and aching, and drunkenness did not come. There was only thirst and desire, and a salty satisfaction in playing the fool. At midnight he stared in fascination as the red nails clawed the three hundredth ticket. Sometimes she said, "Wanna dance?" And sometimes he asked, "Drink?" Sometimes she squeezed his hand and asked, "Having a good time?" And always he answered, "Very good time."

Searching for a match, his fingers touched something hard and square in his pocket.

He brought out the jewel box that held the engagement ring. It was a single diamond set in white gold. He held it under her eyes.

"You like?"

"Beautiful."

"I buy for girl. She die."

"Automobile accident?"

"Just die. Sick. You want ring, you keep."

"I couldn't."

He slipped it on her finger. She tilted it to and from the light, laughing as it sparkled.

Three times the bell clanged, but she forgot the roll of tickets. Then she looked at him again, studied his delicate nose, his fine lips. She lifted his hand and pressed a kiss into the calloused palm.

"You can take me home. That is, if you want to."

He stared into his empty glass, twirled it around and smiled at the memory of the little speech he had prepared that afternoon, the words he planned to say when he slipped the ring on her finger.

"Don't you want to?"

"I like, very much."

"Do you have a car?"

"We take taxi."

She pushed her chair closer to him, so that they sat crowded side by side. She held his hand in both of hers, pressed it, played absently with his fingers.

When he suggested one more bottle of champagne, she frowned. "It's for suckers."

"I am sucker."

"You're not either. You're nice," she said.

"I have friend," he said. "Name Julio Sal. He know you."

"The guy that writes all them crazy letters? He must be nuts."

"Ya. He nuts."

He looked at the clock over the bar and wanted to sigh; instead a sob shook itself from his throat. It was twelve-thirty. The dream was dead.

"I wait for you at door downstairs," he said.

He got up and left her sitting there. It was warm in the street. He walked a few doors north to a small, hole-in-the-wall, all-night grocery store. Boxes of figs and grapes were tilted toward the street. The sight of them increased the acrid, cigarette-and-champagne dry-ness of his mouth. He bought a bunch of grapes for a nickel, waved the clerk aside about a paper sack. The grapes were Black Princes, big and meaty.

He put one of them into his mouth, felt it burst between his teeth, tasted the sweet juice that filled his mouth. A grape from Sonoma County, from the vineyards around Santa Rosa. He had picked grapes in Sonoma — who could say, perhaps from the very vine upon which this bunch had grown.

Eating grapes, Julio Sal walked a block to the Terminal Building, took his overcoat and grips from the ten-cent lockers, went down the stairs to Los Angeles Street and the bus depot. The ticket agent nodded.

"One-way ticket, Santa Rosa," said Julio Sal.

A SMATTERING OF BLISS

By *Virginia Faulkner*

HAL VENNER balanced a cigarette carefully on the palm of his hand and attempted to catapult it into his mouth by smacking his wrist forcefully with his other hand.

"Nice try," said his wife, Lorry, retrieving the cigarette from under the piano. "I think you're improving."

"No kidding?" said Hal.

"Absolutely. They stay in the same room now."

"I've never been any good at tricks," said Hal discontentedly.

"Oh, I don't know," said his wife. She turned to their secretary. "Where are we now, Miss B.?"

"George and Louise are in the bathroom," said Miss B. "George has just said: 'Oh-oh! Seven years' bad luck.'"

"Do you know how to pick up broken glass without cutting yourself?" inquired Hal. "You wet a piece of cotton."

"I love cotton," said Lorry. "Listen, Hal, how would this be? Louise takes off her pump and shatters the medicine-cabinet mirror with one good wallop. Then she gives George an arch look and says something like: 'Well, that's seven years for me, too, baby.' Close shot of George's pan as it finally penetrates that she loves him. Then he turns on a big grin and says: 'Maybe we'll get time off for good behavior.' Camera pulls back to a two-shot of the clinch, and fade-out."

"Oh, I like that," said Miss B. enthusiastically. "I think it's sort of nutty and cute."

"Let's not work any more today, darling," said Hal. "Let's just sit."

"Where, for instance?"

"Somewhere indoors, in case of high fog."

"We're indoors now," Lorry reminded him, "and you need have no qualms about sitting. This is Liberty Hall."

"Sitting here would be too easy. I can't relax unless I've asserted myself."

"You heard him, Miss B.," said Lorry. "When you've typed up those notes, you may scram."

"Ten o'clock tomorrow?" asked Miss B.

"Or so," said Hal. "Better make it at the studio instead of here. It's just as well to give that place a good punch in the time clock now and then. Farewell, Miss B." He slumped down on the sofa, fetching a large sigh. "I wish I were a bricklayer."

"What's stopping you?" asked Lorry. "I bet you'd be a good bricklayer. I hear you were a strong child."

"Half a dozen feet of rusty muscle, that's me," said Hal. "Lorry, let's run away and join a circus. Let's let someone else write movies."

"Oh, goody; let's," said Lorry.

Hal kicked a pillow onto the floor. "Why don't you ever argue with me?" he demanded.

"Listen," said Lorry, "ever since I reached the age of dissent I've argued with people. I've been shrewish and selfish and unpleasant. If I want to be nice to you, I guess I've earned the privilege."

"Would you really walk out on a contract because of a husband's whim?"

"Why not? Your slightest whim is law. Have a slight whim and see."

"I know what you're doing," said Hal. "You're humoring me."

"I can humor a man as well as the next girl," said Lorry complacently. "Matter of fact, if you don't humor a man, the next girl will. The trick is to beat her to the punch. . . . Shall I instruct one of our retinue to call up for plane tickets?"

"Maybe tonight," said Hal, "and maybe tomorrow, and maybe not. Come on; let's pack up some dollars and some field glasses and wend our way to Santa Anita."

Loretta Erskine — no one, even after she had been married two years, called her Loretta Venner — had made a success of playwriting since she was twenty-five, but primarily she had established herself in the public eye, ear and hair as a professional wit, a brilliant and merciless commentator on the topics and personalities of the day. Her elopement with Hal had provided columnists with fireworks ample for a month of Roman holidays, since most of the Erskine plays were based on the proposition that all men are created evil, and that marriage, at least among the leisure classes, is an expensive and rather horrid pastime. Moreover, at the time of the elopement, Lorry was thirty-three and Hal only twenty-six.

As her old friend Sim Bailey told her, "It is all right for some women to be inconsistent, but, sweetie, not you. Hordes of people have been hoping and praying for years that you'd slip and break your damned tongue, and this would give 'em just the chance they've been waiting for. They'll rip you to pieces."

"The Grand Old Lady of Gall and Wormwood takes a groom," mused Lorry. "Why, listen to me! I'm my own worst enemy."

"Listen to me," insisted Sim. "If you have to get married — I use the expression in its narrowest sense, of course — why Hal Venner? He's not even a good writer; he's not even as good as I am."

"You're bald."

"I'm taking treatments," said Sim, "and at least I'm a grown man. If we went to the altar, there would be no unveiled accusations of cradle-snatching. Why don't you take him on a trip and get him out of your system?"

"Because it isn't just a question of that," said Lorry. "Hal and I are what underwear salesmen used to call a good combination. And I want to make it official. I want to step right up to home plate and promise to love, honor and cherish Mr. Venner. Because he's the one, see?"

"Oh, dear," said Sim. "My poor friend, you are never going to be the same."

"I guess that will be all right with everyone."

"You wait," warned Sim darkly. "You wait until you're on the receiving end of a few nifties."

"He who lives by the sword must perish by the sword," said Lorry cheerfully.

"You don't know what you're up against, marrying a younger man."

"Maybe you're right about that," said Lorry, "but if ignorance is you-know-what, I'll take a smattering of bliss."

So far, it had been more than a smattering. The first six months they spent on Lorry's farm in Maryland while Hal finished a book. Then they went on a long cruise around South America and, on their return, wrote a play together. The book got good notices; the play ran fourteen months. It looked as if the drinks were on the belittlers in the back room, for it is uphill work to crack wise in the teeth of a hundred and fifty grand, which was the sum Hollywood plunked down for the rights to The Triple Standard. And how the bowl brimmed with sour grape juice when the Venners took off for the Coast to do the picture adaptation, and giving off an unmistakable aura of marital felicity.

"You know what I think we ought to do, since we're in Hollywood?" said Hal as they were driving back from Santa Anita. "I think we ought to have one of those Hollywood parties where everybody comes in slacks and sarongs, or as Franz Josef."

"With real Japanese lanterns," supplemented Lorry, "and platinum hat checks. A white-tie barbecue."

"That's the idea," said Hal. "Everything very R.S.V.P. and *de rigueur mortis*."

"Who'll we have?"

"Well, for a starter, how about the cast of the picture? We might say the party was in honor of Desire Hamilton, since she's starring."

"Desire Hamilton? Pardon my rising inflection, but you wouldn't be wanting her autograph, would you?"

"Maybe," said Hal smugly, "she wants mine."

"Look here, my boy. Has she been ogling you?"

"Well, you know Desire," said Hal. "And I'm a healthy male."

"Say no more; I'll put that minx from Minsky's in her place."

"I can defend my honor okay myself," protested Hal. "You're not my ol' shotgun-totin' grandpappy anyway."

Lorry looked at him a moment. "You're the boss," she said at last.

"That's the girl," said Hal, relieved. "Promise, now, no cracks?"

"I won't say a word about you," said Lorry. "I'll just be nasty along general lines."

As the prettiest and most important person at the Venner barbecue, Desire Hamilton could sit in a reclining chair, confident that drinks, cigarettes, matches, compliments and conversation would all be tendered to her without the necessity for any of that ungraceful exertion which lawn furniture seems expressly designed to provoke. To successive suggestions that she join in games of badminton, tennis, ping-pong and bowling, she responded with a shake of her lovely head.

"I'm crazy about sports, though," she said. "Did you know I have an indoor ski slide in my rumpus room? It's the only one in Brentwood."

"It's swell that you ski," said Hal. "We won't have to use a double in the Sun Valley sequence."

"Oh, Sam — Sam Fleishauer, he's my agent — won't let me take a chance with my poor little legs," said Desire, regarding her superb gams with affection. "As he so often says, where would I be without them?"

"Where you are most of the time anyway," said Lorry.

"Oh, I don't go out much," said Desire, after a little thought. "I'm slaving at the studio all day long, and you know when you come home exhausted and dead to the world, all you want is a bed. That's why I like an ocean voyage. Because of the rest. And on the train. I always just stay in bed from Pasadena to Harmon. That's what I've got against flying. You don't get that three days in bed."

"You might just fly around for three days," said Lorry.

"Oh, but the vibration. These new ships are wonderful, though. I dedicated one, and they made me an honorary stewardess. I want to make a picture about an air stewardess and call it Air Stewardess, but Sam says the flying-picture cycle is over. He wants my next picture to be something where I can be a sort of a female Paul Muni, like Pasteur and Zola. There was one girl scientist, the one that found radium, but M-G-M owns her."

"Madame Bovary?" suggested the hostess.

"That's her. But do you know what I really want to do? I want to play the wife of Genghis Khan!" Desire sat up straight in the long chair. "You know, the Mongolian Hitler. I see myself as a barbarous dancing girl who gains this strange power over Genghis and unwittingly saves civilization." She sank back. "Of course they'd have to be careful not to give Genghis too much to do; he's a strong character."

"It's an inspiration, don't you think, Hal?" said Lorry. "Desire as Puree, the Mongrel Dancing Girl."

"It's a very interesting idea," said Hal reprovingly. "I've often wondered why there's never been a play about Genghis Khan."

Desire turned toward him, giving him the full benefit of her enormous blue eyes and enchanting smile. "I have the greatest respect for picture making," she said very earnestly, "but there are times when it just doesn't satisfy me. There is something so quickening about a real live audience. I mean it quickens you; it helps you give. If I could just find a really intelligent play. Something with something to it; not just two hims and a her. And I mean all we people who have come to Hollywood really have a debt we owe to the stage because it is the Mother Art."

"If you're really serious about doing a play," said Hal, "perhaps Lorry and I might whip up something for you."

"There's nothing I'd rather do than a play," said Desire, "but I'm so tied up with contracts and all these silly options and commitments. I mean that's how it's been."

"I know," said Lorry sympathetically. "You couldn't call your soul your own, not even if you had one."

"I think," said Hal, "that those people who just came in are looking for you, Lorry dear."

"What do you want me to do? Leave a paper trail or put up some illuminated arrows?"

"Surely you can work out something simpler than that, pet," said Hal. "A clever girl like you."

"The velvet hand in the iron glove," explained Lorry to the others. "He means he wants me to excuse myself and receive guests."

The party was a great success: three mink coats were stolen, several studio deals were negotiated, and a distinguished character actor was pushed into the swimming pool, so the Venners could consider themselves fairly launched should they care to pursue a social career.

Nevertheless, "I'm glad that's behind us," said Lorry as they relaxed in the kitchen. "You never really know what's going on when you give a large party. I wish it wasn't conventional to thank the hostess. I'd much rather guests would come clean, because then you could be sure whether or not anyone had fun."

"I had fun," said Hal.

"Pooh, you don't count. You weren't a guest."

"Incidentally," said Hal in a far from incidental tone, "you behaved like a perfect stinker to Desire Hamilton."

"Am I to construe that as a criticism?"

"She was a guest in your house."

"It's a rented house; and anyway, she's so dumb she didn't catch on."

"Then why did you bother to blast her?"

"Oh, force of habit. Or maybe I'm jealous of her legs."

"Your legs are all right."

"What a fellow you are for pretty speeches! Shall we 'whip up' a play around them?"

"Lay off," said Hal. "I had to say something after all those cracks you made."

"I guess I'm a mean lady," said Lorry. "Well, I'm off for my Thropplestance Wonder-Rest Mattress — and that ain't hay. Do you think prexy will be furious if we cut chapel tomorrow? I want to sleep late."

"You do that. I sort of got myself into going over to Desire's to see her new ski slide. Of course I can get myself out of it. If you have anything planned, that is."

"Frankly, I can't think of anything, offhand, but you won't catch me a second time. *Bon soir,* baby. I'll see you in my dreams." *If I can sleep,* she added to herself, for it was a maxim of Lorry's that when you give a man enough rope, it is a 100-to-1 shot he will wind up on the next reservation.

Despite her forebodings, the subject of Desire Hamilton did not recur in the Venner household until several days following, and Lorry had relaxed to the extent of keeping her fingers crossed on one hand only. Then, at lunch, apropos of nothing but a dreamy silence, Hal observed that Lorry was not right about Desire.

"In other words, you mean I was wrong."

"Yes, if you must have other words. She's not as dumb as you think."

"Is she dumber?"

"She knew you were making fun of her the other night."

"Oh, Desire never could have worked that out by herself. Somebody's read her the papers." And, as Hal looked baffled, "There was an item in Beau Brash's column saying we girls were feuding."

"Then I definitely think we ought to have her over for dinner. We don't want to be bad friends with our own star," said Hal. "Anyway, these Hollywood feuds are so infantile."

"And what makes you think she'd come to dinner?"

"Well, as a matter of fact, I've asked her, and at first she said no, but I fixed things up. I told her —— "

"You told her it was 'just my way.' I say things like that to all the girls."

"Anyhow, I fixed it up. I'm sorry if she bores you, but as you yourself have said, even if all the people bore you some of the time, and some of the people all the time, still a schizophrenic like yourself always has each other."

"Oh, I wouldn't be bored," said Lorry. "I just don't like to look at her, that's all."

"But I've heard you say she was one of the few truly beautiful women in Hollywood!"

"Well, I like the Winged Victory, too, but if I was a sculptor I'd hate to have it around the house."

"I fail to get it."

"Comparisons are odious when you come off second best."

"Are you worrying about your legs again? Because don't. I like your legs."

"Oh, I'm perfectly satisfied with them; I'm not complaining. They do fine in ordinary competition, but this dame is a pro."

"I see what's in your mind," said Hal cautiously, "and you're all wrong."

"To err is human; that's what makes things so tough," said Lorry.

"Well, what shall I do?" said Hal. "I've asked her."

"Take her to Ciro's or some other fleshpot. You're a big boy now. I have to go to New York anyway."

"Now, look here," said Hal.

"It's just a coincidence," said Lorry. "I'm not making anything out of this, honest I'm not. I promised Sim I'd come back for the tryout of his new play, and it opens in New Haven Friday."

"We'll both go."

"No, one of us must stay here on account of the picture. It's in the contract that we hang around until they've finished shooting. Cheer up, I'll bring you a present. A nice scout knife or something."

Sim's play was only a semisuccess, and Lorry stayed with it on the road to help with the doctoring. After two weeks they brought it in, and, if the critics were right, the salvage job had done the trick.

The morning after the New York opening Lorry had late break-fast at Sim's apartment to inspect the notices and to discuss with him the elimination of a scene in the second act, but instead of getting to the business at hand, Sim greeted her with a reproachful air.

"Holding out on me, huh?" he said. "I thought you weren't hang-ing around New York just on account of my *beaux yeux*." And he extended a paper folded open to a two-column cut of Lorry and De-sire at the track. The caption was simple and provocative. RENO-BOUND? was all it said.

"Any comment, Erskine?" inquired Sim.

"There's a question mark," said Lorry serenely.

"I thought it was a typographical error."

"Well, I'll tell you," she said. "Hal has had a little crush on De-sire."

"I can see why," said Sim, eyeing the picture.

"I wouldn't have thought too much about it, but he started sticking up for her when I got smart with her at a party. He even hinted we'd write a play built around her legs and Genghis Khan."

"Ouch!"

"But I really got the wind up when he asked her over for a family dinner — the Jolly Threesome gambit, as I call it."

"What's wrong with that? You could keep an eye on them."

"That ain't the pernt. It showed me Hal's state of mind was dangerous. He was trying to convince himself that there was noth-ing wrong in his seeing Desire. He reasoned that if it was all open and aboveboard, it was harmless. Therefore I checked."

"Gaining what?"

"Plenty. Do you think I'm fatuous enough to try to vamp Hal with that nymph-sized package of dynamite around?"

"So you figured that without you there he'd get bored?"

"Oh, eventually, but it would be quite a while until the first **yawn**. I thought I'd better nip it in the buderoo."

"You're going great," said Sim, looking at the paper again.

"Oh, I counted on that kind of thing," said Lorry. "You see, the very day I left for New York, Hal took Desire to dinner, and you know how they are out there about putting two people together and getting something barely fit to print. Anyway, after they'd been out together some more — I knew they'd have dates because Hal was smitten, and Desire is sore at me — this was bound to happen." She indicated the picture. "Curtains."

"Yes, but for whom?"

"For them," said Lorry impatiently. "Tantamount has just signed Desire to do a picture with Jack Wiley, and she's supposed to be crazy about him. Besides, she's had two divorces in three years, and the studio doesn't want this kind of publicity."

"Even so —— "

"Even so, nothing! Don't kid yourself about Desire; it's career first with that tomato, and Hal isn't a producer. She'll slip him the black spot without a second thought. He'll be furious — the hurt-pride angle — and that's the end of Desire Hamilton as far as the Venner family is concerned."

"It sounds all right," began Sim.

"It works too," said Lorry. She produced a telegram and read dryly:

"FLYING TO NEW YORK TO FLY BACK TO HOLLYWOOD WITH YOU. THAT'S TEN WORDS SO HAVE NO SPACE TO ADD LOVE HAL AND YOU MUST GUESS WHO THIS IS FROM.

"I wish people didn't always feel obliged to be cute in wires."

"Congratulations," said Sim. "In the absence of a hat, I take off my toupee to you."

"Let me see," said Lorry, examining it. "I thought I spied a gray hair." She handed it back to him. "Premature, of course, and so were your congratulations. Desire was only a symptom. You know how guys are. They start looking, and they keep on looking until something happens. My trials have just begun."

"But Hal loves you. Or doesn't he?"

"He certainly does," said Lorry indignantly. "Do you think I'd be taking all this trouble if he didn't? I expect you think I'm a scheming woman fighting a losing battle to keep a young husband — not a pretty picture. But, Sim, I'm going to keep right on scheming. I don't want anything to happen to our setup. We've got love and we've got money; we have health and an absorbing interest in common. The fly in the ointment — and every marriage has some handicap — happens to be that I am brighter than Hal. Not that he isn't bright, but I'm just about the brightest woman in the world."

"You been hanging around Bill Saroyan?" asked Sim suspiciously.

"My being brighter wouldn't matter if I was an ordinary woman and Hal was an ordinary man," continued Lorry, after an involuntary *moue*, "because he wouldn't know it. But owing to my reputation, and because Hal is no fool, he does know it. And even though this is 1941 and equality between the sexes is so established it's old hat, that doesn't alter the fact that in happy marriages it is the gentleman who wears the breeks."

"Hooray for men's rights," said Sim. "One day we lads shall get the vote, just wait and see."

"I bet you do too," said Lorry generously. "Didn't you take the place of the horse? Anyway, for my money, the male — as he is called — has to believe that he dominates the female, because if he doesn't, and is a real guy, he'll hunt around until he finds a dame or dames he does dominate. This is technically known as 'being on the make,' which describes Hal's condition at present. The only cure is to convince him that he's the king of the Venner family, and not just a puppet monarch either."

"I never thought to see you honing for a back seat," said Sim.

"One thing on my side is that we work well together. Hal has a lot of warmth and humanity, which I lack, and he's got a sound plot sense; while I have certain perceptions which are missing in his make-up, and can turn a phrase in any direction. Most important of all, we speak the same language. That's a cliché most people don't bother to figure out, but it means an awful lot. It speeds up things when your minds work contrapuntally; it's as exciting a synchronization as lateral passing in football. You get an idea and you go down the field whipping the ball back and forth until you carry it over. So I don't worry about Hal feeling subordinate in our collaboration, even though the critics and the public persist in handing me top billing. He knows that he's pulling his weight, and that's all that matters to him. As I may have hinted to you, he's a very superior citizen."

"It makes sense," said Sim. "The Triple Standard was a lot more mature and human than the plays you wrote solo."

"And you might add, so am I," said Lorry. "Darn it all, Sim, this marriage is the answer for both Hal and me, and I've got to make it work. It isn't good enough just to go along stuffing up chinks in the armor, pulling fast ones when I see Hal has a yen coming on. The yens don't matter; it's what Hal feels for me that's important.

If things are really right between us I can say nuts to all the other women in the world. Every honest-to-God guy has a dash of the chaser; that can be discounted. You just have to make sure that the chase doesn't take him too far away, and that he always wants to come back."

"There's an old saying," observed Sim, "that they never come back."

"Men go where they feel they belong. Of course I don't include congenital so-and-so's, because the main reason they're so-and-so's is that they don't know where they belong. To a man, 'belonging' means someone's belonging to him rather than his belonging to someone else, and he has this feeling of possession only when he is sure that he is absolutely necessary to the other person. So there you have my difficulty. You see, Hal — being the guy he is — is brimming over with chivalry and the protective instinct, but, unfortunately, he knows I am quite, quite capable of taking care of myself."

"Hal protecting you," said Sim, "would be like a butterfly escorting a Stuka."

"It isn't funny," said Lorry. "Unless I can find a use for that strong right arm of his — unless I can convince him that I'd be sunk without him — I might as well kiss my boy good-by."

"That oughtn't to stump you; all you have to do is play dumb and helpless."

"Sim, use your head! Supposing for the sake of argument that a leopard can change his spots without causing a commotion, if he blossomed out in green and red stripes even a dope would know someing was radically haywire; and my metamorphosis into fluff and nonsense would be just as noticeable.

"I can get away with a lot, but playing dumb isn't on the list."

"Had it occurred to you, dear, that maybe you aren't as smart as you think you are?"

"That's the idea I have to sell Hal," said Lorry. "Because the minute he finds out I'm not as smart as I think I am, then he's smarter than I, and everything will be hunky-dory. If he can't protect me from anything else, he can protect me from myself." She sighed.

"The trouble is I am as smart as I think I am."

Sim stared at her.

"Of course I adore you, Erskine," he said thoughtfully, "but it wouldn't hurt you to have your ears knocked down a couple of yards. It wouldn't hurt you at all."

A woman's place — or anyway, one of a woman's places — being the home, Lorry was glad to return with Hal to their complicated nest in Brentwood, a neo-Goldwyn rancho. The light touch was employed by both husband and wife in their comments on the Hamilton episode, Hal stating that Desire's I.Q. could be totted up on the fingers of a single hand, and Lorry supplementing his observation with the remark that he was too generous; in her opinion, Desire's was the first known case of a negative I.Q. They also agreed that no man was safe with Desire except her own husband, and this disposed of Miss Hamilton as a topic of conversation until, some three weeks later, Lorry announced that they had received a wire bidding them to a revel at Desire's mansion, the occasion being a supper party to commemorate the première of The Triple Standard — retitled for picture purposes, Three's a Crowd.

"We'll regret with pleasure, I presume?"

"I've been meaning to break it to you," said Hal; "we have to go. It's for us."

"What deviltry is this?"

"The studio, probably," said Hal uneasily. "They want us to write her next picture. Seems she's got it in her contract that they let her make that story about Genghis Khan, and she has the idea that I — that we're authorities on the subject."

"I hope you told them to take that bee right out of her bonnet and return it to the hive."

"Oh, sure," said Hal. "I said it was out of the question."

"Good. I suppose we'll have to accept this then," she waved the telegram, "but ask if we can bring Sim Bailey. He's getting here the nineteenth, and I promised to show him Hollywood. If there is a Hollywood, it'll be at Desire's."

Lorry was correct. After the première — which Sim said was a cross between a coronation and a football rally — picturedom's peerage and four-letter men betook themselves to Sleepy Hollow, the name Desire had selected for her residence from a contest held by her fan clubs. It was, as Lorry did not fail to point out, a name more descriptive of the interior of Desire's head than the scale-model country club which it adorned. The hostess, looking more beautiful than a press agent's dream, received at the foot of her ski slide, informing all comers, as was her wont, that it was the only one in Brentwood. Before she could repeat this fact to the Venners, Lorry observed that they were already in possession of the news. "I half expected to find you in a ski suit," she concluded. "A chinchilla one."

"Did you really?" said Desire. "I suppose you get your information on my wardrobe from Hal."

"We don't talk clothes," said Lorry.

"Oh, darling, you should," said Desire, with a glance that summed up and flicked away Lorry's toilette. "I hope you'll make yourselves at home."

"That will take a bit of doing," said Lorry.

"Hal can show you around," said Desire. "Can't you, pet?"

"Yes," said Hal, without enthusiasm.

"I thought you said she was dumb," remarked Sim as they walked away.

At supper, the Venners found themselves on either side of their hostess, who explained that she had seated them there because they were her guests of honor, and she was sure they wouldn't mind her being between them this once.

"I thought you made a habit of it," said Lorry.

"I haven't any habits," said Desire. "I'm too restless."

"Just call me volatile Sal," murmured Lorry. "What about cohabiting? Or don't you indulge?"

"That's a play upon words, isn't it?" said Desire. "It must be wonderful to be a writer. I've often wondered where on earth you get some of your ideas."

"Sometimes from the papers."

"Do you really believe what you read in the papers?"

"Oh, occasionally they get a fact or two straight, the way I look at it. Or don't you believe in the law of averages?"

"I don't think it applies to me," said Desire, with a disarming smile. She turned to Sim, who was sitting on Lorry's right. "I know Miss Erskine finds me awfully dull to talk to. I've never bothered to learn repartee. If I have anything to say, I just say it. And if there's something I don't know, I ask. You see, there are so many clever people in the world, it's always easy to find someone to explain."

"It's an angle," admitted the embarrassed Sim.

"What I mean is: why do things the hard way? When I've got a beef, I spill it; I say what's on my mind. For instance, when I think someone's been making passes at my husband — the times I'm married, that is — I just go right to her and tell her to lay off or I'll pull out every hair on her head. You don't need any vocabulary for that, and in the end it's more effective than all this repartee that just makes everybody uncomfortable and louses up a perfectly good party. Maybe I'm dumb — I know Miss Erskine thinks so — but what's the matter with being dumb? The Bible or something says ignorance is bliss, and God knows I'm doing all right."

"I guess you are, at that," said Lorry quietly. "I apologize. For various things. And, if you'll excuse me, I think I'd like to go."

"Sure, if you want to," said Desire. . . . "Nobody feels so hot after they apologize," she explained to Sim. . . . "But you don't have to go!" she exclaimed as Hal pushed back his chair.

"Of course he doesn't," said Lorry.

"Don't be silly," said Hal, starting after her. Then he hesitated and turned. "Uh — good night, Desire," he said politely. "We had a lovely time."

Sim did not see Hal and Lorry again until the day he was leaving for the East. They had gone to Arrowhead, and had just returned that morning. He found Lorry and Miss B. sorting out scripts on the terrace; Hal would be there presently, Lorry explained; he was talking on the phone to the studio.

"How did you like Desire's party?" she asked. "You haven't thanked me for taking you."

"I thought it might be a delicate subject."

"Well, it is, rather," said Lorry. "By the way, have you noticed anything different about me?"

"Such as what?" hedged Sim.

"Ears are being worn lower this year," said Lorry demurely. "Hal thinks they're awfully becoming."

"Oh, Miss Erskine," said Miss B., "excuse me for interrupting, but shall I send this screen test to the studio?"

"What screen test? We haven't written any screen tests."

"Why, this is the one you worked on by yourself right after your trip to New York, don't you remember? The scene between the two women at the dinner table where they —— "

"That's nothing; you can tear that up," said Lorry hastily.

"Just a minute," said Sim, grabbing it from Miss B., and warding Lorry off with one hand. " 'I've never bothered to learn repartee,' " he read aloud. " 'If I have anything to say, I just say it. And if there's something I don't know, I ask. You see, there are so many clever people —— ' Well, I'll be damned!" He gazed at Lorry with awe and admiration. "You framed yourself," he accused. "Smart. Very smart. But how did you get Desire to do it?"

"Oh, she's a quick study — for a moron."

"You know what I mean. How did you persuade her to co-operate? With a club?"

"We made a deal. And I will say for Desire, she drives a hard bargain."

"But what —— "

"Pipe down! Here's Hal."

"Sorry to be so long, darling. . . . Hello, there, Sim. . . . That was B. J., Lorry, and he wants us to have something to show him this afternoon. . . . Now where were we, Miss B.?"

"At the Mongol camp," said Miss B. "Genghis is trying to make Miss Hamilton."

"Who," said Sim, cocking an eyebrow at Lorry, "drives a hard bargain indeed."

She combined a nod with a warning frown. "So now you know how screen plays are born," she said. "Run along, Sim. Mr. and Mrs. Venner have work to do."

AN EGG FOR THE MAJOR

By C. S. Forester

THE MAJOR commanding the squadron of light tanks was just as uncomfortable as he had been for a number of days. For the officer commanding a light tank there is a seat provided, a sort of steel piano stool, but, in the opinion of the major, it had been designed for men of a physique that has no counterpart on earth. If one sat on it in the normal way, with the part of one which Nature provides for sitting on on the stool, one's knees bumped most uncomfortably on the steel wall in front. And contrariwise, if one hitched oneself back and sat on one's thighs, not only was the circulation interfered with to an extent which led to cramps but also the back of one's head was sore with being bumped against the wall of the turret behind. Especially when the tank was rolling over the desert, lurching and bumping from ridge to ridge; on a road one could look after oneself, but it was weeks and weeks since the major had set eyes on a road.

He left off thinking about the sort of shape a man should be who has to pass his days in a light tank, and gave the order for the tank to stop. He climbed out through the steel door with his compass to take a fresh bearing. Out in the desert here an army had to navigate like a ship at sea, with the additional difficulty that inside the steel walls, with the spark coils to complicate matters, a compass was no use at all. The only thing to do was to get out of the tank, carry one's compass well away from its influence, and look over the featureless landscape and mark some patch of scrub, some minor rise in the ground, on which one could direct one's course. He walked stiffly away from the tank, laid the compass level and stared forward. This was perhaps the five-hundredth time he had done this, and he had learned by long experience the difficulties to be anticipated. There was never anything satisfactory directly ahead on which he could direct his course. There would be fine landmarks out to the right or left where they were no use to him, but nothing straight ahead. He would have to be content with some second best, the edge of that yellow patch on the brown, and he knew quite well that it would appear quite different when he got back into the tank again. Furthermore, it would appear more different still when they had traveled a little way toward it — there had been times long ago, when the desert was new to him, when he had found at a halt that he was more than ninety degrees off his course. He was far more experienced now; five months of desultory warfare and now this last tremendous march across the desert had accustomed him to the difficulties.

Experience taught him to empty his mind of the hundreds of previous landscapes which he had memorized, to concentrate on this one, to note that yellow patch whose edge would be his guiding mark for the next ten miles, and to look back and absorb the appearance of the country in that direction as well. Then he went back to the tank, decided against the piano stool, slammed the door shut, and climbed up onto the roof before giving the word to start. On the roof he could lie on the unyielding steel to the detriment of hip and elbow, anchoring himself into position by locking his toe round the muzzle of the machine gun below him. After a time his leg would go to sleep at about the same time that his hip could bear it no longer; then he would have to change over; three changes — two turns with each foot and hip — would be as much as he could stand, and then it would be time to take a fresh bearing and go back to the piano stool and the other problem of which part to sit on.

He lounged on the steel roof while the tank pitched and rolled under him; it was as well to keep that foot firmly locked below the gun muzzle to save himself from being pitched off. It had happened to him sometimes; everything had happened to him at one time or another. The wind today was from ahead, which was a mercy; a gentle following wind meant that the dust of their progress kept pace with them and suffocated him. He looked away to the left and the right, and he could see a long line of great plumes of dust keeping pace with him as the other tanks of the squadron plowed their way across the desert. The major was an unimaginative man, but that spectacle never failed to move him. That long line of dust plumes sweeping across the desert had menace and sinister beauty about it. There were the high yellow clouds, and at the base of each a little dot, a nucleus, as it were, sometimes concealed from view by the inequalities of the ground, and every cloud indicated the presence of one of the tanks of his squadron. There were other clouds behind, when the major turned his gaze that way; they showed where the stragglers were trying to regain their places in the line after some necessary halt. The ones farthest back were the ones who had had track trouble or engine trouble. There could be no waiting for them, not in the face of the orders which the wireless brought in, insisting on the utmost speed in this dash across the desert.

Already in the major's mind the total of days already consumed in the march was a little vague. If he set his mind to it, he could have worked it out, but he felt as if he had done nothing all his life except lead this squadron across the desert. Something enormous and of vital importance was happening to the north, he knew — Sidi Barrani and Tobruk had fallen, but his command had been plucked out of that attack and sent off on this wide flanking sweep, and were already a little in the dark about the situation. These Italian maps were of no use at all. They showed things which simply did not exist — he could swear to that from bitter experience — and, in consequence, the major did not know within twenty miles where he was. But somewhere ahead of him there was the sea, across the great hump of Northern Africa which he was traversing, and beside the sea ran the great road which Mussolini had built, and he knew he had only to arrive on that road to start making things unpleasant for the Italians. What the situation would be when he did arrive he could not imagine in the least, but the major had absorbed the philosophy of the desert, and left that problem to be solved when it arose, wasting no mental effort on hypothetical cases which probably would have no resemblance to the reality he would encounter sooner or later.

The squadron was moving on a wide front, impressive on account of the distant plumes of dust, but even so, the width of the front was nothing compared with the immensity of the desert. They had marched five hundred miles so far, and a thousand miles to the south of them the desert extended as far as the plains of the Sudan. Sometimes the major would allow his imagination to think about these distances, but more often he thought about eggs. Tinned beef and biscuits, day after day, for more days than he could count, had had their effect. Nearly every idle thought that passed through his mind was busy with food. Sometimes he thought about kippers and haddock, sometimes about the green vegetables he had refused to eat as a little boy, but mostly he thought about eggs — boiled eggs, fried eggs, scrambled eggs — mostly boiled eggs. The lucky devils who were doing the fighting in the north were in among the villages now which Mussolini had peopled with so much effort; they would have a hen or two for certain, and a hen meant an egg. A boiled egg. For a day or two, eggs had formed a staple topic of conversation when he squatted at mealtimes with the gunner and the driver, until the major had detected a certain forbearing weariness mingled with the politeness with which his crew had received his remarks about eggs. Then he had left off talking about them; in this new kind of war, majors had to be careful not to become old bores in the eyes of the privates with whom they lived. But not being able to talk about them made him think about them all the more. The major swallowed hard in the choking dust.

The sun was now right ahead of him, and low toward the horizon; the sky around it was already taking up the colors of the desert sunset, and the brassy blue overhead was miraculously blending into red and orange. To the major that only meant that the day's march was drawing to a close. Sunsets came every day, and eggs came only once a year, seemingly.

When darkness came, they halted; each tank where it happened to find itself, save for the outposts pushed forward in case the Italians should, incredibly, be somewhere near and should have the hardihood to attempt operations in the dark. The driver and the gunner came crawling out of the tank, dizzy with petrol fumes and stiff with fatigue, still a little deaf with the insensate din which had assailed their ears for the whole day. The most immediate duty was to service the tank and have it all ready for prolonged action again, but before they did that they washed their mouths round with a little of the precious water taken from the can which had ridden with them in the tank all day. It was at blood heat, and it tasted of the inside of a tank — indescribably, that is to say. But it was precious, all the same. There was always the possibility that their ration of water would not come up from the rear; and if it did, there was also the chance that there had been so much loss in the radiators during the day that no water could be spared for the men.

Once, long back, there had been a heavenly time when the day's ration had been a gallon a head a day. That had been marvelous, for a man could do simply anything with a gallon a day; he could shave, wash his face, sometimes even spare a little to wash off the irritating dust from his body. But the ration, now that they were so far from the base, was half a gallon, and a man, after a day in a tank, could drink half a gallon at a single draught if he were foolish enough to do so. Half a gallon meant only just enough water to keep thirst from coming to close quarters; only the most fussy among the men would spare a cupful for shaving, and the days when the radiators had been extra thirsty, so that the men's rations were cut in half, were days of torment.

The major and the gunner and the driver settled down in the desert for their supper. Long habit had blunted the surprise the major had once felt at finding himself, a field officer, squatting in the dust with a couple of privates, and, fortunately, long habit had done the same for the privates. Before this campaign opened they would have been tongue-tied and awkward at his presence. It had not been easy to reach adjustment, but they had succeeded — as witness the way in which, without saying a word, they had caused him to leave off talking about eggs. He was still "sir" to them, but almost the only other way in which his rank was noticeable in their personal relationships was that the two privates both suspected the major of being the guilty party in the matter of the loss of one of their three enameled mugs.

They had not ventured openly to accuse him, and he remained in ignorance of their suspicions, taking it for granted that the gunner — a scatterbrained fellow — had been at fault in the matter.

It was an infernal nuisance, being short of a mug; two mugs among three of them called for a whole lot of organization, especially in the morning, when they had to clean their teeth, and sometimes to shave and sometimes to make tea — and the gunner liked his strong, and the driver liked his weak, and the major was the only one who did not want sugar in it. If ever the three of them were to quarrel, the major knew it would be over some difficulty arising out of the loss of the mug. Yet he did not see nowadays anything odd about a major worrying over the prospect of a disagreement with a couple of privates over an enameled mug.

And tonight he was additionally unlucky, because the rations for the day were a tinned meat and vegetable concoction that he particularly disliked. But the gunner and the driver were loud in their delight when they discovered what fate had brought them tonight. They ate noisily and appreciatively, while the major squatting beside them made only the merest pretense of eating and allowed his thoughts to stray back to memories of dinner at the Berkeley and the Gargantuan lunches at Simpson's in the Strand. And also of eggs.

It was dark now, and cold — before supper was over the major had to reach out for a blanket and wrap it round his shoulders as the treacherous desert wind blew chilly. The stars were out, but there was no moon yet and the darkness was impenetrable. There was nothing to do now except sleep. The major chose himself a spot where the scrub grew not too thickly, and where the rock did not jut entirely through the thin skin of earth which overlaid it. He spread his blankets over his fleabag and crawled in with the dexterity of long practice without disturbing the arrangement. The bit of tarpaulin stretched from the side of the tank to the earth kept off the dew, if there should be any, and the joints that had suffered on the steel piano stool and on the steel roof snuggled gratefully against the more kindly contact of the earth. And long habit was a help.

He awoke in the middle of the night with a shattering roar in his very ear. The driver had his own system of keeping his beloved motor warm enough to start. He slept only under two blankets, and when the cold awoke him he knew that it was necessary to warm up the motor. He would crawl out of bed, start it up, allow it to run for five minutes, and then switch it off. That meant that the light tank was always ready for instant action, but the major had never been able to acquire the habit of sleeping through the din of the motor. The only habit he had been able to form was that of cursing to himself at the driver, feebly, half awake, and then of turning over and completing his night's sleep. The gunner, on the other hand, slept stolidly through the whole racket, snoring away stubbornly — the major suspected him of dreaming about eggs.

Before dawn they were up and doing. Two inches of sand in the bottom of a petrol tin made an admirable wick; petrol soaked into it burned with an almost clear flame and heated the water for their tea in a flash. They had grown cunning lately and brushed their teeth after breakfast, using the remains of the tea for the purpose; that gave them an additional two swallows of water apiece to drink at the midmorning halt for filling up. The motor started, shatteringly noisy as usual. Then they were off, the long line of tanks heaving and rolling over the desert, the familiar plumes of dust trailing behind them, the familiar weary ache beginning to grow in the joints of the major as he settled himself on the piano stool.

The major's calculation of his position was a hazy one, and through no fault of his own. Erratic compasses, ridiculous Italian maps and strict wireless silence combined, after a march hundreds of miles long, to make it very doubtful where they were. But the major was philosophic about it. British light tanks were capable of fighting almost anything in Africa, and what they could not fight they could run away from; they had learned that lesson in innumerable untold skirmishes in the old days of the beginning of the war. The major felt ready for anything that might happen, as he stared out through the slit of the conning tower across the yellowish brown plain.

Yet all the same it is doubtful if he was really ready for the sight that met his eyes. The tank came lurching and rolling up a sharp slope. It heaved itself over the crest — the note of the motor changing ever so little as the gradient altered — and a new landscape was presented to the major's eyes.

First of all he saw the sea, the blue sea, the wonderful blue sea, flecked with white. The major wriggled on the piano stool and yelled involuntarily at the top of his voice when he saw it. That marvelous horizon, that beautiful color, that new-found sense of achievement and freedom — they were simply intoxicating. The driver and the gunner were as intoxicated as he was, screwing their necks round to grin at him, the fluffy immature beard of the gunner wagging on his chin.

And then they cleared the next curve of the crest, and the major saw the road, that long coastal road for the construction of which Musssolini had poured out so much treasure. The major had expected to see it from the moment when he had seen the sea — in fact, he was craning his neck for a sight of it. But he was not ready for the rest of what he saw. For twenty miles the road was black with the fleeing Italian army — an enormous column of men and vehicles, jamming the road from side to side, hastening westward — Bergenzoli's army escaping from Bengasi and from the wrath of the English behind them. From a point nearly ahead of them away off to the right stretched that hurrying column. From his point of vantage the major could see it looping like some monstrous water snake along the curves of the road. Now he knew why his squadron had been hurled across the desert at such a frantic speed. It had been planned to cut off Bergenzoli's retreat, and the object had been achieved, with no more than ten minutes to spare.

Those ten minutes were only to spare if the major did the right thing on the instant. But twenty years of training had prepared the major for that very purpose. He was still a hussar, even though his squadron's horses had long ago been replaced by light tanks. His mental reactions were instantaneous; there was no need to stop and ponder the situation. The trained tactical eye took in the lie of the land even while he was shouting into the wireless transmitter the vital information that he was ahead of the Italians. He saw the road and the ridge beside it, and the moment that the information had been acknowledged he was speaking again, quietly already, giving his orders to the squadron. The long line of tanks wheeled and swooped down upon the road.

So close was the race that they were barely in position before the head of the column was up to them. An hour later and the Italians would have been able to post a flank guard behind whose shelter most of them would have been able to slip away. As it was, the major just had time to give his orders to his two troops as the head of the Italian column came down upon them.

The tanks bucked themselves into position and the machine guns spoke out, pouring their fire into the trucks packed with infantry which were so recklessly coming down upon them. It was slaughter, the dire punishment of a harebrained attack. The major watched the trucks swerve off the road, saw the startled infantry come tumbling out while the machine-gun fire cut swaths through them. Truck piled upon truck. The poor devils in them were deserving of pity. At one moment they had thought themselves safe, rolling along a good road back to Tripoli, and then the next these gray monsters had come darting out of the desert across their path, spraying death.

With the checking of the head of the column, confusion spread up the road. The major could see movement dying away as each successive section bumped up against the one ahead; the sudden outburst of firing, taking everyone by surprise, was rousing panic among the weaker individuals. So much the better. From the major's point of view, there could not be too much panic. Somewhere up that column there were field guns and there were heavy tanks, and to neither of them could he offer any real resistance. The more confusion there was in the column, the longer would it take to extricate these, the only weapons that could clear its path. Time was of the utmost importance; he turned and looked back over his shoulder at where the sun was dipping toward the horizon and the blue sea. This time, by some curious chance, his mind was in a condition to take in the fact that the approaching sunset would be red and lurid.   He was smiling grimly as he turned back to his work.

Someone over there was trying to urge the unarmored infantry to the attack — to certain death, in other words, in the face of the two grim little groups of tanks that opposed them.   Some of them came forward to the certain death too.   And the sun was nearer the horizon.

Farther back down the column frantic officers were clearing a path for the artillery.   There were eddies and swirls in the mass.   Trucks were being heaved off the road as the guns came through.   The major took his glasses from his eyes and gave another order.   The tanks curvetted and wheeled, and next moment they had a ridge of solid earth between them and the guns.   There was a dreary wait — the major had time for another glance at the sun sinking in a reddened sky — before the shells began to come over.   Then the major could smile; they were shrieking over the crest and a good two yards above his head before they buried themselves in the ridge behind him.   But there was infantry creeping forward again; there was still the chance that he might be forced sideways out of his position and have to leave a gap through which the mob might escape.   He looked at the sun again, and then out to his right, the direction from which he had come, and he felt a glow of relief.   The rest of the advance guard was coming — a battalion of motorized infantry with their battery of antitank guns.   Now they had a chance.   But where were the cruiser tanks, the only weapons in Africa that could stop the heavy tanks when they should be able to make their way out of the column?

It had been touch and go in the first place, when the light tanks had cut off the retreat of the column.   It was touch and go now, when the light tanks and five hundred British soldiers were trying to stop the advance of fifty thousand Italians.   But night was close at hand.   Darkness blinded the Italian gunners and paralyzed the efforts being made to clear the road for the heavy tanks.   The major neatly withdrew his tanks over one more ridge, in case of a night attack — in all his extensive experience with the Italians they had never ventured a single operation in darkness — and went round his squadron to see that they were as well prepared as might be for a battle on the morrow.

The major always remembers that night as one when there was nothing he found it necessary to do. The British soldier was on the offensive. The veriest fool could see victory just ahead, victory of a crushing type, nothing less than annihilation of the enemy, if only the force of which the squadron formed a part could hold back Bergenzoli until pressure on his rear and the arrival of help to themselves should convince Bergenzoli of the hopelessness of his position. With victory depending on the proper lubrication of their tanks, on their precautions against surprise, they needed no telling, no inspection, to make them do their duty. The major was not an imaginative man, but something in his imagination was touched that night when he talked to his men. The final destruction of the Italians was what they had in mind; the fact that they would be opposed tomorrow by odds of a hundred to one, and that there was more chance of their being dead by evening than alive, did not alter their attitude in the least.

The major walked from one little group to another; the once khaki overalls worn by everyone, even himself, had been bleached almost white by exposure, and the oil stains somehow did not darken them in a bad light, so that the men he spoke to showed up as ghostly figures in the darkness. There was laughter in the voices of the ghosts he spoke to — laughter and delight in the imminent prospect of victory. And in the stillness of the desert night they could hear, across two valleys, the din of the heavy Italian tanks roaring up to take up positions for the charge that would try to clear the way for the Italians next day. That was the lullaby the major heard as he stretched out in the desert to try to snatch a couple of hours' sleep, side by side with the driver and the gunner. Only in the grave did officers and men sleep side by side until this war came.

Dawn — the first faint light that precedes dawn — showed, looming over the farther crest, the big Italian tanks which had been somehow forced forward during the night along the tangled column. They came forward ponderously, with fifty thousand men behind them, and in front of them there was only a thread of infantry, a single battery, a squadron of light tanks whose armor was only fit to keep out rifle bullets. It was as if the picadors and the matadors in the bull ring had to fight, not a single bull but a whole herd of bulls, all charging in the madness of desperation.

There is an art in the playing of a charging bull, even in the handling of a whole herd. Through a long and weary day, that was just what the major's squadron and the rest of the British force succeeded in doing. Since time immemorial — from Alexander to Hitler — it has been the fate of advance guards to be sacrificed to gain time for the maneuver of the main body, to be used to pin the enemy to the ground, so that his flank can be safely assailed. Only troops of the highest discipline and training can be trusted to fulfill such a mission, however. The Italian tanks which were recklessly handled were lured into the fire of the battery; the timid ones were prevailed upon to procrastinate. The slow retreat of the British force was over ground marked with crippled tanks and littered with Italian dead; and there were British dead there, too, and knocked-out British guns, and burned-out British tanks.

It was an exhausted British force that still confronted the Italians. The line had shrunk, so that on its left flank, toward the sea, there was an open gap through which, among the sand dunes, some of the Italians were beginning to dribble on foot, creeping along the edge of the sea in the wild hope of escaping captivity. And then, at that last moment, came the decisive blow. At least to us here it seems the last moment. That can only be a guess — no one can dare say that the British had reached the end of their resistance. But it was at that moment, when British riflemen were fighting hard to protect their headquarters, when two thirds of the British guns were out of action, when the major's squadron was reduced to three tanks, that help arrived. From out of the desert there came a sweeping line of huge British cruiser tanks. They came charging down on the Italian flank, enormous, invulnerable and terrifying. It is impossible to guess at the miracle of organization, at the prodigy of hard work, which had brought these monstrous things across sands which had scarcely even been trodden by camels.

From out of the desert they came, wreathed in dust, spouting fire, charging down upon the tangled mass of the Italian army pent back behind the thin dam of the British line. The Italian tanks wheeled to meet them, and then and there the battle was fought out, tank to tank, under the brazen sky, over the sand where the dead already lay. The dust clouds wrapped them round, dimming the bright flames — visible even in the sunshine — which streamed from the wrecked tanks, the Viking pyres of their slain crews.

When it was over, the whole battle was finished. There was no fight left in the Italians. The desert had already vomited out three fierce attacks — first the major's light tanks, then the infantry, and last the cruiser tanks, and no one could guess what next would come forth. And from the rear came the news that the pursuing British were pressing on the rear guard; at any moment the sea might bring its quota of death, should the British ships find a channel through the sandbanks which would bring their guns within range of the huddled army. Front, rear and both flanks were open to attack, and overhead the air force was about to strike. Nor was that all. Thirst was assailing them, those unhappy fifty thousand men massed without a single well within reach. There was nothing for it but surrender.

The major watched the fifty thousand men yield up their arms; he knew that he was witness to one of the great victories of history, and he was pleased about it. Through the dreadful fatigue that was overwhelming him he also was aware that he had played a vital part in the gaining of that victory, and that somewhere in the future there would be mentions in dispatches and decorations. But his eyelids were heavy and his shoulders drooping.

Then came the gunner; his faded, oil-stained overalls made more shocking than ever by the stains of the blood of the wounded driver, and that horribly fluffy yellow beard of his, like the down on a baby chick, offending the sunlight. Now that they had reached the sea, the distillation plants would supply them with a sufficiency of water and that beard could be shaved off.   But the gunner was grinning all over his face, his blue eyes nearly lost in the wrinkles round them, lines carved by the blinding light of the desert.   The gunner had heard a cock crowing down beside the solitary white farmhouse toward the sea on the edge of the battlefield, and he had walked there and back on stiff legs.   The gunner held out a big fist before the major, and opened the fingers like a man doing a conjuring trick.   In his hand was an egg.

SIT IN THE SUN

By Zachary Gold

MY HUSBAND KANIG, if you can believe it, came home one sunny spring day and retired. A man of sixty. In the old days, in my father's days, a man of sixty was a boy.

Three hundred and sixty-five days a year Kanig comes marching up the stairs, six, a quarter past six — the latest — and sits down at the kitchen table for supper. Who could know this day was different? Did the sun stop shining? Did the world stop turning?

"I'm retiring," Kanig said.

My husband Kanig, you understand, is a man who talks a lot; my husband Kanig likes the sound of his own voice.

"Fine," I said.

I pinched the peas with a fork; Kanig's peas must be just so. I basted the roast. I took the hard tomatoes out of the icebox and began to slice them. God forbid a tomato should be soft. Kanig would throw it on the floor.

"I'll do a little work around the house," Kanig said.

"The house is all right," I told him.

"I'll plant flowers in the back garden."

"Flowers!"

Fifteen years we've been living in the same house; from the beginning Kanig was going to plant flowers in the back yard. Then winter came and it was too cold, and in the summer it was too hot; in the spring it was too nice, and in the autumn it was a shame to work on such fine days. My husband Kanig is a man sensitive to weather.

I took the rolls out of the bag and put them in the bread pan. Salt and pepper were already at the table. Kanig broke an onion roll in half and chewed on the crust; my husband doesn't know what it

means to sit ten minutes in the house without nibbling on something.

"I'm going to build a bench," Kanig said.

"Only a bench," I said. "Why not a sofa?"

"I'm going to read Tolstoy again."

Fine! It was all settled. Kanig always has something to talk
about. My husband Kanig is a man with a million ideas. I shut
the gas off under the roast and ladled the soup into plates.

"Wash your hands, Kanig," I said. "We'll eat."

After supper, Kanig sat down with his newspaper. From eight
o'clock to ten you don't see his face. He sits in the Morris chair and
all you see is a headline. He snaps on the radio and if it plays, it
plays; and if it doesn't, my husband Kanig doesn't know the difference. Music, static, talk — it's all the same. Kanig reads his newspaper.

I was knitting a sweater for my grandchild. My son, the doctor,
has a little girl — a picture, a doll. Outside, the boys were running
up and down the alleys, yelling like Indians; such games they play
these days. Next door, in the upstairs apartment, Mrs. Tolman was
washing her daughter's stockings. A night like a hundred other
nights.

Maybe I closed my eyes for a minute, so what? Was it a tragedy?
I am not so young as I used to be. God forbid, I'm not an old woman
yet, but a little rest never hurt anybody. When I opened my eyes
again, it was after eleven; the knitting was on the floor and Kanig was
fiddling with the radio.

"Kanig," I said, "are you going to stay up all night?"

"It's not late," Kanig said.

"After eleven and not late? You'll be like a sick goat in the office
tomorrow."

The radio coughed. "Listen," Kanig said.

"Lonely Joe," said the fellow on the radio, "up there in Pat's Diner
in the Bronx wants to hear Melancholy Lullaby. Okay, Joe, here it
comes."

"Did you hear that?" Kanig said.

The way Kanig plays a radio, loud enough to wake the dead —
may they rest in peace — you'd have to wear ear muffs not to hear.

"A wonderful thing," Kanig said. "In the old days, a man was
lonely, what could he do? Sit in the house and mope. Now for a
nickel he calls up and a fellow talks to him, an orchestra plays, a girl
sings him a song. Marvelous."

Marvelous today, marvelous tomorrow — it didn't get me to sleep.
"Kanig," I said, "how long are you going to stay up?"

"A few more," Kanig said.

A few more, by Kanig, could mean all night. I put my knitting
back in the bag and straightened the lace doilies on the arms of the
chair.

"Mac, the cabby, wants to hear Drive Me Home, Four to the
Measure. I'll look, Mac —— "

Mac! Joe! My husband Kanig listens to anybody.

In the morning I woke up with the sun on my face. After nine! I
reached for the clock and put it to my ear. Running! What kind
of business was this? In my mother's days a woman was up with
the sun. Who heard of not preparing a meal for your husband in
the morning? I jumped out of bed.

"Kanig!" I called.

He wasn't washing; I ran into the kitchen.

No Kanig. There was nothing on the stove, not the coffeepot,
not a pan of hot water. My husband Kanig for the first time in his
life left the house without a piece of dry bread to put in his mouth.

Ah, I'd hear from Kanig. My husband is not a man without a
tongue. Did it mean nothing to me that he left the house hungry?
Kanig would talk about it for weeks.

But what's done is done. I'd make him a black-bean soup tonight,
some fricassee or stuffed cabbage. A man with a good meal in him
is like a dog on a rope; he runs around a little, he barks a little, but
after a while he sleeps.

So I dressed. I had a cup of hot tea. I cleaned up the house a little. Then I slipped on my coat and picked up the garbage pail to bring it downstairs. I opened the door.

Kanig was painting the foyer stairs.

"Kanig," I said, "what's the matter?"

"Look out," Kanig said. "You'll leave footprints."

"Kanig," I said, "it's ten o'clock. Did you call the office?"

"I'm retired," Kanig said.

So much a person can take and no more. Talk is one thing; talk until you're blue in the face — fine. It's a free country, say what you want. But to do a thing like this out of nowhere, out of a clear sky ——

"Retired!" I said. "Have you got stocks you can live on? You own a bank? Can you go to Miami tomorrow if you wanted to? That's retired!"

Talk to a wall.

I didn't know what to do. I went back and ran down the side stairs like a woman out of her mind. Mrs. Hirschmann, my neighbor downstairs, called me; I didn't answer her. Did I have time for talk?

Out in the street I pulled the coat around me. I straightened my hair. Did I need Kanig to paint the foyer stairs? Union painters weren't working, maybe? Retired!

For his mother, I am proud to say, my son always has a minute. People come to him from all over, only too glad to sit and wait; but for his mother, almost from around the corner, my son always finds time. Children like him I wish on anybody.

"You've been running," he said. "Sit still for a minute."

I sat still.

"All right," he said. "Now tell me what happened."

I told him everything. He knew how Kanig talked. Was that anything new? I told him how I got up late in the morning, shame on me. His father Kanig was retired, I told him.

My son, the doctor, laughed.

"Tell me the joke," I said. "What's funny?"

"Now, mom," he said, "don't get yourself excited."

"Is Kanig an old man?" I said. "Has he lost all his teeth? Do his hands shake so he can't hold them straight?"

"Just let him be," my son said. "You know how he is. He'll get tired of it himself."

"Do you know what I think?" I said. "Something is the matter with Kanig."

My son stood up; he is a man six feet tall, a giant. "I'll look him over next time we come for supper. What's on the menu?"

"Black bread and water for Kanig," I said.

Go examine a wild animal; but my son, the doctor, said there was nothing wrong with Kanig. Nothing wrong? Is it right for a grown man to sit around doing nothing?

People talked. Mrs. Hirschmann, my neighbor downstairs, asked me, "What is your husband doing these days? Is he sick?"

"Kanig is building a bench," I told her.

What if the foyer steps didn't come out just so? Could Kanig help it if he ran out of paint and the second can wasn't the same shade? What if the bench came out lopsided because Kanig cut the legs to different sizes? So we don't sit on it. But my retired husband Kanig, you understand, had a bench and a swollen finger where he got a splinter.

When I went shopping, Kanig followed me like a puppy dog. He smelled everything — the smoked fish, the cheese, the vegetables.

"Get some sturgeon," he said. "It smells good."

Does a man eat with his nose?

Kanig was under my feet. In the morning he sat in the street. He sat like an Indian. He slept and he sat in the sun. He walked around the house, he read a little and he listened to the radio. My husband Kanig — I am ashamed to admit it — became an old man, puttering around the house. It made me sick. "Get out a little, Kanig," I said. "If you won't work, go see things. Go to places. You're a retired man; you have plenty of time."

"There's enough to see here," Kanig said.

"What is there to see?   The leaves on the trees?"

"I watch the boys playing," Kanig said.

"Do something," I said.   "Go see uncle in the Bronx."

"I would waste the day," Kanig said.

Watching children play games isn't wasting a day.   To argue with a man like Kanig ends in aggravation only.   "Kanig," I said, "put on your hat.   Go see uncle."

I marched him to the foyer.   I gave him a quarter for carfare; my husband Kanig gave up carrying money when he retired.   What does a man need money for, he said; Kanig, you heard, is a man who talks a lot.

"Give uncle my regards," I said.

Ten minutes later Kanig was sitting on the stoop in front, in the sun, reading a joke book; a joke book full of colored pictures.

"Kanig," I said, "why aren't you in the Bronx?"

"I bought this instead," Kanig said.

My husband Kanig, who was going to read Tolstoy, reading joke books.

"In this book, Etta," Kanig said, "is a man who has to get somewhere in a hurry.   So he jumps in the air and flies.   He just sticks out his hands."

"It's a story," I said.   "It's for children.   No one is asking you to believe it."

"A man like that, you'd think that at least once something would happen to him.   He'd fall, he'd break an arm, he'd scratch a finger. For the risks he takes, that isn't unreasonable."

"Who makes you read it?"

"It's interesting," Kanig said.

This is my husband, you understand; this is Kanig.   Once, believe me, he was a man.   Ask anybody in the neighborhood.   They all know Kanig.   "Kanig?" they'll say.   "A fine fellow, a fine man."

Ask at the office, they'll tell you.   Top-notch.   A-No. 1.   Take a man like Kanig, give him a garment, and in ten minutes he'll give you the production price within two cents.   He'll tell you how many stitches you need to an inch.

Kanig, I remember, was like the wind when he was young. Kanig could talk to you and make you feel that the world was a knickknack to put in your parlor. Walking down the street with Kanig was like being on a stage. People looked at you; people whispered; people had eyes for the girl with Kanig. A man like that reading joke books!

"Kanig," I said, "throw the book away. Give it to the children."

"Etta —— "

"Do you want everybody laughing at you? Do you want them to call you 'Kanig, the old fool'?"

"Why should anyone care what I do?"

"Throw it away!"

Kanig bent his head and began reading again.

Enough is enough! I marched up the stairs. I slammed the door. I didn't talk to him that night. I gave him his supper and that's all.

The sun comes up and the sun goes down. Nothing stands still. My husband did what he wanted; I did my work. If, suddenly, it was quiet in the house, whose fault was that? What did I have to say to my husband Kanig?

Once a week my son, the doctor, and his wife came to the house. Once a week, at least, I made a meal like old times.

My son works a good day; a piece of bread is not enough for him.

"Have some more meat," I said to him. "You don't look so well."

"For Etta," Kanig said, "you have to look like Tarzan to be healthy."

"Kanig," I said, "eat what you have and keep quiet."

It is good to have a man in your house to eat your food. Kanig once was a man like that. But now a dib of this, a dab of that, a smell from this can and a glass of milk, and he has enough. Kanig eats like a bird.

"How are you feeling?" my son said to him.

"For the doctor?" Kanig said. "Or for the son? For the son I'm feeling fine."

"A little restless?"

"Why should I feel restless?"

"Want to get back into harness?"

"Does a horse want to leave pasture?" Kanig said. He dipped into the stewed prunes and pursed his lips. "Good," he said. "Your mother is a good cook."

Who asked him anything about the prunes?

After supper I just cleared away the table. I left the dishes in the sink. When my son comes to the house, he takes me to the movies. He is a son among sons.

"Come with us," he said to Kanig this night. "You haven't anything against the movies."

"It's a good place to sleep," my husband Kanig said.

The movie was about people. This man wanted to marry the girl, and the girl wanted to marry another man, and the other man, I should know why, wanted to go invent something. So first they talked and then the man invented and then something blew up — a terrible scene. So, between one man and the other man and the girl and the invention, it took up an hour and a half.

"Like it?" my son, the doctor, said to me.

"A fine picture," I said. "Only tell me, which one did the girl marry?"

"The inventor," my son said. "Didn't you see it?"

"I got mixed up," I said.

The lights were going on and I picked up my bingo card. I play from habit. Sometimes I get three across and sometimes I get four; winning is out of the question entirely. But I play; after all, accidents happen.

Tonight, even bingo had to wait. Somebody was giving away a plane trip to California. I should know who. These days in the movies it's like Coney Island. Everybody wins.

They spun the wheel on the screen.

"The winning number is eight hundred and thirty-one," the man on the stage said. "Eight three one."

I reached for my son's ticket. He had eight hundred and thirty-two. I looked at my ticket — eight hundred and thirty. Three across, four across — my family never wins. I nudged my husband. "Kanig," I said.

He woke up. Planes, bingo, pictures — Kanig sleeps.

"Kanig," I said, "your number."

"What number?"

"On the little card when you came in."

"I put it in my pocket," Kanig said.

He reached for it and took it out. I held up his hand so I could see.

"Will the person who has number eight hundred and thirty-one please step forward?"

"Kanig!" I shouted. "Kanig, look!"

A wonderful machine! Clean as the stove in my kitchen. Shiny! Spotless! With a machine like that, let the birds keep their feathers; Kanig could laugh at eagles. A piece of iron and a turning stick. My father, may he rest in peace, wouldn't believe it if he saw it.

"Why should I go?" Kanig said. "Do I know anybody in California?"

"It'll do you good," my son, the doctor, told him.

"Let Etta go."

"Get on the plane, Kanig," I said. "Where is your bag?"

"You'll enjoy the trip," my son told him. "Meet new people. See the Pacific."

"Are the people shaped different?" Kanig said. "The Pacific, the Atlantic — an ocean is an ocean. If I want to look at oceans I can go to Coney Island."

"Kanig," I said, "are you afraid?"

We took him by the hand, like you lead a little boy to school. We put him on the plane; I made the seat comfortable. My husband Kanig doesn't know what's good for him.

"Have a good time," I said.

With a noise like thunder, with the wind of a storm, the machine began to move. It was something to see, believe me. In another minute, it seemed, it would go into the trees. But then, suddenly, it was in the air, getting smaller and going higher until it was just a mark in the sky. My husband Kanig was flying with the clouds.

"It will be a wonderful thing for Kanig," I told my son, the doctor.

Not every day does something like that happen in a family, I assure you. What things he would see; what sights, what places! Places in another world. My son, the doctor, got a map for me — Illinois, Kansas, New Mexico, Arizona. In the old days a man wouldn't see so much in three lifetimes.

He would have stories to tell, my husband. Kanig is not a man without a tongue; Kanig is not a man without wisdom. Albuquerque! Who on the block even knew there was such a place? The Ackermans? The Tolmans? The Hirschmanns? It was a word to them, and that's all. But who saw it with his own eyes? My husband Kanig, believe me.

I made a dinner for the night he came home. A roasted chicken, a noodle soup with *mundel,* a chopped-onion-and-egg salad. Everything was just so. It was all ready when he came in with my son. Kanig was home. We sat down to a holiday meal in our house that night.

He ate slowly; there was no hurry. A trip to California gives a man a good appetite; you can understand that. He finished one dish; I gave him another.

I sat on pins and needles. He didn't look different, but when a man has traveled that far there is a change. We would hear from Kanig; Kanig could see with his tongue. But when a man eats, he eats; an empty stomach means a silent tongue.

Kanig said, "A little tea, Etta?"

"And sponge cake, Kanig."

My husband Kanig could live on sponge cake, made with a little cinnamon, a few chopped almonds and walnuts. He ate the cake, he sipped the tea. He leaned back in his chair.

"Now, Kanig," I said, "tell us."

"It was a nice trip," Kanig said.

"What happened?"

Kanig is not a man without words, you understand; Kanig is not blind.

"When I got into the airplane," Kanig said, "the girl asked me if I wanted anything. What could I want?" He sipped his tea. "In Chicago I had a cup of coffee."

"How was Arizona?" I said.

"It was evening, Etta. We were flying very high. It was hard to see anything."

"Did you like the desert?" my son, the doctor, said.

"It was nighttime. I was tired. I slept."

"The mountains, Kanig?"

"Coming back," Kanig said, "I saw the mountains. There was a little hole in the clouds, and looking down I could see white. The girl told me it was snow. Maybe it was just another cloud. The planes move so fast."

"In California, Kanig?" I said. "What did you do in California?"

Kanig sipped the tea and bit into the sponge cake. "In California," Kanig said, "it was raining."

"But what happened, Kanig? All the time you were gone, what happened?"

"We flew," Kanig said.

"You flew!" I shouted. "A man goes three thousand miles! A man goes over all of America! He goes from here to California and back, and all he can say is he flew!"

"Etta —— " Kanig said.

"Are you a fool, Kanig?" I cried. "Maybe all you can do is sit in the sun. Maybe your eyes have stopped seeing and your ears hearing. Maybe you're just an old man waiting to die."

"Enough!" Kanig shouted and pushed his chair back. "Enough!"

He got up and walked into the bedroom. I heard him snap on the radio. My son, the doctor, put his arm around me. "Sit down," he said. "Sit down for a minute. It was a big trip. Maybe pa is just tired."

A half glass of tea and a piece of sponge cake were still on the table. My husband Kanig didn't finish his meal.

I was ashamed. I sat on the bed, looking at Kanig. He leaned back with his eyes closed, listening to the radio. In the old days, in my mother's days, a woman didn't talk that way to her husband.

"Kanig," I said, "I'm sorry."

"Don't be sorry," he said. He got up and reached into his bag. "Here, I brought this back for you."

It was a round wooden ash tray.

"It's redwood," Kanig said. "It grows out there in trees so big you can't see the top. Put it in the parlor. It will look nice next to your chair."

"Kanig," I said, "you're mad at me?"

"Why should anyone think a man wants to die, Etta?"

"Kanig!"

"Is it wrong to want a little quiet sometimes? Is it wrong for a man to sit in the sun?" Kanig's hand was on the radio, fiddling with the knob. "Look at me, Etta. Am I an old man?"

My husband Kanig, I am proud to say, stands with his back straight. His hand is like a rock. His eyes are clear. An old man?

"No, Kanig," I said.

"What should I do, Etta? When you're young you want to do things to see if they can be done. But when you've done them? What then?"

What hasn't my husband Kanig done?

The man on the radio was talking, "For Mary Phillippo we play Lover Come Back to Me."

"Listen," Kanig said. "The boy will come back. The girl will be happy. Or it will be with another boy. A voice in the air has accomplished a wonder. I have listened to a miracle. What more can I want?" He reached over and snapped off the radio. "Does it mean so much that I didn't see the mountains?"

Is Kanig a baby, for me to tell him where to look and what to see? "Let the mountains fall down," I said to him.

"The desert, Etta?"

"A handful of sand."

"What did I miss on the trip? Another city? Another mountain? What is it, Etta? I sit in the street and I watch the neighbors. I talk with my friends or I do a little work. I watch the sun on the trees and I think for a little while —— "

My husband Kanig, I've told you, has many words; my husband Kanig knows the sound of his own voice. Maybe, sometimes, I don't know what he means. But Kanig is not a fool; if he is retired, he retired with a reason.

So let it be. A man goes three thousand miles to the other side of the world and he brings back a piece of wood. A man goes across all of America and he thinks of his house and his wife. That is something, you understand. That is more than a piece of wood.

There are no quarrels in my house. If Kanig wants to paint the foyer stairs, let him paint. If Kanig wants to plant flowers, he plants them. In the mornings I do my work and I prepare meals fit for a man. And in the afternoons, sometimes, I sit with Kanig in the sun and watch the children playing in the street.

MISS BRONSKA

By Gene Henry

No ENGLISHWOMAN would have had the effrontery to do what little
Miss Bronska did. The few who knew as many of the facts as leaked
out gave thanks for the results. But the British soul must always
feel itself abraded by knowledge that those things which are not
done have been done. British courtesy would not discuss the thing,
except to say, "You know, Miss Bronska's Polish" — which is to say,
"There lies between us a gulf which cannot be bridged." And it is
true the bridge of bombs between the two was not of English make.

No one knew how little Miss Bronska happened to be in London
unless, in fact, she had been blown there by the first bomb dropped
on Warsaw. Miss Bronska herself could not have told you, for how
can one chart a nightmare? And she wouldn't have tried, for why
speak of an unpleasantness when one may, at almost any hour of the
day, run out into the London Streets and watch the British war birds
gaily fighting Jerries overhead?

In the hiving underground canteen where Miss Bronska darted
about, handing out cigarettes and sausages-with-mashed and other
heartening commodities, not all of which could be rung up on the
cash register, where you were yesterday was not nearly so important
as where you might be tomorrow. Busy and neutral, Miss Bronska
suggested a sparrow. She was almost as small-boned as a sparrow,
just a remnant of dull skin stretched over something so indomitable
you couldn't put a name to it. The suggested comparison, and the
fact that the sparrow is practically indestructible, may have accounted
for the fact that the sight of her, darting about picking up and putting
down plates and cups, was pleasant to the weary stretcher bearers and
details of Air Raid Precautions men who drifted into the canteen in
the grim hours of dawn. Tired eyes lighted as they watched her, be-

cause she never looked tired. She could work twenty-four hours at a
stretch and be as bright at the end of it as she was at the beginning.
This may have been because the only bright thing about her was her
two black eyes, and these were inextinguishable.

She was so much a part of the canteen itself that the first time she
was noticed as an individual was the first time she took an afternoon
off. She had been so small and so colorless that no one had had the
faintest notion how much actual work she'd got away with until she
wasn't there to do it. They wondered where she was, but no one
thought to worry whether she might be ill. You couldn't think of illness when all you could remember of her was those two unquenchable
black eyes.

Miss Bronska had gone to a hospital housing casualties from one
branch of the Royal Air Force. In some way she had learned there
was in the hospital a Polish boy. True, he'd been born in America
and was called an American boy. But, to Miss Bronska, America
was a discovery, and being an American was a state of mind having
nothing to do with one's bloodstream.

Having calculated to the penny what she could save by going without her dinners for a week, Miss Bronska had purchased, to take with
her, a carton of cigarettes. They were not the cheapest cigarettes.
They were the ones she liked best. Miss Bronska had the quaint
habit of using as gifts only the things she liked best.

As she came up onto the street, she found it was a nice day with a
watery sun shining. It is traditional with Londoners to be pleased
that the sun shines in late fall. They have a new feeling now. They
burrow up from air-raid shelters and subterranean canteens and greet
the sun as a unique experience. Unique because this one lovely sight
of the sun may be their last. Miss Bronska had gone beyond that.
When she greeted the sun she knew that it and she were the only
survivors from a certain little group who had started out together in
Poland. They had both reached England, and here they meant to
stay.

She was on the bus when the sirens sounded. Her mind having
already gone forward to her destination, she went placidly on with

her knitting, and was recalled to her surroundings only when a girl across the way moved abruptly in an effort to look out and upward at the sky.   It occurred to her then that the occupants of the bus were as unimpressed by the daily loosing of the iron hounds of hate as was the vehicle in which they rode.   She understood that their indifference was not a pose, but a simple balancing upon a pivotal center.   Her own experience had taught her that when a man learns he can trust no manhood save that within himself, all his forces flow inward to corrode or galvanize, depending upon the metal of the core.   It seemed only logical to her that this should be cumulatively true of a nation.

Outside the hospital, she looked hopefully upward.   As there were no planes in sight, she pattered in to breast the fumes of ether, antiseptics, and the sweet reek of pain.   A preoccupied nurse took her in tow and led her up stairs and down corridors to the ward where the Polish boy lay.   It was a small ward, almost, she was moved to feel, a cozy ward, unless one remembered that so much of the fighting of the Royal Air Force was over foreign soil, and that many who were undoubtedly casualties never reached an English hospital.

Miss Bronska entered a bit breathless.   This gave her a shy look as she pattered after the brisk nurse down the lane between the rows of beds.   But there was nothing shy about the black eyes darting from boy to boy.   When a bland blue eye gave her a sober and conclusive wink, she smiled and nodded and resolved to stop and have a chat on her way out.   As it transpired, she didn't wait that long.

The nurse waved her to the bedside of the Polish boy, paused to jerk a blanket straight, flicked a clinical eye about, and went where she was needed.

The ward stirred to interest.

The Polish boy had both legs amputated just above the knees.   He was a mess of bandages and cages and casts.   But he had one good hand.   Miss Bronska offered him her thin claw and her bright smile. "I'm Juliana Bronska," she said.   "I thought I'd drop in for a little visit."

It was curious the way the ward reacted to the little Polish sparrow. They were young. They were so very young, with the piping lustiness of youth which seems most innocent when it is most ribald. They could defer in disconcerting unison to authority, to patronage or to the plain bore. For little Miss Bronska they disbanded into spontaneous individuals, eager and impetuous and affectionate. The Polish boy told her he was called "Legs" because he'd lost both legs. The boy three beds down was "One-Leg" because he'd lost only one. There was "Lungs" across the way; "Head Case" there; "Fin," who'd smashed one arm; and "Fins," who'd lost both arms.

Miss Bronska acknowledged the introductions formally, speaking the brave names proudly. She pattered from bedside to bedside, shaking such hands as could be shaken, breaking open the packages of cigarettes and dividing them with mathematical justice, making sure that one was set alight in each mouth. Without apology or embarrassment, she seated herself beside "Fins," who had no arms and therefore no hands, holding his cigarette and chattering as cheerfully as a sparrow. They loved her. And Miss Bronska had a beautiful time.

They had heard the sirens, and knew she must have crossed the city during a raid. They demanded information. They had heard only a few distant bombs. "Did we chase them off?"

Miss Bronska felt guilty because she'd seen no spectacular fight she could report. There was a wireless in the room. Later they would get the official report. But they wanted immediate talk of their own division of the service. And they were eagles, while she was a sparrow. They would not care for the crumbs of rumor or gossip she'd picked up in the canteen. So she did what no other visitor had had the wit to do. She begged them to tell her of their own fights, only they did not know that this was what she asked.

Miss Bronska was well aware that not in this war nor the last would fliers talk of their own exploits, or of those of their fellows. But she knew also that if there is one thing any boy, of any race and any profession, would rather talk of than another, it is some bit of attempted heroism which backfired, causing embarrassment to the would-be hero and joy to his fellows. So she told them about the stretcher bearers who'd rushed out after a night raid to gather in the casualties.

They'd come upon two women huddled in a doorway. One of the women was obviously in writhing pain. But when the men made to take her on the stretcher, both women shrieked and screamed them off. It was, of course, black as the inside of their helmets, and impossible to tell how badly wounded was the one in pain. But from her groaning and writhing they were convinced her life would be a matter of minutes if something wasn't done at once. So they became official and commanding, and had actually got the screaming woman onto the stretcher when they were forced to the realization that they were about to be present at a birth. They abandoned the stretcher and ran.

Miss Bronska brought her story to an end amid howls of laughter. Then she said innocently, "I don't suppose, in the Air Force, you ever get yourselves into embarrassing difficulties."

She got something then. They yelled one another down to be the first to tell the good one on Fins or Lungs; the boner Legs had pulled, or the time Head Case got the entire squadron in bad with the brass hats. And to make their ribald stories understandable to their guest, they sketched in stark details of aerial warfare which no other necessity could have dragged from them. They entertained her with the best they had. And because she was such a sympathetic audience, they even howled hastily expurgated bits of songs with whose composition they had whittled away the slow pain of the hours. Miss Bronska particularly liked the one that went:

> *Said Legs to Fin,*
> *"As a Siamese twin*
> *We'd make one man sound and merry;*
> *With an arm to spare*
> *You could scratch my hair*
> *While I comb out a Jerry."*

So they gave her:

> *When the great Herr Hitler,*
> *With his mimsey mustache,*
> *Set out to chop the British*
> *Into stinking German hash,*
> *He forgot to warn the blighters*
> *Who'd lined up to do his work,*
> *We're as hard to kill in England*
> *As we were at Dunkirk.*

When she rose to go, she shook hands all around again. Fins held his breath until she'd passed him with a bright smile and a courteous nod, and he was assured she wouldn't spoil it with the sort of grave-digger's pat to which his soul was raw.

Then he grinned and yelled, "Come again, sweetheart!"

To the very end she refused to twitter over pillows. When Legs slipped down in reaching for her hand, and hunched his shoulders at the pillows, she gave them a punch, remarking, "Why is it that hospital pillows always seem to be stuffed with mashed potatoes?"

Nonetheless, the ward was wary, and braced itself for the last lingering chief mourner's look from the door which cut them like a fall against a taut wire. When Miss Bronska pattered through and closed the door without one single backward glance, they sighed and settled back in deep content and quiet pride.

Between the ward door and the stairs going down there was a single room. The door of this room stood ajar for better ventilation, and was blocked with a screen for privacy. Privacy has little meaning to a woman who has crossed a frontier locked in a cattle car with thirty assorted refugees, and spent three weeks in the bowels of a Greek tramp with the unwashed of every nation. Miss Bronska peeped around the screen. There was one bed in the room, and in the bed, propped up with pillows, a male creature differing from the boys in the ward only in that his head was completely swathed in bandages, leaving exposed two nostrils and a mouth.

It did not occur to Miss Bronska that this man's isolation might be due to rank and a resounding title, and that one does not walk up to rank and a resounding title and slap it on the back. Miss Bronska was as single-minded as a matrimonial agency. All she saw was that here was a man with a mouth and no cigarette in it. She rummaged in her bag, hoping there might be one left from her sparse personal supply. It was a cheap cigarette, and not a tidy one. But Miss Bronska smoothed it out expertly and pattered to the bedside, chirping, "Smoke?"

The man gave a spasmodic jerk and bit his lips to stifle a groan.

Miss Bronska had no way of knowing that, lying there quietly blind, he'd been staring into the laughing faces of his boys that one by one exploded in blood and silent agony.

"If you'll just open your mouth," she suggested briskly.

Accustomed to the periodic administration of thermometers, the man opened his mouth, coming back reluctantly from his officers' hell.

Expecting the thermometer, he had to catch himself to keep from mangling the cigarette. But his muscles were not muscles. They were merely insulation covering nerves trained to juggle tons of roaring metal between the bullets of machine-gun fire.

Miss Bronska lighted his cigarette and glanced brightly around. On a metal stand across the room stood a wash basin holding a metal soap dish. Removing the soap, she took the dish and placed it on his knotted fist. "Here's an ash tray," she said. She didn't add that it was high-sided, so he wouldn't spill ashes on his bed. She took it for granted that those sensitive fingers would discover this as soon as they unclamped.

Miss Bronska drew up the single hard chair and sat down beside the bed. Dragging a neat roll of wool and shining needles from her bag, she said, "I'll just get on with my knitting, if you don't mind," and proceeded to click industriously. Obviously she couldn't leave him with a lighted cigarette. He might set those head bandages afire.

The man smoked in a cold concentration of fury. This couldn't have happened to him. It was an outrage as personal as his blindness. Every member of the hospital staff had strict orders to admit no visitor to his room. And he was accustomed to having his orders obeyed. Removing the cigarette from lips as stiff as the wings of his plane, he asked, "Would you mind telling me who you are?"

"I'm Juliana Bronska." She didn't add anything more, because she didn't think it would interest him.

He fell back upon the only weapon constantly at the disposal of an English gentleman, a total black-out of the offensive presence. It was not a good cigarette, but at least it was tobacco. The little brass box on his bedside table was full of fine cigarettes, but he hated to ask a nurse to light one for him, feeling that while she stood by to make sure he didn't set himself alight he might be keeping her from one of his boys in need of something more important. When he'd smoked this one until it burned his fingers, he stubbed it out in the metal soap dish to which his hand had clung.

Miss Bronska stuffed her knitting into her bag, emptied the soap dish, washed it out and replaced the soap. "Good afternoon," she chirped, and pattered out. But she took something with her, some bit of the inviolably private hell which had encased the man. And she left with him the prickling fear that she might come again.

Miss Bronska came again the following week. As before, she went first to the ward, where she was hailed with shouts of joy. This time she brought them little round, hard, brightly colored sweets that could be made to last a long time if you sucked them slowly. She fed them also a little Polish woman's description of last night's raid, which she had stood in the street to watch for them. Since they were friends, they howled at her ignorance of terms and tactics, and proceeded to give her an actual description of the thing her eyes had seen but hadn't understood.

Just before she left she said, "There's a man in a room, just there. His head's all bandaged up."

Silence fell upon the ward. It was not an uncomfortable silence. It was a silence vital with the close-concealed affection of the British-born, streaked with uncontrollable currents of pride and loyalty and battle brotherhood.

It was Legs, the Polish-American boy, who told her, "That's old J. G."

These delicate currents all but unnerved Miss Bronska as she entered J. G.'s room a moment later. She did not consider herself a brave woman, and she had to steel her sparrow-boned frame for a task she knew to be too big for her, but one that no one else seemed to be doing. When Miss Bronska faced a task that needed doing and that no one else seemed to be doing, she usually contrived to do it.

She chirped a bright "Good afternoon" from the doorway, so she wouldn't startle him and make him jerk and bite his lip as he had done before. Then she pattered in, drew the single chair to the bedside and perched upon it. She didn't tell him who she was. She'd told him that already. Juliana Bronska was of no importance. The thing she was there to do was as important as the service in which he'd given up his eyes. It required as accurate a hand and as unflinching a heart. She wasn't sure she had these, but she was used to forcing makeshifts into serving any moment's need.

"I believe I've figured out a way for you to light your cigarettes without setting fire to your bandages," she said to a figure stiffening rapidly into a black-out. How dared the woman force herself inside the private agony of his helplessness?

She took from her bag a single package of expensive cigarettes and set it on his knuckle-whitening fist. "If you'll just put one in your mouth," she suggested.

The box slid off a fist which jerked in outrage. "I do not care to smoke," he offered shortly.

"You needn't smoke it now," she assured him, adding, "They're rather better than the one I gave you last week."

Damn and blast the woman! How dared she put him into the position of refusing her cigarettes because they were not good enough? He considered ringing for the nurse and having her remove the pest. But one never rang for a nurse except in case of actual necessity. His right fist opened spasmodically, and a finger whacked against the box of cigarettes. It occurred to him that at least she'd had the perception to let him extract his own cigarette. The nurse always took one from the brass box and poked it into his open mouth. It saved time, he presumed. But it did make him feel a fool.

He opened the box with a sense of reluctant pleasure, meticulously smoothed back the foil, and offered the result to his guest with "Will you join me?"

"Pleasure," she assured him, extracting a cigarette with fingers so claw-light as scarcely to be felt.

He stuck a cigarette into his own mouth and dropped his hands in the hateful gesture of helplessness to which he was trying to inure himself.

"I expect I shall explain it badly," she chirped, "but if you would be so good as to try the experiment. I've done it myself with my eyes tight shut with every cigarette I've smoked the past week. It sounds rather silly, but it works."

It made his nerves crawl, the thought of some unknown female aping his helplessness. Damn and double damn her flaming impertinence!

"If you'll just plant your two elbows tight against your sides and take hold of the far end of your cigarette with the thumb and forefinger of your left hand, keeping the remaining left-hand fingers stretched straight out —— "

Despite his fierce disinclination, for the life of him he could not keep from doing as she said. But his taut nerves hummed like wing struts in a dive.

She thrust a long wooden match between the thumb and forefinger of his clenched right hand. "Here's a match. It's lighted. Place the tip of the right-hand little finger hard against the tip of the left-hand little finger."

He began to shake all over. It was a shocking thing that a lighted match in a blind hand could do that to pulped nerves. He brought his little-fingertips together and suddenly went still. He was astounded. He saw the thing at once. Saw that the match in his right thumb and forefinger had come miraculously in steady line with the tip of his cigarette.

"It's a sort of three-point lighting," she chirped. "If you remember that during the whole maneuver you keep unmoved the two elbows and the joined tips of the little fingers. The left thumb and forefinger, holding the tip of the cigarette, give you the altitude of the

match. Lower the match an inch or more, and bring it toward the
cigarette until the flame begins to burn your left thumb and forefinger. Release them instantly and spread them wide, but do not
move the little fingers."

It worked. Not since he had lifted his plane off the ground in his
first solo flight had he known such devastating satisfaction. He
could light his own cigarettes.

"If you'll turn the lighted end of your cigarette inside your left hand
and place the first knuckle of that hand against your chin, then place
the big knuckle of your right thumb against your left-hand fingers,
you can blow out the match without getting it near enough to en-
danger your bandages."

He obeyed with the smooth, sure ease of making a left bank.

"There's quite a large ash tray just where your right hand will come
down onto the bed if you don't move your elbow."

It was an ample ash tray. It had cost Miss Bronska her cheap cigarettes for three days. He moved it to his lap, keeping hold of it with
his right hand. She watched him turn the cigarette straight up in
his left hand, bring that hand down until the reaching fingers touched
the right arm, then slide it forward and flick the ash accurately into
the tray. The job was done. He would manage now.

Then Miss Bronska wrote herself an irrevocable invitation to enter
old J. G.'s room. She chirped, "I'm so sorry. I've let my cigarette
go out. (Actually, she'd never lighted it.) Could I trouble you for
a light? The matches are three inches to the left of your right hand."

"Juliana Bronska," he assured her fervently, "nothing would give
me greater pleasure than to give you a light."

Smoking together in silence, they became conscious that a raid
was going on outside. The appalling shriek and grunt and wham
of bombs was so near that they heard the following clatter and
whang of masonry coming down. The dogged bark and chatter
of guns was reassuring.

He said, "They seem to have the range."

"With all the pots and kettles thrown in," she agreed.

It was an ancient joke, but, coming from Juliana Bronska, it sounded ridiculous. He laughed. And laughed again, because to laugh once more was like breathing air after a long stay under water.

When she got up to go she said, "I expect there are going to be lots of amusing things you'll work out for yourself, such as dropping your right hand straight down and bringing it up under the bedside table to get a starting point for reaching things on top. I've put the cigarettes and matches four inches from the front corner of the table."

"You'll come again?"

"This day week," she promised. She would have liked to come sooner. But she felt it wasn't fair to take too much time off from the canteen. Besides, it would take six days of scamping to save enough to buy a little treat for the boys in the ward and another box of good cigarettes for J. G. She was even moved to regret that some of her meals were furnished by the canteen, though how she could have saved anything by going without meals she couldn't have paid for didn't occur to her. Nor did it occur to her to come without a gift. She thought it was the unexpected that broke the monotony, and she knew there was nothing unexpected about the sight of the same little old Polish face.

Miss Bronska did not present the cigarettes to J. G. when next she called. He answered her warning "Good afternoon" with a hearty "Come in. Come in. You'll find the chair just there" — pointing. "Sorry it's not more comfortable."

He had, in fact, slipped out of bed for the first time as soon as the nurse had tidied him up after lunch that day, had found the chair by fumbling about till he barked his shins against it, had learned, by sitting in it, just how hard it was, and had placed it beside the bed so accurately that he could point straight at it with assurance.

Then he dropped his right hand straight down, brought it up gently against the bottom of the bedside table, reached up unwaveringly to grasp the small brass box on top, opened it, and presented it with pride.

"You must allow me to be host today," he said.

Miss Bronska accepted a cigarette with pleasure. When he offered a lighted match, she touched a clawlike hand to his wrist to inform him as cigarette and flame made contact. She murmured "Thank you," and smiled to see him build his fists against his chin to blow out the match without endangering his bandages.

By the time of Miss Bronska's next visit, the nurses were finding little to do for old J. G. He was making his own way to the showers; was shaving with an electric razor such newly exposed bits of his face as the retreating bandages made available, and doing it without snarling the thing in the bandages. He was feeding himself with amazing tidiness, and discussing the progress of the war with zest.

There was just one thing he couldn't do. He could not go into the ward to see his boys. He loved those boys. Loved them as only a man who has been a boy and knows the workings of a boy's mind and heart and nerves could love the eaglets who had sat aloft with him, each a mechanized yolk in the silvered shell of the night, each poised to hurl his own embryo of force against the full shock of steel-hatched death.

The yearning to see them twisted his vitals. If he could have slipped into the ward at night and looked down upon each of them in his sleep, with time to check each one's hurt and read each one's answer to that hurt in the lines of his sleeping face, it would have been well. But to go fumbling in to them with no eyes to read what they would never tell, no guard against their pity or their horror of his blindness — this, he felt, was more than he could face. His ears had told him that Miss Bronska visited the ward. He had heard their shouts of greeting and farewell as she opened the ward door to come and go. But she brought him no word of the ward. And he was grateful for her silence. They were his boys. No stranger could interpret them to him.

Because it was so painful to think of his boys, he thought a great deal about Miss Bronska. Who was she, how did she look, whence had she dropped? Judging by her manners and the faint and charming accent of her speech, she might be a young and lovely Russian countess. Judging by her intuition and her ageless wisdom, she might be a Greek oracle straying from an ancient dream.

When she got up to go one day, he asked, "Would you mind telling me why you bothered about me?"

Miss Bronska had long ago placed this man. Having placed him, she did not anticipate his asking this question. Nor had she formed its answer in her conscious mind. She had to dig it up from under the surface as doggedly and carefully as men dig up a time bomb. She was quite prepared to have it explode in her hands. But it did not occur to her to offer an exploded shell when he had asked for the bomb.

She was silent so long he feared she'd gone without hearing the question. And when she spoke, her voice, for the first time, was strained. "I'm afraid you'll think me very impertinent."

He was startled and curiously stirred. To cover it he asked shortly, "Well?"

"I had to make you see."

It did explode, with him, in worse than death. God! She had to make him see! See what? That he'd been in a bloody funk, without the guts to save himself?

It was anger that saved him, good, cleansing rage against a meddling, gnat-brained female who imagined she'd done him a service in teaching his hands to see to light a cigarette when all he wanted to see was his boys. And he had thought her something special.

As his outrage wore itself out against her imagined image, futility cooled him. He'd never see her. He'd never see anyone. He'd go on through life, presenting himself as a ghastly spectacle for the eyes of other people, without the revenge of seeing them.

He was brought up short by the realization that she had never actually seen him. All she had seen was a man swathed up to his mouth in bedding and hospital gown and bandages, and down to his mouth in more bandages. Yet she knew him. After three minutes with him she knew him to be a dead man, knew how to galvanize him into life even if she had seared him with the current. And he knew nothing about her.

"God," he groaned, "if I could only see her!"

Trying to analyze this sudden, almost penitent desire to see her, it came to him that he did know Juliana Bronska. Knew her with such a clear certainty that he couldn't face it. His wish to see her was defensive, an instinctive urge to dim a light too bright to look upon. It was suddenly clear to him that this inner knowledge is the only vital knowledge. He saw that it is this toward which, and against which, men strive throughout their lives, and which they miss because their eyes are filled to blindness with externals.

He was shy about seeing Miss Bronska again. He knew it would not be necessary to say to her those things no Englishman can say. But he shrank from the feeling of being spiritually unclothed before her. He'd forgotten she was Polish. Had forgotten she might have been a Greek oracle straying from an ancient dream.

She clothed him, at once, with confusion, because she came first to his room, and because there came with her the creak of a wheeled chair and the cheerful tinkle of bottles knocking together. It was only later that he learned the bottles held vodka. Miss Bronska liked vodka best, and she had the quaint habit of using as a gift only the things she liked best. At home in Poland she had liked to take, now and then, a tiny glass of vodka "to warm her quivering stomach." There were a half-dozen bottles, bought with her last ring, the one she'd saved to bury her when the time came. But it was easy and inexpensive to be buried in England these days. Often the Huns did it for a dozen at a time with just a single bomb. A happier way to spend the jewel was in giving a party.

"I thought the boys would like a party," she chirped. "It's a surprise. They don't know you're coming. . . . The chair's six inches to your left."

He was shaken to his depths. His blind eyes burned with liquid fire. He was glad to be able to sit down in the wheeled chair. He knew why she'd brought it. Knew he could have walked, but would have felt a fearful fool stumbling about the unfamiliar ward.

He was going to see his boys. Was going to *see* them.

When she set the basket in his lap, his hands caressed the smooth sides of the clinking bottles. "It is a party," he laughed.

Miss Bronska was so sparrow-small they didn't see her as she wheeled him through the ward door. Their astonished eyes saw only the beloved figure coming toward them, wearing the smile each had carried with him on his last flight. For an instant, the wave held poised. Then it broke in roaring triumph. The walking cases swarmed around him; casts were strained and healing stumps were waved.

As they unloosed the inevitable "For he's a jolly good fellow," Miss Bronska slipped away and down the stairs. Miss Bronska had given them the party. And she had the quaint habit of using as gifts only the things she liked best.

TO WHOM IT MAY CONCERN

By *Edward Hope*

"WHAT's the use of hiring them," Ted asked, glinting his round spectacles at her and folding The Times for emphasis, "on one chance in a hundred? Aside from keeping you upset all the time, it's expensive. You get a woman to come out from New York. You pay her fare and the agency fee. You do her room over and buy a lot of new stuff for the kitchen. She arrives, and before I'm sure of her name, she either leaves or you fire her. Then we get Mrs. Mullins in at sixty cents an hour —— "

"I know," Betsy agreed, hating Hulda for the studied surliness she had assumed for the last few hours of her incumbency, and trying to plan a menu for tomorrow night — the Staffords were invited for dinner — that would not overtax Mrs. Mullins' culinary gifts.

"It's perfectly simple," Ted went on. Everything about the house was perfectly simple, when Ted explained it. "If these women knew all about us and Oak Hill — what we expect of them and what they're up against — it would save everybody a lot of trouble. The ones we don't want wouldn't come to us, and the ones who did come would get off on the right foot. Do you see?"

"I do try to tell them, only it's hard, when you're interviewing a woman, to describe —— "

He put down the paper and leaned forward over it. "Precisely. By that time it's too late. My idea is that we've got to make the employment agencies see the picture. Perfectly simple. Then they can select the probable ones for you. Save time. Save money. Save mistakes. You call up an agency and say: 'This is Mrs. Trivet. I need a general houseworker. You have a letter in your files that describes my requirements.' They refer to the letter, choose two or three women who —— What the dickens do you suppose Hulda used for coffee this morning? Gah-h!"

"I suppose she made it yesterday and warmed it up. I'll be glad to see the last of that one."

"Mrs. Mullins coming in tomorrow?"

"Yes. And I thought I'd go to town Monday or Tuesday and look for another. Sometimes I think I must have tried them all, but I suppose new ones keep escaping from the asylums."

Ted looked at his watch and got up from the table. "Write a first draft of that letter today," he said. "I'll go over it with you tonight. When we've licked it into shape, we'll send copies to all the best agencies."

Betsy walked with him to the front door for the ritual good-by kiss.

"You will write it, won't you?" he asked, setting his hat at the correct angle.

"I'll try."

"It'll work," he assured her. He waved and strode down the front walk. She could see from the swing of his shoulders that he felt better, now that he had solved the servant problem for her.

Dear —— : I am afraid we need another general houseworker already, and this time ——

[She took a fresh sheet of Ted's typewriter paper.]

Dear —— : We are looking for a general houseworker, and it will save time and trouble if I give you the picture of the household and our requirements, to guide you in selecting a woman for the place.

The family consists of Mr. Trivet, our four-year-old son and six-month-old baby girl, the Scotch nurse who takes care of the children, and myself. Our house is on a small, quiet street, just on the edge of Oak Hill, which is forty-seven minutes from New York by the best trains and a little more by the others. Mr. Trivet takes two and a quarter minutes from the house to the station bus, but ordinary people do it more slowly. We live just beyond the end of the bus line, and busses connect with most of the good trains, although the service ——

[She scratched out a few lines and sat chewing the pencil's eraser, which reminded her of the liver Hulda had cooked for dinner Tuesday evening.]

—— forty-seven minutes from New York and the house is ten minutes from the station by bus. The same bus goes to the business center of Oak Hill, where there are two movie theaters, several small but adequate stores, a hairdresser, a restaurant that serves liquor, a diner, and other conveniences. An Army camp, which has been of the greatest interest to several of our recent maids, is only ——

[No, no, no. Not so chatty and not so roseate. She rejected nearly all of that passage.]

The same bus goes to the shopping center of Oak Hill, where there are movie theaters and small shops that fill most ordinary needs. Our maid has Sunday afternoons and evenings off, and, if she likes, can take every Thursday, from shortly after breakfast until any time before breakfast the next morning, which gives her a whole afternoon and evening in New York, if she catches the midnight train back to Oak Hill. Or, if she prefers, she can take two full days a month, leaving after an early dinner one night and being back to get breakfast on the third day following. We pay one round-trip fare to New York per month, and we consider that enough, as the house is not really so isolated as it seems. We have sidewalks now and we are promised street lights some ——

—— one round-trip fare to New York per month.

Mr. Trivet is in the advertising business in New York. He leaves the house every morning at 7:46, and likes to have fifteen minutes for breakfast. He returns each evening at 6:24, and we have dinner at seven. Mr. Trivet is a man of very regular habits and likes everything precisely organized, and the schedule — particularly as to meals — strictly followed. I think it is important that we have a general houseworker with steady nerves and a habit of punctuality. Mr. Trivet tries not to interfere in the running of the house, but when ——

—— and we have dinner at seven. I am particular about neatness and punctuality and I insist on meals being served on time.

We do not demand or even want fancy cooking. We want a good plain cook who can do ordinary dishes well and serve them appetizingly. Rich sauces and fancy desserts are never necessary, as we follow a simple diet Mr. Trivet himself has worked out, with carbohydrates, starches, fats, and so forth, in just the proper proportions. All we ask is that our general houseworker be able to prepare the usual meats and the ordinary vegetables in the simplest ways. Mr. Trivet's mother had such a woman when Mr. Trivet was young — though she has since died and gone to heaven — and we are looking for someone who can compare, even unfavorably, with his recollection ——

—— as we follow a simple diet.

The general houseworker is expected to keep the ground floor of the house neat and clean, and to do the stairs and the upstairs floors once a week. The nurse looks after the children's room and her own, and I do the room Mr. Trivet and I occupy, as I have learned just how he likes everything and it is hard to explain to anyone else. There is a special way of making a bed that Mr. Trivet learned as a young man and has taught me, which keeps the under sheet exactly smooth all night. Wrinkles in the under sheet keep Mr. Trivet awake and, after a sleepless night, he ——

—— and I do the room Mr. Trivet and I occupy.

The Scotch nurse prepares the children's food and takes her meals upstairs with them, but eats the same food as is served in the dining room. The houseworker carries trays for the nurse and the children and washes their dishes. I am anxious to find a woman who has an even, cheerful disposition and is able to get along with other people who may at times seem a trifle exacting. Nanny brought up Mr. Trivet's younger sister and has been in the Trivet family for more than twenty years, and she is naturally a little set in her ways. In fact, she expects more damned ——

———— and washes their dishes.

The nurse has been in Mr. Trivet's family for more than twenty years. She is faithful and efficient, and gets along well with anyone in the house who does the work as it should be done. On Nanny's days off, I take her place myself, doing the children's cooking, and so on. This makes it necessary for me to be in the kitchen a good deal on these occasions, and I expect the general houseworker to carry on her work as usual in my presence. If she doesn't like my being in the kitchen, she can take the same days off as Nanny or keep her blasted trap shut, instead of flying at me, as a Swedish ————

———— doing the children's cooking, and so on.

I am anxious to find a houseworker who is cheerful and of an even disposition, which is a thing whose value in our household cannot be overestimated. The work is not unreasonably hard and I try to make the place as pleasant as possible under the circumstances, with ————

———— and I try to make the place pleasant. A cheerful woman can be such a help in a home where there are children. Our little boy, who takes after his father, is high-spirited and brilliant, but given at times to mischief that demands tolerance and understanding from all of us. A few months ago, when he put glue in our — then — general houseworker's ————

Dear ———— : We need nine or ten more general houseworkers to carry us through to Christmas, and I wish you would start lining them up for me now, to avoid long waits between their terms in our little purgatory. The average length of a general houseworker's stay with us is six days. The shortest was two hours and twenty minutes, and the longest, in the ten months since we came to Oak Hill to live — as we call it — was seven weeks. That, however, was a Lithuanian refugee, and I have always thought that she believed she had been sentenced to our home instead of to a concentration camp. She ran away, finally, leaving her possessions behind, and I, for one, didn't blame her.

Mr. Trivet feels that any general houseworker who considers coming to us ought to be given the picture of our household in advance, and I agree with him. So let me explain how things are, and you can pass the word along, so that any woman who comes out here will have only herself to blame. I think what we need is either a very strong character who can stand up to Mr. Trivet and Nanny and take no nonsense, or else an idiot girl who won't notice. An idiot girl might find the place quite congenial.

We live on the stony edge of Oak Hill in a development that didn't develop, and we have it all to ourselves since the real-estate man shot himself last June. If there had been a few more suckers like us, the bus line would have come right to the door and there would have been street lights and a garbage-collection service and other lovely amenities, about which Mr. Trivet is still writing wistful letters to the town. There is a decent train to New York every morning and another back every evening, but the other trains stop at every cow, and take from an hour and a quarter up. There is a bus that usually meets the good trains and runs at other times on a highly erratic schedule, especially to our end of the line — a brisk five-minute trot from the house — where it only comes to turn around, anyway.

I think most of our general houseworkers leave on account of Nanny, though it is hard to say, with so many reasons for leaving to choose from. One told me last spring that she was leaving because she could not stand Mr. Trivet's —— face, but that was a special case. He was advertising some sort of soap powder at the time and he took her to be an Average Domestic and kept asking her questions. He has caused two or three others to resign because he keeps bringing home things he advertises and insisting on their being tried in the house. But I don't think he is the principal cause of dissatisfaction. Not to the general houseworkers.

It is true that Mr. Trivet had a remarkably happy boyhood and retains unusually vivid memories of it. His mother's general houseworkers, for instance, were jewels from the first to the last, and we never seem to find anyone who can cook anything as they did. If they did. They were also models of cleanliness, eagerness to work, and the right attitude toward their employers, which is unfortunate too. Mr. Trivet used to watch them cook and believes he learned a lot about cookery from these jolly childhood experiences. I often think that, if he had been kept out of his mother's kitchen, as he should have been, and if he had not gone camping and learned to fry eggs and make pancakes, we might have more luck with our servants.

Nanny is part of Mr. Trivet's boyhood. She brought up his younger sister — the one who had such bad luck with the chauffeur when she was seventeen — and has been working for and on Trivets for more than twenty years. She calls my husband "Mr. Teddy" and stays on with us mainly to keep an eye on me. She will stay if it kills her, but I am afraid it won't.

Nanny has a long chin like a snowplow, which she sticks out at people. She is never impertinent to me or quarrelsome with the general houseworker. She merely says what she has on her mind, sticks out her chin, and turns away with a little sound like a wet fingertip on a hot iron. An Italian general houseworker we had last winter chased Nanny around the house with a carving knife, but did not catch her and had to be discharged.

Nanny is very kind to the children, however, and that accounts for the general venomousness of our little boy. It is a constant source of amazement to me how spoiled a child can get in only four years, though he behaves rather well on Nanny's days off, when he knows what is good for him. Little Teddy is another problem for the general houseworker.

Nanny, of course, cannot watch him constantly, being busy so much of the time at her little extra duties, such as listening on the extension when I telephone, finding dust on and under furniture and calling attention to it, and exchanging gossip with the nurse from the big house up the hill. So Little Teddy is often left to his own devices, which are something. If he wants to put flypaper in the soup or to ride on the carpet sweeper when it is being used, and is prevented from doing so, he plants his feet and screams, knowing that this will convince Nanny — and his father, when he is home — that Somebody Has Been Slapping The Child.

Mr. Trivet is, as he often says himself, a reasonable man, but he likes things done as they should be. He insists on having breakfast on the table at 7:31 — because he leaves the house at 7:46 — and his dinner served at 7:00 exactly. At 7:30 in the morning and at 6:59 at night, he is comparatively cheerful; at 7:32 A.M. and 7:01 P.M., if his meals are not ready, he takes a decided turn for the worse. It is, as he says, perfectly simple to have things on time, and if the general houseworker we have at the moment can't do it, we'll find someone who can. His mother's cooks, I understand, never deviated from their schedules by more than thirty seconds.

Mr. Trivet's office is open only five days a week, so he is around the house all day Saturday as well as Sunday, and our week ends are different not only from weekdays but from each other. Mr. Trivet's theory is that the best relaxation is found in doing something out of the ordinary, and he spends his — and my — week ends yielding to his whims. Unless he has brought work home to do — in which case he does it at his desk in the living room, usually just when the maid has started to clean, and insists on a breathless silence from cellar to attic — he starts whimming fairly early Saturday morning and keeps it up until Sunday night.

A whim may lead him to dismantle the kitchen range, or to invite fifteen or twenty people for cocktails, or simply to produce tools and lumber and build something large and wooden in the middle of the living room. I have known him, on a whim, to give the baby her bath — she was all right in a few days — and three weeks ago he spent all of a Sunday morning in the kitchen, making ice cream as his mother's cooks used to. Something went wrong with it, you will perhaps be glad to know, and there wasn't anything else ready for dinner, so we had to go out to a restaurant, which was not part of his whim.

I think this will be enough to give you a rough but fundamentally sound idea of our household, though I see I have omitted one interesting detail: Mr. Trivet's mother is still alive and remarkably active for her age, and we keep a spare room always ready for her unannounced visits. If, after reading this, you feel that it is worth the trouble, I shall be glad to come to town and interview any pro-spective general houseworkers you believe suited to the place. I still wonder whether a young female imbecile might not fit in nicely.

Very truly yours

[The note, on Betsy's gilt-monogrammed notepaper, lay on top of the heap, held down at the four corners by four pebbles from the col-lection Ted had started one Saturday.]

Dear Ted: Here is The Picture. I guess you shouldn't have asked me to paint it. I have given Nanny the day off, so that you could read this before she did, but she will be back, with that triumphant expression at the corners of her mouth that means she could have told you so.

The children and I are going to visit Aunt Grace, who has taken a house in Santa Barbara for the winter. I'll send you the address and you can write and tell me when you have disposed of Nanny — the kindest thing would be to shoot her, but I suppose there might be talk; anyway, it's your sister Ellie's turn to take her for a while; Nanny ought to be rather good with horses — and palmed off the house on somebody. Maybe poor crackbrained Mr. and Mrs. Poppendyke are still willing to buy it, if they haven't been put away before this.

There is still that cold lamb in the icebox. Why don't you run up a curry, the way your mother's Katie used to do it?

BETSY

IT'S A FREE COUNTRY

By Colin G. Jameson

I GUESS a lot of people thought grandmother was crazy. But the milkman was the first person I ever heard say so. It was a jolt, too, because I was fond of Harry, the milkman's horse, and it seemed now as if I shouldn't give him any more sugar.

I was ten at the time, and my family had unloaded me on grandmother — "Mamu," I called her — while they went to Canada on a two months' business trip. They didn't want to take me out of school, and they thought the winter would be milder in Chicago.

It wasn't very mild, though. We had one blizzard after another. I can still close my eyes and see the dry snow eddying about that narrow, grimy street. And I have an unforgettable picture of other things — of the twinkle in Mamu's shrewd old eyes, of the mustang gallop that was her normal pace, of the startling histrionic gifts with which she plagued her neighbors.

For years she had conducted a special feud with that gray Mrs. Byrnes who lived next door — the one whose appearance and disposition led the neighborhood kids to dub her "Nosy Nose." And it was to Mrs. Byrnes that the milkman confided his impression. The two of them were standing on her front stoop, because the elevated embankment prevents the houses on the north side of the street from having rear entrances. I was in a drift under our steps, pretending I was a polar bear in a snow cave. I could hear them without being seen.

Nosy Nose said, "I'll have a quart of buttermilk, too, if it isn't frozen the way it was last time."

The milkman said, "I'm sorry, ma'am. I gave my last bottle to the lady next door. She wanted it for the boy."

Mrs. Byrnes snorted. "Buttermilk for the boy? How idiotic!"

The milkman laughed. "Well, she said he liked it and it wouldn't do him any harm."

"Won't fatten him up, either. The woman is a half-wit."

"I guess she is a little crazy, at that," he admitted.

"She ought to be locked up," Nosy Nose said primly.

That was the end of the conversation, because Harry, the horse, had wandered down to the corner to get out of the biting wind from Lake Michigan. The milkman hurried after him, slipping and sliding on the packed snow.

I was cold, too, so I stopped being a bear and went into the house. I found Mamu in the little garret that was on a level with the platform of the L station. She was sitting in a creaky rocker by the window. An old red shawl was wrapped around her head like a turban. The rest of her was swathed in a yellow Mexican tablecloth that grandfather had brought back when he helped lay out a branch of the National Railroad.

She looked so weird that I stood and stared without saying a word, which was most unusual. Before long an L train stopped at the station with a great squealing of brakes. Mamu picked up great-grandfather's Civil War sword off the floor and started sharpening it on the steel that belonged to the carving set. The edge of the platform was only about ten yards from the window, and a lot of the passengers paused to gape at her. She seemed to be unaware of their existence.

Finally I said, "Mrs. Byrnes and the milkman think you're crazy, Mamu. I just heard them say so."

She hadn't seen me come in, because she jumped, and the sword clattered to the bare floor.

"Crazy?" she said. "Well, why shouldn't I be? It's a free country. Now go change your shoes. They're sopping wet."

Another train came along, and she went back to her sharpening.

That evening I was down in the kitchen, which was in the basement, watching Mamu get supper. It was a fascinating procedure that I never missed. As she banged the pots and pans around and dropped things, she suddenly burned herself.

"Great leaping coals of fire!" she exclaimed. "There I go again!" A guilty look stole over her face. "I shouldn't swear, should I?" she said; then added brightly, "But I didn't, did I? Go get the butter out of the dumb-waiter."

She put a gob of it on her fingers. Her hand was so greasy that when she seized a frying pan it leaped out of her grasp and skittered under the sink.

I retrieved it and said, "Why do they call the dumb-waiter that?"

She said, "I expect the name refers to the ninny who invented it. My heavens, what a dirty face!"

She made me wash at the sink. Meanwhile the smoke began to pour through the cracks in the oven door. Mamu managed to rescue the spoon bread with only minor burns. She put it in the dumb-waiter and we climbed upstairs.

The dining room was a tiny, high-ceilinged cell that dated from after the Chicago fire of 1871. It had an oversized hearth of cracked and blackened marble, with a coal-burning grate. Every time the elevated shook the house, the fireplace smoked. Over the mantel was a terrible, sour-faced portrait of great-grandfather with a good deal of soot on it. Mamu worried about the soot, but she didn't dare stand on one of those jiggly chairs to mop the old gentleman off.

She put the spoon bread and things on the Lazy Susan and reminded me for the nth time about the speed limit. You had to go easy with her Lazy Susan, because it was badly warped and sometimes hurled dishes into space like so many clay pigeons.

We assaulted the spoon bread, but it proved to be too burnt for anybody but the covey of smart sparrows that haunted the two-by-four back yard. So I got out the aged toaster, and we had raisin toast and the cherry jam that some cousin in Iowa sent every Christmas.

For dessert there was candy, also left over from the holidays. Silence fell, because we both started with a caramel. As I chewed, my thoughts reverted to Mamu's sword-sharpening stunt. It was only the latest of a series of monkeyshines that had been perpetrated in that third-floor garret. I recalled the time there was a thaw and big puddles in the back yard. Mamu got out an old yellow rain hat that had belonged to grandfather and sat in the window and fished with one of his rods.

Another time she struggled into a prehistoric red dress with innumerable ruffles and a huge bustle. She secured the gaps with safety pins, and piled her hair on top of her head, and cocked a stained little sailor hat over one ear. Next she rouged and mascaraed her face till it looked like something out of De Maupassant, and paraded up and down in front of the window with a tattered parasol over one shoulder and a long Russian cigarette in her mouth.

These activities puzzled me. "Mamu," I said, "why do you get all dressed up the funny way you did this afternoon? To scare the people on the elevated? Maybe that's why Mrs. Byrnes and the milkman think you're crazy."

"Gracious!" she cried, rather fuzzily. "Almost lost my teeth on that caramel. Dressing up? Well, you dress up, don't you?"

"Yes," I admitted.

"And people don't say you're crazy, do they?"

"No, but —— "

"Well, it's a free country. I'll dress up if I want to. Besides, those people need something to jog them now and then. It's a public service I render to the stuffy citizens of Chicago."

"What do you mean, 'stuffy'?" I asked.

She got up to take away the dishes and tripped over the cord of the toaster, in which she had been burning one out of every three pieces of raisin bread. The ancient machine crashed to the floor and scattered crumbs over a large area. She gave it a resounding kick and resumed her place at the table, breathing hard.

"Where was I?" she inquired. "Oh, yes. When you eat too much turkey and cranberry sauce and pie and things at Thanksgiving, and you're so full you can hardly wiggle, your mother says you're stuffed, doesn't she?"

"Yes, sometimes."

"Well, those people's heads are so stuffed with stupid little thoughts that their brains can't wiggle. They need a shock."

"You're funny," I said, and I came round the table and gave her a kiss. "What do you mean, 'shock'? Electric shock?"

"In a way," she said. "Or this," and she whacked me behind.

After supper Mamu always locked the outside front door and put the chain on it. She double-locked the inner door too. Often she would discover that she had left her galoshes out on the stoop, and she would have to fumble around and find the keys and do everything all over again.

The principal other room on the ground floor was the parlor. It wasn't much bigger than the dining room and was drafty and bare, and we didn't sit in there much. Its sole attraction was a rickety upright piano — one of those ornate things with Corinthian pillars and lion's feet. The treble sounded like somebody dropping bits of broken glass into an empty ashcan, and a number of notes didn't work at all.

Some evenings Mamu would get a lot of Morocco-bound music out of the hall closet and play scraps of Beethoven and Mozart and Chopin. Mostly Chopin, though Mozart suited the piano best. Other times she would dig up some volumes of opera and sing the contralto parts, accompanying herself on the piano. She had the remains of a grand voice, and she could still send the chills down your spine when she wanted to. I think they sometimes went down hers, too, and then she'd forget the accompaniment.

I loved it when she'd leap to her feet in the middle of a phrase of heroic Wagner, and seize the broom she'd forgotten behind the hall curtains, and dash about the room being Brünnhilde or somebody. In the love scenes she'd snatch up a pillow and sing the tenor part to it, and then reverse characters and do the soprano about an octave too low. She was mistress of all the "glunks" and sob stuff, and I usually ended up with the hiccups after a couple of these duets.

The evenings when we went straight upstairs, she'd turn on the radio in her sitting room. The instrument was primitive and predisposed to thunderous displays of static. But it would get Chicago, and that was all that mattered. If someone made a speech, Mamu would argue the points with the speaker. If someone sang, she'd sing alto. And if it was drama, she'd pretend she was in the show. She had an enthusiastic hatred for announcers. When an unctuous voice would come out with something like "And now I'm going to give you special news about Smith's Breakfast Food," she'd retort, "That's what you think!" and flick the switch.

When the radio was shut off for good, she'd go to the wall desk and dip a scratchy, post-office pen into the ink bottle. That was the signal for me to go to bed. She read every word in the Tribune, and each night she wrote aggravated letters to the paper or to individuals who had excited her wrath. In the morning I'd see one or two of them lying on the hall table, addressed to somebody "Esquire." Never "Mr." or even "Esq." The rest of the evening she spent working over the stack of different-sized, weather-beaten notebooks that stood on the desk.

The first night I was in the sitting room, those notebooks caught my eye, and I asked what they were.

She said, "Some of them are diaries, and some of them are my autobiography."

I asked what a diary was.

She said, "It's a record of all the foolish things you used to do when you thought they were smart."

"What's a auto-whatever-it-is?"

"It's a book where you try to make all the foolish things in the diary sound as if they weren't foolish after all."

I wanted to know why there was so much diary and autobiography for only one person.

"Well," she said, "when I was on the stage I managed to do a lot of foolish things, and it takes a tremendous lot of writing to make them sound smart."

"You're grown up," I said. "You don't have to do it, do you?"

"I'm trying to bore myself to death," she explained. "They claim it is a painless way."

I knew she was spoofing me. "You're just saying that, Mamu," I protested. "Will it really be a book that I can read?"

"I doubt if your mother will approve of your reading it," she said solemnly, but her eyes were twinkling. "It *will* be a book, though. At least that's what the publisher says."

"Is he going to pay you for it?"

"Pay me?" She got up and did a decorous little minuet around the room. "He certainly is going to pay me," she said with a final creaky curtsy. "And then I'm going to put a charge of dynamite under this ancestral mansion and blow it to smithereens."

An L train shook the house just then, and she added, "I hope I take a chunk out of that thing too. After that I'm going down to Florida and be a bathing beauty. Now scat! It's bed-time."

I remembered about the dynamite when I saw Mrs. Byrnes the morning after the milkman had agreed that Mamu was crazy. I was on my way to school, and old Nosy Nose was sweeping the snow off her front steps.

I don't know now if I really thought Mamu was sincere about her plan or if I was just trying to scare Mrs. Byrnes. Anyway, I told her that my grandmother said she was going to blow up our house, and that I suspected the Byrnes house might get blown up too.

Nosy Nose looked flabbergasted. I continued down the street with my chin in the air.

When I got home, it was snowing again. Two men were standing on our front stoop, banging on the door and flailing their arms to keep warm. As I approached the steps, Mamu put her head out of the upstairs window.

She said, "Good afternoon, gentlemen. I can't find the key to the inner door, so I'll have to let you in through the basement."

She shut the window, and a few moments later she was rattling the rusty lock of the basement door. It finally swung open, and one of the men took a shiny badge out of his pocket.

"Great leaping coals of fire!" Mamu cried in alarm. "So you're the police!"

The men said that was right.

Her face froze. "Then you can't come in after all, unless you've got a warrant. And I don't suppose you have." She yanked me inside and slammed the door.

I couldn't understand this at the time. She always let everybody else in. If a poor colored man or a tramp came by and asked for a dime, she'd hustle him into the kitchen and make him a cup of coffee and a sandwich, and stand there smoking a cigarette while he ate. She'd question him about his family and his troubles, and sometimes she'd go fetch one of her notebooks and read out of it. When the man was through, she would fish a quarter out of the spoutless teapot where the grocery money was kept and say, "Now you can go ahead and get that drink. At least you've got a base."

In an hour those policemen came back. Mamu insisted on scrutinizing the warrant before she would let them in, though she didn't have her glasses and couldn't read a word of it.

The leader seemed to sense this. He said, "We understand you're storing explosives without a permit."

Mamu had been cleaning the kitchen. She was wearing a dilapidated man's hat that was several sizes too large for her, to keep the dirt out of her hair.

She pulled it down over one eye and put a hand on her hip and said, "Them's fightin' words, stranger. But I surrender. You may search the house. You'd better search it thoroughly. They might be anywhere. I can't remember anything."

The policemen gave each other a knowing look and began with the basement. We dogged their every footstep, and Mamu kept making suggestions and pointing out nooks that they had overlooked. After a spell of this, they became sweaty and exasperated.

The leader said, "Lady, come clean. Where are they?"

"Where are what?" she said, all innocence.

"Them explosives, of course."

"What explosives? I never said there were any."

"But, lady, you did so!"

"I said nothing of the kind, my good man," she retorted haughtily. "I pointed out that I couldn't remember anything about any explosives, and that therefore they might be anywhere. If I were a secret explosives storer, I wouldn't be a piker about it. They'd be all over the place."

The men got red in the face and muttered restrained oaths and departed. Mamu rushed into the parlor and played "My country, 'tis of thee, sweet land of liberty" on that cracked old piano. She made such a racket that the floor shivered as if a continuous L train were going by.

There was a last defiant discord. "Great leaping coals of fire!" she said. "I'd forgotten all about supper. And I'll bet there isn't a thing in the house but lamb broth and corn muffins and cherry preserve and apple betty with hard sauce."

"But I like all those, Mamu," I said, somewhat perplexed.

"Do you?" she said in an astonished voice. "Well, isn't that lucky?"

Just then the cigarette she had laid on the piano began to work on what was left of the varnish. She grabbed it and burned herself and said "Ow!"

"You're always burning your fingers, Mamu," I said. "I should think they'd get used to it and you wouldn't have to say 'Ow!' any more."

She took the damaged finger from her mouth and winked. "My fingers are used to it," she said, "but I'm not."

The next day was Saturday. Right after breakfast Mamu started to repair the doorbell wire that ran through the front hall. Soon she discovered that she'd accidentally cut the telephone cord. She worked feverishly to put it back together again before the company found out. Of course telephone lines have three sections, and you have to juggle the wires around till you get the right ones connected up. When you succeed, you get Central. Or you did in the days before dial phones.

Mamu finally got the cord fixed and started to tell Central a long, involved story to explain why the line had been dead, though this had probably never been noticed.

She said she'd left the receiver off by mistake and gone to the grocery for half a pound of bottom round ground twice. The sight of a dirty-faced child in the store reminded her that she'd forgotten to tell her grandson to take a bath because he was invited out for lunch, and she called back to tell him so, and the phone didn't work, and she was afraid the house was on fire, because she heard a siren, and she hurried home.

At this point there was a loud pounding on the front door.

Mamu shouted "Traitor!" into the mouthpiece and hung up. As she hesitantly approached the door, I asked why the "traitor."

She said, "That two-faced Central has been holding me on the line just long enough for the repair man to get here and catch me with tools and bits of wire scattered all over the hall."

"But you were doing all the talking," I objected.

"And you're doing all the question asking," she snapped.

It wasn't the repair man, after all. It was a pasty-faced young fellow in a chesterfield and derby who announced that he came from Mamu's publisher. When she heard that, she snatched his coat and hurried him into the parlor and plopped him into the only decent chair.

A little red spot of embarrassment appeared in each of his chalky cheeks. "I'm afraid I haven't got very good news for you," he said. "Mr. Ritchie has decided he can't take the book, after all."

Mamu collapsed on the piano bench and suddenly looked old and tired. Then her eyes narrowed, and she stuck out her jaw.

"What's the matter with it?" she demanded. "Mr. Ritchie said the first ten chapters were amazing. That's his very word — 'amazing.'"

The visitor shifted about uncomfortably in his chair. "Well, there are two or three things. One is that paper prices are going up."

"Heard that one before. What are the real ones?"

"Well," he said reluctantly, "Mr. Ritchie has decided the book hasn't — ah — a professional ring to it."

"Poof!" she said. "It's what you write about that counts, not how you write it. Why doesn't he have some of his smart young men brush it up, if it's so amazing?"

"The subject matter is another thing. There are episodes that Mr. Ritchie thinks are — er —— "

The pasty-faced young man paused and looked at me, standing in the doorway, all ears.

"Too gaudy for the old Puritan, eh?" Mamu said scornfully.

"Of course if you'd like to tone it down, he might recon —— "

"Never!" Her old eyes blazed.

That was the end of the interview.

After he'd gone, I said, "But what are you going to do now?"

"Do?" she cried, puffing furiously on a cigarette. "Great leaping coals of fire! I'll make that fusty old Ritchie eat his words, that's what I'll do! Go take that bath."

That evening when Mamu picked up her pen and told me to scat, I said, "I wrote a diary a couple of days ago."

"You did?" she said. "Well, it's undoubtedly a trick to stay up longer, but let's hear it."

So I went to my room and got my composition book. The diary read somewhat as follows:

"This morning I went to school. Miss McCarthy said I was late, and I was. I was late because I was mad at Mrs. Byrnes because she thinks Mamu is crazy. I told her we were going to blow up our house and probably hers would get blown up too."

Mamu shouted with laughter. "So that's it! Well, when you next see Mrs. Byrnes, you tell her that grandmother presents her compliments, and that she will meet Mrs. Byrnes behind the L embankment at dawn. Skillets at twenty paces. But you won't remember all that."

I did, though. And Mrs. Byrnes wasn't angry. She just said, "Poor, poor boy," and patted my head. I was glad I had on my knitted wool cap.

When I got home, I reported her peaceful attitude to Mamu. The old lady said, "Hmpf!" and continued about her business, which happened to be the resetting of the rat traps in the basement. I followed along. We found two sprung traps by the garbage pail, but no casualties. Mamu picked up one of the traps and started to reset it. I watched her maneuvers closely, and neither of us said a word for a minute. Later we figured that there must have been a rat at the pail when we came downstairs.

We got between him and his hole, and he hid till he thought from the silence that we had gone back up. When Mamu was setting the second trap, he made a dash for it. He came round the furnace at full speed and collided with one of her ankles.

She jumped into the air and yelled, "Aroint thee, witch!" The trap in her hand went off with a murderous bang. Luckily it didn't catch her fingers. But her leap ended right on top of the one on the floor, and it clamped down on her toes.

She squawked and shouted, "Vile vermin, vamoose!" and heaved the furnace poker in the general direction taken by the rat, who was probably safe at home and telling his children about it by that time. After that she hopped around on one leg with the trap banging on the floor because she was unwittingly favoring the wrong foot.

At length she began to unlace her high black shoe to see what had happened to her big toe.

"If it has been amputated," she said, "I shall wrap it up in white tissue paper and red ribbon and send it to Mrs. Byrnes."

It was only bruised, which disappointed me a little, I'm afraid.

Next morning Mrs. Byrnes was on her front steps, as usual. I said, "My grandmother got caught in a trap yesterday afternoon."

Old Nosy Nose looked astonished, also as usual, and said, "What's she setting traps for? Witches?"

"How did you know?" I asked. "Mamu did call it a witch, but I think it was a rat, really."

Mrs. Byrnes' jaw dropped, and she fumbled at her front-door latch quite a time before she could get in.

Nosy Nose had an unusual opportunity to collect further data on Mamu's insanity on the Friday before my family returned from Can-

ada. Late that afternoon the old lady took some newspapers and
stuffed them into a suit of grandfather's and stitched the collar around
the base of a cracked bust of Julius Caesar that used to stand at the
head of the stairs. She dug up a long, moth-eaten wig in the hump-
backed trunk in the attic and glued it to Julius' head. She hung him
in front of the window of the third-floor garret with a piece of clothesline round his neck, and she pulled down the shade and fixed the
lamp so it would throw his shadow against it.

When she was satisfied that all was shipshape, she sent me downstairs to put on my galoshes and overcoat. Eventually she joined me
in the front hall. She was wrapped up in a huge gray Austrian cape
with a hood.

We went to the L station around the corner and paid twenty cents
to get up on the platform opposite our window. There was quite a
crowd there, watching the horrid sight etched so blackly on the illuminated shade.

One dried-up little man spoke to us out of the growing dusk. "It's
the end, all right," he said. "She's finally hung herself."

With a catch in her voice, Mamu said, "No, no. I'm afraid it's
even worse than that. Don't you remember how the poor soul used
to threaten her neighbor, Mrs. Byrnes? We must call the police."

There was the customary haggling and indecision, and then the
whole group of twenty or thirty people surged down the steps and
besieged the policeman on the corner. Mamu kept discreetly in the
background, away from the rays of the street lamp, while everybody
else talked at once.

Someone suggested that the insane lady was probably armed.

"Of course she is," the dried-up man said nervously. "Furthermore, maniacs always have superhuman strength, so you'd better be
careful, officer."

The policeman was. He called the riot squad.

When it arrived, we all trooped to the house, with Mamu gallop-
ing along in front of the crowd, right behind the five policemen.
Mrs. Byrnes joined the procession and urged that the door be broken
down without delay. Nobody seemed to remember that she was the
supposed victim.

Door battering proved to be unnecessary, because Mamu had thoughtfully left the house wide open. The police rushed upstairs with Mamu and me in their wake and the other people stringing along diffidently at a safe distance. The men burst into the little room on the third floor, and I went in, too, but Mamu disappeared. I was watching the "corpse" being cut down when a loud scream came from the doorway.

The police whirled with drawn guns. There stood Mamu in a long purple dress covered with rhinestones, looking very regal indeed.

"What is the meaning of this?" she said coldly to the sergeant. "Cannot a lady take a nap without having hoodlums in uniform burglarize her house?"

The sergeant holstered his weapon and mopped his brow.

"Listen, lady," he said wearily. "What's the idea of hanging that thing in there and scaring people half to death, and all them other things I hear you been doing in front of that window?"

"Get out of my house!" Mamu commanded. "Get out of my house! Have things come to such a pass that an authoress cannot create a mood without playing host to the entire elevated public?"

She seized upon me and said, "Darling! That your immature nerves should be shocked this way! *Shocked*, I said."

She smacked me behind, where nobody could see, and burst into tears.

The bravest citizens had reached the third floor by this time. They scuttled down again, looking foolish. Mamu followed with the five policemen, and I came after them. There were pictures on the wall all the way down both flights of stairs — those little ones of too-thin horses and blurry old people with wooden faces — and faded violets under glass, and a stuffed owl in a niche on the second-floor landing. As we passed each item, Mamu paused and said something like, "I want to draw your particular attention to this splendid El Greco." Or, "My half brother found it necessary to shoot this owl during our last barnstorming tour, poor dear. I mean my brother, not the owl."

The police herded everybody out of the house. They said

they were going to have to arrest Mamu for disorderly conduct.

She said, "My maiden name was O'Rourke," which was untrue. "I would like to see you gentlemen in the kitchen for a moment. . . . You may go up and play."

That meant me.

A grin stole over the sergeant's face. He beckoned to his companions and followed her down the narrow basement stairs.

About half an hour later Mamu appeared at the door of my room, singing:

> "*I've never been-on*
> *The banks of the Shann-on,*
> *But I've kissed the Blarney stone.*"

"Are they going to take you to jail?" I asked excitedly.

She smiled and shook her head.

I felt vaguely disappointed. "But how did you get rid of them?"

"In one of the most efficient ways I know," she replied. "I let the coffee and fudge cake run out."

The next morning there was a news story in the Tribune about the events of the previous night. Mamu read it aloud at the breakfast table with considerable satisfaction. I think the headline was:

AUTHORESS "CREATES MOOD" AND PANICS L PATRONS

It was Saturday, so I was home all day. Toward noon a darkhaired, weaselly-looking young man came to see Mamu. She sent me upstairs. I watched at the window till he had left, and came down again. Mamu looked like a cat that's found a saucer of cream.

"Do you know what a reporter is?" she said.

"It's one of those men who write things for the paper."

"Well, that little pipsqueak was one. Tomorrow there's going to be a feature article about your eccentric grandmother and her elevated Grand-Guignol. There will be pictures dating from the nineties and all the trimmings."

"Will my mother let me read it?" I asked.   The family was coming home on Sunday.

"I'll read it to you myself," she said.   "And we'll buy an extra copy of the paper for Mrs. Byrnes.   Poor thing!   She never allows herself to absorb much culture."

My mother and father were expected in the evening.   Mamu spent the early morning getting a room ready for them and trying to gather together a reasonable percentage of the clothes I had brought with me two months before.   Suddenly she dropped the pillow she was putting in a clean case.

"Great leaping coals of fire!" she exclaimed.   "The Sunday paper. Here's twenty cents.   Dash out and get two of them."   We didn't subscribe for the Sunday edition.

I ran to the L station and back, and she grabbed one of the papers with trembling hands and opened it to the drama section.

I looked over her shoulder.   There were three photos of her in her heyday, and she must have been a beauty all right.   A half page was devoted to the pictures and to her life story and to a glowing account of her long-forgotten career on the stage.   None of the names and places meant much to me, except the fact that she'd once played 444 nights in London.   I could sense the importance of that.

She read me every word.   At the end it said something about her autobiography "coming out soon."

"But your book isn't coming out soon, is it?" I asked.

"That remains to be seen," she said mysteriously.

It didn't remain long.   Before lunch the phone rang twice.   Each time Mamu snatched it up eagerly.   As she listened, her face fell, and she said in a cold voice, "No, not interested."   Afterward she fidgeted about and looked unhappy.

About three, it rang again.   She answered, and this time she smiled triumphantly.

"Yes, Mr. Ritchie?" she said in a carefully controlled voice.   "Who is publishing my book?   Oh, I don't think I could tell you that, Mr. Ritchie.   It wouldn't be professional, would it?"

She paused, and I could hear Ritchie's pleading words rattling in the receiver. She let him suffer for a long time.

Finally she said, "Well, all right, Mr. Ritchie. I'll see what I can do. But you'd better rush that young whippersnapper out here instanter, or I'll change my mind."

She jumped up and did her little minuet around the room.

"It's sold!" she shouted. "And this time I get his name on a contract, so he can't back out!"

"But I thought you'd sold it to somebody else," I said.

"Oh, you did? Well, isn't that odd? And I suppose you think I've been making a special silly out of myself and letting police crawl all over the house just to shock the public?"

"I thought you said that's why you did it."

"Publishers and public are equally shockable," she chuckled. Then a faraway look came into her eyes. "Speaking of shocking," she mused, "I can hardly wait till old Nosy — I mean Mrs. Byrnes — gets her autographed copy. I have an unrighteous and utterly delightful suspicion that it will shock her worse than the dynamite would have."

BREEZE O' WIND

By *Alexander Key*

I NEVER seen nothing like that summer when I was fifteen. The Gulf
was every kind of blue and green, and so alive with color it took
your breath away, and all through the long, burning days there'd
be great mountains of clouds boiling up from the river swamps behind town, and moving seaward in snorting squalls that often turned
to waterspouts. Late in August the sea changed. It lay silky and
still under the heat, and there was something sort of hanging in the
air that made you uneasy. Sounds carried a great distance, and you
could hear the put-putting of the shrimp trawlers clean out to the
island pass; stingarees swarmed along shore, and most any time you
could watch sharks or tarpon chasing mullet right up into the shal-
lows near the house. Never did the oleanders bloom so heavy, and
never were the figs so large and sweet. And you felt somehow that
all of it was wrong. The days were like rich poison fruit turning
ripe, and they seemed to put a spell on everybody and everything.

I remember it was three weeks since I'd missed my trip with Matt
on the Angelus; my foot was a heap better and I was able to walk all
right if I didn't step too hard. Mom was in the kitchen frying
grouper and hush-puppies, and I could hear her talking to herself
as she rolled the hush-puppy batter into cones and dropped them into
the hot grease with the fish. I knowed she was worrying about
Fiddler. Somehow it didn't seem right, because with the Angelus
a week overdue, it looked like Matt was the one she should 'a' been
thinking about. Cap'n Ned never stayed out more'n a couple weeks.

"You'd better wash up for supper," she called. "What's happened to Fiddler?"

I knowed she didn't want the truth, so I didn't say nothing.

"Micky Joe, answer me!" mom snapped. "Did he go shrimping today?"

"I never seen his boat go down the channel."

"That boy!" She always got a different tone in her voice when she was talking of Fiddler, like he could do no wrong. I reckon it was because he favored pa so much. His nickname didn't come from being musical, though you'd 'a' thought he was the Pied Piper, the way the girls took after him. I think it started from his being quick, like those little fiddler crabs that swarm over the mud flats. He was the quickest big feller I ever seen.

Mom came to the screen door, her brow all wrinkled up, while she wiped her big hands on her apron. "He must be still working on that engine. You better go find him, Micky Joe."

"Aw, I ain't his watchdog," I grumbled.

She kicked the screen door open and slung a pine knot at me. I ducked it and went off the porch fast, and kept on through the palm tangle at the corner of the yard. It was the first time she'd heaved anything at me in months.

"You trifling rascal!" she yelled. "You go find Fiddler, you hear me? And bring him home, or you don't get a bite to eat!"

I limped on down to the boardwalk that follows the beach. Finding Fiddler might be easy enough, but bringing him home was another matter. He's six-foot-two and redheaded, and there ain't nobody on the coast, not even a deep-water Greek, wants to get in his way when he's had a couple drinks. I was just as sure as anything that he was getting wound up for trouble, because he'd had a row with his girl and hadn't come home last night.

I didn't know what to do. I stood there hating mom and hating myself, and trying to figger what it was that had got into everybody. It was even working on Cap'n Hook, as we call grandpa, for during the last ten days he hadn't spoke a word to any of us. He just sat on the upper gallery, where ninety years of Beales had watched their boats come in, and stared out at sea. It was the longest silent spell he'd had since pa sailed to the snapper banks and never come back.

If Sissie had been home, it would have helped a lot. She's got a way with mom, and she's Cap'n Hook's darling. But she'd had a falling out with Johnny Tacon and gone to visit some of mom's folks in Georgia, and we didn't know when we'd see her again.

She'd left the day I was due to sail with Matt and Cap'n Ned, and things had been going wrong ever since. I'd never been out on the Angelus, and at breakfast mom got to wailing about "her baby being took away and drowned like his pa," and it started an argument that ended with her chasing Matt and me out of the house. That baby stuff always got me; I was towheaded and freckle-snouted, and at fifteen I could lick my weight in anything.

I went stomping into the water to cool off, and darned if I didn't go and step on the biggest stingaree alive. That sting tore into my ankle like a red-hot iron, and I reckon I went clean out my head. Most people do. Matt and Fiddler carried me back to the house, and Cap'n Hook slit the wound and doused it with soda and kerosene while I howled. He don't believe much in doctors, and I remember him glowering at the barometer afterward and grunting, "Hump! Some fool thing always happens on a low glass!"

That sting messed up everything for me, and I even had to stop helping Fiddler and Angel on the Sanderling. You can't ever trust a stingaree wound; they're troublemakers long after they're healed.

I couldn't go home and I didn't want to tangle with Fiddler; the dog flies kept me moving, so I followed the boardwalk around to the ferry dock at the river mouth. And all the while I prayed that Matt would come back; he's the oldest, and I thought if he would only come back, that things would get all right.

It was a terrible hot evening and the sunset was smearing everything a dirty red. The tide was higher than it had been all summer. Out in the river, Cap'n Dash Lundy was backing the East Bay ferry towards the slip, and cussing a Tarpon Springs sponger trying to keep off his bow. Another sponger was coming up the channel — the fifth today.

A Greek don't run to cover for nothing. And the Angelus was a week late. It made me kind of sick inside. I never noticed the

Partridges' old flivver rolling up till the brakes squealed and Serena jumped out. Serena's Fiddler's girl.

She caught my arm and pulled me over to the side of the dock where the loafers couldn't hear us. She was scared — and that was something new for Serena, who used to play ball with the high-school gang before she grew up. She's slim and black-eyed, and plenty to look at in white. Fiddler was plumb crazy about her.

"I didn't dare go by the house," she whispered. "You know how your mother is. I —— "

"What's the matter?"

"Oh, it's that darned fool, Fiddler! Micky Joe, you've got to find him. You've —— "

"What's he done?"

"He tried to beat up Johnny Tacon after the dance last night. If I hadn't stopped it —— "

"What'd you stop it for? Johnny's been gittin' in his craw for years."

"Will you shut up and listen to me? I broke a date with Fiddler last night and went out with Johnny. Now do you see?"

"Oh." I blinked at her. I wanted to kick her.

"Don't look at me like that. I had plenty of reasons."

"Yeah, I know your reasons! You an' Fiddler'd had a row an' you figgered you'd go out with Johnny an' make 'im jealous. Well, you done it! He never come home last night. Now if he gits drunk an' catches Johnny, why — why, he'll kill 'im!"

"For heaven's sake!" she cried. "Don't waste time arguing about it now! Johnny's carrying a gun — and I just learned that Fiddler's in Dad Hunter's place. You've got to get him out of there, Micky Joe! You've got to make him go home!"

"You're the guy started it! Why don't you?"

"But I can't!" she wailed. "I'm leaving on the ferry right away. Auntie's sick across the bay and alone tonight, and on top of it I promised to meet Sissie and drive her home tomorrow. It just looks like everything's happened all at once!"

"I didn't know Sissie was coming home tomorrow."

"She didn't intend for you to. It was partly on her account that I —— " She broke off as the ferry whistle blew, and suddenly kissed me on the cheek. "Please, honey," she pleaded. "You've just got to do something! I — I'm depending on you."

She ran to her car and drove aboard, and I stood rubbing my cheek while the ferry pulled out. I had the doggonedest feeling, like the earth was dropping away from under me. She'd sure started something. Going out with Johnny Tacon might have worked all right with some fellers, but with Fiddler it was next to messing with dynamite.

And Fiddler was at Dad Hunter's place. I knowed what that meant. All of a sudden I was plenty scared, too, and I lit off towards Dad Hunter's place as fast as I could make my feet work.

Fiddler wasn't there. But lying by the counter was a shrimp hand with an eye swelled shut, and there were some others standing over him trying to bring him to with a bucket of water. Nobody spoke, and there wasn't no need to. It's always the same story when Fiddler's been taking on ballast. Fellers just get in his way and forget how quick he is.

"Where's he gone?" I asked Dad Hunter.

Dad only shrugged and spread his hands.

"Was he likkered yet?"

"Jest started. He never got none here."

Dad's the only rascal in town sells that panther sweat right over the counter in broad day, and everybody knows it.

"Sometime," I promised, "I'm agoin' to shove your yeller teeth out through the back o' your neck. If Fiddler gits in trouble —— "

"You git out o' here!" snarled Dad Hunter.

I cussed him good and went out into the middle of the street, looking every which-a-way. It wasn't quite dark, and it didn't help my feelings none to see the sou'east warning flags hanging from the weather tower. A sou'easter coming — and Fiddler on the loose.

I figgered he might head for his boat, so I forgot my bad foot and ran all the way down to the Magnus wharf, where the Sanderling was tied. Somebody was aboard, all right, but it turned out to be his shrimp pardner, Rico Angelini.

"Hey, Angel!" I called down the hatch. "You seen Fiddler?"

"Feedler? Na, I fix-a da mote." He stuck his round head above the hatch, blinking like a hairy baboon. "Huh, what'sa da mat'?"

"Plenty's the mat'. Fiddler's gittin' likkered! Come on; you gotta help me find 'im!"

Angel gaped, then shook his head fast. "Na, na, na, na! You t'ink I cr-r-razee? Feedler fine boy sober. Drunk? Whuff! I gotta beega family — seex-a li'l' girl to feed — Rosa, Carlotta, Amelita, Seraphina, Maria —— "

"Never mind that; we gotta keep Fiddler out o' trouble! If he gits likkered he'll kill Johnny Tacon!" I grabbed his shoulders and pulled him on deck. "Now, you come on!"

He came, grumbling. "I no like. Ev't'ing wrong. Feedler he drink. Tide she too high. Glass she too low. Flag say sou'easter she come. Dat no sou'easter! Leesen. You hear?"

It was dark now, the water front quiet. There wasn't a breath of wind, but far off I could hear a great roaring, like an express train in the distance. That's what it sounded like — a sort of monster express roaring with destruction.

I think my hair uncurled a little when I realized what caused that sound. It was the pounding of the surf against the island beach, seven miles across the bay. No ordinary sou'easter ever pushed a sea like that ahead of it.

II

We searched everywhere for Fiddler that night, but not a soul had seen him, not even Old Man Jim Dooley, the town marshal. We never thought of trying the hotel, simply because it had been full of Federal officers all week. What we didn't know at the time was that the officers had left on the afternoon ferry, and that nobody had dared sell Fiddler a drop till they were gone. Otherwise he'd have been likkered a lot sooner.

Finally Angel went back to the Sanderling, promising to lock the hatch on Fiddler if he came aboard. I limped home, found the house dark and Fiddler's room empty, and sneaked upstairs and crawled in bed. I hadn't eaten since noon, but I was too jumpy and worried to care about it now, and I had that awful feeling of something crowding close and getting ready to happen.

My room faces the beach, and all night long I could hear that surf pounding the island. I kept thinking of the Angelus out there somewhere, and whenever I dozed off I'd suddenly wake up staring in the dark, thinking I'd heard Matt cry out in trouble. At dawn the whole sky was an ugly bloody red, and the tide was up over the beach. The queer thing was the wind, which was northeast and quartering offshore.

I dressed and went down to the kitchen, and in a few minutes mom came down. She had on an old pink wrapper over her nightgown, and her eyes were puffy.

"What happened to you last night?" she laid into me, real cross. "Why didn't you come home?"

"I got a cramp in my bad foot. I couldn't walk till it left."

"You're lyin' to me! What's Fiddler done? Where's he gone?"

"I think mebbe he went to Carrabelle for some motor parts. I dunno. My foot —— "

"Why do you lie to me like that? I know when you're lyin'!"

She slammed around in the kitchen and finally got breakfast on the table. Cap'n Hook came down, looking grim, and we ate. At least Cap'n Hook and me ate, but mom didn't. First thing I knowed, she had her head in her hands and was crying. Cap'n Hook stood up, tall and gaunt and gray, and rubbed his gnarled hands on his baggy serge britches. He put me in mind of an old buck eagle disgusted with everything in sight. He started to leave, came back and glowered at mom. Suddenly he took a hitch in his sleeve holders and broke his ten-day silence.

"Hump!" he grunted. "Every tom-fool thing in creation happens on a low glass. She's twenty-nine twenty now, an' fallin'!" He straightened. "Sarah Beale," he ordered, with a rasp that made the windows rattle, "ye've got to git aholt on yourself! There's a big breeze acomin' an' we've got to make ready for it!"

I gaped at him. Mom sat up like she'd been shot. "You — you mean to say we're goin' to have a — a —— Oh, my God!"

"Last night," I said, "there was only a sou'east warnin' up."

"Sou'east hell!" he snarled. "There's a real breeze o' wind makin' up out yonder; this hull coast is goin' to catch the wrath o' God soon. Micky Joe, go find that scamp Fiddler. If he's likkered an' mean, knock 'im on the head an' —— "

"The idea!" mom gasped. "Fiddler don't drink!"

" —— an' tell Jim Dooley to lock 'im up, so he can't hurt nobody. An' tell the boys to git the boats up the river. Lively! I want ye back to help batten down the house."

I left fast. When I reached the Sanderling she was riding so high her deck was above the dock. Nobody was aboard. During the night all the snapper fleet had come in from outside — all, that is, but the Angelus. I felt pretty sick, but I hurried along the docks, spreading Cap'n Hook's word while I looked for Angel. The sou'-east warning was still flying, yet the wind was freshening in the northeast. But it was Cap'n Hook's opinion that counted, and boat after boat began casting off and heading for the swamps.

Angel was over by the post office with Cap'n Dash Lundy and the weatherman. "I've no orders to change the warning," the weather-man was saying, and Cap'n Dash was blowing through his whiskers and boasting that he'd never yet allowed a weather scare to keep him off the bay.

"Ya, you fresh-water man," Angel told him. "You never see real breeze o' wind. She come dis-a-way, I tell you! An' when she come, she come queek an' bad. Hit dat chicken-coop ferry, mebbe drown ev'body! Ya, you watch-a da barom'. Be damn careful!"

"Crazy Dago," growled Cap'n Dash. "Always hollerin' about the weather."

"Angel's right," I put in, suddenly remembering Sissie was coming home today. "You'd better be careful! Cap'n Hook says we're go-ing to catch it!"

He cussed me for an impudent young'un, and stomped off. I didn't care. I just hoped to heaven Sissie and Serena would come back before the old fool began his afternoon trip. His son Jed ran the ferry mornings and was a pretty good man, but Cap'n Dash was always taking chances.

Angel grabbed my arm. "I find Feedler! He safe now."

"Huh? You found 'im? Where?"

"He gotta da room in Rick's Hotel where he go drink. Me an' Mist' Jeem Dooley lock door. He no git away."

A weight seemed to melt off my middle. I told him to take the Sanderling up the river, and headed home myself to help Cap'n Hook.

Mom was getting lamps and candles ready in case the lights went out later, and Cap'n Hook had caught him a nigger somewhere and was making him nail battens over the shutters.

"Where's Fiddler?" Cap'n Hook demanded right off.

He blew up when I told him. "An' ye think a hotel door kin hold a red-headed Beale? Git back there fast! Git Jim Dooley to help! Git Angel — the Magnus boys! Hurry!"

I laid a straight course for the hotel — and the second I hove in sight of it I seen I was too late.

The porter was sitting on the sidewalk, spitting blood, somebody inside was hollering, and there was a crowd on the porch looking goggle-eyed down the street. Fiddler had busted loose and gone.

Now I'm in for it proper, I thought.

I ran on, tracing Fiddler's course by the people staring in his wake. He'd turned the corner past the poolroom and was making for the docks. To head him off, I cut into the alley behind the weather tower, came out by the post office, and was just in time to get caught in the whole thing.

I never will forget how it was at that moment: the sticky heat and the sun's glare on the tin roofs and the shell streets; people grouped on every corner and looking ornery, like they wanted to kick a hole through something; and Old Man Jim Dooley standing spraddle-legged and cussed above the crowd about the post-office steps, black hat over his turtle face and big silver star gleaming on his white shirt. I remember a hound dog come ayelping from behind the post office, with a fishhouse cat riding its back; Old Man Dooley yanked out his pistol and started to take a shot at them; then he stared at a commotion farther up the street and let his pistol dangle. And suddenly everybody was staring. Men were jumping to get clear of something coming, and I spotted Johnny Tacon hurrying towards the post office and looking back over his shoulder. Johnny was scared; his long legs were going fast and his green shirt was streaked with sweat.

Then I seen Fiddler coming. Fiddler was swinging straight down the middle of the street, feet apart, shoulders back, spine stiff, bare to the waist and looking bigger than the Manassa Mauler and nine times as mean. The sun was glinting on his great wedge of shoulders, his red hair was blazing like fire, and he didn't even have a list. But he was carrying a terrible load — I could tell it by the way his chin was down and his head was tilted. He was clean off and crazy, and there was a fish knife in his belt and his right hand was curved on the handle of it.

I ran to him and spoke, and tried to take him easy by the arm. He swung me rolling across the shells. I got up and came back at him.

"Fiddler," I said again. "Fiddler."

"Go way, Micky Joe," he said, real soft. "Go way. I'm goin' kill a feller. I'm goin' kill that Johnny Tacon. I'm —— "

"Fiddler! Please, for God's sake!"

"Go way!" he snarled, and he wasn't my brother Fiddler now. The best feller in the world, the swimmer who'd saved more lives than anyone on the coast.

He wasn't even handsome now; his eyes were narrow and red. He was a tiger. He slapped me, and he was that quick I never seen it coming. I was out before I fell.

When I come to, he was going up the post-office steps. Old Man Dooley was trying to stop him with his pistol, and I could see Johnny Tacon's long legs sliding out the side window.

But you can't stop a tiger with a word and a threat; Fiddler kept right on up the steps, and Old Man Dooley shot. He shot twice, fast — only Fiddler's hand was already on the barrel. The pistol went flying. There was the smack of a fist on flesh; Old Man Dooley's feet jerked stiff in front of him, and he spun over into the flower bed and lay still.

Fiddler turned, sort of slow and deliberate, like he was getting his bearings, then he spied Johnny Tacon running towards the end of the street, where Johnny's boat was tied. Fiddler pulled his knife and come down the steps like the wind.

The crowd had fanned out in every direction. But right in Fiddler's path was an old Greek woman who'd tripped in her skirts and fell, and an oysterman in sea boots who'd got confused. I thought he was going to knife the oysterman, but he was saving that knife for Johnny. He flattened the oysterman with a left you couldn't see, stepped careful over the Greek woman, like he was walking on eggs, and ran on.

He wasn't six jumps behind Johnny. I scrambled up and followed, and I'd almost reached the dock when I stubbed my foot and a cramp shot through the stingaree wound. My leg doubled under me like it was hit with an ax, and I went sprawling.

I laid there and clawed the oyster shells. And I seen the flash of Fiddler's knife, seen it turn red, and then Johnny was stumbling across the stern of his boat and blood was streaming down his green shirt. Fiddler drove him over the rail and they went under together.

Johnny's head appeared. Then Fiddler's. And between them drifted a shrimp boat that had just cast off for the swamps. The crew hauled Johnny aboard, and Fiddler was left splashing in the propeller wash.

For a long time I couldn't do nothing but fight my cramp. Fiddler had swum off someplace down the dock, and I sat there thinking, *Now he's in bad trouble. The law will be on him, and if Johnny dies, they'll hang him.* Fiddler was my brother, and I had to help him. I had to stay with him till he sobered, and hide him. He'd do the same for me if I got in trouble.

Finally I managed to wobble to my feet and limp over to the dock. During the last half hour the weather scare had spread over the whole town; they'd forgot Fiddler, and everywhere I could hear the racket of hammering and men shouting and hurrying to get ready for the wind. All along the water front they were working like the devil to move gear out of the buildings to higher ground, and at the Magnus place they were heaving stuff from the upper windows to sails spread in the street, and a black gang was dragging it back and piling it in the old sponge exchange. The tide had reached dock level, and Heppy Magnus was having fits.

I yelled to Heppy. He come arunning, eyes popping and shirt hanging out over his fat belly. "Yonder!" he screamed, pointing up the river. "Dat Feedler, he crazee in de head! He steal my pretty Maris to chase Johnny! See? See? He'll wreck her! I know he'll wreck her!"

The little blue Maris was a half mile up the river.

"I'll follow him!" I cried. "I'll take Johnny's boat! I gotta catch him! Mebbe I can make it to the creek in time!"

Johnny's old oyster sloop was the only boat left at the dock. I got the motor going, headed across the harbor; then the motor died and I had to drop the board quick and jump for the halyards.

The wind was sweeping over miles of salt marsh and driving straight across the upper bay and the river mouth; it hadn't changed a point all day and now it was beginning to howl. The mains'l banged full; the sloop heeled to her hatches before I could ease the sheet, then she went skipping upstream like a singed cat.

All of a sudden there wasn't any sun, and a line of rain squalls come astreaking over the marshes.

Before they hit I got a glimpse of two things I'll never forget. One was the ferry putting out for her afternoon trip, and the other was the weather tower with two square red flags flying from it, stiff as boards. It was the hurricane warning.

Then the rain blotted everything from sight, and I had my hands full till I reached the swamps. I dropped sail at the cypress creek where all the boats go in a blow, and drifted on in. And there was the Maris dead ahead, her nose wedged among the other boats. Her pilothouse was empty.

Hurrying, I made lines fast to the tangle, grabbed a shark club from the cabin rack, and began crawling forward from deck to deck, searching for Fiddler.

The creek was jammed tight with boats as far up as I could see, and the crews were making a holiday of it. A swamper was busy peddling a bateau of likker. The frogs were hollering, the wind was howling in the cypress tops, rain was flooding over everything, and nobody gave a hoot.

Not a soul had seen Fiddler. I crawled onto the landing, and found Angel and a seine-boat crew trying to turn a truck around on the timber road. The tide was up over the road and they were splashing through it like kids, Angel lit like the rest.

"Meeky Joe!" he cried. "Where you come from?"

He sobered quick when I told him about Fiddler. "Didn't any of you see him?" I asked.

"I seen Johnny," said one of the seiners. "Bleedin' like a stuck pig. They took him to town on the other truck."

"I 'member!" Angel burst out. "There was 'nother feller — beeg feller, no shirt — try catch dat truck. Look lak Feedler."

"Did — did he catch the truck?"

"No see; rain too hard."

"Let's git to town!" I cried.

We got the truck turned around, piled aboard it, went bouncing through the swamp to the piney woods, and headed lickety-split towards town. I was sick to my middle and desperate; it looked like I'd failed in everything.

One of the seiners said, "Wind's still nor'east. Think she'll back around before we catch it, skipper?"

"She may never back around," growled the skipper, spitting rain. "She's blowin' forty now."

I thought we'd never reach town. We finally made it to Main Street, turned towards the docks, and then all of a sudden the sky opened wide and it seemed like solid water was being slung out. It stopped the truck dead in the middle of the street.

"She's come early!" the skipper hollered. "This is it!"

III

We tumbled from the truck, and it was suddenly every man for himself. I ran after Angel and grabbed his arm and begged him to stay with me.

"Damn dat Feedler!" he cried. "I gotta seex-a li'l' girl; dey cry for papa! I go home. You go home too!" He tore away, running fast.

And there I was alone. I hugged a palm till the first squall passed, and managed to reach the lee of the store buildings before the next one hit. It was turning dark, though I couldn't believe it was that late. Figgering Fiddler would return to the hotel, I laid my course for it, and that was when the wind took aholt and settled things for itself.

It knocked me down, it rolled me along the street; and when I tried to struggle up and fight against it, I couldn't. It was still in the same direction, slamming at my back and across town like a great hand, slamming harder and harder. It had a deep, slatting, thundering roar to it, with a scream mixed in, and once when it flung me over I got a glimpse of fish houses going to pieces, of swells smashing through buildings and racing up the street to the post-office steps. And high over town whirled a big tin roof like a monster bat.

I went panicky then, and I thought, *I'm in the middle of a hurricane, and if I don't get home I'll sure be killed.*

My foot was full of hot knives, but somehow I made it through the park and reached the boardwalk above the bay. Then my foot caved in. I hung on to Doctor David's picket fence, and I was thinking that nothing worse could happen, when I seen something in the bay that curdled me all inside.

It was Cap'n Dash Lundy's ferry. He'd been swept past the river mouth, and now he was trying to edge the ferry into shore and beach her. But the land curves here, and the wind was blowing off the bluff. Seas were smashing white over her pilothouse, and the slamming wind was driving her backward, farther and farther from shore. She was beyond any help, and before the rain blotted her from sight, I made out plain as anything the two cars on her after deck. It didn't take but a glance to recognize one of them. Serena was bringing Sissie home today. They were both on board.

The ferry had hardly vanished when a couple fellers come running from Doctor David's place, struggled through the gate beside me, and stared at the bay.

"Did you see her?" one of them yelled. "Wasn't that our ferry?" It was Jed Lundy, Cap'n Dash's son.

I nodded. My throat wouldn't work.

The other wore a torn green shirt, and there was a fresh bandage on his left arm. Johnny Tacon! If I'd seen him five minutes earlier it would have made a heap of difference, but Johnny didn't matter much now.

"Sissie — she — she's aboard!" I managed to say.

"What's that?" Johnny suddenly whirled on me like a wild man. "How d'you know she's aboard? You sure?"

I told him. He clutched the pickets and I thought he was going to fold up. It come to me that he was a lot crazier about Sissie than he'd ever let on, though he was such a stubborn, homely duck I never could figger what she seen in him.

All at once he got a grip on himself. "Come on!" he yelled. "We'll follow the beach! Maybe — maybe —— " Then he was tearing along with the wind, Jed Lundy right behind him.

I tried to go, too, but my bad foot wouldn't let me. Then one of the pickets tore loose and I went rolling over the walk. I couldn't stand, so I grabbed on to a fallen cedar, got to my knees and crawled. That's how I made it home. I kept crawling right on through our side yard and to the lee door of the sun room. It was black dark when I opened it and fell inside.

The draft from it brought mom running. The lights were out and she was carrying a small ship's lantern.

"Oh, my Lord!" she cried. "Cap'n! Micky Joe's hurt!"

I tried to tell her I was all right, only I couldn't get it out. I kept seeing the ferry blowing away in the rain, and Johnny Tacon running like a crazy man along the bluff.

Cap'n Hook came and helped haul me into the living room. It was the most protected spot in the house, but the rain was flying straight and driving under the shingles and through the weatherboarding; water was running across the floor and dripping from the ceiling and even running down the stairs. Mom had the rugs rolled up and stacked in a corner, and she'd brung a lot of bedding and clothing down, and piled it on chairs under tarpaulins, so it wouldn't get soaked. Candles were sputtering in the big glass hurricane lamps on the mantel, and extra lanterns were rocking on the old teak table that had come off Cap'n Hook's brig. The wind had a more terrible sound here inside, and the whole house kept atrembling like it was having a spasm.

"Where're ye hurt?" Cap'n Hook demanded.

"Just my foot; it went bad on me."

"Where's Fiddler?" mom begged, her cheeks white and sagging like biscuit dough.

Just to ease her, I said he was at the hotel. I'd 'a' died before telling her about the ferry with Sissie on it.

"Sarah," Cap'n Hook snapped, "take a hitch in your worries an' git the boy some coffee an' a change o' clothes. He looks worser'n a drowned rat. The house won't blow away. She was put up by master shipwrights; been ridin' out breezes since 'forty-two!"

"Oh, Lordy," mom moaned. "Why'd I ever leave Georgia an' marry a Beale?" She flung some clothes at me and I stripped and changed. She come in with coffee and fish, and her voice went higher. "Just listen to it!" she wailed. "An' they're all away from home! All but my baby!"

"Aw, fer —— Don't call me that now."

"Why don't they come home to me on a night like this? I wouldn't keep them worried so. Matt, he's been gone twenty-two days. Why, his ice would all be melted."

"Sarah," said Cap'n Hook.

"You leave me alone! All you Beales are alike. Won't stay off the water! I done lost Nick — an' this time I know it's Matt. I just know it! Mebbe Fiddler too! Oh, Lord in heaven!"

Cap'n Hook laid down his barometer, and his gaunt old eagle face was grimmer than ever. "Sarah," he said quiet like, "these things happen. Ye've got to learn to face them when they come. No blood o' mine would ever want to die in bed with a nightshirt round him. There ain't no better end for a man than to go down at sea. I hope I kin go that way, an' I know Matt an' Fiddler be the same." With that, he broke out the card table and ordered us to draw up our chairs. "There'll be no sleeping tonight," he said. "We'll have a round o' rummy."

The game seemed to keep mom's mind off things, like Cap'n Hook intended. It didn't help me none. While the wind slammed and roared harder and harder outside, I tried to figger where the ferry would go if it stayed afloat — only I couldn't see it staying afloat at all. Then I happened to look up, and there on the mantel between the hurricane lamps was Sissie's picture. The large one she'd had taken when she graduated from high school. She was a happy little thing and not a bit like the rest of us Beales. Her hair was all shining gold, and the photographer had sort of clouded it about her face so that she looked like an angel.

I didn't know I was sniffling till Cap'n Hook snapped, "Here, here! What the devil ails ye?"

"Nothin'," I gulped.

"Then watch the game," he ordered. . . . "Play, Sarah."

We played, and now the rain was a terrible solid thing against the house. Water streamed down the cypress paneling; it poured like a fountain down the stairs and gushed black from the fireplace.

One of the hurricane lamps teetered and crashed on the hearth. Mom dropped her cards and screamed.

I got up and put my arm around her, but she didn't quiet till Cap'n Hook took the battens off his tongue and began to talk — about himself. It was something he'd never done before.

He held up his long gnarled hands, all covered with scars. "Ye see them scars, Sarah? I got 'em on the Guinea Coast when I was a lad."

Mom asked, "Wh-what were you doin' on the Guinea Coast?"

"Blackbirdin'. The skipper got likkered an' somebody sold 'im a bunch o' cannibals with filed teeth. They busted loose. That was a night! An' blowin' near as bad as this. Ye know, a breeze down under the line blows opposite from what it does here. It whirls same as the clock."

"The idea! But — but what about those cannibals?"

"They bit," snarled Cap'n Hook, rubbing the scars. "Some was kilt, but we got 'em stowed, and got a fair wind later. Seventeen days goose-wingin' the Trades, bound for Brazil. An' then we run slap onto a Yankee gunboat alayin' for us."

"They — they catch you?"

"They sunk us! Within sight o' shore, an' two hundred niggers under the gratings. That's a Yankee for ye! Damn 'em! I was fifteen, but they'd 'a' hanged me jest the same if I hadn't swum for it. I could swim well as ary one o' the boys in them days. I mind once in sixty-four — "

And so it went till the candles burned down to nubbins.

Then suddenly he stopped and sat up, and the spell on us broke. A wet draft roared through the house.

I near swallered my tongue when Johnny Tacon stumbled in upon us, dripping water, gasping. He had the awful staring look of a drowned man. He'd lost the bandage off his arm and blood was welling through the stitches.

"Where's Fiddler?" he croaked. "Tell me quick! I gotta find 'im!"

"Easy," said Cap'n Hook, rising. "Fiddler ain't here. What ails your arm?"

"Never mind the arm!" cried Johnny. "Find Fiddler! He's the only one kin do anything! The ferry's gone down near Green Point!

Jed Lundy an' me sighted her just before dark, awash to her pilot-house, everybody packed in it — Sissie, Serena —— "

"Sissie!" screamed mom, and dropped in a heap. Cap'n Hook froze.

"Tried to launch a boat! Smashed it in the dark! Jed's gone for another! But it's no use till somebody swims it first with a line! If — if we kin only find Fiddler —— "

IV

I was already up and running for the door, and if there was anything wrong with my foot, I never felt it.

"Hold it!" Cap'n Hook barked. "We can't save a soul by tearin' off half cocked. Luff up, Johnny; ye're in bad shape. I'll fix that arm while I figger what to do."

In two shakes he'd ripped up one of my shirts and bound Johnny's arm, and then he was herding us into the storeroom and loading us with coils of rope and crab line. Johnny had fought the wind most of the night to reach us, and he said Jed Lundy was rounding up the seiners near the point. "They ought to be draggin' a boat through the woods now. It's near daylight."

"Your pa's truck handy?" asked Cap'n Hook.

"In the barn, but it'll never run in this rain!"

"She'll have to run! There's nary 'nother way to find Fiddler an' git out there in time! Make for the truck — lively!"

We followed him out the sun-room door into the dim morning. The wind rolled us in a heap; we got up, butted our heads against it, and falling and rising with the gusts, fought our way to the lee of the oleanders and the alley fence. I don't know how Johnny stayed with us, after fighting the thing so long and being hurt in the bargain.

We made it to the Tacon barn, pried the battens off the doors, and then a miracle happened.

The rain stopped. The wind gave a little moan and died. In the sudden dead calm there wasn't a sound save dripping water and the rumbling of the surf. Mrs. Tacon's old red rooster limped from the barn, ruffled his wet feathers, and went through all the motions of crowing without making a squawk.

I was gaping at the mangled trees when Cap'n Hook bellowed, "Hurry! Git that truck rollin'! We're in the center!"

We got under way, but with the down trees and wreckage in the streets I thought I'd never reach the hotel. I didn't know where else to look for Fiddler, and as I finally whirled the truck up in the rear of the place and we piled out, I had a sudden horrible fear that Fiddler hadn't come back here at all; that he was still slogging through the swamp, drunk and crazy.

The calm was still with us — a calm so dead and empty it felt like the end of the world. We shoved into the kitchen, where the colored cook was trying to mop up and brew coffee, and dashed for the back stairs. At the turn of the upper hall we saw a door hanging on a hinge. We ran to it.

It was Fiddler's room — and Fiddler had come back to it. He was spread out on the bed, bare to the waist, as I'd seen him last, wet and dirty, and clutching half a baked ham he'd snitched from the kitchen. Everything was soaked and in a mess, and Fiddler was snoring through it all as peaceful as a lamb, his mop of curls making a red halo about his head.

We fell on Fiddler, shaking him, slapping him, begging him to get up. I slung a washbowl of water in his face, and he knocked the bowl across the room and sat up, cussing. Then he caught sight of Johnny, blinked, and swung to his feet like a bolt of lightning.

We grabbed his arms and hustled him into the hall and down the stairs. Johnny ran ahead to get coffee ready, and Cap'n Hook snarled, "Git aholt to yourself, Fiddler! The ferry's gone down an' little Sissie's on it!"

"An' Serena too!" I hollered, hauling him into the kitchen. "We gotta git a line to 'em before they drown! You hear me, Fiddler? Can you do it?"

The tiger had gone. He looked so rocky it scared me. He leaned on my shoulder, staring at Johnny. "You say —— "

Johnny could hardly stand. He thrust a mug of coffee into Fiddler's hands. "Drink it!" he ordered. "Git your fool drunken head clear! We can't launch a boat till you swim out with a line. I tried it. Might 'a' made it if you hadn't cut me up! You git that, Fiddler? Now it's up to you — if they drown —— " Johnny clutched the table. All of a sudden his knees buckled and he crumpled on the floor.

It hit Fiddler hard. "Please, God," he prayed. "Please, God, forgive me!" Then he stiffened as the hotel rocked in a blast of returning wind. The calm was over. The wind had turned.

We let Johnny lay and rushed to the truck.

Before we were well under way the wind was on us in a banging roar, and the truck was fighting it like a ship in a head sea, and barely moving. Things that had stood the strain from the northeast were whipping the other way and tearing loose. We reached the old coast road, and all we'd lost was a fender; I don't know what hit it. Stinging spoondrift was blowing off the bay, and for a while the high banks of palmettos protected us. Then we swung around a curve and I was so blinded with the stuff that I drove slap into a tangle of broken pines. The motor stopped, and that was the end of it. We piled out.

We were just on the edge of Green Point hammock. Way off in the flooded pines to the left, like shadows in the flying salt spray, I could make out people moving.

It was Jed Lundy and the seiners with a boat. We grabbed our gear and pushed towards them. And it was a job, for pines were falling all the time and there were hundreds down as far as I could see, all lying in two directions, like a giant had slapped them first one way and then the other. The tide was washing through the woods in long surges, and a couple dozen men were struggling in it to clear the boat — a big seine skiff that was jammed in a tangle of pine tops. The bad news had spread, and more men were hurrying behind us to help.

Fiddler was wide awake now, and wild. He got things going. You could hear him yelling above the wind, and fellers who'd jumped from him yesterday fell to and worked like demons. They freed the boat. They dragged it after him to a palm grove near the point. The wind was on us full force and the last few yards were a battle.

The palms were all leaning like umbrellas blown inside out, and fellers were clinging to them and staring at something out in the bay. The ridge here was awash, and beyond it where the marsh had been were great smashing seas with a few splintered pines showing above the crests. Way off by the point was a dim black object near lost in the spray — the ferry's pilothouse.

Sissie was in there — Sissie and Serena and a lot of other people. Packed in there all through the night, waiting for it to go to pieces.

I didn't see how even a fish could swim in it, for the point juts south here and the wind was driving across it to the upper bay. But lines were rigged between the broken trees and swimmers were trying to battle out beyond shore. It was hopeless.

Fiddler went lunging through the grove in a sort of frenzy, and every eye was suddenly on him. He was out of his clothes in a flash, and, grabbing the end of the crab line, he cast a bowline in it and threw the loop over his shoulder. He never took his eyes off the ferry, and he never stopped moving.

I was right behind him, keeping the crab line clear. The idea was to get the crab line to the ferry first, then haul out the heavy rope that was to pull the boat. It was the only way.

At the sight of Fiddler, the others jumped to help, clearing the snarl of ropes, making the new ones fast, getting the crab line ready to pay out. They believed in Fiddler. They knew he could do it. He was the greatest swimmer on the coast.

He looked it, with his big shoulders and the long muscles rippling down his back. But he was rocky from that likker. And that little crab line was going to feel like a ton, with the seas against it. Fiddler would never give up as long as he could draw breath — and I knowed he'd drown if he didn't have help.

I was already tearing off my clothes as fast as I could. When he plunged in, I took the line in my teeth and followed.

V

He got out past the trees, then a big sea smashed him back. Now he did what none of the others had thought of trying. Just before the next one hit, he dove and stayed under.

I jerked in slack from behind and dove, too, and I stayed under as long as I could. It worked. We could swim under water when we couldn't swim on top. That's why the rest had failed.

The only thing that worried me was my bad foot; I was scared it would play out before I could do Fiddler much good. But I'd always been able to swim under water better'n on top, and that sort of put us even.

When I came up for air I spotted him for an instant far ahead; a flash and he was down again like a porpoise. I pulled in more slack and slid after him. There were stobs and briers down here, raking my belly, but there wasn't any wind and sea to throw me back. Finally there was saw grass, cutting like razors. I didn't care. We were over the marsh, making progress.

When I felt sand under me I figgered we had a chance. For we were out of the marsh and in the bay.

And then I lost the line. I don't know how it happened. One second I had it in my teeth, and the next second I didn't. I kept thrashing around and diving, and when I did find it, it was worse than losing it. For it wasn't the bight of the line I found, it was the loop that Fiddler had been carrying. Then I thought I would go crazy. Fiddler was gone, and I was alone. It was awful.

Then a sea rolled me over and I got a glimpse of the pilothouse. I was so close I could see the broken windows and people's faces staring out.

I dove, and the picture of those staring faces kept me going. One of them was Sissie. Down deep was slack water, and I went kicking and clawing over the sand till my lungs were splitting and my bad foot was afire. The crab line over my shoulder felt like it was dragging the weight of the world behind it. I was done for when I touched wood.

I managed to push to the surface, and there was the ferry's lee cap rail, and not a foot from my nose. I tried to reach out and grab it. I couldn't. I was plumb used up. A sea smashed over me and I knowed I was a goner. And that was when something grabbed me by the hair and pulled. I didn't know for a long time that it was Fiddler.

After he'd lost the line in some drift, he spotted me swimming with it up to wind'ard. He was too weak to catch me, so he come on as best he could, and caught on the broken hawser trailing over the ferry's bow. Just as he pulled himself up, he seen me floating past.

I never could figger how he managed to hold to me with the seas smashing over us, and slide along the cap rail to the lee of the pilothouse. He done it all right, for that's where we were when I come to. Even so, we were in a bad fix, and too tuckered to crawl on deck. Cap'n Dash or his engineer should 'a' given us a hand, but they never appeared. I didn't learn why till next day.

It was Serena that crawled out to us and pulled us over the rail. Serena, she's sure got what it takes. The pilothouse was full of men what could have come out, only they was a bunch of Holy Rollers on a picnic; they'd hollered all night for God to help 'em, and now they were on their knees crying about Judgment Day.

It took all three of us to haul in the crab line trailing the heavy rope; and when the rope was fast to the bitts, Fiddler had to rout out some of those crazy Holy Rollers and make 'em help drag the boat to us. We heaved our heads off before the boat appeared. There were four big oarsmen in it, straining on the oars for all they were worth, and an extra man in the stern sheets going like mad with the bailing bucket.

Then the Holy Rollers made a dash to get aboard, and Fiddler had to lay into them with both fists so we could load their women first. Serena dragged Sissie out and put her aboard — Sissie had got a crack on the head and couldn't stand. It took two heartbreaking trips to get everybody ashore, and Serena wouldn't go till the last.

She still had enough scrap in her to finish her two-day-old fight with Fiddler.

"Think I'd live with a drunken fool?" she screamed at him. "I'd rather drown!"

"Come on!" he yelled at her. "She's breaking up!"

"Not till you promise to stop it!"

"I promise, damn it!" And he threw her into the boat.

We trailed ashore on the rope. It went slack as we reached the palms, and when I looked back the ferry was gone.

The breeze blew on inland that afternoon; I missed seeing the worst of the damage, for I slept the clock around and Cap'n Hook made me stay in bed four days. Fiddler was up the next morning helping look for Cap'n Dash. They told me that the ferry's engine stopped just before she went aground, and that to keep from capsizing, Cap'n Dash and his nigger went aft to roll the cars off the stern. A big sea swept the deck and carried them away. Their bodies never were found.

Fiddler had the law to think about for a while. But nobody would testify against him, least of all Johnny, so he got off on probation. And Serena made him keep his promise.

There've been breezes since, and some were bad, but I'll never see one that left so deep a mark. I remember those days of waiting afterward, when I'd be helping Fiddler clear the driftwood from around the house, and how we'd turn and study every sail that hove in sight, staring at it a long time while we tried to tell ourselves that it was the Angelus, and that Matt would be home soon. And up in the gallery Cap'n Hook sitting grim and silent, watching too. We kept waiting and praying for the Angelus, but she never come in.

Early on a Sunday a month later, when the tide was at ebb, Father Donovan held final service for the Angelus and all the lost ones down at the river mouth, and everybody in town came and brought flowers and cast them into the water, and sang that old, old song, The Golden Shore, while the tide carried the flowers out to sea.

THE YORKSHIREMAN FLIES AGAIN

By Eric Knight

IT ALL happened in a perfectly normal way — that is, normal for Sam Small, that right, good, loyal Yorkshire hero who had not only flown under his own power, as you might say, but had performed other wondrous feats that surpassed the laws of science and man.

Sam just woke up one morning, and there he was in a strange room. And when he got up and happened to see himself in the mirror over the dressing table, he was somebody else.

Who else he was he didn't know at first. The face he saw wasn't his; that much he knew. Because it didn't have any long, gray handle-bar mustaches. But it looked faintly familiar.

Just then a lad came in, a servant chap, and said, "Heil, Hitler. Did you sleep well, sir?"

"Heil Hitler, I don't know," said Sam, who, although puzzled as you might expect, was keeping his wits about him.

Then this servant chap helped him get dressed — and a fancy business it was, what with being shaved and powdered and getting on a very posh sort of uniform. After that, breakfast was served, which was at least a phase of the situation that Sam, or any other Yorkshireman, could cope with.

While he ate, Sam gave the situation a bit of a going over.

Now, Sam, he said to himself as he champed away with right Yorkshire aplomb and sang-froid, *tha's been i' plenty o' peculiar situations afore and come out all right. So courage — and watch thy step, and happen this'll turn out all right too. Since they're heiling Hitler, tha's in Germany. So tha'd better go right on pretending tha's this other chap — whoever he is. But who is this chap tha's turned into?*

That's what worried Sam — and it would no doubt have worried you under the same circumstances. Who was he?

It wasn't until the private-secretary chap came in that Sam found out.

After breakfast this lad came in and said "Heil Hitler" and "Good morning."   Sam heiled Hitler and good-morninged right back, and the chap opened a portfolio and put down a lot of letters for Sam to sign.

And that's how Sam found out who he was — for at the bottom of each letter, typed in below the space where he was to sign, was the name: RUDOLF HESS.

Oh-h-h, my gum, Sam breathed to himself. *So that's who I've turned into.   That's undoubtedly why I looked familiar in the mirror.   I'm the chap that's sort of captain of the second team in Germany.*

He looked up, and the secretary chap was waiting.   Sam picked up the pen.   He was just going to sign when his forehead broke into a rash of perspiration.   No doubt this chap would know the real Hess' signature, and would spot a forgery right off the bat.

Sam was in a pickle, but at last an inspiration came to him.   He had always heard these German leader chaps were temperamental.   So he waved his arms suddenly and said, "Take 'em away.   The stars say it ain't a good day for signing aught."

The secretary lad didn't show the slightest morsel of surprise at this, so Sam drew a breath and raced on to the next fence.

"Now, lad," he said, "what's next on my schedule?"

"Oh, just inspecting a few troops and reviewing a parade or two — the usual routine stuff," the lad said.

"Let's get on with it, then," Sam said.

So off he went and kept himself quite busy, and no one seemed to suspect him at all.

But around teatime the telephone rang.

"Hello," said Sam.

"Heil Hitler, is that you, Rudolf?" said the voice.

"Aye, heil Hitler, it's me," Sam said.   "Who's this?"

"Heil Hitler, it's me."

"Who?"

"Hitler!"

"Oh, heil you," said Sam. "How are you?"

"Heil me," said Hitler. "I'm lonesome, Rudy. Hop in your plane and come down to Berchtesgaden to see me."

"Righto," said Sam. "I'll be right there. Good-by."

"Wait, Rudy. You forgot something."

"I catch on," Sam said. "Heil you. Good-by."

"Heil me. Good-by, Rudy."

So Sam got in his plane and flew down to Berchtesgaden, and in he went to see Hitler. "Now, Adolf," Sam said, "what's all the tizzy about?"

"Oh, Rudy," Hitler said. "It's them. It's everyone. They all want something."

"What did they want?" Sam asked politely.

"Oh, secret police. Goebbels was in, and he found out somehow that I'd let Goering have a few more secret police on his private staff, and he says Goering is using them to spy on him. So I had to let Goebbels have some more secret police to spy back on Goering.

"And then the army staff found out, and they wanted more secret police to spy on the other secret police. But I fooled them all. I called Himmler in and let him have a whole lot more secret police to spy on all the others."

"Brilliant," said Sam.

"Oh, Rudy. Do you think so?"

"That I do."

"Ah, Rudy. You're the only one I can trust — really trust, I mean. You don't want any secret police, do you?"

"Not me," said Sam. "I don't like police."

"There. That's what I mean," Hitler said. "I can really trust you."

"Then you're all cheered up?"

"No," said Hitler. "I don't feel good."

"What's wrong now, lad?"

"It's this British business. I don't see why they don't have sense enough to give in. They haven't a chance. We've bombed them enough to make any sensible people surrender."

"That won't make 'em surrender," Sam said.

"Well, how could we beat them?"

"The only road tha'll ever beat the British is by going over there and really beating 'em," Sam said proudly.

"You mean invasion?" Hitler said.

"Naught else, lad."

"Rudy," Hitler said, "you're wonderful. You're the only one who agrees with me. And all the silly generals and admirals keep saying we can't do it. I still think we can. Here, hand me that atlas."

And that's how Sam Small became the chap that planned the invasion of England. When they got the atlas, they put it on the floor, and Sam got that interested in the whole affair, it didn't seem as if he were planning the ruination of his own country. It was just he forgot, like, and did the job as a Yorkshireman does any job — the best he knows how.

And you've got to admit it's a very interesting occupation — planning current history, as you might say.

Well, they talked about what kind of barges they had, and how many men were available, and got all that sort of stuff settled.

"Now, where shall we land? How about Dover?" asked Hitler.

"No," said Sam.

"No?" asked Hitler. "Did you say no to me, Rudy?"

"Aye, I said no," said Sam. "Tha can't make it there — too many high cliffs."

"What a wonderful knowledge of the tactical situation you have, Rudy. Well, how about Portsmouth?"

Sam shook his head slowly. "I wouldn't touch that," he said. "That's a very, very tough nut to crack. Tha sees, it's a navy town, and as many as five pubs in a row on some streets. The British wouldn't retreat from that without a fearful battle."

"Where, then, Rudy?"

"Right at Pevensey — where William the Conqueror landed."

"Good — and he made it, didn't he, Rudy?"

"That he did."

"It's an omen, Rudy. It'll be Pevensey. Now we can be ready in a week. How about, say, a week from tonight, and we'll invade?"

"Now hold on a minute. Hold on," Sam said. "Don't be i' such a hurry. Let's figure dates. That'd be a Thursday night — no good. Here! I got it. A week from Saturday. That's the last o' the month."

"Is that a lucky date, Rudy?"

"Lucky?" said Sam. "Why, figure it out — that's a week end, and moreover, it's the last o' the month — and that makes it pay day. Just think, all the single N.C.O.'s'll be down the wet canteen getting splashed; and the married sergeants, they'll be in tow o' their wives, who'll be getting their pay away from 'em; and the officers, they'll be on their way for a week end in the country; and the enlisted men, they'll be all so busy in the huts playing crown and anchor. And as for the navy — well, tha knows what sailors are like on pay nights. They'll be sloppo — stinko — blotto. It's the only time tha has a chance."

"Rudy, you're wonderful," Hitler said.

And he sounded so delighted Sam suddenly felt sorry Hitler couldn't know he was really Sam Small, and then he could have the credit for himself. It was no use doing a good job when another man got all the credit. But while he was thinking that, Hitler called in his staff and ordered them to invade England. And only then did Sam see what he'd done. He'd planned a foolproof invasion of his own land. And it was too late to do anything about it. Because Hitler was commanding the generals, and the generals were giving orders to aides-de-camp, and the aides-de-camp were phoning orders to other officers, who would give them to noncommissioned officers, who would give them to the soldiers who had to get their feet wet, and there it all was.

You may be sure that Sam was in a pretty pickle. He had to sit there all night and watch his own plans for the invasion of his own country being ordered. And every once in a while Hitler would come over and say: "Er — Rudy, you're sure William the Conqueror made it?"

"Aye, William made it all right, all right," Sam would say ruefully.

"All right," Hitler would say, as if relieved.

Along towards dawn everyone got a bit sleepy, so Hitler suggested that Sam stay over for the night — it being very late, so to speak. And that Sam did.

But he didn't go to sleep. He lay there racking his brains. It seemed perfectly plain that he couldn't stop the invasion now. The only thing left to do was to tip the British off it was coming. But how could he do that?

"Oh-h-h," moaned Sam to himself. "I've mucked things up for fair now. In little more than a week they'll be invading England, and I can't find no way to stop it. What have I done? Eigh, I wish to goodness I had Mully here to advise me. That I do!"

And worried and harassed, poor Sam fell asleep just as dawn came over the big, white-crested mountaintops.

The next morning Sam woke up and he was still Rudolf Hess. And it was then the big idea occurred to him.

If I can't stop the invasion, what I've got to do is get back home and tip 'em off, he said to himself. *That's the ticket.*

So he set his mind on some way of getting home. And that wasn't simple. You couldn't just go right up and say: "I want to book a ticket for London, please."

He decided he'd have to get away by subterfuge.

But every time he tried that during the day, he was foiled.

They had a big staff meeting on the invasion that day. It just went on and on.

Finally Sam said, sort of carelesslike, "Well, everything seems to be going nicely, so I think I'll pop along."

"Why, where are you going, Rudy?" Hitler asked.

"Oh, I thought I'd just pop back to Berlin," Sam said disengagingly.

"Oh, no," Hitler said. "You must stay here, Rudy. There's a lot to do. It isn't fair to go sneaking out on all the work. Besides" — and here he dropped his voice to a pathetic whisper — "you're the only one I can trust — really trust."

So Sam had to stay.

But Sam was determined, and watched and watched until he got a chance to get clean away down the elevator. But he was brought back again, and he and Hitler got into quite a tiff.

Sam was fair stumped, so he put on a real hurt sort of look. "Why, Adolf," he said, "I thought you said you trusted me?"

"I do," Hitler said, "but I don't trust anyone that much. Now, you stay here. And just in case, I've given orders you aren't to fly your plane any more."

Eigh, what a trusting chap, Sam said. But he said it to himself.

After that all he could do was sit there and watch the reports of the generals come in — something like election reports reaching headquarters.

Everything was going with thorough German efficiency, the reports showed. A hundred divisions of troops were already rolling in trains to the invasion ports, moving only at night; engineers, with terrible German skill, had blasted under the French cliffs enough room to house 50,000 concrete barges in which the troops would cross the Channel; guns, ammunition, supplies were moving in a stream; amphibian tanks were rolling to low beaches from which they'd swim across the Channel; Goering's air force was being equipped with special exhaust fixtures, so that 60,000 planes could lay down an artificial fog over the Channel and the coast. There wasn't a thing they didn't think of — and it was all taking place right before Sam's very eyes!

And poor Sam couldn't even send a wireless message. He wished he had a few of Gommy Doakes' racing pigeons, so's he could send a message to Gommy to warn the officials back home. But wishing achieved nothing. He still had no pigeons. He was stuck!

And he stayed stuck — all that day, and all the next, and the day after that. And all the time the horrible date was drawing nearer when — as Sam could tell by all the terrible German efficiency — England was to be "*ausgestruckensunkenstunkenstrafenschmacked.*" Which means it was to be napoo, fini, conked!

Eigh, Sam was that bothered.

There were only three days left before the invasion when it happened. Fate knocked at history's door, as you might say. Sam didn't know it was Fate. All he saw was that Heinrich Himmler had come into the conference room and was whispering to Hitler. And very uneasy Sam got about it, too, because he could see them both looking sideways at him as Himmler talked. He got very uneasy.

Finally, Hitler nodded, and beckoned to Sam, and he and Himmler and Sam left the big room where the generals were planning the ceremony for the final capitulation of the British army, which was to take place in the Tower of London. The three went to a conference room, and Hitler motioned Sam to sit down.

"Rudy," Hitler said, smiling, "what do you say ought to be done to any man impersonating one of our honored leaders?"

Sam began to sweat all over.

Oh-h-h, my gum, so they have found me out, he said to himself. Now how did they do that?

So he swallowed a couple of times, and looked at Hitler, smiling blandly, and at Himmler, smiling not so blandly. Oh, Sam didn't like the way that Himmler smiled.

And while he looked at them he said to himself, *Well, tha's fair copped out, Sam, and tha's had an exciting life, so best tha can do is go down like a true Yorkshireman. But the way yon Himmler's smiling, it could be a nasty death, so let's have a nice, clean, quick 'un.*

Quickly he got up and, almost to his own surprise, flung out his right arm in salute and said, "Any man daring to impersonate you, my leader, should be instantly shot."

"Good, Rudy," Hitler said. "You see, Himmler, I told you."

Then he turned to Sam.

"But it isn't me who's being impersonated, Rudy. It's Rudolf Hess."

So, the jig's up, Sam said to himself. *Well, here goes.*

He got up and took the automatic from Himmler's holster, and held it ready in his hand.

"He should be shot, even if it is me," he said.

And then he turned the gun toward his own chest.

Hitler jumped up happily. "Ah, what loyalty, what trust, what faithfulness, Rudy! You truly are the only one I can trust! . . . Where is he, Himmler?"

"Right downstairs," Himmler said. "My agents found him walking around in his pajamas in Rudolf's Berlin apartment, and knowing Rudolf was here — in fact, that you'd forbidden him to leave here — we brought him down in Rudolf's fighting plane. He's still in the plane at the secret airdrome down below."

"Good," said Hitler. "Let's take a look at him."

"Righto," said Sam, sticking the gun in his pocket.

"Hey! How about that there gun?" Himmler said to Sam.

"Why, of all the suspicious —— Tha doesn't think I were trying to pinch it, does tha?"

"No, but I lost more than one thing that way," Himmler said.

"Heh, I'll bet that's the way tha got it," Sam came back.

"Boys, boys," said Hitler. "Will you stop this squabbling? . . . Now, let him have the gun, Heinrich. Because as a special treat to Rudy — and to show my trust in him — I'm going to let him have the pleasure of personally — er — purging this intruder."

"Me or Streicher could do better," Himmler grumbled.

"No," Hitler said, getting angry. "Am I fuehrer round here or not? Rudy shall purge him."

All this time they had been traveling — down elevators and across courtyards and through tunnels and through an underground airdrome and out to where a plane stood with a bunch of black-helmeted soldiers in a row around it. And there, standing before the plane with an officer holding him, was Sam's double — that is, he didn't look like Sam. He looked exactly like what Sam looked like now. Like Rudolf Hess. In fact, as Sam knew and you may have guessed, it was the real Rudolf Hess.

And there was poor Sam, condemned to shoot this man in cold blood.

"What a good disguise," Hitler said. "See how cunning and ruthless our enemies are, Rudolf. I wonder if we shouldn't examine him some more, as Himmler suggests, to make him confess he's a British agent?"

But Sam had been doing some fast thinking all this time. And an inspiration came. He took out the gun and pointed it at the real Hess.

"No," Sam said. "Let me do a bit of examining first."

"This'll be good," Hitler said appreciatively.

"Now, you pig-dog," Sam said menacingly, putting the gun in Hess' stomach. "How dare you impersonate me?"

And he gave Hess a punch in the nose.

"Why, Rudolf's improving," Himmler said.

Sam punched Hess again, and when Hess made to rush at Sam, the big officer pinned his hands behind his back.

"That's all right," Sam said. "Let him go and stand clear."

The man stood clear, and Sam, with the gun right on the middle button of Hess' silk pajama coat, uncorked a left hook that knocked Hess clean back into the door of the plane. With a cry of rage Sam rushed after him, and gave him a hefty kick that lifted him still farther. And, as Himmler applauded with happiness, Sam kicked the prostrate body clean through the door of the plane, rushed in after it, slammed the door, started the engine and, before the entire amazed assembly, took off with a snarl of powerful engines. There was a bit of popping, and he heard a few bullets go through the tail of the machine, but that was all.

And there was Sam, free at last.

At first, Sam could hardly contain his delight. He felt like singing and dancing. He roared with laughter as he imagined what Hitler and Himmler must be thinking.

Then he heard a movement behind him, and saw Hess sitting up.

"Now, lad," Sam said cheerfully, "sorry I had to belt thee so realistically, but it were the only road to fool 'em."

"Here, turn round and land," Hess said.

He got up quickly, but Sam pointed the pistol at him.

"Now show a bit o' sense, lad," he said. "We're both of us Rudolf Hess, and if we landed, which one of us'd they believe?"

"I am the real Rudolf Hess!"

"Aye, and I can say the same thing as long and as loud as thee. It don't matter which one of us is the real Hess. Thing is they'd never believe nor trust either one o' two of us after this — after me flying away. Think. They'd put us both i' jail, or under observation, or worse. Now settle down and use thy head, lad."

The man was quiet a while. "But where can we go?" he asked.

"That's easy," Sam said happily. "We're sailing for England."

And he began to sing the popular song.

Hess looked at him with admiration and awe. "You mean, to solve the situation, we're going to fly singlehanded against the foe and go down fighting for our country?"

"Summat like that," Sam said. "Here, and to make it simpler, happen tha'd better fly this ship for a while, and I'll keep watch over thee wi' this gun, so's tha'll not change thy mind. Hop along, lad!"

So Hess flew the ship while Sam kept the gun on him and watched the compass to see he played no tricks.

"Put a bit more north in it," Sam said. "We might as well come down in Yorkshire. It's a good place to land, what wi' plenty o' flat moors."

"How much north?" Hess asked.

"Oh, I don't know," Sam said. "Just stick a bit o' northing in it. Yorkshire's such a big county we can't help hitting it."

Now, you may, no doubt, be able to hitch up some of the rest of this story in your own mind.

They got a bit too much northing in their west and so missed Yorkshire altogether and hit Scotland. Sam, in the dusk, did see some sort of a castle, and it looked a bit like the Duke o' Rudling's place.

"We'll land near the Duke o' Rudling's!" Sam shouted. "He'll fix me up!   Has power and all that!"

"You mean he's a secret sympathizer with our great movement?" Hess asked.

"If tha puts it that way — in a sort of road — aye."

"I'll remember the name," Hess said. "In case we get separated I'll ask for him."

"Separated," Sam said. "Why should we get separated?"

"Because it sounds as if we're out of gas," Hess said. "And we can't see well enough to land in this dark. We'll have to jump."

And just then the motor sputt-sputted, and Hess got up and put on the straps of the parachute and opened the door.

"Here I go," he said.

"Good luck, lad," Sam said.

"Good luck to you too," said Hess. "And you'll need it. Because it seems to me that there isn't another parachute!"   And he jumped.

Now, anyone who has made a study of history knows that there is a special Providence that keeps watch over the British Empire.

Time after time in history a grave crisis has approached, all has seemed hopeless, and then, always, the situation has produced the man.

I want you to see how this special Providence that God has provided for his Britons worked in this case. Here is a man — the only Briton alive who carried in his brain the most terribly important news of a crushing threat to the Empire. Here he is, in the pitch dark, in a plunging airplane thousands of feet above a wild terrain. He has no parachute. To stick to the ship will be death. Yet he must escape and live to carry his news to the nation's leaders.

And what other man in the world could Fate have picked for such an important event in history than Sam Small? What other man could have done it? Here was the inescapable situation, and

Providence places in that situation the one man in the entire world who could descend from that plane in safety — in other words, Sam Small, the Flying Yorkshireman. The one man alive who could fly under his own power!

But let us not stand too long in breathless astonishment at the inscrutable laws or whims of Providence and her kindly regard for Britons. Let us shake our heads, perhaps, and leave the whole matter there, where it belongs, amid the galaxy of things unsolved — time, space, the way of a man with a maid, the logic of women, and the Einstein theory. Let us rather return to something we can grasp and believe in. In other words, good old loyal Sam Small.

There he stood, near certain death, and yet his mind worked calmly, smoothly, steadily and ploddingly, in his Yorkshire way.

"Well," he said, "there's naught for it. I promised Mully I'd never, never fly again as long as I lived. But if I must do it, I must, and happen she'll forgive me, this being a very important occasion in my life, as I might say."

So, drawing a breath, he stood at the door.

"I hope I haven't forgotten how to do it," he muttered. "For if I have, I'm bound to land wi' a fearful bloody smack."

And thus, in his Yorkshire way, without any passionate or patriotic exhortations regarding King and country, Sam, without any parachute, jumped!

For a fearful moment he tumbled head over heels in the darkness. The racing wind tore at his arms as he attempted to stretch them out. The air ripped at his clothes and hurtled him over and over. He was just beginning to think he'd lost the knack, when he remembered he must have faith.

"But I can fly," he said. "I could, I have, and I will again."

And, like the stilling of a stormy sea, the tempest of air ceased, the tugging and racking of his limbs ended, and instead of falling helplessly, he was gliding smoothly, beautifully, deliriously, on supporting cushions of air. The feeling was about as ecstatic as — as having someone scratch a tickle on your back where you can't reach.

"Oh-h-h," said Sam. "Eigh, that's good. I'm very, very proud o' thee, Sam, that tha does it so nicely without any practice for many years. Tha's doing very nicely."

Just then there was a sort of a pop and flash far below, and Sam realized that the plane at last had crashed. So he glided down gently toward it and circled over a field where lanterns were beginning to bob.

He glided nearer and nearer, until he heard a voice saying clearly, and in a slightly accented English, "I am Rudolf Hess!"

To which a voice replied, "Hech, Moggie, r-r-roose t' swoddies. Her-r-re's a Gair-rmon come bur-r-rlin' fro' t' skees!"

"What a bloody terrible dialect they gabble i' these parts," Sam said. "It must be Scotland I'm in. And since I don't want to be copped as a German i' this mess, I'd better sheer off. But where can I go?"

Sam was in quite a fix, for he still, you must remember, looked like Rudolf Hess, and was still dressed in a German uniform. He was worse off than the real Hess, who had been dressed, you recall, only in pajamas.

Then Sam had a bright idea. "Fly home to Mully, lad," he said. "Two heads is better nor one, and she'll help thee solve it. Besides, she's sort o' used to wonderful things happening to thee, and won't have to be explained to too much."

So he flipped an arm and, gaining a little altitude, struck south toward Yorkshire. The false dawn was just beginning to show when Sam began to recognize the terrain.

"I must be over Mulford," he said, "for there's The Wagon and Horses, and there's Black Swan. Aye, and there's The Wellington Arms, so I must be over Wuxley . . . and there's the good old Spread Eagle and here's the Green. And there's my cottage. Whoops!"

And there Sam made a mistake. He hadn't flown for a long time, you must remember, and in his joy at being home, he streaked into a sort of power dive, figuring to bank up into a snappy sort of stand-up landing. Instead, he misjudged a bit, came up too late, hit under the lintel of his door so hard it drove his head six inches down into his shoulders, and there, stunned as even a Yorkshireman must be by such a wallop, he lay on his own doorstep, insensible to the world.

When Sam woke up, he heard a familiar sobbing. He sat up, and there was Mully rocking in her chair before the fire, and he was on the sofa with a bandage round his head.

"Mully!" he cried. "Ah, lass, lass! Tha doesn't know how glad I am to be home!"

She got up and turned her tear-stained face on him.

"Lying out there, dead drunk for the world to see thee as it wakes. Makin' a shame o' my home and a mockery o' our good name. Oh, Sam, Sam! How could tha visit this final shame on me? After all I've tried and tried and stood by thee and worked for thee and cooked for thee and tried and tried —— "

"Here, here," Sam said, moving painfully toward her.

"Don't come near me, you drunken, good-for-nothing, nasty old —— "

"Mully, listen," Sam pleaded. "Listen, because I've got to talk fast. I've been Rudolf Hess. I've planned the invasion o' Britain. It comes off i' forty-eight hours or so from this evening."

"Heh!" she said scornfully. "That proves it. Tha's still intoxicated. Go back and sleep it off."

"I'm not drunk," Sam said angrily.

"Well, where's tha been this past week?"

"I tell thee, I been i' Germany. I've been Rudolf Hess. We've got to tip 'em off about the invasion."

"If tha's got any regard for our good name, tha'll stay home and behave. The neighbors have been asking where tha was. And tha wasn't at the Spread Eagle, for I've asked and asked and —— "

"Now have done!" Sam shouted. He stood up, swaying from the bump on his head. "Now, for once, tha'll listen to me — or am I not master i' my own home? Now listen. I left Spread Eagle one evening a week ago, coming home, and I were sober as a judge — or, I'll tell real truth —— "

"Tha'd better for a change!"

" —— I had naught but happen one or two more nor the limit.   And I stumbled i' the dark by that nasty bit of a curb by Braithwaites', and next thing I knew, I woke up, and I were Rudolf Hess, i' Germany. So I got up —— "

And off Sam went, telling her simply exactly what had happened.

When he was through, Mully stared at him a long time, and then shook her head.

"Sam Small," she said, "God knows I've stood as much from thee as any woman ever stood from man.   But this time I can't swallow it."

"Well, this is true," Sam said doggedly.   "Tha must believe me."

"Believe thee," Mully said — in exactly that tone wives use the world over.   "How can I believe thee?   Tha says tha escaped in a plane?"

"Aye," said Sam.

"How did tha know how to fly an airyplane?"

"I don't know," Sam said, "but it's quite logical.   Aye, look, when I were there I spoke German, didn't I?"

"I suppose tha'd have to."

"Well, tha knows I don't know any German.   So, if I could speak German when I don't know any, it's just as logical I could fly a plane when I don't know how to, isn't it?"

"That sounds right and proper to me, Sam," Mully said slowly. "But tha's still got to admit that —— "

Mully halted, for at that moment there came a knock on the door — an excited thundering of a knock.

"Mrs. Small!" cried an old, trembling voice.   "Mrs. Small, is tha in?"

Mully motioned Sam to be quiet.

"Aye, I'm in, Mrs. Wambley."

"Well, did tha hear, Mrs. Small?"

"No, what?"

"Why, Capper read it off the Leeds and Yorkshire Mercury down at the pub first thing.   It says a plane come down i' Scotland, and who does tha think were in it?"

Mully stood up, and at that moment she felt a strange, creeping vibration go over her.

"I know," Mully said quietly. "In it were Rudolf Hess!"

"Oh, somebody already told thee," Mrs. Wambley's voice said, and then they heard her aged feet pattering away to find better fields for spreading news.

For a full minute Mully stood unmoving — and Sam had the sense that any really good husband has, of not taking a second's triumph of the I-told-you-so variety. Then she turned to him.

"Sam," she said finally, "from this moment on, noa matter what happens to thee i' this life, I'll niver, niver, so long as I live, ever doubt thee nor —— "

"Now, now," Sam said. "We've got work to do!"

"That we have," she agreed. "When's the invasion?"

"Tomorrow night," Sam said.

"Well, wash that blood off, and I'll bandage thee and slip on my best Paisley shawl, and we'd better be off and tell the old Duke o' Rudling about it."

"Aye, I thought o' him," Sam said.

From that moment on, life began a blaze of activity for Sam and Mully. For, unfortunately, the Duke wasn't home, having gone to London to see about forming a new company of Home Guards.

So Sam and Mully took the train to London, but when they got there, the Duke had started back.

"Now look here, we can't waste no more time," Sam said. "It's getting too near the kickoff. Happen we'd better see some generals."

So they went to Whitehall to see a general. Finally, after hunting along endless corridors, they got to him and began to explain about the invasion. When they'd explained it all, he shook his head.

"Interesting, what, what, what!" he said. "Invasion, eh? That's under the heading enemy activity — probably G-2 — Intelligence. Not my chicken at all. Better see General Boppingtop. Wouldn't want to trespass in his department."

So they went down more passages, and finally got to see General

Boppingtop, who was very interested, until Sam told him that they lived in Yorkshire.

"Ah, sorry. Then that'd be Northern Command, what, what, what!" Boppingtop said.

"But could tha do aught — if they invade —— "

"You civilians can't understand," the general smiled, pulling at his long mustache. "In the army — place for everything — everything in its place. That's military way. Must follow channels. See Toppingbop — GSO-5, GTH-3, VII Corps, Northern Command. Good man, Toppingbop. Tell you exactly what to do."

By the time Sam and Mully got out on the pavement of great, roaring London, it was already dusk, and people were scurrying for home before the raids started.

"Well, routine's routine," Sam said. "And we must respect law and order, so —— "

"We'll do nothing of the sort," Mully snapped. "If we go on this way, we'll be all wearing swastikas afore we get our story told. I know what to do. We'll call a bobby!"

"Now, I don't want to have aught to do wi' bobbies," Sam protested.

But, nevertheless, they went over to a policemen, who listened to them and then telephoned for a Black Maria, which came and took them to the police station.

When the sergeant there examined them, he nodded his head and put down on the page before him: "Two suspicious characters, by their accent undoubtedly Dutch or Rumanian. Booked under the D.O.R.A."

Then he had them put in cells.

The next morning they came up for trial, and the magistrate warned them not to let it ever happen again, and fined them costs, and dismissed the case as a first offense.

Sam and Mully both kept their mouths shut, but when they were on the pavement again, Sam started to laugh.

"So finally it's thee that lands us behind the bars," he chuckled. "It were thy idea calling a bobby. I've always told thee never to have aught to do with bobbies."

Mully tucked her shawl tighter about her chin.

"My gum," she said. "For two pins I'd go back home and let 'em invade these nasty people down i' London. I don't see why our good King and Queen ever live down here and —— "

"That's it," said Sam suddenly. "Why didn't I think o' that afore."

"That's what?" Mully said.

"We'll go tell the King. Here. Probably he's right at home at Buckingham Palace now."

So they walked over to Buckingham Palace and Sam said to the sentry at the gate, "Mr. and Mrs. Sam Small to see His Majesty, the King."

The sentry turned in his box and rang the telephone.

"Mr. and Mrs. Sam Small to see Your Majesty," he said.

"Well, send 'em right up," said the King. "Don't leave 'em standing there, lad."

The sentry took Sam and Mully up to the palace, and the King said, "Sit right down with me and the Queen and have a cup o' tea; it's that chilly and raw out today."

So the Queen poured Sam and Mully a cup of tea, using only one lump of sugar, which Mully recognized was because of wartime, and then the King said, "Well, Sam, lad. Always glad to see thy face. Now what's up this time?"

"Well, there's off to be an invasion tonight," Sam said.

And then and there Sam explained the whole matter, telling about how he had been Rudolf Hess.

"By gum," said the King, "what a peculiar metamorphosis. But I'm glad tha managed to change back in the nick o' time. Now, about stopping that invasion. . . . Where's my head general?"

"Here, Your Majesty," said the general, sort of springing up from nowhere and saluting. He wasn't at all like General Boppingtop, being much younger.

"Good," said the King. "And where's the head of my air force?"

"Present, sir," said the air-force general, saluting.

"And where's my head admiral?"

Being the silent service, the admiral didn't say anything. He just popped up and saluted.

"Good," the King said. "And now, where's Winnie?"

"I've been here all the time," Churchill said, lighting another cigar as he came from behind a curtain.

"Fine," said the King. "Now, Sam Small tells me they're off to pull an invasion tonight."

"Eigh," said the general, "what a nasty, nasty time to invade. Right on pay night — and a week end too."

"Aye, that's why I planned it for tonight, in the first place," Sam moaned. "I don't want to say aught about British soldiers and sailors, especially in front o' generals — and Your Majesties —— "

"Oh, I know what my brave soldiers and sailors are like," the King said. "They'll get a little rosy on pay nights."

"Rosy?" said the generals.

"Stinko," Sam suggested.

"Very, very awkward time to invade," the generals said. "What can we do?"

"I have it," Sam said. "How about sending out an order that pay day is shifted until Monday morning?"

"Oh, can't do it," said the general. "The law. It specifically states in King's Rules, Regulations and Orders, pay day has been pay day in the British army for four hundred years. It's the law."

And there they might have been stuck yet, despite Sam's good idea, except for the King.

"Well, my gum," the King said. "Can't I have a law passed that the foregoing is all true except in case of invasion?"

"That you can," said Churchill. "Leave that to me."

And off he popped to have the law passed, and off went the generals and the admiral.

And everyone heaved a sigh of relief, because they knew that the British army and navy would be cold sober for the invasion. More than that, they'd be so mad about missing their pints of beer — the birthright of every Briton — that they'd mop up any unfortunate German army that managed to get into England.

And that's how the invasion of England was foiled.

And this, and this only, is the true account of what really happened, and the only true explanation of why Rudolf Hess landed in Scotland too.

After this war is over, you can go to Mr. Churchill and ask him if it isn't so. I request any doubter to do just that, and I wager anything you want he'll agree with me.

As for Sam, the King was ready to reward Sam with medals or anything he wanted, but Sam was real Yorkshire where rewards went — he didn't want any.

"Well," said the Queen graciously, "there's no reward greater than the knowledge that you've saved your country from a terrible fate."

"Thank you kindly, ma'am," said Mully, dropping a neat curtsy.

Then the King gave Sam his final compliment. "Aye," he said. "What would Britain do without the common men and women of Yorkshire?"

"I don't know," Sam said. "But it'll be a sad day if they ever try it."

A KISS FOR MR. LINCOLN

By Louise Kennedy Mabie

THE CITY was iron-gray in color, iron-bound with cold. Smoke from the tall new chimney of the rolling mill down on the Flats made a tent above the chill small city. Flakes of soot settled on snow-covered sloping lawns. Along the aristocratic stretch of Lake Avenue, lace curtains, washed, starched and put up in September, were turning gray. But the Kennard residence shone white far back among its cedars, its Venetian-lace curtains hung delicate and clear; to combat the wintry dusk there was a glow of lamps and firelight, and upstairs in the front bedroom young Mrs. Kennard was dressing.

Mr. Kennard had been particular. He had said, "A Mr. and Mrs. Murdock, of Mayfield, are coming to supper with us on the ninth. These guests are important. Mr. Murdock is a railroad man."

"What is a railroad man?" young Mrs. Kennard had asked.

"A railroad man is a man who builds railroads," Mr. Kennard had answered crisply. "Steam cars to compete with the boats between here and Buffalo. A railroad man," said Mr. Kennard, "is a man of courage, of quick decisions, of daring, sway, vision and influence. Mr. Murdock has a plan for making use of the old Ohio road, the road on stilts, and for linking our cities together from Toledo to Erie, and even on to Buffalo itself."

"Has Mr. Murdock a beard?" asked Mrs. Kennard.

"Mr. Murdock has not," Mr. Kennard replied. "Mr. Murdock is still a very young man."

"You are only thirty-five years old," Mrs. Kennard had said, "and you have a beard."

"I am a banker," said Mr. Kennard; "the youngest bank president in the state. Bankers are expected to wear beards. In fact, I am hoping to have my bank finance Mr. Murdock's railroad."

"You wish it?"

"I said I hoped. But above all, I wish to gain the vote and influence of Mr. Murdock for Mr. Lincoln."

"You wish Mr. Murdock to vote for Mr. Lincoln — to use his influence to elect Mr. Lincoln President — more than you wish to finance his railroad?"

"I do."

When Mr. Kennard said "I do," things were important. Always young Mrs. Kennard felt caught up, lifted by that crisp "I do" into realms of power and action that she never at any other time entered, but about which she sometimes thought. The outside of Mr. Kennard's bank was imposing, solid, strong and proud. You drove past the Weddell House on the corner.

"The Weddell House," young Mrs. Kennard had said lightly, balancing to look behind her at the sweep of her gray silk skirt. "When Mr. Murdock comes to supper, will he sleep afterwards at the Weddell House?"

"For you to think where Mr. Murdock will sleep is indecorous," said Mr. Kennard. "And why do you not sit? Why do you walk up and down?"

"A lady can be told by her carriage."

"A lady can be told by her shape — not fat, not thin, but rounded, slim and resilient," said Mr. Kennard.

Mr. Kennard's eyes rested on Mrs. Kennard's shape and Mrs. Kennard stood still at once. She stopped looking behind her at the sweep of her gray silk dress with the ruchings around all the edges. There was Honiton lace at the throat. She stood erect and shameless, and she folded her hands tightly together; a second wife, young, and not only young but very beautiful. She had been married to Mr. Kennard two years ago and it had happened so quickly that beforehand she had not had much time to think. But lately she had begun to think a little.

"I walk up and down, Henry," she said slowly, for she was thinking it out as she spoke, "to get a little away from you — and from your voice. Because it — penetrates me. I was not thinking of Mr. Murdock actually as he slept, and even if I should have, wouldn't his wife be with him? What I was really thinking of, Henry, was sheets."

"Sheets!" pronounced Mr. Kennard, outraged.

"If Mr. Murdock should stay overnight here, whether our sheets would be good enough for such a railroad man."

"Our sheets are made of Irish linen," said Mr. Kennard. "Our sheets would be good enough for Mr. Lincoln." Mr. Kennard's voice was raised. He was angry. Mrs. Kennard's shoulders drooped. She bent her head to the storm. "Mr. Murdock will stay at the Weddell House, as usual, and his wife will most certainly be with him. It seems to me, Delight, that you have almost too much of an indelicate interest in Mr. Murdock."

"Is Mr. Murdock a handsome man?" asked Mrs. Kennard.

"He is!" shouted Mr. Kennard and left the room.

So now, tonight, everything was all ready for Mr. and Mrs. Murdock except Mrs. Kennard, and she was almost ready.

Her hair was done, which was a comfort. Mrs. Kennard's hair was bright and brown, and as it curled over her proudly held Kennard head there were deep crinkles in it which Mother Nature had put in with an iron. Mrs. Kennard's eyes were gray and unawakened, her skin was white, her nose tilted, and her mouth was both rich and generous. Tonight she had stained her mouth red with a geranium flower from the glassed-in plant room. Tonight Mrs. Kennard wore a ruched dress of fawn-colored silk which had been made for her in Paris on her wedding tour with Mr. Kennard, and with it she wore coral-colored satin slippers and cream-colored silk stockings with clocks embroidered in coral. The dress was cut low and the low part, being French, had not been filled in with mull or lace, and tonight Mrs. Kennard had not covered up the low part with a necklace. But from her small ears she hung carved coral earrings, and on her small wrists there were thick coral bracelets, and in her hands, although the night was cold, Mrs. Kennard carried a tiny fan made of coral feather tips.

Mr. Kennard was dressing in his room, and in between their two rooms were folding doors made of heavy black walnut. These doors were nearly always closed, and Mr. Kennard slept in the small single bed in his room, so as not to disturb Mrs. Kennard. Mr. Kennard said it was better that way, that his morning exercises would wake her up. "They do anyway," Mrs. Kennard had said. But tonight Mrs. Kennard knocked on the intervening walnut door.

"Henry! I'm all dressed. Want to see me?"

"I," said Mr. Kennard, "am busy."

"But I have on my Paris dress!"

"I," said Mr. Kennard, "have seen it."

"Never with my corals!"

"I," said Mr. Kennard, "can wait."

So Mrs. Kennard left her room and walked down the stairs holding up the train of her dress carefully in her hand, and in the long parlor she touched the flowers, pulling them more delicately into shape, and in the dining room she lighted the candles, and in the kitchen she pirouetted for the maids and showed them her corals and the clocks on her stockings. And at once the maids, of whom there were two, were fired with an enthusiasm which entered into them from somewhere outside themselves. The cook showed Mrs. Kennard the turkey in the oven and lifted the lid from the bean porridge on the stove, and Mrs. Kennard not only sniffed but she did a little dancing step with her skirts held up, so they could see the lace on her petticoat, and the Bohemian hired girls, first and second, were both shocked and diverted, and everything went well.

Mr. Kennard did not join Mrs. Kennard until after their guests had arrived, so Mrs. Kennard had to meet them alone.

A carriage door slammed. There was the prance of hoofs on the drive — two horses. Mrs. Kennard opened her front door herself, and the first thing she noticed was that Mrs. Murdock had white hair. Mrs. Murdock wore a long sealskin cloak over her black lace dress, and Mrs. Murdock was no longer young. Then Mrs. Kennard's eyes lifted to look at Mr. Murdock, and there they rested, for Mr. Murdock was not only much younger than Mrs. Murdock, but he was remarkably handsome. And he was smiling. He was hearty. He seemed to reach out. He was tall. He was big. He was dark and dashing.

"Well, well," he said, and his glance ran down from Mrs. Kennard's face to her neck and then down to the tips of her coral-colored slippers. "Is this Mr. Kennard's daughter?"

"I," said Mrs. Kennard with dignity, "am Mr. Kennard's wife."

"My dear," said Mrs. Murdock, and she held out her hand. At the same moment Mr. Murdock held out his hand, so Mrs. Kennard was, for the moment, a link between them. Then Mr. Murdock's hand crushed Mrs. Kennard's hand so tightly in his that she cried out and dropped her feather fan. Mr. Murdock picked it up. Mrs. Murdock removed her sealskin cloak and folded it over a chair. And for a moment nothing was said.

"Henry!" Mrs. Kennard called up the staircase. "Henry!"

"Is that for help?" asked Mr. Murdock, and Mrs. Murdock walked on into the long parlor with the effect of leaving them together behind her. "Fans are for flirtations," Mr. Murdock said at once, quietly, rapidly. "Do you know that much?"

"I don't know — how much I know," hesitated Mrs. Kennard.

"You must know that you're beautiful," said Mr. Murdock. "Dazzling. What have you done to your mouth?"

"Geranium."

"Why?"

"To look — prettier."

"Prettier!" said Mr. Murdock, and he bent to look at her mouth. "Does it taste?" he asked, and he put his hand under her bare elbow. For there was speed, power, force to Mr. Murdock, and Mrs. Kennard drew her elbow away. Mrs. Kennard put up her fan to cover her mouth. She felt breathless, she felt afraid, but not afraid. She thought, *Henry,* and just then Henry came down the staircase.

"Good evening," he said in his dry voice. "We are honored, Mr. Murdock. How has the weather been with you in Mayfield?"

"Changeable," said Mr. Murdock, who was breathing quickly, who

hardly looked at Mr. Kennard as he shook hands with him, so oc-
cupied was he in looking at Mrs. Kennard. But Mrs. Kennard was
looking at Mr. Kennard. She was staring at him with her geranium-
tinted mouth open. Mrs. Kennard had gone a little pale.

"Henry!" she said faintly, and she fanned herself with her tiny fan.
"Your — your beard —— "

"Well," said Mr. Kennard crisply, dryly, as if annoyed. "I admit it.
I have no beard. Suddenly I tired of my beard, so I got rid of it. It's
gone. Why make an issue of it?"

"Because you look different," said Mrs. Kennard faintly. "I feel
queer. I — I have never seen you without your beard. You're —
you're new to me, Henry. You're like a — stranger to me."

"That," said Mr. Kennard, "may prove to be an advantage. Or it
may not. . . . Have you had a cold fall in Mayfield, Mr. Murdock?"

"Changeable," said Mr. Murdock. "I stick to that."

"Henry! You haven't even a mustache," said Mrs. Kennard.
"You look so clean."

"But I have always been clean," said Mr. Kennard.

"So young," breathed Mrs. Kennard. For Mrs. Kennard had had a
shock. She was very pale. She glanced up to Mr. Murdock for help,
and at once she received it. Mr. Murdock enclosed her bare elbow
with his warm hand, and he did not relinquish her until she was
safely seated on her sofa in her parlor beside Mrs. Murdock. Mrs.
Kennard sat there quietly enough, but she still breathed quickly, as if
there wasn't enough air in the room.

Sherry was brought in. Mr. Kennard toasted Mrs. Murdock. Mr.
Murdock toasted Mrs. Kennard. Mr. Kennard toasted Mr. Lincoln
and watched when Mr. Murdock set down his glass without drinking. The fire blazed under Mr. Kennard's ministration. Mr. Murdock sat on the arm of the sofa nearest Mrs. Kennard, and he didn't
bother with Mr. Kennard at all. Or with Mrs. Murdock. He only
bothered with Mrs. Kennard.

He said, "Kennard, you have a most beautiful wife. And have you
noticed that she has stained her mouth red with a geranium flower?"

"That," said Mr. Kennard, "is unheard of."

"But she told me —— " Mr. Murdock began smilingly. Mr. Murdock was a smiling man. He stopped speaking when Mrs. Kennard touched his arm.

"Henry, it's true," she said. "I did stain my mouth."

Mr. Kennard set down his sherry glass. Mr. Kennard was not so tall as Mr. Murdock, but when he drew himself up to his full lean height he was almost as tall. He drew himself up now.

"I knew that Mr. and Mrs. Murdock — our guests — were important to you, Henry," said Mrs. Kennard. "That you wanted everything to be very nice — to give them our best — the turkey — the apple pudding — our best — so I just brightened up my mouth."

Mr. Kennard said, "In my mind, there was no question of your giving your mouth. I cannot conceive," said Mr. Kennard, "of your having thought of such a thing."

"I didn't. I haven't. My mouth was incidental, like — like having the curtains washed and the decanter polished. I know how important Mr. Murdock is to you, Henry — you want to finance his railroad — but that even beyond and above money I know how much you want Mr. Murdock's vote — his influence — to help elect Mr. Lincoln for President."

"Supper is ready, Mrs. Kennard," said the second hired girl from the doorway.

Mr. Kennard stood as if he had been struck, caught, tied. Then he moved suddenly, as if he had been untied, and crossing to Mrs. Murdock he bowed before her.

"Mrs. Murdock, may I have the honor?" he said.

Mrs. Murdock stood up, placing her hand in the crook of Mr. Kennard's outstretched arm, and they moved toward the dining room. Past Mrs. Kennard on the sofa and Mr. Murdock on the arm of the sofa. Eyes front. Stiff.

"Henry, you told me so!" cried out Mrs. Kennard desperately. "You made it clear to me!"

They passed on into the dining room. Mrs. Kennard pounded her foot noiselessly on the floor.

She pounded on her knee with her closed fist, until Mr. Murdock, leaning down, caught up her closed fist and kissed it.

"Thanks," said Mr. Murdock. "You warned me. You are unique."

"When he gets angry with me," said Mrs. Kennard breathlessly, "he — just — walks away."

"If you belonged to me," said Mr. Murdock, "and I were angry with you, I wouldn't walk away. I'd knock you down."

"That — would be better. I could understand that," said Mrs. Kennard. "That would be more — personal."

"You and I," said Mr. Murdock, "are violent, lawless people. We match."

"Without his beard," said Mrs. Kennard, "he's a stranger to me. I have had a shock. I'm trembling. My brow is all — damp."

"Are you coming, Brit?" called Mrs. Murdock from the dining room.

"Yes. In a moment." And to Mrs. Kennard he said, "You're as clear, straightforward and definite as a child. As cruel too. Do you realize what such candor can do to people?" Mr. Murdock pulled Mrs. Kennard to her feet, took away her fan and laid it on the table, took out his fine handkerchief and held it against her forehead, looked down at her red mouth and then deliberately into her uplifted beautiful eyes. Her eyes had tears in them.

"I'd give a great deal to kiss you," said Mr. Murdock, "but there is such a thing as honor."

"Yes. There is," said Mrs. Kennard.

"You are my host's wife and they are waiting. If I kissed you once I'd kiss you again. It might take time."

"Yes. It might," said Mrs. Kennard.

Mr. Murdock sighed. With his hand under her chin, he turned Mrs. Kennard's face away. Then, with her hand on his arm, pressed by his arm tight against him, Mrs. Kennard and Mr. Murdock proceeded to the dining room where, after a moment of hush, everything became very hearty.

Mr. Kennard, serving the bean porridge from the covered silver tureen, told his story of the farmer's boy and the sack of potatoes.   Mr. Murdock told his story of the mongoose on the railway coach, at which Mrs. Murdock laughed heartily.

"I always laugh at Brit's old stories," she said.

But she is so nice, thought Mrs. Kennard, looking at Mrs. Murdock very carefully.   *She has a husband who is not faithful, and she knows it.   She laughs at his old stories.   She covers up.   I wish I could cover up.   She is a better wife than I am,* thought Mrs. Kennard.

Everything was delicious.   Mrs. Murdock said so.

At intervals Mr. Kennard mentioned Mr. Lincoln.

"Too raw, awkward, unschooled," said Mr. Murdock.

"But a master of men," said Mr. Kennard.

"This country doesn't want a master of men," said Mr. Murdock.

"This country doesn't want slavery," said Mr. Kennard.

"Part of it does."

"Do you?" cried out Mr. Kennard, arresting his fork in the air.

"I do not, sir," ejaculated Mr. Murdock.

Mr. Kennard, appeased, continued his supper.

Mr. Kennard spoke of Mr. Lincoln's debate with Douglas, to which, he said, the entire country had paused to listen.

"Mr. Lincoln clarifies," he said.   "He does not confuse.   His exact speech hits his meaning in the center."

"I am not interested in politics," said Mr. Murdock.

"But this goes beyond politics," insisted Mr. Kennard.   "This is an affair of terrible responsibility.   We need a man with the power of mastery — a man with insight, heart, pity —— "

"May I trouble you for the gizzard, Mr. Kennard?" asked Mr. Murdock.   And he added blandly, "My favorite bit."

The coffee was served last in small cups, *as is fashionable,* Mrs. Kennard thought with satisfaction.   Mrs. Murdock asked for the recipe of the apple pudding.   The ladies arose and left the gentlemen to themselves and their cigars.

Alone together, the ladies settled themselves on the sofa in the parlor, and from the weather and the servant problem they moved, with a growing mutual liking, to more intimate things. No, Mrs. Murdock had no children.

"Except Mr. Murdock," she added with a laugh.

Mrs. Kennard hadn't any children either, but she had been married only two years. She hoped for a girl or maybe a boy.

"Doesn't Mr. Kennard care for children?" asked Mrs. Murdock.

"I don't quite know. I've never asked," confessed Mrs. Kennard.

"But, my dear," said Mrs. Murdock. "A thing like that — the most important thing —— "

"Yes. I know," said Mrs. Kennard. "Our marriage is rather formal. Somehow, we have never discussed it."

"Make him," said Mrs. Murdock placidly.

"But Mr. Lincoln has insight, courage!" cried out Mr. Kennard heatedly from the dining room. "He came up from the meanest poverty, from a rough frontier! From old processes Mr. Lincoln has wrung himself out to be a greater type of man."

"Than whom?"

"Than Douglas!" cried out Mr. Kennard. "I tell you Mr. Lincoln is not in this fight for himself!"

"Mr. Kennard, politics bore me," said Mr. Murdock, "and argument does not persuade. Let's join the ladies."

"One moment, Mr. Murdock," said Mr. Kennard. "One more moment. I see that I must bring myself to speak more personally, to — to explain. What my wife told you before supper, Mr. Murdock, was the exact truth," said Mr. Kennard stiffly. "My bank does wish to finance your railroad, and not as a favor to you. We go after business that is good business for us, new business, legitimate business — in this case, revolutionary business. We keep our eyes forward. We believe in the future of our country. You and I can reach agreement on business to our mutual advantage, if you wish, downtown in my office. But the reason I asked you to my home tonight, Mr. Murdock, goes farther, higher, digs deeper than business, since it was to try and secure your vote, your great influence politically throughout the state, for Mr. Lincoln."

"So she spoke embarrassing truth," said Mr. Murdock.

"She spoke truth," said Mr. Kennard.

"What were your prepared to offer me for my vote," asked Mr. Murdock bluntly, "when you asked me to come here?"

"I hoped to persuade."

"Persuade! Hell!" said Mr. Murdock. "When I deal I deal." And there was the sound of a pushed-back chair.

The ladies relaxed, and then stiffened as Mr. Murdock, followed by Mr. Kennard, appeared in the doorway, for Mr. Murdock's face was flushed, his hair was rumpled, his white tie was crooked, and his shirt front bulged.

"Get your cloak, Margaret," he said to his wife. "We are leaving."

"But, Brit!" said Mrs. Murdock.

"Do as I say, Margaret," said Mr. Murdock.

The ladies clasped each other's hands, and the hands of both were trembling.

"But the evening has just begun!" cried Mrs. Kennard. "I've been looking forward to showing Mrs. Murdock the house! We — we have an Italian chest upstairs, carved, with cupids blowing trumpets; we bought it on our wedding tour. Later, we were going to play cards, and have mulled wine and little frosted cakes. The little cakes are waiting!" burst out Mrs. Kennard. "I had it all planned!"

"Mrs. Kennard's plans," said Mr. Murdock, "Mr. Kennard's persuasions — they are neither of them good enough. I am angry," said Mr. Murdock reasonably. "I come in good faith to have my good supper with friends, and I find myself in the midst of a conspiracy."

"You have had your good supper," said Mrs. Kennard. "Aren't you big enough, powerful enough to best any conspiracy?"

"You bet I am," said Mr. Murdock.

"Especially after I told you," said Mrs. Kennard. "Now, my husband," said Mrs. Kennard proudly, "is too honest to conspire. He tries to reason. He believes so deeply in Mr. Lincoln himself that he cannot understand how others more shallow than himself cannot so believe. But I am not too honest to conspire, Mr. Murdock, and neither are you. What we really want from you, Mr. Murdock, is your vote for Mr. Lincoln. You will see that we value our country above money. Do you?"

"I have my own scale of values," said Mr. Murdock. . . . "Margaret, this must be painful for you," said Mr. Murdock. "I asked you to get your cloak and go out to the carriage."

"But Mrs. Murdock wants to see our Italian chest upstairs," said Mrs. Kennard.

"Do you?" Mr. Murdock asked his wife.

"Why, yes," said his wife. "I believe I do."

"Where is it?" Mr. Murdock asked Mrs. Kennard.

"In the front bedroom. I'll show her."

"Go up and see it, Margaret," Mr. Murdock said. "Examine it well. Ascertain whether or not it is an older Italian chest than ours. Then come down, get your wrap and join me in the carriage."

The ladies stood up, Mrs. Murdock walked past Mr. Murdock and out through the wide doorway into the hall. Mrs. Kennard was going with her, but as she passed Mr. Murdock he stopped her. "Not you," he said. Mrs. Murdock continued on up the staircase. Mrs. Kennard stood still.

"What will you offer me?" Mr. Murdock asked Mrs. Kennard rapidly, directly, and Mrs. Kennard moved back a little. When Mr. Murdock came nearer, Mrs. Kennard put up her hand to push him back, so Mr. Murdock took her hand in his and kissed her palm. Nobody had ever kissed Mrs. Kennard's palm.

"What will you give me?" Mr. Murdock asked huskily. "I mean you, yourself."

"For what?" asked Mrs. Kennard.

"For my switch to Mr. Lincoln — my influence. When I deal I deal."

"You mean a bribe?" asked Mrs. Kennard faintly, and she looked over her shoulder swiftly at Mr. Kennard.

"Call it anything. We have only a moment."

"But only a moment," hesitated Mrs. Kennard, "would not be — worth while."

"It would to me," said Mr. Murdock. "I promise you."

"You mean here, now?"

"Where else?"

Mrs. Kennard shut her eyes, for if she looked at Henry she could not do it. Then Mrs. Kennard swayed forward and held up her mouth. He lifted her clear of the floor, like a trophy, a triumph. She was captured, taken, kissed lightly, then heavily, then deliriously, shamelessly, completely, by Mr. Murdock before she was torn away from Mr. Murdock by her husband. Mrs. Kennard couldn't breathe. She couldn't think. She was someone else than herself — someone shameless and young. Nothing was locked any more, nothing not understood. This was what she had been born for and had reached at last. There was Mr. Murdock lying on the floor, for her husband had knocked Mr. Murdock down. There was Mr. Murdock on the floor, beginning to shake his head, to feel his chin blindly with his hand, and Henry standing over him.

All Mrs. Kennard said weakly was, "Henry, your morning exercises —— "

"Get up," Henry said to Mr. Murdock, "and get out."

After an instant, Henry pulled Mr. Murdock to his feet, and with a strong arm around Mr. Murdock's middle he guided Mr. Murdock's wandering steps to the door.

" 'S all right — Mr. Lincoln," Mr. Murdock murmured hazily on his way.

"Damn Mr. Lincoln!" said Henry breathlessly. "Damn you! Damn the whole world!" said Henry.

Mrs. Kennard ran to open the door. They were out on the porch now, down the steps. Mr. Murdock was in the carriage now. Mrs. Kennard had time to run back, straighten the rug, set up an over-turned chair, tidy her hair before the mirror and wipe her mouth swiftly with the back of her hand before Mrs. Murdock came deliberately down the staircase. Mrs. Kennard went to meet her.

"Your — husband," Mrs. Kennard said breathlessly, "has gone — out to the carriage."

"Yes," said Mrs. Murdock.

"The rug — I'm afraid he fell a little — tripped — but nothing serious. I didn't mean —— When one is untried and devoted — one
blunders."

"Devoted to whom?" asked Mrs. Murdock.

"To one's husband — unalterably — as I am."

"Yes," said Mrs. Murdock pleasantly, and she held out her hand.
"Your cupids are very fine."

"Cupids?" said Mrs. Kennard stupidly.

"Perhaps, since Mayfield is so far away, you will mail me the recipe
for the pudding."

"Oh, I will — I will," said Mrs. Kennard.

Finally they were gone. The light over the step was safely out.
Mrs. Kennard plumped up the pillows on the sofa. Mr. Kennard
broke up the last log in the fireplace. The lamps were out. Mr.
Kennard turned off the lights in the crystal chandelier, and Mrs. Kennard, following him on tiptoe, pinched them off again for perfect
safety. Mrs. Kennard preceded Mr. Kennard up the staircase. Nothing was said. Mrs. Kennard went into the front bedroom, Mr. Kennard went into his room and both their doors into the hall were closed.
The heavy walnut doors between their rooms were already closed.

Mrs. Kennard undressed slowly, listening for sounds in the other
room. Mrs. Kennard got out a fresh nightgown — the French one
with just puffs at the shoulders — the low-necked French one that
was too delicate to wear. It smelled French and wicked, for it had
lain in sachet for months. Mrs. Kennard was a little frightened when
she saw herself in the long mirror, but she just shut her eyes and went
on brushing her hair. She looked at herself again when she got her
hair braided, but this nightgown was not made for braided hair, so she
shut her eyes, unbraided her hair and brushed it all over again. She
had to knock twice on the door before he answered.

"Yes?" he said.

"Henry, I'm coming in," said Mrs. Kennard. "I — want to talk to
you — explain."

"There can be no explanation," said Mr. Kennard.

Mrs. Kennard's heart, which had practically stopped until he answered, went on again.   It was such a relief that he had spoken at all. One can combat speech.

"Henry, I didn't like him," said Mrs. Kennard.   "I just liked — it!"

"You," pronounced Mr. Kennard through the door, "are a shameless woman!"

"Who cares about a little thing like shame when one is fighting for one's life?" cried out Mrs. Kennard.

"You are not fighting for your life," said Mr. Kennard.   "Your life is quite safe!"

"But my happiness is not," cried out Mrs. Kennard, "and happiness is more to me than life!   Henry, I'm coming in!"

Mrs. Kennard opened the door.   He was sitting up in his bed with both pillows behind him, with a book in his hand, with the lighted lamp on the night table beside his bed shining down on his closed book.   Henry's face was in shadow, but even in shadow Henry looked very handsome, very young, with his eyes so bright with anger and his face so white.

"It wasn't the man," said Mrs. Kennard at once.   "It was the — awakening.   Henry, it's wonderful."

"Without love?" shouted Mr. Kennard.

"I thought of you."

"You could not have, at a moment like that — possessed.   I keep seeing you — abandoned to him.   The sight seared my eyeballs."

"You cared?"

"What am I made of — flint?   Of course I cared.   I am sick with it — I am sick with longing.   But I am bound by my own will.   I shall not abandon myself — take advantage.   Only an overpowering love —— I have tried to be honest, to be upright —— "

"But, Henry!   It's natural to abandon yourself to me.   It's upright. It's honest, if you really love me.   I don't mean pleasantly, I mean terribly — not able to get along without — the house dead when you're away — dread of an illness, a separation — pushing the clock ahead to make it hurry.   I even love the pillars outside your bank — Bank Street — my favorite street — your step on the stairs, so light and fast, as if you wanted to reach me — your hands — the way your hair grows at the back of your neck, like a little boy's — your honesty. I'd steal for you, Henry. Of course I kissed him. I'd lie — I'd do anything for you — anything."

Mrs. Kennard was crying. She threw herself forward across his bed and sobbed. It was cold in Henry's room with the window open — even in rain, even in snow, open. Mrs. Kennard shook with the cold in her thin French nightgown and tried to curl her small feet up piteously beneath her for warmth. And Mr. Kennard had never wanted her to be cold. To Mr. Kennard she had been almost too rare and delicate to touch, a treasure to set up above him on a shelf and admire, an object to cherish, to keep safe from harm, to hurry home and look at, even covet, but not to touch, for it was not possible that anyone as cool and beautiful as she was could want him to.

But now it came over Mr. Kennard with a bounce that that was what she had wanted all along, for she had said so, and she had never failed him in stating almost more than he wanted of the truth. And now he found that he had wanted all her truth, had longed for it, depended on it even when it blazed up so bright and fierce that it seared him and he had to turn away. For her truth was the heart of herself which he had dared momentarily to doubt, and doubt of her he could not stand. She was his only love, his weakness, his pearl. And there she was, within reach, sobbing, and shaking with cold. Henry got up out of his bed and closed the window. Then he lifted her up from where she was and placed her in the exact warm center of his bed and covered her up. Then he went down on his knees beside the bed on the cold floor and put his head down beside hers on the pillow and hushed her.

"There, there, I love you more than anything in this world or out of it, but I revere you too."

"I don't want to be revered; I want to be kissed. Not like him — not for Mr. Lincoln, like you and me —— "

And when Henry kissed her, delicately at first, and then vigorously, and then wildly, she turned more closely against him and sighed, "That's the way — that's it."

And in the night, sleeping close beside Henry in his narrow bed, she woke up once to pull up the blankets warmer, higher over Henry's shoulder. And to someone far beyond the open window, far across the great stretch of quiet land, she said, "Thank you, Mr. Lincoln."

TOLERANCE

By Ray Millholland

EVERY day for a solid week now, twelve Superaviation fighting-plane engines had passed Final Test. Every engine had been passed by the entire staff of gimlet-eyed Air Corps inspectors, to whom a variation from specifications of two tenths of a thousandth of an inch was treason.

All of which Blue Chip knew better than anybody else. He also knew what the rest of the aviation industry had predicted — at the time he had taken over as plant manager of Superaviation — that not even a magician allowed to use his own trick mirrors could ever build those engines to the merciless specifications demanded by the Army.

But instead of sitting there at his desk in his air-conditioned office and admiring his own achievement of the impossible, Blue Chip was doing some hard thinking under that battered hard straw hat cocked back on the southeast corner of his brains. Sure as little green apples, the Army would soon be yelling for more engines per day. And with good mechanics almost impossible to hire any more, there were only two ways of getting them — by persuading the men, through their natural leaders, to speed up their effort; and by training apprentices in the shortest time possible.

Across the desk from Blue Chip, and wearing an alertly suspicious look, sat Billy Anderson, the bandy-legged little toolmaker who ran the big seventeen-thousand-dollar jig borer out on the gear-housing line. Incidentally, Billy commanded the respect of his fellow tool-makers for his swiftness and accuracy, while the younger and less experienced men considered it a mark of distinction merely for Billy to stop, look at the work they were doing and pass on without snorting in caustic contempt.

"Billy, I was just thinking," said Blue Chip, pretending he was admiring the rising blue line of the production chart on his office wall, but all the time keeping track of how the little toolmaker was taking it. "I was thinking just before you came in what a jam the Army boys would be in for engines if it wasn't for a few old-timers like you and Pat Shacko and a few more like you."

"It's about time us old-timers who served our regular apprentice time instead of robbing our trade got a little credit. You wasn't here when they opened this dump and started hiring green kids for mechanics, so you'll have to take my word for it. Me and Pat Shacko braces the employment man for a job. He takes a look at the few gray hairs over my ears and that limp Pat's carried ever since a crane sling broke and put him in the hospital, and says, 'Sorry, boys, but the rules are we can't hire men over thirty-five.'"

All Blue Chip had to do was nod silent agreement and Billy was off again. "You should 'a' seen the junk this joint shucked out the first three months, when that mob of young punks tried to work to a four-tenths tolerance. Anyways, they didn't get an engine past the Army inspectors until they threw up their hands and called in me and Pat Shacko and a few other old-timers to do the fussy operations. Yeah, know what some of those young punks said, first day you showed up in that old straw crown?"

All Blue Chip had to do was look blank and receptive, and he heard, "Well, one of them young punks points at your back and says to me, 'Now I know where they got the idea for the Foxy Grandpa cartoons in the funny paper.'"

"Uh-huh, I heard him make that crack," grunted Blue Chip, both elbows resting on the arms of his chair, and pretending to be concentrating on a report on his desk blotter. "Got a something here that says we have less than five hundred all-around machinists out of nearly seven thousand men on the pay roll."

"If you mean guys who can run a planer or a boring mill, make a lathe sit up and cry, write his name with a milling-machine dividing head or make any kind of a part a dizzy designer can draw — well, you ain't got near that many," insisted Billy.

"Billy" — Blue Chip hoisted his bushy eyebrows and pinned his man to the back of his chair with a steady look — "between you and me, we aren't getting out, by half, the engines Washington will be squawking for the minute the country finds out how bad a jam we're in. What are we going to do for more mechanics like you and Pat Shacko?"

A horrified look froze on Billy Anderson's face. "Mean we got to double the size of this joint?"

"Something like that," admitted Blue Chip, shaking his head. "But where I'm going to get the mechanics, I don't know."

"Nuts, Blue Chip. Nuts!" Billy Anderson snapped his half-finished cigarette clear across the room into the drip bucket under the water cooler. "I mean you're plain nuts worrying yourself into an early grave. You got dough in the bank, enough to take it easy in Florida and spend your time fishing the rest of your life. Why worry? If I was in your shoes, I'd tell the flat world to go climb up a rope."

That is just what Blue Chip had planned doing when the lid blew off the witches' caldron over in Europe. But now he was shaking his head. "We can't do it, Billy."

"Don't 'we' me into it," was the quick reaction from Billy Anderson. "I'm already sick of stumbling over fifty green punks around the tool-crib window, waiting for somebody to tell 'em what size drill to use, when it's marked plain on the drawing. I'm quitting right now and getting me a job in some alley shop. Me and Pat Shacko both, if you want to know."

Blue Chip started punching dots in his desk blotter with a pencil point. "I suppose you could make — overtime and all — your sixty to eighty bucks almost any place nowadays. But how would you and Pat Shacko like knocking down a hundred a week on a couple of soft jobs?"

"Only worry jobs pay that kind of money," was Billy's instant and cynical reaction. "I knew a cross-eyed Russian planer hand who went clear bats just dreaming of being a foreman someday. What loosened his gibs, permanent, was worrying about the worry part of the job he didn't even have yet."

Blue Chip dropped his pencil into the tray on his desk, like a man who has just made a mistake there is no use trying to rub out.

"Have it your way, Billy. Thought you might like to be interested in keeping your wife from asking why her man isn't making the big money Mrs. Pat Shacko's is."

"Okay, I'll kick your April fool's plug hat once, anyways," Billy said. "What's the job you're trying to hang around the neck of a coupla broken-down toolmakers?"

"Figuring on making you and Pat apprentice masters over a new bunch of boys we've got to start training," explained Blue Chip mildly. "You raised three toolmakers out of four, yourself. It ought to be a hay job for you."

"Five," snapped Billy. "I raised my sister Flora's three boys too. Only one went off and worked his way through college. But then, his old man saw funny spots in front of his eyes too."

"Not asking you to turn out all-around toolmakers this time," went on Blue Chip, reaching for his telephone. . . . "Walters, in Personnel. . . . Haggerty speaking. Tell Professor Bickman I am transferring my two best toolmakers to the apprentice-school staff. They will report in the morning."

"Who's this Professor Bickman?" demanded Billy, the moment Blue Chip had hung up.

"Expert on adult education Washington is lending us to help you and Pat get the school started," answered Blue Chip.

Not even Blue Chip, who had spent twenty-five years as superintendent of a lathe works for old Gus Banks before coming to Superaviation as plant manager — which should have made him an expert on unpredictable situations — dared guess how Professor Bickman was going to get along with Billy Anderson and Pat Shacko. But there was one thing Blue Chip was sure of — that Professor Bickman was going to be a lucky and wealthier man if Pat Shacko did not blarney him into investing at least a month's salary in Pat's rotary-valve-engine patent.

The first repercussions from the new arrangement arose from a different, though not unexpected, quarter. Martin, the general foreman of the machine shop, waylaid Blue Chip with loud complaints that his two best mechanics had been taken from him.

Joe Williams, Blue Chip's young master mechanic, who happened to be present, took a drawing pencil from his vest pocket and prodded Martin's burly shoulder for his attention. "What is this business of you claiming Billy Anderson and Pat Shacko as your men? They're both listed on the pay roll as toolmakers. That makes 'em my men."

"Okay, if you want to be technical about it," Martin jerked back at Joe Williams. "And suppose you work this out on your slide rule too: Who's going to knock out the two extra gear housings a day we get from Pat and Billy, to make it twelve engines instead of ten?"

"Wrong," said Blue Chip, taking his grease-spotted hard straw hat off and wiping his brow with a bandanna. "Twelve a day isn't a candle to what the Army is expecting."

"Call it fourteen then," conceded Martin stubbornly. "In two more weeks you could of had 'em if you guys had let me keep Pat and Billy to break in another pair of operators for the new jig borer we've been going to get 'tomorrow' for the last six months."

"Now you're arguing on our side — with Blue Chip and me," shot back Joe Williams. "Our bottleneck is skilled operators that can hold frog-hair tolerances and still make their machines walk the dog."

"I can use a hundred like that, right this minute," retorted Martin. "They can hang by their tails from the roof trusses and eat peanuts, just so they can read a micrometer to a tenth of a thousandth."

Having allowed Martin the satisfaction of arguing himself into a tacit admission that the machine shop would benefit greatly from the new apprentice school, Blue Chip restored his hard straw hat to an almost perfect horizontal position on his head and continued his morning round of inspection.

As he walked along the broad aisles, bounded by four-inch black lines painted on the floor, and even traffic police at important inter-sections to prevent the scurrying electric trucks from crashing into one another — Blue Chip was unconsciously contrasting all this with the way things used to be in the old days when he was serving his time. In the old days there was almost as much machinery bolted upside down to the roof trusses, in the way of countershafts and belt shifters and the like, as there was on the floor. Like as not, too, there was a razor-edged, belt-lacing hook flapping around your lathe step-cone pulley that would lay your arm open from wrist to elbow if you got careless. But now there stretched acres and acres of busy machines all around him with not a belt flapping, because they were all driven by individual motors tucked away out of sight in the lower part of each machine.

Blue Chip paused by a polished iron surface plate where a white-haired inspector was checking a newly finished crankshaft. The inspector was working without spectacles.

"Your eyes got mine beat, Bob," said Blue Chip, "if you can check close work like this without your cheaters."

The old inspector shook his head. "I don't trust even as good eyesight as mine." He lifted his right eyebrow and clamped it down on a jeweler's magnifying glass and bent over the instrument he was using.

He said nothing for a moment, then took his jeweler's glass from his eye and reached for an "O.K." inspection tag. "There isn't a single dimension on one of these cranks where a mechanic dares miss it a thousandth; and fifty of 'em he has to split a thousandth into tenths. It sure beats my drum how these green youngsters ever do it."

Blue Chip hurried on. There was too little time in a day of twenty-four short hours to stop and admire superfine workmanship. His business was cracking bottlenecks — riding grief jobs until they were licked. Above all, there was the endless job of training men for exacting jobs — operators to run the machines, foremen who had to be constantly on the alert to prevent spoiled work and yet not to be so obvious in their supervision that the men became nervous and lost control over their machines.

Farther down the aisle, a smart-looking youngster of barely twenty stumbled blindly from between two machines and collided with Blue Chip's heavy bulk. "Sorry," said the youngster, and stooped down to pick up his tools, which had spilled from the rolled-up canvas apron under his arm.

"No harm done, bud," said Blue Chip. He waited for the youngster to finish picking up his tools, then added, "Getting a transfer to another department?"

Then Blue Chip saw the boy's face for the first time. Young lips were clamped shut and tears were being held back by sheer will power.

"No, sir. I — I'm quitting to join the Army."

"Mind if I see your draft-board notice?" asked Blue Chip.

"It isn't that." The youngster clutched his tool roll tighter under his arm and tried to break away. "As far as the draft board is concerned, I guess I could stay here forever. I'm just no good for this kind of work. I'm joining the Army!"

"Hold it, son." Blue Chip slipped a big hand under the youngster's arm and fell in step with him as they walked toward a battery of time clocks near an employees' exit. "Now just what struck you all of a sudden to blow your job building plane engines to lug a gun around? Nothing against guns, understand. I'll bet you're a good rifle shot already that any captain in the Army would be tickled pink to have in his company. But did you ever stop to think that there's ten good squirrel hunters for every one good mechanic nowadays?"

The youngster said, "Not the kind of a mechanic I am. I just spoiled ten cluster gears that the inspector said cost a hundred bucks apiece. I haven't got any business around a place like this."

Just then they were passing the inspection bench on which stood a row of sparkling cluster gears. Each bore a flamboyant red rejection tag.

"This the grief?" asked Blue Chip.

"Yeah." The boy's eyes could stand only the briefest look at his shame.

"Bob" — Blue Chip beckoned to the inspector — "what's wrong with these gears?"

"All ground undersize on the ball-bearing-seat diameter."

Blue Chip examined tag after tag and noted the inspector's comments. "M'm'm. All ground exactly twenty-five thousandths undersize, it seems."

"Yes," answered the inspector. "Every one exactly wrong by twenty-five thousandths, to the tenth. But junk just the same."

There was a knowing twinkle in Blue Chip's eye as he nodded to the youngster. "I remember making a bull like that, first job as a toolmaker I ever got after serving my time. I was turning up a special tap for my new boss. What did I do but turn it exactly twenty-five thousandths small, just like you've done. Felt like two cents' worth of dog meat, too, just like you feel."

A smile brightened the youngster's face. "Bet you did just what I did — read your micrometer one whole turn of the barrel too much."

"That's right, son!" agreed Blue Chip, waving to the row of ten spoiled gears. "But I doubt if I would have made ten pieces in a row exactly wrong to the tenth. Fact, I know I couldn't have done that good."

Blue Chip turned the youngster around and pointed over his shoulder toward the machine he had just left. "It takes a bang-up mechanic to make something exactly wrong without a miss, ten times running, son. Now go back there and read your mikes, like you've learned how by hard experience."

Already ten minutes late for his promised visit to Professor Bickman's new apprentice-training school, Blue Chip took the next cross aisle and strode through a miniature canyon formed by two rows of tall drilling machines. Just as he was passing the last machine in the line, he heard the shrill scream of a rapidly rotating tool from which the flood of coolant had been accidentally shut off.

In the wink of an eye the tool grew overheated and seized in its closely fitting guide bushing. Instantly the relentless power of the machine started whirling the work-holding fixture and beating a thunderous tattoo on the iron machine table. The middle-aged operator of the machine tried to reach past the dangerous, whirling mass of steel to shut off the power.

Blue Chip was just in time to jerk the operator out of danger. But not quite fast enough to prevent a jagged corner of steel from ripping a gaping wound in the man's arm. A punctured artery spurted.

In one continuous jerk, Blue Chip ripped the injured man's sleeve from cuff to shoulder. He then clamped his thumb on the inside of the elbow and forced the wrist back to the shoulder.

"Roll up your apron and jam it up in his armpit!" he barked at another operator who had come to help. "Higher! . . . That's it!" Then to the injured man, "Easy now. Let me hold your elbow tight against your side."

"Am I bleeding to death?" gasped the injured man.

"Not while we've got this artery kinked in two places, you won't," Blue Chip assured him.

In another moment Martin, the machine-shop foreman, was there, with two of his clerks carrying a stretcher and a first-aid kit. "I heard the racket and never stopped to look," he grunted at Blue Chip. "Doc and the nurse are already on the way. I left two of my men phoning for them."

Ten minutes later Blue Chip was walking beside a wheeled stretcher to the ambulance. Steady eyes looked up from the pillow at him. "I heard doc and the ambulance intern say I would have been dead before they got there, if you hadn't known what to do. Thanks."

Blue Chip scribbled a note and handed it to the ambulance intern. "Have 'em call me every fifteen minutes, either here or at my house, until Mac is in the clear. . . . I'll be seeing you myself, Mac, in the morning."

"Look after my micrometer, will you?" asked the man on the stretcher. "It flew out of my hand when —— "

"Got it all safe, right here," assured Blue Chip, patting his vest pocket. "I'll send it to the gauge room for a checkup, just in case it got sprung."

Now it was three-thirty. Blue Chip's call had been clanging continuously for the last half hour from the factory signal system.

He stopped in at the first-aid clinic and picked up the telephone from the nurse's desk. "Haggerty," he said, and held out his cuff toward the nurse. "See how much of that you can get off before it dries in, will you, please? . . . Yes, Haggerty speaking."

It was P. G. Ashurst, chairman of the board of Superaviation, calling from an all-day conference with Army officials in Washington.

"Listen, Blue Chip. Our easygoing schedule of twelve engines a day is out the window. Across the pond they're yelling they've got to have a minimum of twenty of our new fast fighters a day or the jig is up. I've promised them fifteen a day on my own responsibility. But Colonel Flightsby wants it direct from the horse's mouth. Here's the colonel now."

"This isn't a question of well-intentioned promise, Haggerty," came the colonel's grave voice over the wire.

"Fifteen a day, beginning the first of the month," promised Blue Chip. "And twenty a day, sixty days from right now."

"I'd like to believe that fifteen-a-day promise," replied Colonel Flightsby. "But you can't do it. You'll have to put on a thousand more skilled men. And where are you going to get 'em?"

"We'll be on schedule with fifteen engines a day," insisted Blue Chip.

And so Blue Chip was a full half hour late for his appointment to inspect Professor Bickman's apprentice-training school.

"How are the two new instructors, Pat Shacko and Billy Anderson, doing?" Blue Chip asked Professor Bickman.

The professor, who had voluntarily emerged from retirement to offer his talents as an engineer and teacher to aid the national-defense program, unhooked one earpiece of his spectacles and let them dangle from his ear while a quizzical smile flitted across his chubby pink-skinned face.

"Interesting, to say the least," he drawled. "The one with a slight limp — impediment in his stride — especially."

"That will be Pat Shacko," said Blue Chip. "Pat isn't gabby, but when he does say something —— "

"I beg to differ slightly there," sighed Professor Bickman. Rather sheepishly, he slipped a hand under his desk blotter and drew out a grease-smudged stock certificate. "Sounds rather amazing. But somewhere during our first interview I gave Mr. Shacko my personal check for one hundred dollars and became a stock-holder to the extent of one thousand ten-cent shares in his — ah — remarkable rotary-valve engine."

"You got company there," admitted Blue Chip, but did not go so far as to admit how close he, too, had come to owning one of those grease-smudged stock certificates.

Blue Chip followed the professor down the corridor and across an open alleyway to one of the older buildings of the plant which had been converted into a training school.

"As you see," explained the professor, nodding toward one class visible through a glass partition, "we have divided the apprentices and older semiskilled men whose skills we are attempting to elevate into groups of fifty. This class is studying elementary shop geometry and the simpler principles of trigonometry."

Blue Chip saw one gray head among the class and asked, "Do the older men have trouble picking up mathematics?"

"They are measurably slower than the youngsters," admitted Professor Bickman. "However, our best examination paper last week was turned in by a fifty-year-old cabinetmaker we are training to become a metal pattern-maker."

Next they came to a larger room, equipped with rows of small metal-working machines. At the time Blue Chip and the professor entered, the entire class was perched on rough bleachers and more or less respectfully listening to a blackboard demonstration by their instructor, one Pat Shacko.

"Accuracy is what you birds got to get in your noodle the first thing," Pat Shacko was saying. "You don't make even half-baked flying-machine engines, like what we build here, without you can split a thousandth ten ways."

Pat seized a bit of chalk and proceeded to do a remarkably good sketch of an internal-combustion engine on the blackboard. "When I mean accuracy, I ain't blowing bubbles in my beer, neither. Now, you take this here picture of my rotary-valve engine. She's gotta be built to closer tolerances than ordinary. But when she is, I'm here to tell you Uncle Sam's boys will have something that'll chase the Krauts down their ratholes. Thing for you guys is to pay attention and practice accuracy. Then someday, when this war scare is all washed up, you'll be the kind of mechanics I need in my new factory to build my rotary-valve engines."

Professor Bickman's eyebrows went into a restrained flutter, and he glanced obliquely Blue Chip's way. But Blue Chip was stolidly listening to Pat Shacko's further remarks.

"You birds is all anxious to start cutting metal," Pat was saying. "Okay, we'll begin this afternoon. For a project, we'll build us a single-cylinder model of my rotary-valve engine."

Professor Bickman coughed apologetically behind his hand and said, in a low whisper, to Blue Chip, "I'll have a word with Mr. Shacko immediately after class is dismissed and persuade him to assign a more suitable project —— "

Blue Chip pondered for a moment, then shook his head. "Maybe it isn't a bad idea to let Pat build his rotary-valve model. If it's his baby he is trying to teach 'em to machine the parts for, he'll make 'em turn out accurate work."

They arrived at the next classroom just in time to hear Billy Anderson, the erstwhile toolmaker and star operator of the largest jig borer in the Superaviation plant, beat a tattoo on a steel plate.

"All you punks, front and center!" commanded Billy in a voice adrip with exasperation. The apprentices dutifully shut down their machines and trooped hilariously to the bleachers for an unscheduled lecture.

"What have I got in my hand?" demanded Billy, scornfully holding up a micrometer.

"Looks like, from here, a C clamp for gluing two pieces of wood together," piped up a red-headed youth from the back row.

Teacher Billy Anderson skewered the offender with a caustic eye. "Smart guy, huh? Okay, we start all over from where we begun this morning. This gimmick in my hand is a micrometer, graduated to read in tenths of a thousandth of an inch. It's what you measure your work with so's you stay inside the tolerance some overeducated baboon drawing pictures in the engineering department puts down to worry the guys in the shop."

Professor Bickman cast silently prayerful eyes toward the ceiling and refrained from looking at Blue Chip. Had he done so, he might have seen the general manager of Superaviation unconsciously nodding approval.

Teacher Billy Anderson warmed to his subject of tolerance, "The idea of tolerance is that one guy bores a hole in one piece and another guy makes a shaft what's supposed to fit in that hole. That's all this big plant is trying to do — fit two pieces together and another piece to them, until we got a finished engine. But if the guy that bores the hole plays it safe and makes it a hair too small and the guy making the shaft to go in that hole makes his piece a hair too big, why, they won't go together. . . . Now go back to your machines. And the first dim-wit that brings me a shaft turned a thousandth too big or too little from what his drawing calls for, I'll — damned if I won't send him up to the drafting room along with the rest of the baboons!"

Professor Bickman let out a faintly worried sigh. "I'm afraid, Mr. Haggerty, that Mr. Anderson is a little narrow in his definition of tolerance. He — er — appears to believe our engineering department is — er —— "

Blue Chip smiled and interrupted, "The worst manhandling I ever took, when I was a young toolmaker myself, was the time I called a young draftsman about my own age an overeducated baboon. Didn't find out till after I'd used a dollar's worth of beefsteak on my eyes that he was a champ heavyweight boxer at college."

As they started back to Professor Bickman's office, Billy Anderson hustled his apprentices back to their machines and caught up with Blue Chip out in the hall.

"Listen, Blue Chip, I'm quitting this teacher-dear stuff and going back to my old job on the jig borer. Right away in the morning. See?"

"Better think it over a little, don't you think, Billy?" Blue Chip was stalling for time. He had seen how the youngsters turned back to their machines, exchanging winks and grins. Regardless of how it might have appeared to Professor Bickman, it was plain that Billy Anderson was already the hero of his pupils. "Why, I thought you were doing fine. Those boys really understood what you meant by tolerance. It's the first thing they have to learn before they can be trusted out in the shop."

"I like the kids too," admitted Billy Anderson, though without yielding an inch. "But it ain't what I like or what you like, Blue Chip. I been elected the chairman of the shop grievance committee. It ain't going to look right, me wearing a white collar along with the bosses and then fronting for the boys in the shop when they got a kick to make."

"So now I got a grievance committee along with all my other worries, huh?" Blue Chip nodded slowly. "The boys sure picked the right chairman. You got the best eye for a grievance of any man in the shop."

Billy Anderson flicked a crackling eye across at Blue Chip. "When you start reaching for your crying towel, 's time for the other party to call out the Marines if he wants to keep his shirt. I've known you too long, Blue Chip. You never give away anything that belonged to the company yet. But you can't lick seven thousand men this time. See?"

"How soon is your grievance committee fixing to jump me, Billy?"

For a moment Billy Anderson squinted suspiciously, as if debating whether a straight answer was giving aid and comfort to the enemy. "We got a committee meeting tonight. We won't be keeping our squawk on ice long, you can bet."

"M'm'm," said Blue Chip. He dug out his stubby pipe and squeaked shrilly into the mouthpiece, then tapped the bowl on the heel of his huge hand. "In that case, I'd better stick on the job all night tonight. Got to figure out some way of hitting fifteen engines a day by the first of the month. Then, next month, I've promised Uncle Sam we'll be turning out twenty fast fighting engines a day."

"Fixing to pull the old speed-up on us, huh?" was Billy's caustic reaction.

"Nope." Blue Chip thumbed his pipe full and struck a match.

"Just worrying where I can pick up another thousand men who can work to the tolerance we've got to have to build these engines. On a guess, Billy, how many of the new boys in the school, would you say, will be fit to turn loose in the shop after a month's training?"

Billy Anderson got up, disgusted with such daydreaming. "Maybe six kids outta two hundred, you'll get. And as for a thousand new men what would know a machine-shop mike ain't a radio gimmick — well, I'll board free at my house every good mechanic you hire between now and the Fourth of July."

Billy stamped out. Blue Chip sighed and returned to his spacious chrome-trimmed office. It was five o'clock and he said to Miss Brown, his secretary, "Tell the cafeteria cashier to send me over a roast-beef sandwich and a glass of milk, about six."

Miss Brown took off her hat and hung it back on the bronze hat tree. "In that case, I'm staying too. If I don't, you'll keep on working until midnight or after, like you've already done three days this week."

"You run along," said Blue Chip gruffly. "I've got some thinking out loud to do. And some of it isn't going to be Sunday-school words."

Miss Brown pushed her typewriter into her desk with a rebellious thump. "I know a few words, too, I'd like to say to whoever it is that is working you to death, Mr. Haggerty. Look how slack the front of your vest is already, and you haven't had that new suit a month yet!"

Blue Chip relighted his pipe and reached for a mass of interoffice mail he had neglected all day. Acrid layers of thick blue tobacco smoke drifted to the far corner of the room, then dived silently into the bronze exhaust grill of the air-conditioning system. . . . At nine, Blue Chip reached for the sandwich on the aluminum tray that had been brought in without his noticing when. But instead of eating the sandwich immediately, he thumped the aluminum tray with a forefinger and wondered how soon it would be before he would have to send those thousands of trays in the cafeteria to the foundry to be recast into lightweight engine parts.

Ten o'clock came. The high-pitched hum of machine gears grew louder in volume as someone opened Blue Chip's office door. He thought it was the night janitor coming in to clean out the wastebaskets and dump the ash trays. His attention remained fixed on the sketches and sheets of figures covering his desk. The facts were there — hard facts that could not be sent to fit a man's wish or that cocksure promise he had made over long-distance to old P. G. Ashurst and Colonel Flightsby.

"Well!"

Blue Chip looked up and grunted with surprise at seeing Billy Anderson standing there at that time of night. Billy was not alone. Four other men in well-pressed suits and wearing neckties and looking the prosperous men they were stood behind Billy.

"Meet the grievance committee, Blue Chip," said Billy Anderson, flipping a jerky wrist toward his colleagues. "That's Pat Shacko in his new forty-dollar suit, case you don't recognize him outta his apron. . . . Mallory from Green Test, next. . . . Doc Baker from Gears. . . . And Conover from the Crankshaft line."

Blue Chip shifted his position in his chair to ease his cramped neck muscles and said, unperturbed — outwardly at least, "The sooner the better, I suppose. What's burning you, boys?"

"We had our first meeting tonight of the grievance committee," began Billy Anderson, chewing nervously on a half-smoked dead cigar. "First thing we took up was that bad accident to old man McCoy on the drill-press line."

"The hospital says he is getting along fine," interposed Blue Chip, then nodded for Billy to go on.

"Yeah, we phoned the hospital ourselves," said Billy coldly. "The main thing, that accident should 'a' never happened."

"He forgot to turn on the coolant before he started his tool into the work," explained Blue Chip, matter of fact. "The tool heated up and grabbed in the guide bushing and started the jig to flying around."

"He shouldn't have to remember not to forget stuff like that," retorted Billy. "Machines should be fixed so all a man has to keep his mind on is holding his tolerance.   And that's plenty when you're fighting tenths."

"That's a fair grievance," admitted Blue Chip, making a note. "I'll have the master mechanic's department put automatic control valves on all the coolant lines.   Anything else, boys?"

"Yeah, the big one." Billy stepped forward and leaned over the desk, rapping Blue Chip's notes with a knuckle.   "About this business of pushing twenty motors a day out of this shop by the end of next month.   We talked that over tonight.   You ain't going to get 'em with no thousand green men dumped in on us guys and borrowing our tools and bothering us when we're trying to split a tenth."

Blue Chip lifted his heavy eyebrows.   "We sure are going to make a stab at it, boys.   Every engine more per day we put out of this plant makes it just that much more certain we will continue to live in a country where a grievance committee can walk in and get it off their chest like you boys are doing right now.   Did you ever think of that side of it?"

Pat Shacko, standing at Billy's elbow, pocketed his own dead cigar and fished out a fresh one.   He bit off the end and expelled it with an impatient breath.

"C'mon and tell Blue Chip what we been jawing about together tonight, Billy."

Billy restored the shredded end of his cigar by stroking it with a forefinger while he looked sharply across the desk at Blue Chip.

"We all know you from way back, Blue Chip.   You're a driver. See?   The bosses pay big dough to a guy like you with the savvy that can make a shop hump."

A dull flush crept up Blue Chip's neck.   He got up slowly, stiffly, ponderously from his chair.   "What d'you think building fighting engines is — a strawberry festival?"   He swung a forefinger like a club under the committee's noses.   "I can put on an apron again and take over any machine in this plant and knock out a third more work than I've seen out of any of you.   And I can do it without raising a sweat."

"Yeah, and we know it!"   Billy Anderson broke out in a slow grin.

"That's just what we got on our chest, Blue Chip. So can we put out enough more. But who's going to make all the extra dough? Just the bosses?"

Blue Chip's anger cooled as if it had been doused with a bucket of ice water. "Now you're talking down my alley. You get me fifteen motors a day by the first of next month, and keep humping until I can get more men and machines, and there's ten per cent ante in it for every man's pay envelope. Except for the deadbeats and bums. I'm not paying for what I don't get!"

Billy Anderson turned to his now grinning colleagues of the grievance committee. He jerked his thumb over his shoulder at Blue Chip. "Didn't I tell you right? A boss that can see the makings of a good mechanic in a kid that's just spoiled a thousand dollars' worth of work has got something between his ears besides his hard nose." Billy Anderson stopped short, self-conscious at his unaccustomed show of sentiment. "Beat it, you guys, and get some sleep. It ain't no strawberry festival in front of us tomorrow."

But Pat Shacko did not leave with the others. He edged a step closer to where Blue Chip was standing and laid a dog-eared stock certificate on the desk blotter. "That's for being quick when Tom McCoy got hurt today. He's my brother-in-law, and I'd of had my sister and her three kids to look out for if —— It ain't worth much now, but soon's my first model rotary-valve engine is finished, it'll be like you owned that much of Henry Ford's stock."

Billy Anderson turned back and gave Pat Shacko a nudge with his thumb. "Get going and let this night owl go to roost." He lingered long enough to wink at Blue Chip and whisper, "I got some of that stock of Pat's too. Is it on the level that you're gonna let his apprentice class make a model of his screwy rotary-valve engine?"

"He's the boss there," said Blue Chip noncommittally.

"In that case," said Billy with a resigned shrug, "maybe I'd better have the kids in my class work on it too. Y'never can tell when one of these nut inventors is gonna hit for a million."

SIX P.M., P.S.T.

By Eddy Orcutt

THE CLOCK said 4:48. "Four forty-eight, Pacific Standard Time — four forty-eight, P.S.T.," mom told herself. "An hour and twelve minutes yet." In New York, by Eastern Time, Daylight-Saving Time, it would be nearing nine o'clock. There, where Ernie was, it would be night, all the streets and high buildings blazing their million lights against the summer dark. The fight mob would be already jamming the Garden, jamming the floor and the balconies and galleries, clamoring its million mob noises into the half-dark around and above the floodlighted ring. And Ernie was there. There where the night was, where the lights and the noises and the mob were, and the roped-in square of canvas under the ring lamps.

Mom was afraid suddenly, and alone.

". . . a motherly little woman in a comfortable Ingleside home," Jimmy Porter's column that morning had called her.

This home fronted a lawn and a quiet street where the trees were very old. This living room was dark and high and old-fashioned, smelling a little of dad's pipe tobacco, and of roses left overnight on the center table, and of sun-dried eucalyptus leaves from the trees outside. A strip of westering sunlight shone beneath mom's new Venetian blinds, and the room still held thin heat and the perfume of mown grass from the airless California day.

The clock said 4:49. Another minute gone.

"But I want him to win — I want him to!" mom said. She said it aloud, though, in this empty room, and her fear was that it was a lie. Her fear was that she wanted her own boy to lose tonight, to be beaten. And then, crowding up out of the dark place where she had kept it locked for so long, came another fear. The fear that

Ernie might win, that he might be champion, that he might not be her own boy any more. That fear came, and loneliness.

Champion. Middleweight champion of the world.

The two fears mingled, fused, crowded up out of the dark, and mom fought to bring her mind's eye back to this home, to this room. She fought to keep her own sudden panic from speeding out into the New York night, into the fight mob, into the Garden's lights and high shadows. She fought to keep it from speeding to the place where Ernie waited, fought to keep it from touching Ernie, hurting him.

Ernie Conlan. Tuffy Conlan. Mom's baby. ". . . the tough, crowding left-hooker, trial horse of the middleweights, who gets his big chance tonight in the Garden ring."

The phone rang, out in the hall. Mom reached it quickly, wanting to feel the instrument solid in her hand, a thing to hold on to. She made her voice calm. ". . . No, not at all. No trouble at all. . . . Just fine," mom said. . . . "Yes, of course, we think he'll win — we hope so." Handling a part of her job, one more chore in the day's routine, mom steadied. . . . "Just one more fight," mom said — the routine phrase, the routine smile. And when the call ended, she added, unhurriedly, one more name to the list on the phone pad. Mrs. Shane. Harry Tobey. Bill Wright. Ken McCabe, of the Register. Mrs. Laws. Half a dozen others. But then, after the new name was added, there was another moment empty of things for Ernie's mother to do. Until dad came home — until dad and the young ones came, gathering here for the fight broadcast — mom's work was done. For a moment she stood there by the silent phone, trapped by this emptiness and afraid of her fear.

But they'll be here any time now, she told herself.

A breeze moved outdoors, and a draft stirred in the hall. It had the homey smell of the old house in it, and the smells of mom's house-keeping — cedar and soap and cleanser and fresh linen, and a cool hint of kitchen smells, like the aroma of bread fresh-baked. All day, since the stroke of seven, mom had kept busy in the house. But that was ended now, and the house was ready — the house was waiting.

"That's the tough part — waiting. That's really tough." It was Ernie, mom remembered, who had said that.

And in New York now, in the dressing room, Cop Robinson would be wrapping Ernie's hands. Mom knew how those hands looked. She knew the pattern of the white gauze, thin strips of adhesive between the knuckles, and the final shape of the bandage on the hard, square-cut fists. In a sudden, unexpected way, she could see Ernie. Ernie, and the boy's crooked eyebrow, the small quirk of his upper lip. Only now the kid would be sullen, intent, no trace of the grin so much like dad's. He would be holding his hand steady, helping the Cop turn a width of gauze around the thumb, clenching a fist slowly for a snug fit, not too tight. Somebody from Stanley Krovac's corner would be there, watching. The Cop would work slowly, exactly, taking his time. And they would be waiting, all of them. The tough part. Waiting.

In the living room the clock chimes played their music-box tune, and the slow gong struck five. An hour. One hour more.

"Not yet! Not quite yet!" mom said.

In that other moment mom had wanted the family to come quickly. Claire first, probably. Then dad, ducking the office early. Then Bob and Marian, Marty and Irma — to be here tonight, Marty had traded shifts on the dispatcher's board at the union airport. Mom had wanted them here. She had wanted them to crowd this house and the empty room, settle themselves, talk to her, keep her busy. But now her lips moved silently and she asked them to wait. To wait just a minute. To give her one last chance to remember Ernie and all the story that would end tonight in the Garden ring. To-night at six P.M. In an hour. Six P.M., P.S.T.

He'll win; I know he will. The fear ached with loneliness.

Ernie was the baby, the little fella. Claire was two years older, and Bob was five years older. Marty, Jr., the oldest, was now thirty-four, seven years older than Ernie. And Ernie somehow had been the one who got the bad breaks, the solitary one, the one who did not quite belong. "It was our fault," mom said, and she had said it a thousand times. The story was hers too. Dad's. The family's.

Ernie had been only eight when dad moved the family down to Central Avenue, his first big job for Zellermann's markets. Dad had won his promotion to Westlake seven years later.

Seven years. Mom remembered the weary mornings before daylight, hundreds of them, endless numbers of them, when dad's day at the store began at 6:30. She remembered him in the mornings, walking to work, and the gray fatigue in his face at night, getting home after dark. Seven years of it. Those years, and so many others, were warm now with heartache and pride and regret.

On Central Avenue, in the tough edge of the Terminal district, Marty and Bob had been big enough to help mom look out for Claire. Ernie's way of helping, mom knew later, had been to look out for himself. And the rough lessons Ernie learned there were later the seeds of trouble. At Westlake, when the family finally moved, Ernie suddenly was grown up — fifteen then, a sophomore transfer at Jefferson High, a silent kid, sturdy, sober-faced. "Tuffy. Tuffy Conlan, the bad man from Central Avenue." He played football against lads who outweighed him forty pounds, and the smart kids at Jefferson tagged him with his nickname, "Tuffy Conlan, the bad man —— "

"Well, if he wants to fight," the gray policeman said, "why not let him? Why not learn him how?"

Some of mom's memories hurt. Truant officers and vice-principals and the smart gals from the probation office had failed, and there was a day when a policeman brought Ernie home from school. That was the Cop — Cop Robinson — Special Officer J. N. Robinson, he was then. Tonight the Cop would be handling Ernie's corner in the Garden, taking a cut of his purse. But mom remembered that first meeting, the Cop's gray glance, and the odd, harsh warmth of his tone to the kid.

"Why be a chump?" the Cop had asked. "Why fritz yourself up with a bunch of high-school punks? You could really fight."

Eleven years ago. Nearly twelve.

The clock said 5:04. And now, when mom wanted it to lag, time hurried and the memories crowded one another, jumbling the years.

With Cop Robinson, Ernie had begun going down to the Garvanza
A.C., afternoons and Saturdays, tackling the tough textbook that the
gray policeman had conned in his own young days. The Cop was
not so old as he looked, and he had crawled through the ropes against
Wolgast and Britt and Willie Ritchie and Mexican Joe Rivers. . . .

"This is a jab — like this, mom. . . . With a sidestep, you pivot
on the left and step off on the right, see? Watch my left foot. . . .
Mom, if I got to be a real good fighter, you wouldn't mind?
I wouldn't ever be just a dumb slugger." The time had come when
Ernie, the little fella, had bits of shop talk to bring home to mom.
Like Marty, years before, exploring the Morse code with a dime-store
buzzer, or Bob, with his nitrate-stained fingers, coming home late and
hungry from the chem lab at S.C. Tech. Or like the gangling young
grocery clerk mom had married so many years ago, lying awake
sometimes after a fourteen-hour day to talk about some new angle
dug out from the drudgery. . . . "Once I get the left hook down
pat, mom — look, it murders these right-hand punchers!" Awkward, bashful bits of shop talk, at first. Mom smiled a little now,
remembering.

Swiftly, in mom's daydream, the story grew. Ernie, the strange
trade he followed, places glimpsed through Ernie's eyes, bits of shop
talk, names. . . . Frankie Muma, the Sacramento Kid. Schoolboy
Frayne. Lefty Murdoch. . . . "You can't jab a southpaw — you
got to trade best hands with 'm." . . . A post card from Rube Taylor's old-time gym in San Francisco. Stillman's in New York.
Mother Showley's camp at Jersey Lakes. Murray's Rink in the
Bronx, and the dressing rooms on a winter night. The Stadium,
Chicago, with a pipe organ playing between bouts. Mom knew these
things — in imagination, from glimpses, from endless talk — as she
knew the signal tower in the Terminal Belt Line yard, where Marty
got his first job, or Bob's cubby at Western Chemical, high above the
battery of digestion vats, or dad's downtown office in the new Zellermann Building. Twelve years. Nearly twelve years.

Ernie was there, vivid in the daydream. He had needed her so
much, in small, homey ways, through all those years. He had come
home to her so often. He had been so much hers. Mom's boy.

"But this is the big one, mom! They figure I got no chance, but I might fool 'em! I might lick this fella!"

And now the fear, too, was vivid. Fear that the boy might win — fear that the big win, the fool title, would somehow end the story. Mom's odd smattering of ring lore made the title a cruel, mystic thing, with an aura of big money, champagne, girls, the night spots in the big town. A champion would not be needing mom's way of setting out a platter of ham and eggs, her way of pressing a necktie in a hurry, her way of settling the boy down in the kitchen for a long talk, just the two of them.

"Don't let it end! Don't!" mom said.

But a clock ticked and the time hurried. At a stroke of the clock, at a time set, Ernie would touch gloves with Stanley Krovac, champion, under the ring lamps. Ernie. The little fella. "Just another fight," mom had been telling people, but it was not true.

"Champion," the echo said. "Champion of the world."

Mom went hurriedly into the hall. Claire should be here now. Dad would be on the way, surely. Marian, Bob's wife, would be stopping for Bob at Western Chemical. Marty and Irma. Mom saw them all in her mind, saw each of them. For them, in this home, she would have to be calm and steady — they would be needing that, the way a fighter needs a calm and steady man behind his corner when the bell rings. But now in mom's mind that fear bred other fears. She began a prayer, "Please, our Father in heaven —— "

A car was sliding into the driveway, and mom was glad, suddenly, that she did not have to know what the rest of her prayer might be.

"Claire's right behind me; I passed her," dad said.

Dad came toward her along the walk flanked by slender tree roses and flooded with level sunlight. He grinned up at her, flushed with excitement. A stocky man, gray, now fifty-four years old, but with an odd, boylike simplicity about him. The later, easier years bring that look, sometimes, to a man who has missed boyhood.

"How are you, mother — all right?" he asked.

"Fine," mom said. "I'm just fine."

* * *

They gave mom the wing chair beside the radio. "Lean back, mom. Relax," they told her. But now her laugh was easier than theirs, quieter, and hers was the steady voice in the room's hush and the queer tension.

". . . perpetual care," the radio blared. "Wurfel's Elysian Memorial Field —— "

Bob, at the dial, clicked it off. Dad leaned forward from his place on the couch, across the room.

"Don't cut it too fine, Bob. We want to get all of it," mom said. The clock showed 5:57.

Bob's grin was nervous. "Three minutes to go yet."

Marian, Bob's wife, giggled suddenly.

"Three minutes more," Irma said, "and I'll be screaming."

"That'd be the first time," mom told her, chuckling.

Irma, tall and blond, the prettiest of the three girls, tried an answering smile. Dad, sitting between Irma and Marian, grinned a little, and Marty laughed. Marty stood tall in the doorway, his hands locked behind his back. Tension came quickly back into the room. They were waiting.

"Better turn it on again," mom said evenly.

The radio gave out organ music from Wurfel's Elysian Chapel.

"You asked for it," Bob cracked. But the corny music blurred away into a fade-out, and mom glanced up at the clock.

". . . every Monday, Wednesday and Friday evening at this same hour," the radio announced. "And now good night."

"Everybody quiet!" dad ordered suddenly.

His voice was high-pitched, harsh, and the foolish command was not like him.

"Take it easy," mom said, holding the shape of a smile.

Mom shut the fear far back in her mind, locked it away, hiding it from the people in this room, as she would have kept it hidden from Ernie. KNMT gave them station identification, network identification, then a distant, empty hum before the Garden ringside came in.

A good corner man don't get excited, except maybe on purpose, mom remembered.

"Good evening, fight fans of America!"

It began callously, briskly, on the chimes' foolish tune and the slow stroke of the clock. It bridged three thousand miles, branched in a million directions.

"Here we go," Irma said.

Dad edged farther forward.

". . . the bell for the last round of the semifinal. And here beside me, ready to give you the blow-by-blow picture —— "

"Who cares!" dad muttered. "Who cares!"

For mom the crowd's noise now smothered the talk from the ringside. Into this room came overtones from that last round in the distant ring, overtones from the mob — a cruel, urgent, growing clamor — and all the noises blended now into a nightmare noise. The last moment of Ernie's wait was now ending. Ending hurriedly, too soon, the crowd's clamor smearing the swift, intent, relentless movement of time. In this moment, mom knew, she might be in Ernie's mind, as he was in hers. Then the moment would end. Then he would be alone. Then he would be gone. That word echoed. That fear hammered in the noises, thinly, far back. Mom realized that she made some small sound.

The radio covered it: ". . . decision to Izzy Retzlaff, the Brooklyn boy — a mighty tired boy now. Let's listen to the crowd give him a hand!"

Mom gripped the wing of her chair. *I want Ernie to win. I want him to.* Not aloud, this time. Not fearing it for a lie. Not knowing it for the truth. Saying it, though. Saying words.

And then Madison Square Garden's great roaring filled the room: ". . . the champion, Stanley Krovac, moving down the aisle. . . . And now the challenger, the California boy, reaches the ring ledge. His gray-haired manager spreads the ropes for 'm. . . . He's entering the ring now!"

"That's Ernie!" dad said loudly.

This home, this room with sunset glinting the ivory bands of the blind at the west window, merged, now, with an arena three thousand miles away. In the ring of that arena Ernie Conlan walked to the resin box, scuffed his ring shoes in it, tested his ring shoes on the stained canvas.

"Ernie Conlan — Tuffy Conlan, they call him — has been around quite a while, and he came up the hard way. As a welterweight, the California slugger — he's the club-fighter type, and a crowd-pleaser — fought boys like Dan Latzo and Barney Cool. In the middleweight division, though, he reached national ranking only a few months ago, when —— "

Angry, dad repeated, " 'Slugger! Club fighter!' "

"He'll fool 'em!" Bob said, too loudly.

Mom looked at them. In this room now, they were all ringsiders, and mom searched with a glance for some last glimmer of a feeling like her own. Bob. Marian. Claire. Marty. Irma. Dad. Ernie's dad was a man watching the ring, staring up into the ring lamps, waiting for the bell's clang.

"Krovac, the champion, is one of the wickedest punchers in the ring today. A build like you read about. Dead-white skin, dead-black hair, black eyes. Poker-faced, coming out from his corner now, like a jungle cat pacing a cage!"

The room and the arena merged. The mob crowded in, and the noises of the mob, and mom was alone.

At the ringside, engineers tinkered their gear. The mixers brought in the crowd's roar, then cut to the ring: ". . . both you boys are familiar widda rules; I do' need t' go inta 'm. I wanna see a good, clean exabition now. I wanna see ya —— "

The referee was talking to Stanley Krovac, talking to Ernie, standing very close, talking. Mom held her breath, hoping to hear Ernie breathe, hoping to hear a word from him, standing so close.

"Turn it up higher, Bob."

And then mom heard the bell.

"Tuffy Conlan comes out fast, half crouching, but Krovac meets 'm in the center of the ring. Krovac jabs his left — a left to the face! Another left! Another — moving away! Conlan wants to get in

close — wants to crowd in — but Krovac jabs, breaks back! He
shoots a left to the face! The boxing master with dynamite in his
right hand! Tuffy still tries to move in —— "

"Ah-h-h!" dad snarled.

The ringside call went gunning ahead, choppy, staccato with excitement: "That jab again! Krovac with a left to the head! Another! Tuffy Conlan takes it, bores in . . . another jab!"

But mom took a quiet breath, and her hand on the chair arm slowly
unclenched. Ernie's waiting was ended. He was working at his
trade now. Fighting.

"Now it's Conlan! A hard left to the body, but Krovac goes away,
still jabbing! Conlan runs him into the ropes. No damage."

The first round ended. But even when the gong rang for the next,
mom leaned back, her mind alert, but her body relaxed. The fight
went on.

The fight was a sharp, hammering pattern of noise. A break at
the round's end, and a change of announcers. A change of pace.
Then the ten-second buzzer. Then the bell's distorted clang. Then
the fight again — the machinegun staccato from the ringside, the
sounds in the ring, the mob's obbligato.

In that pattern of noise, mom saw the fight.

Through the second, through the third round, Ernie bored in
against the champ's flashing left hand. The champ flicked that left,
or drove it straight, tormenting Ernie or jolting him off balance. In
the third, though, when the champ threw his right hand, it was high.
He threw it again, and missed. He charged in, shooting that right,
but Ernie got under it, in close. And mom began to sense a kind of
logic — a stubborn, sweated, frightening logic — in the noise the
fight made.

"Ernie ain't untracked yet. He ain't fighting his fight," dad said.
Mom heard his high, uneven voice, and other voices.

At the end of the third, there was an edge of anger in the mob's
noise — anger at the plugging, battered logic in Ernie Conlan's
march. The mike blotted it suddenly: ". . . and I know that you
men will be glad to hear a cordial invitation, at this time, from Stein-

beck, the Nation's Tailor." A third announcer mooed through the commercial.

"Ernie! Come on now, Ernie!" dad groaned.

But mom knew, with a chill that was like joy and like shame, that the champion was measuring Ernie for that right-hand blast again.

Round four.

Later — long later, it seemed to mom — came the sudden shift in the pattern of the noise. The stubborn march led Ernie into the dynamite's path, and there was a flash of time when mom saw him breaking back into the ropes. The mob's yell went high and shrill. The champ whipped his right hand over in long, raking blows, and Ernie staggered. Further along, toward the end of the sixth, mom saw the boy stumble, sink back to the canvas. Then, very slowly, he got to his knees.

"Six! . . . Seven! . . . Eight! . . . He's up! He's boring in again, bulling his way in, trying to clinch! Krovac fires another terrific right to the head! High! Tuffy ties 'm up!"

And then there was the queer moment at the end of a round — at the end of the eighth — when Ernie's mother added up all the noises, all these flashes of the fight, and knew what the end would be. Knew finally, without question, desperately afraid.

"He'll snap out of it!" dad cried. "He'll —— "

Mom looked at the people in the room. They were afraid too.

The bell rang. "And here's round nine! Round nine, Tuffy Conlan and Stanley Krovac, for the world's middleweight title! And here comes Krovac! Coming out like a panther!"

But now mom was waiting — not for the end, but for what might come after the end. "That's the tough part — waiting."

Ernie did not go down in the ninth. In the ninth Krovac hammered at him savagely, whistling the right across. The crowd's yell was high, incessant, screaming.

"That's it! No, a little high! Tuffy's breaking back, staggering! . . . That right hand! He's got Tuffy on the ropes! Tuffy's away again!"

The noise yelled for the knockout, the kill. But the ninth ended, and the high screaming went on into the tenth.

And in the tenth. A sudden shock. Silence. A silence incredibly swift, incredibly brief. Then, in the Garden mob and in the room where mom sat, the roar was a solid thunder. There in the tenth, with Stanley Krovac finally throwing all that he had, throwing it savagely with his right hand and following it for the kill, there was the thin edge of a split second when Ernie set himself, shifted and hooked his left. Then that shock of silence. Then that thunder.

"Kovac's down! The champ is down!"

Mom waited.

Stanley Krovac went down slowly. Slowly, still a champion, he got up again. He got up at "seven." The thunder pounded on. The keening terror of the mob's blood yell topped it. And in the last, relentless logic of the fight's cruel pattern, Ernie Conlan cut the champion down, slaughtered him with left hands and a chopping right.

The end came. The knockout.

"Two twenty-nine of the tenth! Two twenty-nine! They're carrying Krovac to his corner. And now, up in the ring —— "

Through the clamor of other noises, the radio carried the announcer's booming, official voice: "The . . . winner! . . . And new . . . champion —— " And in the ring, in Ernie's corner, they were going to get Ernie's own voice on the air: "Tuffy! Tuffy Conlan —— "

Now, in the room dad was throwing his arms around mom, hugging her. The young ones were all but yelling in her ear, the boys pawing at her with clumsy hands, frolicking like young animals. "Mom! Mom! You booted him home again! Mom!"

With a queer, tardy thrill, mom recaptured that high moment in the ring — remembered Ernie, the little fella, the long years, the tough plugging and the stubborn battles. Then that climax when the little fella had tricked a champion into a crazed, reckless, right-hand attack. That gasp of silence, and the thunder and the mob's high screaming.

"Mom!" they cried, in the room. Deep in mom's heart the thrill died, and her boy was gone, and the terror was like a weight of metal, cold.

"Listen! Listen, Ernie's coming on!"

And for mom, when they made their breathless, proud hush in this room, when they looked at her, making the room exultant and secret for her, a desperate, swift hope flared. Now Ernie would say hello to her. "Hello, mother," he would say. "Hello, mom." That was routine — part of the fight broadcast, mom knew. But tonight — tonight it would be Ernie. It would be different. Listening desperately, mom hoped that some word of his, one word, a tone in his voice, would bring the boy close again, let her know surely and secretly that he still was hers.

The radio's dial glowed in the darkening room, faces turned toward mom, and mom listened.

Ernie's voice came over. The voice was flat, gasping, hurried. "I think I beat a great champion . . . a great fighter, a good guy, a great champion. If I can be a great champ like he was . . . well, I'd like to do it. I — I got to duck out now, Mac. I got to hurry. Thanks, Mac. . . . Thank you, everybody out there."

Then the ring noises, the noises from the ringside again, and the announcer going briskly into the summary and the sign-off.

And in the room, a moment with no sound at all.

". . . returning you now to your local stations."

Mom lied to them, taking care of them. Taking care of Ernie, too, in a way — covering up for him. "I never did want that 'Hi, mom' stuff," mom said. "Ernie knew it; I asked him not to." Some final spark of her own magic gave warmth to her lie, and her lie brought warmth again suddenly into the room. "A champion! A champion in the family!" mom said. "What do you think of the baby brother now?"

In the hall the phone began to ring.

"I'll get it!" dad cried. . . . And mom led the laugh at dad's broad grin, at the small-boy glow in dad's eyes.

Mom stood up. Ernie would send a wire; he might even telephone, she told herself. Somehow he still might reach her, mom told herself.

"Now for supper!" mom said. She did not give up her waiting. But she kept her waiting hidden, deep down and secret, in the place where her fear had been.

Into the phone dad yelled, "Oh, boy! Oh, boy! . . . No, no, listen! We knew he'd pull something! That kid! That Ernie!"

In the dining room the girls put out the big family platter of cold cuts, the big bowl of green salad. Marty sliced the long loaves of rye bread.

The telephone rang again. "Hello. . . . Hi, hello!" dad yelled.

Mom answered the doorbell — the Martins, from across the street.

"Oh, isn't it great! Isn't it marvelous!" Mrs. Martin gushed.

And mom laughed with her. "Yes, it's great."

Now the house was noisy, strangers were coming in, and mom's waiting was easier to hide, but lonelier.

A telegram came. Dad sang out, "Look! Here's one from the boss — one from old Zellermann, up in San Francisco!"

The phone rang again.

From the dining room Bob called, "Come an' get it!"

The doorbell.

"Did you hear from Ernie yet?" Mrs. Martin asked.

"Heavens to goodness! Tonight?" mom countered.

At eight o'clock mom heard the clock chimes — midnight in New York. Champion. Big money now. The big time. Lights glowing in the night spots, new friends crowding in, girls, handshakers, big shots. A night to celebrate — the end of a long, tough climb. The end. Mom shut the picture out of her mind. . . . "Hello! Hello. My, it's nice of you to come in!" She greeted neighbors, other friends, a grinning young reporter from the Register. Into the telephone she heard dad say, "That knockdown? That was just a stall. Erni was leading 'm on!" Mom winked at the reporter. More telegrams came in, five in one bunch.

"You people that haven't eaten; step right up! It's on the house!" Bob called. "Victory Cafeteria!"

Eight-thirty passed. Nine o'clock. Ten.

The word from Ernie did not come.

"It's been great! Gee," dad said, "it's been great!"

Because time passed, and the confusion ebbed finally, and sheer weariness blurred the end of mom's waiting. The crowd was gone at last. The young ones, and the wives, and the outsiders. All the people were gone at last, and the doorbell silent and the phone silent. "Gee! Gee, it's been great!" And the end of mom's waiting was gone too.

Dad fell asleep like a tired boy, and mom rested, finally, watching a panel of slow moonlight move across their bedroom wall. Outside, that high moonlight would be a bridge in the sky, blending the night here with morning in the East. For a moment she envied Marty, in the airport tower, looking toward New York, toward morning.

Morning. In the morning.

And in the morning — late morning, nearly noon — mom came to know the strange, new feel of the house, this home, now that Ernie was finally gone. Telegrams came, tardy phone calls, interrupting her work, but none from Ernie, and finally mom had the house clean and shining again, aired out, its open windows shaded against the sun. She had the feel of clean bedrooms in the house, polished bathrooms, fresh linen, floors dust-mopped and gleaming. All the house was quiet, with coolness in it, a breath of air stirring through it from the lawn and the tall trees outside. And in the empty house there was a kind of quiet pride, all its waiting ended and all its loneliness concealed. Now it was mom's house.

Mom set coffee to perking in the kitchen.

"Salad's best the morning after," she told herself, opening the icebox, trying to believe that food would cure her hunger.

The doorbell rang again. Mom closed the icebox. Mom schooled herself to accept another telegram, sign for it unhurriedly, wait until the boy had gone before she tore open the envelope. Mom went carefully into the hall.

Ernie said, "I figured it right!"

He had opened the screen door and come in. The wide oblong

of bright sunlight was behind him, and a taxicab moving slowly, backing out of the drive.

"Eight hundred and fifty bucks," Ernie said. "I missed the airliner — had to charter a plane. I'd have wired you, mom, but I —— " Against the doorway, he was very tall. He was taking in the clean pattern of mom's house dress, the quiet of the cool room, the smell of coffee from the kitchen. "Look, I kind of wanted to celebrate. I wanted to catch you alone. You know, just you and me. I —— " That crooked eyebrow of his made a frown, and he got the words out fast. Ernie grinned at mom suddenly, his lip still puffed from a champion's gloves and those ten rounds in the Garden ring. "Hi! Hello, mom!" Ernie said.

The bright blur of the sun was in mom's eyes then, but her two hands reached out. Ernie's broad shoulders were very broad. His arms were very strong.

"Hello, Ernie," mom said. "Hello, champion!"

THE WEDDING GIFT

By *Thomas H. Raddall*

NOVA SCOTIA, in 1794. Winter. Snow on the ground. Two feet
of it in the woods; less by the shore, except in drifts against Port
Marriott's barns and fences, but enough to set sleigh bells ringing
through the town, enough to require a multitude of paths and bur-
rows from door to road, to carpet the wharves, and the decks of
ships, and trim the ships' yards with tippets of ermine. Enough
to keep fires roaring in the town's chimneys, and blue wood
smoke hanging in a cloud low over the roof tops in the still December air. Enough to squeal underfoot in the trodden places, and
to muffle the step everywhere else. Enough for the hunters, whose
snowshoes could now overtake with ease the floundering moose and
caribou. Even enough for the always-complaining loggers, who
could now take their ox sleds anywhere in the woods. But not
enough, not nearly enough snow for Miss Kezia Barnes, who was
going to Bristol Creek to marry Mr. Hathaway.

Kezia did not want to marry Mr. Hathaway. She had told Mr.
and Mrs. Barclay tearfully that she didn't want to marry anybody.
But Mr. Barclay had taken snuff and said "Ha! Humph!" in the
hard way he used when he was displeased; and Mrs. Barclay had
sniffed and said it was a very good match for her, and revolved the
cold blue eyes in her fat moon face, and said Kezia must not be a little
fool.

There were two ways of going to Bristol Creek. One was by
sea, in one of the fishing sloops. But the preacher objected to that.
He was a pallid young man, lately sent out from England by Lady
Huntingdon's Connexion, and seasick five weeks on the way. He
held Mr. Barclay in some awe, for Mr. Barclay had the finest pew in
the meetinghouse and was the chief pillar of godliness in Port Mar-

riott. But young Mr. Mears was firm on this point. He would go
by road, he said, or not at all. Mr. Barclay had retorted "Ha!
Humph!" The "road" was twenty miles of horse path through
the woods, now deep in snow. Also the path began at Harper's
Farm, on the far side of the harbor, and Harper had but one horse.

"I shall walk," declared the preacher calmly, "and the young woman
can ride."

Kezia had prayed for snow, storms of snow, enough to bury the
trail and keep anyone from crossing the cape to Bristol Creek. But
now they were setting out from Harper's Farm, with Harper's big
brown horse, and all Kezia's prayers had gone for naught. Like any
anxious lover, busy Mr. Hathaway had sent Black Sam overland on
foot to find out what delayed his wedding, and now Sam's day-old
tracks marked for Kezia the road to marriage.

She was a meek little thing, as became an orphan house help
brought up in the Barclay home; but now she looked at the preacher,
and saw how young and helpless he looked so far from his native
Yorkshire, and how ill-clad for this bitter transatlantic weather, and
she spoke up, "You'd better take my shawl, sir. I don't need it.
I've got Miss Julia's old riding cloak. And we'll go ride-and-tie."

"Ride and what?" murmured Mr. Mears.

"I'll ride about a mile, then I'll get down and tie the horse and walk
on. When you come up to the horse, you mount and ride him a
mile, and tie him, and walk on. Like that. Ride-and-tie, ride-and-
tie. The horse gets a rest between."

Young Mr. Mears nodded and took the proffered shawl absently.
It was a black thing, and matched his sober broadcloth coat and
smallclothes, and his black woolen stockings and his round-brimmed
black hat. Very sensibly — and it was really Mr. Barclay's suggestion
— he had borrowed a pair of moose-hide moccasins for the journey.
A prayer book in his coat skirts bumped the back of his legs as he
walked.

At the top of the ridge above Harper's pasture, where the narrow
path led off through gloomy hemlock woods, Kezia paused for a last
look back across the harbor. In the morning sunlight the white roofs

of the little lonely town resembled a tidal wave flung up by the sea and frozen on point of breaking against the dark pine forest to the west. Kezia sighed, and young Mr. Mears was surprised to see tears in her eyes.

She rode off ahead. The saddle was a man's, of course, awkward to ride modestly, woman-fashion. As soon as she was out of the preacher's sight she rucked her skirts and slid a leg over to the other stirrup. That was better. There was a pleasant sensation of freedom about it. For a moment she forgot that she was going to Bristol Creek, in finery secondhand from the Barclay girls, in linen shift and drawers that she had sewn herself in the light of the kitchen candles, in white cotton stockings and a bonnet and shoes from Mr. Barclay's store, to marry Mr. Hathaway.

The Barclays had really done well for her, from the time when, a skinny, weeping creature of fourteen, she was taken into the Barclay household and, as Mrs. Barclay so often said, "treated more like one of my own than a bond girl from the poorhouse." She had first choice of the clothing cast off by Miss Julia and Miss Clara. She was permitted to sit in the same room, and learn what she could, when the schoolmaster came to give private lessons to the Barclay girls. She waited on table, of course, and helped in the kitchen, and made beds, and dusted and scrubbed. But then, she had been taught to spin and to sew and to knit; and she was permitted, indeed encouraged, to sit with the Barclays in the meetinghouse at the convenient end of the pew, where she could worship the Barclays' God and assist with the Barclay wraps at the beginning and end of the service. And now, to complete her rewards, she had been granted the hand of a rejected Barclay suitor.

Mr. Hathaway was Barclay's agent at Bristol Creek, where he sold rum and gunpowder and corn meal and such things to the fishermen and hunters, and bought split cod — fresh, pickled or dry — and ran a small sawmill, and cut and shipped firewood by schooner to Port Marriott, and managed a farm, all for a salary of fifty pounds, Halifax currency, a year.

He was a most capable fellow, Barclay often acknowledged; but when, after fifteen capable years at Bristol Creek, he came seeking a wife, and cast a sheep's eye first at Miss Julia, and then at Miss Clara, Mrs. Barclay observed with a sniff that Hathaway was looking a bit high. So he was. The older daughter of Port Marriott's most prosperous merchant was even then receiving polite attentions from Mr. Gamage, the new collector of customs, and a connection of the Halifax Gamages, as Mrs. Barclay was fond of pointing out. And Miss Clara was going to Halifax in the spring to learn the gentle art of playing the pianoforte, and incidentally to display her charms to the naval and military young gentlemen who thronged Halifax drawing rooms.

The dear girls laughed behind their hands whenever long solemn Mr. Hathaway came to town aboard one of the Barclay vessels and called at the big house under the elms. Mrs. Barclay bridled at Hathaway's presumption, but shrewd Mr. Barclay narrowed his little black eyes and took snuff and said "Ha!   Humph!"

It was plain to Mr. Barclay that an emergency had arisen.   Hathaway was a good man — in his place; and Hathaway must be kept there, to go on making money for Mr. Barclay at fifty pounds a year. 'Twas a pity Hathaway couldn't content himself with one of the fishermen's girls at the Creek, but there 'twas.   Hathaway had set his mind on a town miss, so a town miss he must have.   But she must be the right kind, the sort who would content herself and Hathaway at Bristol Creek and not go nagging the man to remove and try his capabilities elsewhere.

At once Mr. Barclay thought of Kezia — dear little Kezzie.   A colorless little creature, but quiet and well-mannered, and only twenty-two.

Mr. Hathaway was nearly forty, and far from handsome, and had a cold, seeking way about him — useful in business, of course — that rubbed women the wrong way.   Privately Mr. Barclay thought Hathaway lucky to get Kezia.   But it was a nice match for the girl, better than anything she could have expected.   He impressed that upon her.

Mr. Hathaway spent two or three evenings courting Kezzie in the kitchen — Kezzie in a quite good dress of Miss Clara's, gazing out at the November moon on the snow, and murmuring now and again in the tones of somebody in a rather dismal trance, while the kitchen help listened behind one door and the Barclay girls giggled behind another.

The decision, reached mainly by the Barclays, was that Mr. Hathaway should come to Port Marriott aboard the packet schooner on December twenty-third, to be married in the Barclay parlor, and take his bride home for Christmas. But an unforeseen circumstance had changed all this. The circumstance was a ship, "from Mogador in Barbary," as Mr. Barclay wrote afterward in the salvage claim, driven off her course by gales and wrecked at the very entrance to Bristol Creek. She was a valuable wreck, laden with such queer things as goatskins in pickle, almonds, wormseed, pomegranate skins and gum arabic, and capable Mr. Hathaway lost no time in salvage for the benefit of his employer. He could not come to Port Marriott for a wedding or anything else. A storm might blow up at any time and demolish this fat prize. He dispatched a note by Black Sam, urging Mr. Barclay to send Kezia and a preacher by return; it was not the orthodox note of an impatient sweetheart, but it said that he had moved into his new house by the wharf and found it "extream empty," and it suggested delicately that while his days were full, the nights were dull.

Kezia was no judge of distance. She rode for what she considered a reasonable amount of time and then slid off and tied the brown horse to a maple tree.

She had brought a couple of lamp wicks to tie about her shoes, to keep them from coming off in the snow, and she set out afoot in the big splayed tracks of Black Sam. The soft snow came almost to her knees and she lifted her skirts high.

The path was no wider than the span of a man's arms, cut out with axes years before. She stumbled over a concealed stump from time to time, and the huckleberry bushes dragged at her cloak, but the effort warmed her. It had been cold, sitting on the horse with the wind blowing up her legs.

After a time the preacher came up, riding awkwardly and holding the reins in a nervous grip. The stirrups were too short for his long black-stockinged legs. He called out cheerfully, "Are you all right, miss?" as he passed.

She nodded, standing aside with her back to a tree. When he disappeared ahead, with the black shawl tassels fluttering in the wind, she picked up her skirts again and went on. The path climbed and dropped monotonously over a succession of wooded ridges. Here and there in a hollow she heard water running, and the creak of frosty poles underfoot, and knew she was crossing a brook, and once the trail ran across a wide swamp on half-rotten corduroy, bare of snow. She found the horse tethered clumsily not far ahead, and the tracks of the preacher going on.

She had to lead the horse to a stump, so she could mount, and when she passed Mr. Mears again she called out, "Please, sir, next time leave the horse by a rock or something, so I can get on."

In his quaint old-country accent he murmured, "I'm very sorry," and gazed down at the snow. She forgot she was riding astride until she had passed him, and she flushed, and gave the indignant horse a cut of the switch. Next time she remembered and swung her right leg back where it should be and tucked the skirts modestly about her ankles; but young Mr. Mears stared at the snow anyway, and after that she did not trouble to shift when she overtook him.

The ridges became steeper, and streams roared under the ice and snow in the swales. They emerged on the high table between Port Marriott and Bristol Creek, a gusty wilderness of young hardwood scrub struggling up amongst the fallen gray snags of an old forest fire.

Now that they were out of the thick softwoods and amongst winter-bare maple and wire birch, they could see a sky. It was blue-gray and forbidding, and the wind whistling up over the plateau from the invisible sea felt raw on the cheek. At their next meeting Kezia said, "It's going to snow." She had no knowledge of the trail, but guessed they were not more than halfway across the cape. On this high barren the track changed suddenly to a mere trickle amongst the scattered hardwood clumps, where the path makers had not bothered to cut, and marked now by yesterday's footprints of Black Sam.

The preacher nodded dumbly. The woods, like everything else in his chosen mission field, were new and interesting, and he could not understand the vague alarm in her voice. He looked at Black Sam's tracks confidently, as if they would stay like that forever.

She tied the horse farther on and began her spell of walking, clutching the bundle containing her two flannel bed shirts, a shift of linen, three pairs of stout wool stockings, and Mr. Barclay's wedding gift for Mr. Hathaway. Her shoes were solid things, the kind Mr. Barclay invoiced as "a Common Strong sort, for women, Five Shillings"; but the soft snow worked into them and melted, and saturated the leather. Her feet ached with cold each time she slid down from the horse, and it took several minutes of stumbling through the snow to bring back the blood warmth.

Now as she plunged along she felt the first sting of snow on her face and, looking up, saw the stuff borne on the wind in small hard pellets that fell amongst the hardwoods and set up a whisper everywhere. When Mr. Mears rode up to her the snow was thick in their faces, like flung salt.

"It's a nor'easter!" she cried up to him. She knew the meaning of snow from the sea. She had been born in a fishing village down the coast.

"Yes," the preacher mumbled, and drew a fold of the shawl about his face. He disappeared. She struggled on, gasping, and after what seemed a tremendous journey came upon him standing bewildered, and looking off somewhere to the right.

"The horse!" he shouted. "I got off him — and before I could fasten the reins some snow fell from a branch — startled him, you know — and he ran off — over there." He gestured with a black-mittened hand. "I must fetch him back," he added confusedly.

"No!" Kezia said. "You couldn't. You'd only get lost. Oh, dear! This is awful. We'll have to go on, the best we can."

He was doubtful. The horse tracks looked very plain. But Kezia was looking at Black Sam's tracks, and tugging his arm. He gave in, and they struggled along for perhaps half an hour. Then the last trace of the old footprints vanished.

"What shall we do now?" the preacher asked, astonished.

"I don't know," whispered Kezia, and leaned against a dead pine stub in an attitude of weariness and indifference that dismayed him.

"We must keep moving, my dear, mustn't we? I mean, we can't stay here."

"Can't stay here," she echoed.

"Down there — a hollow, I think. Some hemlock trees — or are they pines? I'm never sure. Shelter, anyway."

"Shelter," muttered Kezia.

He took her by the hand and half dragged her toward the hollow. The trees were tall spruces, a thick bunch in a ravine, where they had escaped the old fire. A stream thundered amongst them somewhere. There was no wind in this place, only the fine snow whirling thickly down between the trees, like a sediment from the storm overhead.

"Look!" cried young Mr. Mears. A hut loomed out of the whiteness before them, a small structure of moss-chinked logs with a roof of poles covered with birch bark. It had an abandoned look. Long streamers of moss hung out of the shrunken logs, and on the roof patches of bark waved gently in the snow. The door stood half open, and a white drift lay along the split-pole floor.

Instinctively Kezia went to the stone hearth, covered with old ashes sodden with rain down the chimney and frozen now to a cake. "Have you got flint and steel?" she asked.

He shook his head and stared at her. She saw in his eyes something dazed and forlorn, like the eyes of a small boy lost, and was filled with a sudden anger, not so much at him as at Mr. Barclay, and that — that Hathaway, and all the rest of menkind. They ruled the world and made such a sorry mess of it.

In a small fury she began to rummage about the hut. There was a crude bed of poles and brushwood by the fireplace — brushwood so old that only a few brown needles clung to the twigs. A rough bench whittled from a pine log, with round birch sticks for legs. A broken earthenware pot in a corner; in another some ash-wood frames such as trappers used for stretching skins. Nothing else. The single window was covered with a stretched bladder, cracked and dry rotten, but still keeping out snow and admitting a gray daylight.

She scooped up the snow from the floor with her mittened hands, throwing it outside, and closed the door carefully, dropping the bar into place, as if she could shut out the cold with it. The air inside was frigid. The breath hung visible in the dim light from the window.

Young Mr. Mears dropped on his wet knees and began to pray in a loud voice. His face was pinched with cold and his teeth rattled as he prayed. He was a pitiable object.

"Prayers won't keep you warm," Kezia said crossly.

He looked up, amazed at the change in her. She had seemed such a meek little thing. Kezia was surprised at herself, and, surprisingly, she went on: "You'd far better take off those wet moccasins and stockings and shake the snow out of your clothes." She shook her skirts and Miss Julia's cloak, and turned her small back on him and took off her own shoes and stockings, and pulled on a dry pair of stockings out of her bundle. She threw him a pair. "Put those on."

He looked at them, and at his large feet hopelessly. "They wouldn't go on."

She tossed one of the flannel bed shirts. "Wrap your bare feet in that."

He obeyed, in an embarrassed silence. She rolled her eyes upward, for his modesty's sake, and saw a bundle on one of the low rafters — the late owner's bedding, stowed away from mice. She stood on the bench and pulled down three bearskins, marred with bullet holes. A rank and musty smell arose in the cold. She considered them gravely.

"You take them," Mr. Mears said gallantly. "I shall be quite all right."

"You'll be dead, and so shall I," she answered vigorously, "if you don't do what I say. We've got to roll up in these."

"Together?" he cried in horror.

"Of course. To keep each other warm. It's the only way." She

spread the skins on the floor, hair uppermost, one overlapping another, and dragged the flustered young man down beside her,
clutched him in her arms, and rolled with him, over, and over again,
till they were a single shapeless heap in the corner farthest from the
draft between door and chimney.

"Put your arms round me," commanded the new Kezia, and he
obeyed. "Now," she said, "you can pray.   God helps those that help
themselves."

He prayed aloud for a long time, and privately called upon heaven
to witness the purity of his thoughts in this strange and shocking
situation. He said "Amen" at last; and "Amen," repeated Kezia,
piously.

They lay silent a long time, breathing on each other's necks and
hearing their own hearts — poor Mr. Mears' fluttering in an agitated
way, Kezia's as steady as a clock. A delicious warmth crept over
them. They relaxed in each other's arms. Outside the storm hissed
in the spruce tops and set up an occasional cold moan in the cracked
clay chimney, and the down-swirling snow brushed softly against the
window bladder.

"I'm warm now," Kezia murmured.   "Are you?"

"Yes," he said.   "How long must we stay here like this?"

"Till the storm's over, of course. Tomorrow, probably. Nor'-
easters usually blow themselves out in a day and a night, specially
when they come up sharp like this one.   Are you hungry?"

"No."

"Abigail — that's the black cook at Barclay's — gave me bread and
cheese in a handkerchief. I've got it in my bundle. Mr. Barclay
thought we'd reach Bristol Creek in time for supper, and Mrs. Barclay said we ought to be there by three o'clock this afternoon; but
Nabby said I must have a bite to eat on the road. She's a good kind
thing, old Nabby. Sure you're not hungry?"

"Quite. Not hungry a bit. I just feel rather fatigued."

"Then we'll eat the bread and cheese for breakfast. Have you got
a watch?"

"No, I'm sorry," replied Mr. Mears. "They cost such a lot of money. In Lady Huntingdon's Connexion we —— "

"Well, it doesn't matter. The light's getting dim in the window. Dark comes very quick in a snowstorm. It must be about four o'clock."

"Dark," echoed young Mr. Mears drowsily. Kezia's hair, washed last night for the wedding journey, smelled pleasant so close to his face. It reminded him of something. He went to sleep dreaming of his mother, with his face snug in the hollow of Kezia's neck and shoulder, and smiling and muttering words she could not catch.

She kissed his cheek. It seemed a very natural thing to do. Soon she was dozing herself, and dreaming, too; but her dreams were full of forbidding faces — Mr. Barclay's, Mrs. Barclay's, Mr. Hathaway's; especially Mr. Hathaway's. Out of a confused darkness Mr. Hathaway's hard acquisitive gaze searched her shrinking flesh like a cold wind. Then she was shuddering by the kitchen fire at Barclay's, hearing Mr. Hathaway's courtship. In the midst of that sickening wooing she wakened sharply.

It was quite dark in the hut. Mr. Mears was breathing quietly against her throat. But there was a sound of heavy steps outside, muffled in the snow, and felt rather than heard. She shook the young man, and he wakened with a start, clutching her convulsively.

"Sh-h-h!" she warned. "There's something out yonder." She felt him stiffen, straining ears.

"Bears?" he whispered.

Silly! thought Kezia. People from the old country could think of nothing but bears in the woods. Besides, bears holed up in winter. A caribou, perhaps. But caribou went inland before this, to the wide mossy barrens, away from the coastal storms. A moose? Again the sound.

"There!" hissed the young preacher. Their hearts beat rapidly together.

"The door — you fastened it?"

"Yes," she said. Suddenly she knew.

"Unroll, quick!" she cried. . . . "No, not that way — your way."
They unrolled, ludicrously, and the girl scrambled up and ran
across the floor in her stockinged feet, fumbling with the rotten bar.
Mr. Mears attempted to follow, but tripped over the nightshirt still
wound about his feet, and fell with a crash. He was up again in a
moment, catching up the clumsy wooden bench for a weapon, his
bare feet slapping on the icy floor poles.

He tried to shoulder her aside, crying, "Stand back! Leave it to
me!" and waving the bench uncertainly in the darkness.

She laughed excitedly. "Silly!" she said. "It's the horse." She
flung the door open. In the pale dark of a night filled with snow
they regarded a large shape, white-crusted about the back. The shape
whinnied softly and thrust a long face into the doorway. Mr. Mears
dropped the bench, astonished.

"He got over his fright and followed us here, somehow," she said,
and laughed again. She put her arms about the snowy head and laid
her face against it. "Good horse. Oh, good, good horse!"

"What are you going to do?" the preacher murmured over her
shoulder. After the warmth of the furs they were shivering in this
ice-cavern atmosphere.

"Bring him in. We can't leave him out there in the storm." She
caught the bridle and urged the horse inside, clucking expertly. The
animal hesitated, but fear of the storm and a desire for shelter and
company decided him. He came in, tramping ponderously on the
poles.

The preacher closed and barred the door.

"And now?" he asked.

"Back to the furs. Quick! It's awful cold."

Rolled in the furs once more, their arms went about each other instinctively, and the young man's face found the comfortable nook
against Kezia's soft throat. But sleep was difficult after that. The
horse whinnied gently from time to time, and stamped about the
floor. The decayed poles crackled dangerously under his hoofs
whenever he moved, and Kezia trembled, thinking he might break
through and frighten himself, and flounder till he tumbled the crazy

hut about their heads. She called out to him, "Steady, boy! Steady!"

It was a long night. The pole floor made its irregularities felt through the thickness of fur; and because there seemed nowhere to put their arms but about each other, the flesh cramped, and spread its protest along the bones. They were stiff and sore when the first light of morning stained the window. They unrolled and stood up thankfully, and tramped up and down the floor, threshing their arms to life and fighting off the gripping cold. Kezia undid her bundle in a corner and brought forth Nabby's bread and cheese, and they ate it side by side on the edge of the rotten brushwood bed, with the skins about their shoulders. Outside, the snow had ceased.

"We must set off at once," the preacher said. "Mr. Hathaway will be anxious."

Kezia was silent. She did not move, and he looked at her curiously. She appeared very fresh, considering the hardships of the day and the night. He passed a hand over his cheeks and thought how unclean he must seem in her eyes, with this stubble on his pale face. "Mr. Hathaway —— " he began again.

"I'm not going to Mr. Hathaway," Kezia said quietly.

"But — the wedding!"

"There'll be no wedding. I don't want to marry Mr. Hathaway. 'Twas Mr. Hathaway's idea, and Mr. and Mrs. Barclay's."

"What will the Barclays say, my dear?"

She shrugged. "I've been their bond girl since I was fourteen, but I'm not a slave like poor black Nabby, to be handed over, body and soul, whenever it suits."

"Your soul belongs to God," said Mr. Mears devoutly.

"And my body belongs to me."

He was a little shocked at this outspokenness, but he said gently, "Of course. To give oneself in marriage without true affection would be an offense in the sight of heaven. But what will Mr. Hathaway say?"

"Well, to begin with, he'll ask where I spent the night, and I'll have to tell the truth. I'll have to say I bundled with you in a hut in the woods."

"Bundle?"

"A custom the old people brought with them from Connecticut when they came to settle in Nova Scotia. Poor folk still do it. Sweethearts, I mean. It saves fire and candles when you're courting on winter evenings. It's harmless — they keep their clothes on, you see — but Mr. Barclay and the other Methody people are terrible set against it. Mr. Barclay got old Mr. Mings — he's the Methody preacher that died — to make a sermon against it. Mr. Mings said bundling was an invention of the devil."

"But if you go back to Mr. Barclay —— "

"He'll ask me the same question. And I'll have to give him the same answer. I couldn't tell a lie, could I?" She turned a pair of round blue eyes and met his embarrassed gaze.

"No. No, you mustn't lie. Whatever shall we do?" he murmured in a dazed voice.

Again she was silent, looking modestly down her small nose.

"It's very strange — this country," he floundered. "There are so many things I don't know, so many things to learn. You — I — we shall have to tell the truth, of course. Doubtless I can find a place in the Lord's service somewhere else."

"I heard say the people at Scrod Harbor want a preacher."

"But — the tale would follow me, wouldn't it, my dear? This — er — bundling with a young woman?"

" 'Twouldn't matter if the young woman was your wife."

"Eh?" His mouth fell open. He was like an astonished child, for all his preacher's clothes and the new beard on his jaws.

"I'm a good girl," Kezia said, regarding her foot. "I can read and write, and know all the tunes in the psalter. And — and you need someone to look after you."

He considered the truth of that. Then he murmured, uncertainly, "We'd be very poor, my dear. The Connexion gives some support, but of course —— "

"I've always been poor," Kezia said. She sat very still, but her cold fingers writhed in her lap.

He did something then that made her want to cry. He took hold

of her hands and bowed his head and kissed them. "It's strange —
I don't even know your name, my dear."

"It's Kezia — Kezia Barnes."

He said gently, "You are a brave girl, Kezia Barnes. I shall try to
be a good husband to you. Shall we go?'

"I think you'd better kiss me first," whispered Kezia demurely.

He put his lips awkwardly to hers; and then, as if the taste of her
clean mouth provided strength and purpose, kissed her again, and
firmly.

She put her arms about his neck. "Oh, Mr. Mears!"

How little he knew about everything! He hadn't even known
enough to wear two or three pairs of stockings inside the roomy moccasins, nor to carry a pair of dry ones. Yesterday's wet stockings were
lying like sticks on the frosty floor. She showed him how to knead
the hard-frozen moccasins into softness, so he could put them on;
and while he worked at the stiff leather she tore up one of her wedding bed shirts and wound the strips about his feet and legs. It
looked very queer when she had finished, and they both laughed.

They were chilled to the bones when they set off, Kezia on the
horse and the preacher walking ahead, holding the reins. When
they regained the slope where they had lost the path, Kezia said, "The
sun rises somewhere between east and southeast, this time of year.
Keep it on your left shoulder a while. That will take us toward
Port Marriott."

When they reached the green timber she told him to shift the sun
to his left eye.

"Have you changed your mind?" he asked cheerfully. The ex-
ercise had warmed him.

"No, but the sun moves across the sky."

"Ah! What a wise little head it is!"

They came over a ridge of mixed hemlock and hardwood and
looked upon a long swale full of bare hackmatacks.

"Look!" the girl cried. The white slot of the ax path showed
clearly in the trees at the foot of the swale, and again where it entered the dark mass of pines beyond.

"Praise the Lord!" said Mr. Mears.

When at last they stood in the trail, Kezia slid down from the horse.

"No!" he protested.

"Ride-and-tie," she said firmly. "That's the way we came, and that's the way we'll go. Besides, I want to get warm."

He climbed up clumsily and smiled down at her. "What shall we do when we get to Port Marriott, my dear?"

"Get the New Light preacher to marry us, and catch the packet for Scrod Harbor."

He nodded, and gave a pull at his hat brim. She thought of everything. A splendid helpmeet for the world's wilderness. He saw it all very humbly now as a dispensation of Providence.

She watched him out of sight. Then she undid her bundle quickly and took out the thing that had lain there, "and on her conscience," through the night — the tinderbox — Mr. Barclay's wedding gift to Mr. Hathaway.

She flung it into the woods and walked on, skirts lifted, in the track of the horse, humming a psalm tune to the silent trees and the snow.

SOMEBODY HAS TO BE NOBODY

By Budd Schulberg

AT HALF past five Ciro's looks like a woman sitting before her dressing table just beginning to make up for the evening. The waiters are setting up the tables for the dinner trade, the cigarette and hatcheck girls are changing from slacks to the abbreviated cancan costumes which are their work clothes, and an undiscovered Alice Faye who is making her debut tonight is rehearsing, *Oh, daddy, I wanna bran'-new cah, champagne, caviah, oh, daddy.* . . .

A telephone rings and the operator who is suffering from delusions of looking like Bette Davis answers, "Ci-ro's. . . . A table for Mr. Nathan? . . . For six. . . . His usual table?" This was not what she had come to Hollywood for — to take reservations over the telephone — but even the small part she played in A. D. Nathan's plans for the evening brought her a little closer to the Hollywood that was like a mirage, always in sight but never within reach. For, like everyone else in Hollywood, the telephone operator at Ciro's had a dream. Once upon a time, ran this one, there was A Famous Movie Producer — called Goldwyn, Zanuck or A. D. Nathan — and one evening this F. M. P. was in Ciro's placing a million-dollar telephone call when he happened to catch sight of her behind the switchboard. "Young lady," he said, "you are wasting your time at that switchboard. You may not realize it, but you are Naomi in my forthcoming farm epic, Sow the Wild Oat."

Reluctantly the operator plugged out her dream and sent word of Nathan's reservation to André. André belonged to that great international race, headwaiters, whose flag is an unreadable menu and whose language is French with an accent. Headwaiters are diplomats who happened to be born with silver spoons in their hands instead of their mouths. André would have been a typical headwaiter. But he had been in Hollywood too long. Which meant that no matter how good a headwaiter he was, he no longer wished to be one. André wanted to be a screen writer. In fact, after working only three years, André had managed to finish a screen play entitled, surprisingly enough, Confessions of a Hollywood Waiter, which he had written all by himself, in English.

With casual deliberateness — hadn't Jimmy Starr called him the Poor Man's Adolphe Menjou? — André picked out a table one row removed from the dance floor for Mr. Nathan. The waiter whose ringside table was A. D. Nathan's "Usual" raised a protest not entirely motivated by sentiment. In Waiters' Local 17, A. D. Nathan's fame was based not so much on his pictures as on his tips.

"Mr. Nathan will have to be satisfied with this table," André explained. "All the ringside tables are already reserved."

André had to smile at his own cleverness. A. D. Nathan did not know it yet, but André had had him in mind from the beginning as the producer of his scenario. A. D. seemed the logical contact because he remembered André as an ordinary waiter in Henry's, back in the days before pictures could talk. But André knew he needed something stronger than nostalgia to bring himself to A. D.'s attention. Every Saturday night Nathan presided at the same table overlooking the floor. Tonight André would make him take a back seat. Nathan would threaten and grumble, and André would flash his suave headwaiter smile and be "so sorry, Monsieur Nathan. If there were only something I could do." Then, at the opportune moment, just as the floor show was about to begin, André would discover that something could be done. And when Nathan would try to thank André with a crisp green bill for giving him the table André had been saving for him all evening, André's voice would take on an injured tone: "*Merci beaucoup,* Mr. Nathan. Thank you just the same, but André is glad to do a favor for an old friend."

André thought of the scene in terms of a scenario. That was the dialogue, just roughed in, of course. Then the business of Nathan insisting on rewarding André for his efforts. And a close-up of André, shyly dropping his eyes as he tells M'sieu Nathan that if he really wants to reward André, he could read Confessions of a Hollywood Waiter, by André de Selco.

So that was André's dream, and he dreamed it all the while he was fussing over last-minute details, like a nervous hostess getting ready for a big party.

By the time Nathan's party arrived, the big room with the cyclamen drapes and pale green walls of tufted satin was full of laughter, music, shop talk and an inner-circle intimacy that hung over the place like the smoke that rose from lipsticked cigarettes and expensive cigars. Everyone turned to stare at the newcomers, for Hollywood celebrities have a way of gaping at one another with the same wide-eyed curiosity as their supposedly less sophisticated brothers waiting for autographs outside.

Nathan entered with assurance, conscious of the way "There's A. D." was breathed through the room. His figure was slight but imposing, for he carried himself with the air of a man who was used to commanding authority. There was something ghostly about him, with his white hair and pale skin, but his eyes were intensely alive, dark eyes that never softened, even when he smiled. As he followed André toward the dance floor, actors, agents, directors and fellow producers were anxious to catch his eye. It was "Hello, A. D. . . . How are you tonight, A. D.?" and he would acknowledge them with a word or a nod, knowing how to strike just the right balance between dignity and cordiality.

At his side was his wife, a tall brunette with sculpture-perfect features, hardened by a willful disposition. Some still remembered her as Lita Lawlor, who seemed on the verge of stardom not so many years ago. But she had sacrificed her screen career for love, or so the fan magazines had put it, though gossipers would have you believe that Lita was just swapping one career for another that promised somewhat more permanent security.

Accompanying the Nathans were a plain middle-aged couple whom no one in Ciro's could identify, a girl of seventeen who managed to be astonishingly pretty without the aid of the Westmore Brothers, and Bruce Spencer, a young man whom Nathan was grooming as the next Robert Taylor. And grooming was just the word, for this male ingénue pranced and tossed his curly black mane like a horse on exhibition.

André led the party to the inferior table he had picked out for them.

"Wait a minute. André, this isn't my table," Nathan protested.

He frowned at André's silky explanations. He was in no mood to be crossed this evening. It seemed as if everything was out of focus today. First his three-thousand-dollar-a-week writer had turned in a script with holes big enough to drive a tank through. Then he had decided that what he needed was a date with a cute little thing like this Jenny McBride, and instead here he was with his wife, that young ham of hers and those Carters he'd been ducking for months. And to top everything, there was that business in New York.

Impatiently, Nathan beckoned the waiter. "I want a magnum of Cordon Rouge, 1929."

1929, Nathan thought. That was the year he almost lost his job. It was a funny thing. All these people hoping to be tossed a bone never thought of A. D. Nathan as a man with a job to hold. But that year, when the panic came and the banks moved in, he had had to think fast to hold on to that big office and that long title.

He wondered what would have become of him if he had lost out. He thought of some of the magic names of the past, like Major Adams and Eddie Selbert, who could walk into Ciro's now without causing a head to turn. And he thought how impossible it would be to enter Ciro's without the salaaming reception he always complained about, but could not have given up.

But that was nothing to worry about now, as he looked across at Jenny, with that incredibly young face, so pretty and soft, like a marmalade kitten, he thought. He lifted his glass in a toast to her.

"Happy birthday," he said. "May you always be seventeen."

"Seventeen!" Mrs. Carter exclaimed. "I'd forgotten there were any seventeen-year-olds left in the world!"

They all laughed and Nathan looked at Mimi Carter, suddenly shocked to see how old she and Harry had become. He could remember when they were the stand-bys at the Embassy Club and the Cocoanut Grove. Now their eyes were shining like tourists', because they had never been to Ciro's before.

"Is the wine all right, Harry?" Nathan asked.

Harry looked up, his face flushed with pleasure. "All right? I haven't had wine like this —— " He paused to think. "In a long time," he said.

There was a silence, and Nathan felt embarrassed for him. He was glad when Mimi broke in with the anecdote about the time they were leaving for Europe with their Western star, Tex Bradely, and Tex insisted on bringing his own Scotch along because he was afraid to trust those foreign bootleggers.

Nathan was only half listening, though he joined in the laughter, for he found himself wondering, *When is Carter going to put the bite on me for that job he wants? And how am I going to con this Mc-Bride kid?* And though he could not divine André's plans or guess how he figured in the dreams of the telephone operator who looked like Bette Davis, he could not help feeling that Ciro's was a solar system in which he was the sun and around which all these satellites revolved.

"André," he beckoned, "will you please tell the operator I'm expecting a very important long-distance call?" An empty feeling of excitement rose inside him, but he fought it down. The dancers were swaying to a tango. Nathan saw Spencer and Lita, whirling like professionals, conscious of how well they looked together. He looked at Jenny, and he thought, with a twinge of weariness, of all the Jennies he had looked at this way. "Would you like to dance, my dear?"

He was an old man to Jenny, an old man she hardly knew, and it seemed to her that everybody in the room must be saying, "There goes A. D. with another one. Kids like that will do anything to get ahead." But she tried to smile, tried to be having a terribly good time, thinking, *If I want to be an actress, this is part of the job. And if I can't look as if I'm getting the thrill of my life out of dancing with this old fossil, what kind of an actress am I, anyway?*

Nathan could have told her what kind of an actress she was. He had expressed himself rather vividly on that subject after seeing her test that afternoon.

"McBride stinks," he had told his assistants as the lights came on in the projection room that afternoon. "She'll never be an actress and she photographs even younger than she is."

That's what he wanted to tell her. But he was reaching that age when it is reassuring to be surrounded with Jenny McBrides. That meant feeding her the old come-on, tossing her just enough crumbs of encouragement to keep her hopes alive. "I'd like to talk to you about that test sometime soon," was all he had said.

"Enjoying your birthday party, Jenny?" he said as he led her back to the table.

"Oh, I'm having an elegant time, Mr. Nathan," she said. She tried to say it with personality, her eyes bright and her smile fixed. But only her ambition was in it, not her heart.

Her heart was not in Ciro's. Her heart was on Orange Grove Avenue. That's where Bill Mason lived. Bill worked as a grip on Nathan's lot. The grip is the guy who does the dirty work on a movie set. Or, as Bill liked to explain it, "I'm the guy who carries the set around on his back. I may not be the power behind the throne, but I'm sure the power under it."

Jenny thought of the way she and Bill had planned to celebrate her birthday, down at the amusement pier. They always had fun down there together.

"Oh, I'm so sorry, Mr. Nathan," Jenny had told the producer when he phoned, "but this — this happens to be my birthday, and I —— "

"I know it's your birthday, my dear," he had lied wearily. "Why do you think I called? I thought we might have a birthday party — just the two of us."

She hesitated, not knowing what to do. Bill would never forgive her. But this was A. D. Nathan, calling her in person.

"Thanks, very much; I'd love to. But I do have an appointment —— "

"Well, bring your appointment along," Nathan had conceded;

"we'll make a real party of it. How would you like to go to Ciro's?"

She had never been to Ciro's. "Next to heaven," she said, "I can't think of a nicer place."

Bill had looked in on his way home as usual, an energetic kid with laughter in his eyes and unruly brown hair that Jenny was forever scolding him for forgetting to comb.

"Sorry to keep you waiting, Mac," he called from the door. "But that old bag" — he was referring to one of the screen's most glamorous personalities — "blew her lines in the big love scene fifteen straight times. I thought one of the juicers was going to drop a lamp on her!"

He lifted Jenny off her feet the way he always did and kissed the tip of her nose. "That schnoz is too little to work," he grinned. "Too bad you haven't got a nice big practical one like me."

She took a kitten bite out of his cheek. "Aren't you going to say anything?" she pouted.

"That's my cue," he said. "Happy birthday, child. How old are you this year, twelve?"

She shut her eyes childishly and lapsed into baby talk, "I want my serpwise."

She was surprised. Bill was holding up a diamond engagement ring.

"Like it?"

"Oh, it's beautiful. But, Bill —— "

Bill grimaced with boyish embarrassment. "Try it on. What's a little thing like a diamond to us Masons? Know what Leon Shamroy told me today? Said he'd put me on the camera crew, starting the next picture."

He kissed her again, this time for keeps. "I'll run home and slip into something more comfortable, as they say in the movies," he laughed, indicating his blue jeans and work shirt.

Jenny advanced cautiously, fearing the storm ahead. "Bill — Bill darling, do you have any evening clothes?"

Bill stopped at the door. "Evening clothes? We'd look like a couple of jerks, riding the roller coaster in evening clothes."

"But, Bill, we aren't going to the pier.   We're going to Ciro's."

"Ciro's!   Honey, are you crazy?   It costs you five clams just to get a glass of water in that joint!"

"I guess A. D. Nathan can afford it," she said, watching his expression change and hurrying to explain. "Darling, I'd of given anything to get out of it.   But you know how important he is.   I don't want to sound dramatic, but — well, my whole career may depend on this."

"You don't sound dramatic," he said; "you sound touched."   The playfulness was gone from his eyes now, the gaiety between them snapped like a violin string.   "Listen, Mac, you may be kidding yourself, but you can't kid me.   I was on the set when you made that test.   I love you enough to tell you what a lousy actress you are."

Jenny tightened with indignation.   "I suppose you know more about acting than Mr. Nathan?   He says he wants to keep the test to look at again."

"Are you sure he meant the test, and not you?"

Here at this table in Ciro's the waiter was filling her glass again, and she was laughing at something funny and off-color that Bruce Spencer had just said.   But she couldn't forget what she had done to Bill, how she had slapped him, melodramatically handed back the ring, and how, according to the few choked words exchanged at the door, they had parted forever.

Jenny had cried, because she loved Bill.   And then she had stopped crying and called A. D. Nathan, because she had read too many movie magazines.   *This is what makes a great actress of you — sorrow and sacrifice of your personal happiness,* she thought, and she saw herself years later as a great star, running into Bill in Ciro's after he had become a famous cameraman.   *"Bill," she would say, "perhaps it is not too late.   Each of us had to follow his own path until they crossed again."*

By the time Jenny phoned Nathan to say she would come alone, he had already asked his wife.   "Now we have to find an escort," he grumbled.   "Fine chance of finding an extra man at this hour."

"We might be able to get hold of Bruce Spencer," said Lita.   "He

said something about being free when we left the club this afternoon."

Nathan knew they could get hold of Bruce Spencer. Lita and
Bruce were giving the Hollywood wives something to talk about over
their bridge tables of an afternoon. Sometimes he dreamed of putting an end to it. But that meant killing two birds with bad publicity. And they were both his birds, his wife and his leading man.

"All right," he said, "I'll give Spence a ring. Might not be bad
publicity for the McBride girl if we decide to use her."

Lita pecked him on the cheek with preoccupation. Bruce was
dying to get that star-making part in Suicide Squad. This might be
the ideal evening to talk A. D. into it.

And then, since the four of them might look too obvious, Nathan
had wanted an extra couple. He tried several, but it was too late
to get anybody in demand. That's how he had happened to think
of the Carters.

When you talked about old-time directors, you had to mention
Harry Carter in the same breath with D. W. Griffith and Mickey
Neilan. Carter and Nathan had been a famous combination until
sound pictures and TB knocked Carter out of the running. The
last job he had had was a quickie Western over a year ago. And a
year in Hollywood is like an era anywhere else. A. D. had forgotten
all about Carter until he received a letter from him a few months
ago, just a friendly letter, suggesting dinner some evening to cut up
touches about old times. But A. D. knew those friendly dinners,
knew he owed Carter a debt he was reluctant to repay, and so, somehow, the letter had gone unanswered. But, in spite of himself, his
conscience had filed it away for further reference.

"I know who we'll get. The Harry Carters. Been meaning to
take them to dinner for months."

"Do we have to fall back on the Old Ladies' Home?" Lita said,
drawing on a pair of long white gloves that set off her firm tan arms.

"It might not be so bad," Nathan said, giving way to the senti-
mentalism that thrives in his profession. "Mimi Carter always used
to be a lot of fun."

"I can just imagine," said Lita. "I'll bet she does a mean turkey trot."

So that's how it happened chance plucked the Carters out of the obscurity of a bungalow court and dropped them down in the middle of a world they had never expected to see again.

"Harry, I just know this means A. D.'s going to give you a chance again," Mimi Carter whispered as they walked off the dance floor with their arms around each other, and she saw how his eyes were shining and hastened to warn, "Not too much wine, Harry. Be careful. You aren't used to it, and you've got to impress A. D. to-night."

"Don't worry, sweetheart," he answered. "I'm watching. I'm waiting for the right moment to talk to him."

Lita and Bruce were dancing again, and Jenny was alone with A. D. at the table when the Carters returned. It was the moment Jenny had been fishing for. She could hardly wait to know what he thought of the test.

"I don't think it does you justice," Nathan was saying. "The cameraman didn't know how to light you at all. I think you have great possibilities."

Jenny grinned triumphantly, the wine and encouragement going to her head, and Nathan reached over and patted her hand in what was meant to seem a fatherly gesture, though he lingered a moment too long. But Jenny saw nothing but "A. D. Nathan Presents Jenny McBride —— " For this was Jenny's dream, a dream that seemed to be coming true as André presented her with an ornate birthday cake, the orchestra played a special swing arrangement of Happy Birthday and everyone in Ciro's applauded, applauded her, even famous people like George Raft and Betty Grable and Marlene Dietrich. Jenny blew out the candles, candles that seemed to spell "A. D. Nathan Presents Jenny McBride," and she laughed with embarrassment and delight and the thought that *You're on your way, Jenny McBride. If Bill could only see you now.*

Then she looked up and a forkful of birthday cake stopped in mid-air. Bill Mason was seeing her now. He was sitting at the bar with a highball in his hand, staring down at her. As she stared back, he drained his glass, his face terribly red and terribly serious. She had never seen him drunk before. Horrified, she saw him rise slowly and start toward her table, with a desperate effort to preserve his dignity.

He stopped at their table, weaving slightly, bowed low like a foreign director and kissed Jenny's hand.

"Allow me to eentroduce myself," he said to Nathan with mock seriousness. "I am ze great foreign director, Vilhelm von Mason. I yust vant to tell you vat a vunderful actress you haf here. Ven she plays drama, you bust out crying, you are laughing so hard."

"Bill!" she cried. "Bill, what are you doing here?"

"I am getting drunk here," Bill answered. "Drunk enough to get up courage to come over and take you home."

People were beginning to stare, and Nathan hated scenes. "Who is this man?" he demanded. "What is he doing here?"

"I'm nobody you ever heard of," said Bill. "Just a lousy grip who works on your lot. Just the dope this great tragedienne of yours is going to marry."

Everyone looked at Jenny, and she felt her dream smashing up, and she fought to hold the pieces together. She used the old words, but she poured them out as if no one had ever spoken them before, "Get out of here! I hate you! I never want to see you again!"

Bill smiled, sadly and drunkenly. "Don't believe her, A. D. We're a natural, Mac and me. And if you'd just get your mind off that casting couch for a minute, you'd tell her to go home and forget this stuff."

"If you work on my lot, you're fired," Nathan said, and he called to André, "Have this man thrown out of here."

A couple of bouncers closed in on Bill. He waited for them calmly. He was sober now. "Might as well save yourself the trouble, boys. You couldn't keep me here if you gave me the joint. I'm going to a place with real class, Barney's Beanery."

Then he bowed to Jenny and kissed her hand again. "Good-by, Miss Garbo. It's been thrilling to meet you. Don't forget to send me that autographed picture."

The birthday cake was eaten and the champagne was drunk, but it was no longer the same. A. D. continued to stare at Jenny, but the expression in his eyes had changed to thoughtful inspection.

Harry Carter looked at his watch nervously. It was almost time for the floor show. And after that, the party would be over, before he had a chance to talk about that comeback. He looked at Mimi, trying to find the courage to put it up to A. D. But A. D. seemed in no mood to listen. Lita and Bruce were watching, too, wondering how to bring the subject around to Suicide Squad. And André, behind that headwaiter's mask, was thinking, *Only twenty more minutes and I will be speaking to A. D. about my scenario.*

"André," Nathan called, and the headwaiter snapped to attention. "Are you sure there hasn't been a call for me?"

"No, monsieur. I would call you right away, monsieur."

Nathan frowned. "Well, make sure. It should have been here by now." He felt angry with himself for losing his patience. There was no reason to be so upset. This was just another long-distance call. He had talked to New York a thousand times before, about matters just as serious.

But when André came running with the message that New York was on the wire, he could not keep the old fear from knotting his stomach, and he jostled the table in his anxiety to rise.

"You may take it in the second booth on the left, Mr. Nathan," said "Bette Davis" as she looked up from her switchboard with a prefabricated smile. But he merely brushed by her and slammed the door of the booth behind him.

The telephone girl looked after him with the dream in her eyes. *When he comes out I'll hafta think of something arresting ta say ta him,* she decided. *Wouldn't it be funny if he did notice me?*

Five minutes later she heard the door of the booth sliding open and she looked up and smiled.

"Was the connection clear, Mr. Nathan?"

That might do for a starter, she thought. But he didn't even look up as he murmured, "Yes. I heard very well. Thank you," and he put half a dollar down and walked on. He felt heavy, heavy all over, his body too heavy for his legs to support and his eyes too heavy for the sockets to hold. He walked back to the table no longer seeing the people who tried to catch his glance, erect through force of habit.

"Everything all right?" said his wife.

"Yes. Yes," he said. "Everything."

Was that my voice? It didn't sound like my voice. It sounded more like Harry Carter's voice. Poor old Harry. Never forget the days we ran the World-Wide lot together. Or that time I lost my shirt in the market and Harry loaned me fifty G's. Wonder what ever happened to Harry.

Then he realized it was Harry Carter talking, "A. D., this has sure been a tonic for Mimi and me. And I know we didn't come here to talk shop. But you always used to have faith in me and — well —— "

All heads were turning toward the entrance again and Nathan saw Joe Morris, a rival producer, coming in. "Excuse me. I'll be right back," he said, and he rose to his feet in slow motion.

With that same somnambulistic rhythm he walked toward Morris.

"Well, Joe, guess I put one over on you this time. Guess who's going to do my next picture? Harry Carter."

"Harry Carter!" Morris unclenched his cigar. "Why, he's dead, isn't he?"

"You should be so dead. I've got him over at my table now, talking a deal. I just saw a swell little picture he did for Tec-Art. Looks like the old master is better than ever, and we're crying about the dearth of directors."

Joe Morris chewed his cigar irritably. If there was anything he couldn't stand, it was letting A. D. Nathan outsmart him. Then a shrewd gleam came into his eyes.

"Harry and I used to be great pals," he said. "Think I'll walk back to your table and say hello to him."

Carter looked up in amazement as Morris came toward him, with his friendly face on. "Well, Harry, old kid," he greeted him. "Where you been keeping yourself lately? How about dropping in at the beach tomorrow for a drink?"

"You see!" Harry told his wife proudly as they did an especially fancy turn around the floor. "Is Hollywood a crazy place! One minute you're a bum who can't get by the gate, the next minute they're fighting over you."

Jenny and Nathan were sitting at the table alone again. *This will be quick,* he thought — *this will be quick and sharp, like a scalpel cut.*

"Miss McBride," his voice began in a monotone, "what would you say if I were to tell you that your screen test was so bad it even made the projectionist laugh?"

Jenny flushed with the pain of it, and she looked at the emptied magnum of champagne.

"Why, Mr. Nathan, you must be — you must be —— "

"No, I am not drunk," he said, with terrible finality. "You're the one who's drunk. I've filled you full of false hopes that have made you drunk. You see, I have a very bad habit of lying to pretty girls who can't act. So, if you have any brains at all in that very pretty head of yours, you'll run home and marry that grip of yours before it's too late."

He didn't move his head, and his face seemed to show no emotion at all when she gritted her teeth to fight back the tears. But there was a faint, tired smile around his mouth as he watched her jump up from the table and run toward the door.

At the entrance, the autograph crowd pushed forward to see who it was, and when they found it was no one they recognized, they relaxed in disappointment.

"Don't get her!   She's nobody!" someone called out, and suddenly Jenny thought, *Well, I guess somebody has to be nobody,* and she felt better when she gave the cab driver Bill's address on Orange Grove Avenue.

"What did you do to that kid?" Lita asked when the music stopped and she returned to the table arm in arm with Bruce.

"I told her that as an actress she'll make a good wife for a grip," Nathan said.

"I didn't think she had much on the ball," Bruce said, lighting a cigarette, and proud of the smooth way he shifted into, "By the way, A. D., Lita let me read the script on Suicide Squad. That's a terrific part, that aviator who goes blind, but doesn't let anybody know it. Who's going to play it?"

"Any leading man in Hollywood except you," Nathan said.

Bruce looked undressed without his assurance. The silence was awkward, and then Lita said, "But, A. D., that part was written for Bruce."

All the rest of his face seemed to be sagging, but Nathan's hard black eyes watched them with bitter amusement. "There isn't a part in the studio that's written for Bruce. The only thing that kept Bruce from being fired months ago was me. And now there's no longer me."

Lita looked up at him, really frightened now.

"A. D., what do you mean?"

His face was white, white as a ghost, the ghost he was about to become. "I mean I'm out," he said. "Finished. Washed up. Through. Hudson called to say the board voted to ask for my resignation."

"What are you going to do now?" she said.

He thought of the thing he had promised himself to do when his time came — drop out of sight, break it off clean. Hollywood had no use for anticlimaxes on or off the screen. But as he sat there, he knew what would really happen.

Move over, Major Adams and Eddie Selbert, he thought. *Make room for another ghost.*

The floor show was just starting. The undiscovered Alice Faye was putting everything she had into *"Oh, daddy, I wanna bran'-new cah, champagne, caviah."*

And as she sang, André smiled in anticipation. So far everything had gone just as he had planned. And now the time had come to move A. D. up to that ringside table.

WEEP NO MORE, MY LADY

By James Street

THE MOONLIGHT symphony of swamp creatures hushed abruptly, and the dismal bog was as peaceful as unborn time and seemed to brood in its silence. The gaunt man glanced back at the boy and motioned for him to be quiet, but it was too late. Their presence was discovered. A jumbo frog rumbled a warning and the swamp squirmed into life as its denizens scuttled to safety.

Fox fire was glowing to the west and the bayou was slapping the cypress knees when suddenly a haunting laugh echoed through the wilderness, a strange chuckling yodel ending in a weird "gro-o-o."

The boy's eyes were wide and staring. "That's it, Uncle Jess. Come on! Let's catch it!"

"Uh, oh." The man gripped his shotgun. "That ain't no animal. That's a thing."

They hurried noiselessly in the direction of the sound that Skeeter had been hearing for several nights. Swamp born and reared, they feared nothing they could shoot or outwit, so they slipped out of the morass and to the side of a ridge. Suddenly, Jesse put out his hand and stopped the child, then pointed up the slope. The animal, clearly visible in the moonlight, was sitting on its haunches, its head cocked sideways as it chuckled. It was a merry and rather melodious little chuckle.

Skeeter grinned in spite of his surprise, then said, "Sh-h-h. It'll smell us."

Jesse said, "Can't nothing smell that far. Wonder what the durn thing is?" He peered up the ridge, studying the creature. He had no intention of shooting unless attacked, for Jesse Tolliver and his nephew never killed wantonly.

The animal, however, did smell them and whipped her nose into the wind, crouched and braced. She was about sixteen inches high and weighed twenty-two pounds. Her coat was red and silky and there was a blaze of white down her chest and a circle of white around her throat. Her face was wrinkled and sad, like a wise old man's.

Jesse shook his head. "Looks som'n like a mixture of bloodhound and terrier from here," he whispered. "It beats me —— "

"It's a dog, all right," Skeeter said.

"Can't no dog laugh."

"That dog can." The boy began walking toward the animal, his right hand outstretched. "Heah. Heah. I ain't gonna hurt you."

The dog, for she was a dog, cocked her head from one side to the other and watched Skeeter. She was trembling, but she didn't run. And when Skeeter knelt by her, she stopped trembling, for the ways of a boy with a dog are mysterious. He stroked her, and the trim little creature looked up at him and blinked her big hazel eyes. Then she turned over and Skeeter scratched her. She closed her eyes, stretched and chuckled, a happy mixture of chortle and yodel. Jesse ambled up and the dog leaped to her feet and sprang between the boy and the man.

Skeeter calmed her. "That's just Uncle Jess."

Jesse, still bewildered, shook his head again. "I still say that ain't no dog. She don't smell and she don't bark. Ain't natural. And look at her! Licking herself like a cat."

"Well, I'll be a catty wampus," Skeeter said. "Never saw a dog do that before." However, he was quick to defend any mannerism of his friend and said, "She likes to keep herself clean. She's a lady and I'm gonna name her that, and she's mine 'cause I found her."

"Lady, huh?"

"No, sir. My Lady. If I name her just plain Lady, how folks gonna know she's mine?" He began stroking his dog again. "Gee m'netty, Uncle Jess, I ain't never had nothing like this before."

"It still don't make sense to me," Jesse said. But he didn't care, for he was happy because the child was happy.

Like most mysteries, there was no mystery at all about My Lady. She was a lady, all right, an aristocratic Basenji, one of those strange barkless dogs of Africa. Her ancestors were pets of the Pharaohs and her line was well established when the now proud races of men were wandering about Europe, begging handouts from Nature. A bundle of nerves and muscles, she would fight anything, and could scent game up to eighty yards. She had the gait of an antelope and was odorless, washing herself before and after meals. However, the only noises she could make were a piercing cry that sounded almost human and that chuckling little chortle. She could chuckle only when happy and she had been happy in the woods. Now she was happy again.

As most men judge values, she was worth more than all the possessions of Jesse and his nephew. Several of the dogs had been shipped to New Orleans to avoid the dangerous upper route, thence by motor to a Northern kennel. While crossing Mississippi, My Lady had escaped from the station wagon. Her keeper had advertised in several papers, but Jesse and Skeeter never saw papers.

Skeeter said, "Come on, M'Lady. Let's go home."

The dog didn't hesitate, but walked proudly at the boy's side to a cabin on the bank of the bayou. Skeeter crumbled corn bread, wet it with pot likker and put it before her. She sniffed the food disdainfully at first, then ate it only when she saw the boy fix a bowl for his uncle. She licked herself clean and explored the cabin, sniffing the brush brooms, the piles of wild pecans and hickory nuts, and then the cots. Satisfied at last, she jumped on Skeeter's bed, tucked her nose under her paws and went to sleep.

"Acts like she owns the place," Jesse said.

"Where you reckon she came from?" The boy slipped his overall straps from his shoulders, flexed his stringy muscles and yawned.

"Lord knows. Circus maybe." He looked at M'Lady quickly. "Say, maybe she's a freak and run off from some show. Bet they'd give us two dollars for her."

Skeeter's face got long. "You don't aim to get rid of her?"

The old man put his shotgun over the mantel and lit his pipe. "Skeets, if you want that thing, I wouldn't get shed of her for a piece of bottom land a mile long. Already plowed and planted."

"I reckoned you wouldn't, 'cause you like me so much. And I know how you like dogs, 'cause I saw you cry when yours got killed. But you can have part of mine."

Jesse sat down and leaned back, blowing smoke into the air to drive away mosquitoes. The boy got a brick and hammer and began cracking nuts, pounding the meat to pulp so his uncle could chew it. Skeeter's yellow hair hadn't been cut for months and was tangled. He had freckles too. And his real name was Jonathan. His mother was Jesse's only sister and died when the child was born. No one thereabouts ever knew what happened to his father. Jesse, a leathery, toothless old man with faded blue eyes, took him to bring up and called him Skeeter because he was so little.

In the village, where Jesse seldom visited, folks wondered if he were fit'n to rear a little boy. They considered him shiftless and no-count. Jesse had lived all of his sixty years in the swamp and his way of life was a torment to folks who believed life must be lived by rules. He earned a few dollars selling jumbo frogs and pelts, but mostly he just paddled around the swamp, watching things and teaching Skeeter about life.

The villagers might have tried to send Skeeter to an orphanage, but for Joe (Cash) Watson, the storekeeper. Cash was a hard man, but fair. He often hunted with Jesse, and the old man had trained Cash's dogs. When there was talk of sending Skeeter away, Cash said, "You ain't agonna do it. You just don't take young'uns away from their folks." And that's all there was to it.

Jesse never coveted the "frills and furbelows of damn-fool folks" and yearned for only two things — a twenty-gauge shotgun for Skeeter and a set of Roebuckers for himself, as he called store-bought teeth. Cash had promised him the gun and the best false teeth in the catalogue for forty-six dollars. Jesse had saved $9.37.

"Someday I'm gonna get them Roebuckers," he often told Skeeter. "Then I'm gonna eat me enough roastin' ears to kill a goat. Maybe I can get a set with a couple of gold teeth in 'em. I seen a man once with six gold teeth."

Once Skeeter asked him, "Why don't you get a job with the W. P. and A. and make enough money to buy them Roebuckers?"

"I don't want 'em that bad," Jesse said.

So he was happy for Skeeter to have M'Lady, thinking the dog would sort of make up for the shotgun.

The boy cracked as many nuts as his uncle wanted, then put the hammer away. He was undressing when he glanced over at his dog. "Gosh, Uncle Jess. I'm scared somebody'll come get her."

"I ain't heard of nobody losing no things around here. If'n they had, they'd been to me 'fo' now, being's I know all about dogs and the swamp."

"That's so," Skeeter said. "But you don't reckon she belonged to another fellow like me, do you? I know how I'd feel if I had a dog like her and she got lost."

Jesse said, "She didn't belong to another fellow like you. If'n she had, she wouldn't be so happy here."

Skeeter fed M'Lady biscuits and molasses for breakfast, and although the Basenji ate it, she still was hungry when she went into the swamp with the boy. He was hoping he could find a bee tree or signs of wild hogs. They were at the edge of a clearing when M'Lady's chokebore nose suddenly tilted and she froze to a flash point, pausing only long enough to get set. Then she darted to the bayou, at least sixty yards away, dived into a clump of reeds and snatched a water rat. She was eating it when Skeeter ran up.

"Don't do that," he scolded. "Ain't you got no more sense than run into water after things? A snake or a gator might snatch you."

The Basenji dropped the rat and tucked her head. She knew the boy was displeased, and when she looked up at him her eyes were filled and a woebegone expression was on her face.

Skeeter tried to explain, "I didn't mean to hurt your feelings. Don't cry." He stepped back quickly and stared at her, at the tears in her eyes. "She is crying! Be John Brown!" Skeeter called her and ran toward the cabin, where Jesse was cutting splinters.

"Uncle Jess! Guess what else my dog can do!"

"Whistle?" the old man laughed.

"She can cry! I declare to goodness! Not out loud, but she can cry just the same."

Jesse knew that most dogs will get watery-eyed on occasion, but, not wanting to ridicule M'Lady's accomplishments, asked, "What made her cry?"

"Well, sir, we were walking along and all of a sudden she got a scent and flash pointed and then —— " Skeeter remembered something.

"Then what?"

Skeeter sat on the steps. "Uncle Jess," he said slowly, "we must have been fifty or sixty yards from that rat when she smelled it."

"What rat? What's eating you?"

The child told him the story and Jesse couldn't believe it. For a dog to pick up the scent of a water rat at sixty yards simply isn't credible. Jesse reckoned Skeeter's love for M'Lady had led him to exaggerate.

Skeeter knew Jesse didn't believe the story, so he said, "Come on. I'll show you." He whistled for M'Lady.

The dog came up. "Hey," Jesse said. "That thing knows what a whistle means. Shows she's been around folks." He caught the dog's eye and commanded, "Heel!"

But M'Lady cocked her head quizzically. Then she turned to the boy and chuckled softly. She'd never heard the order before. That was obvious. Her nose came up into the breeze and she wheeled.

Her curved tail suddenly was still and her head was poised.

"Flash pointing," Jesse said. "Well, I'll be a monkey's uncle!"

M'Lady held the strange point only for a second, though, then dashed toward a corn patch about eighty yards from the cabin.

Halfway to the patch, she broke her gait and began creeping. A whir of feathered lightning sounded in the corn and a covey of quail exploded almost under her nose. She sprang and snatched a bird.

"Partridges!" Jesse's jaw dropped.

The child was as motionless as stone, his face white and his eyes wide in amazement. Finally he found his voice, "She was right here when she smelled them birds. A good eighty yards."

"I know she ain't no dog now," Jesse said. "Can't no dog do that."

"She's fast as greased lightning and ain't scared of nothing."

Skeeter still was under the spell of the adventure. "She's a hunting dog from way back."

"She ain't no dog a-tall, I'm telling you. It ain't human." Jesse walked toward M'Lady and told her to fetch the bird, but the dog didn't understand. Instead, she pawed it. "Well," Jesse said. "One thing's certain. She ain't no bird hunter."

"She can do anything," Skeeter said. "Even hunt birds. Maybe I can make a bird dog out'n her. Wouldn't that be som'n?"

"You're batty. Maybe a coon dog, but not a bird dog. I know 'bout dogs."

"Me too," said Skeeter. And he did. He'd seen Jesse train many dogs, even pointers, and had helped him train Big Boy, Cash Watson's prize gun dog.

Jesse eyed Skeeter and read his mind.

"It can't be done, Skeets."

"Maybe not, but I aim to try. Any dog can run coons and rabbits, but it takes a pure D humdinger to hunt birds. Ain't no sin in trying, is it?"

"Naw," Jesse said slowly. "But she'll flush birds."

"I'll learn her not to."

"She won't hold no point. Any dog'll flash point. And she'll hunt rats."

"I'm gonna learn her just to hunt birds. And I'm starting right now," Skeeter said. He started walking away, then turned. "I seen a man once train a razorback hawg to point birds. You know as good as me that if a dog's got pure D hoss sense and a fellow's got bat brains, he can train the dog to hunt birds."

"Wanta bet?" Jesse issued the challenge in an effort to keep Skeeter's enthusiasm and determination at the high-water mark.

"Yes, sir. If I don't train my dog, then I'll cut all the splinters for a year. If I do, you cut 'em."

"It's a go," Jesse said.

Skeeter ran to the bayou and recovered the rat M'Lady had killed. He tied it around his dog's neck. The Basenji was indignant and tried to claw off the hateful burden. Failing, she ran into the house and under a bed, but Skeeter made her come out. M'Lady filled up then and her face assumed that don't-nobody-love-me look. The boy steeled himself, tapped M'Lady's nose with the rat, and left it around her neck.

"You done whittled out a job for yourself," Jesse said. "If'n you get her trained, you'll lose her in the brush. She's too fast and too little to keep up with."

"I'll bell her," Skeeter said. "I'm gonna learn her ever'thing. I got us a gun dog, Uncle Jess."

The old man sat on the porch and propped against the wall. "Bud, I don't know what that thing is. But you're a thoroughbred. John dog my hide!"

If Skeeter had loved M'Lady one bit less, his patience would have exploded during the ordeal of training the Basenji. It takes judgment and infinite patience to train a bird dog properly, but to train a Basenji, that'll hunt anything, to concentrate only on quail took something more than discipline and patience. It never could have been done except for that strange affinity between a boy and a dog, and the blind faith of a child.

M'Lady's devotion to Skeeter was so complete that she was anxious to do anything to earn a pat. It wasn't difficult to teach her to heel and follow at Skeeter's feet regardless of the urge to dash away and chase rabbits. The boy used a clothesline as a guide rope and made M'Lady follow him. The first time the dog tried to chase an animal, Skeeter pinched the rope around her neck just a bit and commanded, "Heel!" And when she obeyed, Skeeter released the noose. It took M'Lady only a few hours to associate disobedience with disfavor.

The dog learned that when she chased and killed a rat or rabbit, the thing would be tied around her neck. The only things she could hunt without being disciplined were quail. Of course, she often mistook the scent of game chickens for quail and hunted them, but

Skeeter punished her by scolding. He never switched his dog, but to M'Lady a harsh word from the boy hurt more than a hickory limb.

Jesse watched the dog's progress and pretended not to be impressed. He never volunteered suggestions. M'Lady learned quickly, but the task of teaching her to point birds seemed hopeless. Skeets knew she'd never point as pointers do, so he worked out his own system. He taught her to stand motionless when he shouted "Hup!" One day she got a scent of birds, paused or pointed for a moment as most animals will, and was ready to spring away when Skeeter said "Hup!"

M'Lady was confused. Every instinct urged her to chase the birds, but her master had said stand still. She broke, however, and Skeeter scolded her. She pouted at first, then filled up, but the boy ignored her until she obeyed the next command, then he patted her and she chuckled.

The lessons continued for days and weeks, and slowly and surely M'Lady learned her chores. She learned that the second she smelled birds she must stop and stand still until Skeeter flushed them. That she must not quiver when he shot.

Teaching her to fetch was easy, but teaching her to retrieve dead birds without damaging them was another matter. M'Lady had a hard mouth — that is, she sank her teeth into the birds. Skeeter used one of the oldest hunting tricks of the backwoods to break her.

He got a stick and wrapped it with wire and taught his dog to fetch it. Only once did M'Lady bite hard on the stick, and then the wire hurt her sensitive mouth. Soon she developed a habit of carrying the stick on her tongue and supporting it lightly with her teeth. Skeeter tied quail feathers on the stick, and soon M'Lady's education was complete.

Skeeter led Jesse into a field one day and turned his dog loose. She flashed to a point almost immediately. It was a funny point and Jesse almost laughed. The dog's curved tail poked up over her back, she spraddled her front legs and sort of squatted, her nose pointing the birds, more than forty yards away. She remained rigid until the boy flushed and shot, then she leaped away, seeking and fetching dead birds.

Jesse was mighty proud. "Well, Skeets, looks like you got yourself a bird hunter."

"Yes, sir," Skeeter said. "And you got yourself a job." He pointed toward the kindling pile.

The swamp was dressing for winter when Cash Watson drove down that day to give his Big Boy a workout in the wild brush.

He fetched Jesse a couple of cans of smoking tobacco and Skeeter a bag of peppermint jawbreakers. He locked his fine pointer in the corncrib for the night and was warming himself in the cabin when he noticed M'Lady for the first time. She was sleeping in front of the fire.

"What's that?" he asked.

"My dog," said Skeeter. "Ain't she a beaut?"

"She sure is," Cash grinned at Jesse. Skeeter went out to the well and Cash asked his old friend, "What the devil kind of mutt is that?"

"Search me," Jesse said. "Skeets found her in the swamp. I reckon she's got a trace of bloodhound in her and some terrier and a heap of just plain dog."

M'Lady cocked one ear and got up and stretched; then, apparently not liking the company, turned her tail toward Cash and strutted out, looking for Skeeter.

The men laughed. "Som'n wrong with her throat," Jesse said. "She can't bark. When she tries, she makes a funny sound, sort of a cackling, chuckling yodel. Sounds like she's laughing."

"Well," Cash said, "trust a young'un to love the orner'st dog he can find."

"Wait a minute," Jesse said. "She ain't no-count. She's a bird-hunting fool."

Just then Skeeter entered and Cash jestingly said, "Hear you got yourself a bird dog, son."

The boy clasped his hands behind him and rocked on the balls of his feet as he had seen the men do. "Well, now, I'll tell you, Mr. Cash. M'Lady does ever'thing except tote the gun."

"She must be fair to middling. Why not take her out with Big Boy tomorrow? Do my dog good to hunt in a brace."

"Me and my dog don't want to show Big Boy up. He's a pretty good ol' dog."

"Whoa!" Cash was every inch a bird-dog man and nobody could challenge him without a showdown. Besides, Skeeter was shooting up and should be learning a few things about life. "Any old boiler can pop off steam." Cash winked at Jesse.

"Well, now, sir, if you're itching for a run, I'll just double-dog dare you to run your dog against mine. And anybody who'll take a dare will pull up young cotton and push a widow woman's ducks in the water."

Cash admired the boy's confidence. "All right, son. It's a deal. What are the stakes?"

Skeeter started to mention the twenty-gauge gun he wanted, but changed his mind quickly. He reached down and patted M'Lady, then looked up. "If my dog beats yours, then you get them Roebuckers for Uncle Jess."

Jesse's chest suddenly was tight. Cash glanced from the boy to the man and he, too, was proud of Skeeter. "I wasn't aiming to go that high. But all right. What do I get if I win?"

"I'll cut you ten cords of stove-wood."

"And a stack of splinters?"

"Yes, sir."

Cash offered his hand and Skeeter took it. "It's a race," Cash said. "Jesse will be the judge."

The wind was rustling the sage and there was a nip in the early-morning air when they took the dogs to a clearing and set them down. Skeeter snapped a bell around M'Lady's neck and, at word from Jesse, the dogs were released.

Big Boy bounded away and began circling, ranging into the brush. M'Lady tilted her nose into the wind and ripped away toward the sage, her bell tinkling. Cash said, "She sure covers ground." Skeeter made no effort to keep up with her, but waited until he couldn't hear the bell, then ran for a clearing where he had last heard it. And there was M'Lady on a point.

Cash almost laughed out loud. "That ain't no point, son. That's a squat."

"She's got birds."

"Where?"

Jesse leaned against a tree and watched the fun.

Skeeter pointed toward a clump of sage. "She's pointing birds in that sage."

Cash couldn't restrain his mirth. "Boy, now that's what I call some pointing. Why, Skeeter, it's sixty or seventy yards to that sage."

Just then Big Boy flashed by M'Lady, his head high. He raced to the edge of the sage, caught the wind, then whipped around, freezing to a point. Cash called Jesse's attention to the point.

"That's M'Lady's point," Skeeter said. "She's got the same birds Big Boy has."

Jesse sauntered up. "The boy's right, Cash. I aimed to keep my mouth out'n this race, but M'Lady is pointing them birds. She can catch scents up to eighty yards."

Cash said, "Aw, go on. You're crazy." He walked over and flushed the birds.

Skeeter picked one off and ordered M'Lady to fetch. When she returned with the bird, the boy patted her and she began chuckling.

Cash really studied her then for the first time. "Hey!" he said suddenly. "A Basenji! That's a Basenji!"

"A what?" Jesse asked.

"I should have known." Cash was very excited. "That's the dog that was lost by them rich Yankees. I saw about it in the paper." He happened to look at Skeeter then and wished he had cut out his tongue.

The boy's lips were compressed and his face was drawn and white. Jesse had closed his eyes and was rubbing his forehead.

Cash, trying to dismiss the subject, said, "Just 'cause it was in the paper don't make it so. I don't believe that's the same dog, come to think of it."

"Do you aim to tell 'em where the dog is?" Skeeter asked.

Cash looked at Jesse, then at the ground. "It ain't none of my business."

"How 'bout you, Uncle Jess?"

"I ain't telling nobody nothin'."

"I know she's the same dog," Skeeter said. "On account of I just know it. But she's mine now." His voice rose and trembled. "And ain't nobody gonna take her away from me." He ran into the swamp. M'Lady was at his heels.

Cash said, "Durn my lip. I'm sorry, Jesse. If I'd kept my big mouth shut he'd never known the difference."

"It can't be helped now," Jesse said.

" 'Course she beat Big Boy. Them's the best hunting dogs in the world. And she's worth a mint of money."

They didn't feel up to hunting and returned to the cabin and sat on the porch. Neither had much to say, but kept glancing toward the swamp where Skeeter and M'Lady were walking along the bayou. "Don't you worry," he said tenderly. "Ain't nobody gonna bother you."

He sat on a stump and M'Lady put her head on his knee. She wasn't worrying. Nothing could have been more contented than she was.

"I don't care if the sheriff comes down." Skeeter pulled her onto his lap and held her. "I don't give a whoop if the governor comes down. Even the President of the United States! The whole shebang can come, but ain't nobody gonna mess with you."

His words gave him courage and he felt better, but for only a minute. Then the tug-of-war between him and his conscience started.

"Once I found a Barlow knife and kept it and it was all right," he mumbled.

But this is different.

"Finders, keepers; losers, weepers."

No, Skeeter.

"Well, I don't care. She's mine."

Remember what your Uncle Jess said.

"He said a heap of things."

Yes, but you remember one thing more than the rest. He said, "Certain things are right and certain things are wrong. And nothing ain't gonna ever change that. When you learn that, then you're fit'n to be a man." Remember, Skeeter?

A feeling of despair and loneliness almost overwhelmed him. He fought off the tears as long as he could, but finally he gave in, and his sobs caused M'Lady to peer into his face and wonder why he was acting that way when she was so happy. He put his arms around her neck and pulled her to him. "My li'l' old puppy dog. Poor li'l' old puppy dog. But I got to do it."

He sniffed back his tears and got up and walked to the cabin. M'Lady curled up by the fire and the boy sat down, watching the logs splutter for several minutes. Then he said, almost in a whisper, "Uncle Jess, if you keep som'n that ain't yours, it's the same as stealing, ain't it?"

Cash leaned against the mantel and stared into the fire.

Jesse puffed his pipe slowly. "Son, that's som'n you got to settle with yourself."

Skeeter stood and turned his back to the flames, warming his hands. "Mr. Cash," he said slowly, "when you get back to your store, please let them folks know their dog is here."

"If that's how it is —— "

"That's how it is," Skeeter said.

The firelight dancing on Jesse's face revealed the old man's dejection, and Skeeter, seeing it, said quickly, "It's best for M'Lady. She's too good for the swamp. They'll give her a good home."

Jesse flinched, and Cash, catching the hurt look in his friend's eyes, said, "Your dog outhunted mine, Skeets. You win them Roebuckers for your uncle."

"I don't want 'em," Jesse said, rather childishly. "I don't care if'n I never eat no roastin' ears." He got up quickly and hurried outside.

Cash reckoned he'd better be going, and left Skeeter by the fire, rubbing his dog.

Jesse came back in directly and pulled up a chair. Skeeter started to speak, but Jesse spoke first. "I been doing a heap of thinking lately. You're sprouting up. The swamp ain't no place for you."

Skeets forgot about his dog and faced his uncle, bewildered.

"I reckon you're too good for the swamp too," Jesse said. "I'm aiming to send you into town for a spell. I can make enough to keep you in fit'n clothes and all." He dared not look at the boy.

"Uncle Jess!" Skeets said reproachfully. "You don't mean that. You're just saying that on account of what I said about M'Lady. I said it just to keep you from feeling so bad about our dog going away. Gee m'netty, Uncle Jess. I ain't ever gonna leave you." He buried his face in his uncle's shoulder. M'Lady put her head on Jesse's knee and he patted the boy and rubbed the dog.

"Reckon I'll take them Roebuckers," he said at last. "I been wanting some for a long, long time."

Several days later Cash drove down and told them the man from the kennels was at his store. Skeeter didn't say a word, but called M'Lady and they got in Cash's car. All the way to town, the boy was silent. He held his dog's head in his lap.

The keeper took just one look at M'Lady and said, "That's she, all right. Miss Congo III." He turned to speak to Skeeter, but the boy was walking away. He got a glance at Skeeter's face, however. "Hell," he muttered. "I wish you fellows hadn't told me. I hate to take a dog away from a kid."

"He wanted you to know," Cash said.

"Mister" — Jesse closed his left eye and struck his swapping pose — "I'd like to swap you out'n that hound. Now, course she ain't much 'count —— "

The keeper smiled in spite of himself. "If she was mine, I'd give her to the kid. But she's not for sale. The owner wants to breed her and establish her line in this country. And if she was for sale, she'd cost more money than any of us will ever see." He called Skeets and offered his hand. Skeets shook it.

"You're a good kid. There's a reward for this dog."

"I don't want no reward." The boy's words tumbled out. "I don't want nothing, except to be left alone. You've got your dog, mister. Take her and go on. Please." He walked away again, fearing he would cry.

Cash said, "I'll take the reward and keep it for him. Someday he'll want it."

Jesse went out to the store porch to be with Skeeter. The keeper handed Cash the money. "It's tough, but the kid'll get over it. The dog never will."

"Is that a fact?"

"Yep. I know the breed. They never forget. That dog'll never laugh again. They never laugh unless they're happy."

He walked to the post where Skeeter had tied M'Lady. He untied the leash and started toward his station wagon. M'Lady braced her front feet and looked around for the boy. Seeing him on the porch, she jerked away from the keeper and ran to her master.

She rubbed against his legs. Skeets tried to ignore her. The keeper reached for the leash again and M'Lady crouched, baring her fangs. The keeper shrugged, a helpless gesture.

"Wild elephants couldn't pull that dog away from that boy," he said.

"That's all right, mister." Skeets unsnapped the leash and tossed it to the keeper. Then he walked to the station wagon, opened the door of a cage and called, "Heah, M'Lady!" She bounded to him. "Up!" he commanded. She didn't hesitate, but leaped into the cage. The keeper locked the door.

M'Lady, having obeyed a command, poked her nose between the bars, expecting a pat. The boy rubbed her head. She tried to move closer to him, but the bars held her. She looked quizzically at the bars, then tried to nudge them aside. Then she clawed them. A look of fear suddenly came to her eyes and she fastened them on

Skeets, wistfully at first, then pleadingly. She couldn't make a sound, for her unhappiness had sealed her throat. Slowly her eyes filled up.

"Don't cry no more, M'Lady. Ever'thing's gonna be all right." He reached out to pat her, but the station wagon moved off, leaving him standing there in the dust.

Back on the porch, Jesse lit his pipe and said to his friend, "Cash, the boy has lost his dog and I've lost a boy."

"Aw, Jesse, Skeeter wouldn't leave you."

"That ain't what I mean. He's growed up, Cash. He don't look no older, but he is. He growed up that day in the swamp."

Skeeter walked into the store and Cash followed him. "I've got that reward for you, Jonathan."

It was the first time anyone ever had called him that and it sounded like man talk.

"And that twenty-gauge is waiting for you," Cash said. "I'm gonna give it to you."

"Thank you, Mr. Cash." The boy bit his lower lip. "But I don't aim to do no more hunting. I don't never want no more dogs."

"Know how you feel. But if you change your mind, the gun's here for you."

Skeets looked back toward the porch where Jesse was waiting, and said, "Tell you what, though. When you get them Roebuckers, get some with a couple of gold teeth in 'em. Take it out of the reward money."

"Sure, Jonathan."

Jesse joined them, and Skeeter said, "We better be getting back toward the house."

"I'll drive you down," Cash said. "But first I aim to treat you to some lemon pop and sardines."

"That's mighty nice of you," Jesse said, "but we better be gettin' on."

"What's the hurry?" Cash opened the pop.

"It's my time to cut splinters," Jesse said. "That's what I get for betting with a good man."

YOU COULD LOOK IT UP

By James Thurber

IT ALL began when we dropped down to C'lumbus, Ohio, from Pittsburgh to play a exhibition game on our way out to St. Louis. It was gettin' on into September, and though we'd been leadin' the league by six, seven games most of the season, we was now in first place by a margin you could 'a' got it into the eye of a thimble, bein' only a half a game ahead of St. Louis. Our slump had given the boys the leapin' jumps, and they was like a bunch a old ladies at a lawn fete with a thunderstorm comin' up, runnin' around snarlin' at each other, eatin' bad and sleepin' worse, and battin' for a team average of maybe .186. Half the time nobody'd speak to nobody else, without it was to bawl 'em out.

Squawks Magrew was managin' the boys at the time, and he was darn near crazy. They called him "Squawks" 'cause when things was goin' bad he lost his voice, or perty near lost it, and squealed at you like a little girl you stepped on her doll or somethin'. He yelled at everybody and wouldn't listen to nobody, without maybe it was me. I'd been trainin' the boys for ten year, and he'd take more lip from me than from anybody else. He knowed I was smarter'n him, anyways, like you're goin' to hear.

This was thirty, thirty-one year ago; you could look it up, 'cause it was the same year C'lumbus decided to call itself the Arch City, on account of a lot of iron arches with electric-light bulbs into 'em which stretched acrost High Street. Thomas Albert Edison sent 'em a telegram, and they was speeches and maybe even President Taft opened the celebration by pushin' a button. It was a great week for the Buckeye capital, which was why they got us out there for this exhibition game.

Well, we just lose a double-header to Pittsburgh, 11 to 5 and 7 to 3, so we snarled all the way to C'lumbus, where we put up at the Chittaden Hotel, still snarlin'. Everybody was tetchy, and when Billy Klinger took a sock at Whitey Cott at breakfast, Whitey throwed marmalade all over his face.

"Blind each other, whatta I care?" says Magrew. "You can't see nothin' anyways."

C'lumbus win the exhibition game, 3 to 2, whilst Magrew set in the dugout, mutterin' and cursin' like a fourteen-year-old Scotty. He bad-mouthed everybody on the ball club and he bad-mouthed everybody offa the ball club, includin' the Wright brothers, who, he claimed, had yet to build a airship big enough for any of our boys to hit it with a ball bat.

"I wisht I was dead," he says to me. "I wisht I was in heaven with the angels."

I told him to pull hisself together, 'cause he was drivin' the boys crazy, the way he was goin' on, sulkin' and bad-mouthin' and whinin'. I was older'n he was and smarter'n he was, and he knowed it. I was ten times smarter'n he was about this Pearl du Monville, first time I ever laid eyes on the little guy, which was one of the saddest days of my life.

Now, most people name of Pearl is girls, but this Pearl du Monville was a man, if you could call a fella a man who was only thirty-four, thirty-five inches high. Pearl du Monville was a midget. He was part French and part Hungarian, and maybe even part Bulgarian or somethin'. I can see him now, a sneer on his little pushed-in pan, swingin' a bamboo cane and smokin' a big cigar. He had a gray suit with a big black check into it, and he had a gray felt hat with one of them rainbow-colored hatbands onto it, like the young fellas wore in them days. He talked like he was talkin' into a tin can, but he didn't have no foreign accent. He might 'a' been fifteen or he might 'a' been a hundred, you couldn't tell. Pearl du Monville.

After the game with C'lumbus, Magrew headed straight for the Chittaden bar — the train for St. Louis wasn't goin' for three, four hours — and there he set, drinkin' rye and talkin' to this bartender.

"How I pity me, brother," Magrew was tellin' this bartender.

"How I pity me." That was alwuz his favorite tune. So he was settin' there, tellin' this bartender how heartbreakin' it was to be manager of a bunch a blindfolded circus clowns, when up pops this Pearl du Monville outa nowheres.

It give Magrew the leapin' jumps. He thought at first maybe the D.T.'s had come back on him; he claimed he'd had 'em once, and little guys had popped up all around him, wearin' red, white and blue hats.

"Go on, now!" Magrew yells. "Get away from me!"

But the midget clumb up on a chair acrost the table from Magrew and says, "I seen that game today, Junior, and you ain't got no ball club. What you got there, Junior," he says, "is a side show."

"Whatta ya mean, 'Junior'?" says Magrew, touchin' the little guy to satisfy hisself he was real.

"Don't pay him no attention, mister," says the bartender. "Pearl calls everybody 'Junior,' 'cause it alwuz turns out he's a year older'n anybody else."

"Yeh?" says Magrew. "How old is he?"

"How old are you, Junior?" says the midget.

"Who, me? I'm fifty-three," says Magrew.

"Well, I'm fifty-four," says the midget.

Magrew grins and asts him what he'll have, and that was the beginnin' of their beautiful friendship, if you don't care what you say.

Pearl du Monville stood up on his chair and waved his cane around and pretended like he was ballyhooin' for a circus. "Right this way, folks!" he yells. "Come on in and see the greatest collection of freaks in the world! See the armless pitchers, see the eyeless batters, see the infielders with five thumbs!" and on and on like that, feedin' Magrew gall and handin' him a laugh at the same time, you might say.

You could hear him and Pearl du Monville hootin' and hollerin' and singin' way up to the fourth floor of the Chittaden, where the boys was packin' up. When it come time to go to the station, you can imagine how disgusted we was when we crowded into the doorway of that bar and seen them two singin' and goin' on.

"Well, well, well," says Magrew, lookin' up and spottin' us. "Look who's here. . . . Clowns, this is Pearl du Monville, a monseer of the old, old school. . . . Don't shake hands with 'em, Pearl, 'cause their fingers is made of chalk and would bust right off in your paws," he says, and he starts guffawin' and Pearl starts titterin' and we stand there givin' 'em the iron eye, it bein' the lowest ebb a ball-club manager'd got hisself down to since the national pastime was started.

Then the midget begun givin' us the ballyhoo. "Come on in!" he says, wavin' his cane. "See the legless base runners, see the outfielders with the butter fingers, see the southpaw with the arm of a little chee-ild!"

Then him and Magrew begun to hoop and holler and nudge each other till you'd of thought this little guy was the funniest guy than even Charlie Chaplin. The fellas filed outa the bar without a word and went on up to the Union Depot, leavin' me to handle Magrew and his new-found crony.

Well, I got 'em outa there finely. I had to take the little guy along, 'cause Magrew had a holt onto him like a vise and I couldn't pry him loose.

"He's comin' along as masket," says Magrew, holdin' the midget in the crouch of his arm like a football. And come along he did, hollerin' and protestin' and beatin' at Magrew with his little fists.

"Cut it out, will ya, Junior?" the little guy kept whinin'. "Come on, leave a man loose, will ya, Junior?"

But Junior kept a holt onto him and begun yellin', "See the guys with the glass arm, see the guys with the cast-iron brains, see the fielders with the feet on their wrists!"

So it goes, right through the whole Union Depot, with people starin' and catcallin', and he don't put the midget down till he gets him through the gates.

"How'm I goin' to go along without no toothbrush?" the midget asts. "What'm I goin' to do without no other suit?" he says.

"Doc here," says Magrew, meanin' me — "doc here will look after you like you was his own son, won't you, doc?"

I give him the iron eye, and he finely got on the train and prob'ly went to sleep with his clothes on.

This left me alone with the midget. "Lookit," I says to him. "Why don't you go on home now? Come mornin', Magrew'll forget all about you. He'll probably think you was somethin' he seen in a nightmare maybe. And he ain't goin' to laugh so easy in the mornin', neither," I says. "So why don't you go on home?"

"Nix," he says to me. "Skiddoo," he says, "twenty-three for you," and he tosses his cane up into the vestibule of the coach and clam'ers on up after it like a cat. So that's the way Pearl du Monville come to go to St. Louis with the ball club.

I seen 'em first at breakfast the next day, settin' opposite each other; the midget playin' Turkey in the Straw on a harmonium and Magrew starin' at his eggs and bacon like they was a uncooked bird with its feathers still on.

"Remember where you found this?" I says, jerkin' my thumb at the midget. "Or maybe you think they come with breakfast on these trains," I says, bein' a good hand at turnin' a sharp remark in them days.

The midget puts down the harmonium and turns on me. "Sneeze," he says; "your brains is dusty." Then he snaps a couple drops of water at me from a tumbler. "Drown," he says, tryin' to make his voice deep.

Now, both them cracks is Civil War cracks, but you'd of thought they was brand new and the funniest than any crack Magrew'd ever heard in his whole life. He started hoopin' and hollerin', and the midget started hoopin' and hollerin', so I walked on away and set down with Bugs Courtney and Hank Metters, payin' no attention to this weak-minded Damon and Phidias acrost the aisle.

Well, sir, the first game with St. Louis was rained out, and there we was facin' a double-header next day. Like maybe I told you, we lose the last three double-headers we play, makin' maybe twenty-five errors in the six games, which is all right for the intimates of a school for the blind, but is disgraceful for the world's champions. It was too wet to go to the zoo, and Magrew wouldn't let us go to the movies, 'cause they flickered so bad in them days. So we just set around, stewin' and frettin'.

One of the newspaper boys come over to take a pitture of Billy Klinger and Whitey Cott shakin' hands — this reporter'd heard about the fight — and whilst they was standin' there, toe to toe, shakin' hands, Billy give a back lunge and a jerk, and throwed Whitey over his shoulder into a corner of the room, like a sack a salt. Whitey come back at him with a chair, and Bethlehem broke loose in that there room. The camera was tromped to pieces like a berry basket. When we finely got 'em pulled apart, I heard a laugh, and there was Magrew and the midget standin' in the door and givin' us the iron eye.

"Wrasslers," says Magrew, cold-like, "that's what I got for a ball club, Mr. Du Monville, wrasslers — and not very good wrasslers at that, you ast me."

"A man can't be good at everythin'," says Pearl, "but he oughta be good at somethin'."

This sets Magrew guffawin' again, and away they go, the midget taggin' along by his side like a hound dog and handin' him a fast line of so-called comic cracks.

When we went out to face that battlin' St. Louis club in a double-header the next afternoon, the boys was jumpy as tin toys with keys in their back. We lose the first game, 7 to 2, and are trailin', 4 to 0, when the second game ain't but ten minutes old. Magrew set there like a stone statue, speakin' to nobody. Then, in their half a the fourth, somebody singled to center and knocked in two more runs for St. Louis.

That made Magrew squawk. "I wisht one thing," he says. "I wisht I was manager of a old ladies' sewin' circus 'stead of a ball club."

"You are, Junior, you are," says a familyer and disagreeable voice.

It was that Pearl du Monville again, poppin' up outa nowheres, swingin' his bamboo cane and smokin' a cigar that's three sizes too big for his face. By this time we'd finely got the other side out, and

Hank Metters slithered a bat acrost the ground, and the midget had to jump to keep both his ankles from bein' broke.

I thought Magrew'd bust a blood vessel. "You hurt Pearl and I'll break your neck!" he yelled.

Hank muttered somethin' and went on up to the plate and struck out.

We managed to get a couple runs acrost in our half a the sixth, but they come back with three more in their half a the seventh, and this was too much for Magrew.

"Come on, Pearl," he says. "We're gettin' outta here."

"Where you think you're goin'?" I ast him.

"To the lawyer's again," he says cryptly.

"I didn't know you'd been to the lawyer's once, yet," I says.

"Which that goes to show how much you don't know," he says.

With that, they was gone, and I didn't see 'em the rest of the day, nor know what they was up to, which was a God's blessin'. We lose the nightcap, 9 to 3, and that puts us into second place plenty, and as low in our mind as a ball club can get.

The next day was a horrible day, like anybody that lived through it can tell you. Practice was just over and the St. Louis club was takin' the field, when I hears this strange sound from the stands. It sounds like the nervous whickerin' a horse gives when he smells somethin' funny on the wind. It was the fans ketchin' sight of Pearl du Monville, like you have prob'ly guessed. The midget had popped up onto the field all dressed up in a minacher club uniform, sox, cap, little letters sewed onto his chest, and all. He was swingin' a kid's bat and the only thing kept him from lookin' like a real ball-player seen through the wrong end of a microscope was this cigar he was smokin'.

Bugs Courtney reached over and jerked it outa his mouth and throwed it away. "You're wearin' that suit on the playin' field," he says to him, severe as a judge. "You go insultin' it and I'll take you out to the zoo and feed you to the bears."

Pearl just blowed some smoke at him which he still has in his mouth.

Whilst Whitey was foulin' off four or five prior to strikin' out, I went on over to Magrew. "If I was as comic as you," I says, "I'd laugh myself to death," I says. "Is that any way to treat the uniform, makin' a mockery out of it?"

"It might surprise you to know I ain't makin' no mockery outa the uniform," says Magrew. "Pearl du Monville here has been made a bone-of-fida member of this so-called ball club. I fixed it up with the front office by long-distance phone."

"Yeh?" I says. "I can just hear Mr. Dillworth or Bart Jenkins agreein' to hire a midget for the ball club. I can just hear 'em." Mr. Dillworth was the owner of the club and Bart Jenkins was the secretary, and they never stood for no monkey business. "May I be so bold as to inquire," I says, "just what you told 'em?"

"I told 'em," he says, "I wanted to sign up a guy they ain't no pitcher in the league can strike him out."

"Uh-huh," I says, "and did you tell 'em what size of a man he is?"

"Never mind about that," he says. "I got papers on me, made out legal and proper, constitutin' one Pearl du Monville a bone-of-fida member of this former ball club. Maybe that'll shame them big babies into gettin' in there and swingin', knowin' I can replace any one of 'em with a midget, if I have a mind to. A St. Louis lawyer I seen twice tells me it's all legal and proper."

"A St. Louis lawyer would," I says, "seein' nothin' could make him happier than havin' you makin' a mockery outa this one-time baseball outfit," I says.

Well, sir, it'll all be there in the papers of thirty, thirty-one year ago, and you could look it up. The game went along without no scorin' for seven innings, and since they ain't nothin' much to watch but guys poppin' up or strikin' out, the fans pay most of their attention to the goin's-on of Pearl du Monville. He's out there in front a the dugout turnin' handsprings, balancin' his bat on his chin, walkin' a imaginary line, and so on. The fans clapped and laughed at him, and he ate it up.

So it went up to the last a the eighth, nothin' to nothin', not more'n seven, eight hits all told, and no errors on neither side. Our pitcher gets the first two men out easy in the eighth. Then up come a fella name of Porter or Billings, or some such name, and he lammed one up against the tobacco sign for three bases. The next guy up slapped the first ball out into left for a base hit, and in come the fella from third for the only run of the ball game so far. The crowd yelled, the look a death come onto Magrew's face again, and even the midget quit his tomfoolin'. Their next man fouled out back a third, and we come up for our last bats like a bunch of schoolgirls steppin' into a pool of cold water. I was lower in my mind than I'd been since the day in Nineteen-four when Chesbro throwed the wild pitch in the ninth inning with a man on third and lost the pennant for the Highlanders. I knowed something just as bad was goin' to happen, which shows I'm a clairvoyun, or was then.

When Gordy Mills hit out to second, I just closed my eyes. I opened 'em up again to see Dutch Muller standin' on second, dustin' off his pants, him havin' got his first hit in maybe twenty times to the plate. Next up was Harry Loesing, battin' for our pitcher, and he got a base on balls, walkin' on a fourth one you could 'a' combed your hair with.

Then up come Whitey Cott, our lead-off man. He crouches down in what was prob'ly the most fearsome stanch in organized ball, but all he can do is pop out to short. That brung up Billy Klinger, with two down and a man on first and second. Billy took a cut at one you could 'a' knocked a plug hat offa this here Carnera with it, but then he gets sense enough to wait 'em out, and finely he walks, too, fillin' the bases.

Yes, sir, there you are; the tyin' run on third and the winnin' run on second, first a the ninth, two men down, and Hank Metters comin' to the bat. Hank was built like a Pope-Hartford and he couldn't run no faster'n President Taft, but he had five home runs to his credit for the season, and that wasn't bad in them days. Hank was still hittin' better'n anybody else on the ball club, and it was mighty heartenin', seein' him stridin' up towards the plate. But he never got there.

"Wait a minute!" yells Magrew, jumpin' to his feet. "I'm sendin' in a pinch hitter!" he yells.

You could 'a' heard a bomb drop. When a ball-club manager says he's sendin' in a pinch hitter for the best batter on the club, you know and I know and everybody knows he's lost his holt.

"They're goin' to be sendin' the funny wagon for you, if you don't watch out," I says, grabbin' a holt of his arm.

But he pulled away and run out towards the plate, yellin', "Du Monville battin' for Metters!"

All the fellas begun squawlin' at once, except Hank, and he just stood there starin' at Magrew like he'd gone crazy and was claimin' to be Ty Cobb's grandma or somethin'. Their pitcher stood out there with his hands on his hips and a disagreeable look on his face, and the plate umpire told Magrew to go on and get a batter up. Magrew told him again Du Monville was battin' for Metters, and the St. Louis manager finely got the idea. It brung him outa his dugout, howlin' and bawlin' like he'd lost a female dog and her seven pups.

Magrew pushed the midget towards the plate and he says to him, he says, "Just stand up there and hold that bat on your shoulder. They ain't a man in the world can throw three strikes in there 'fore he throws four balls!" he says.

"I get it, Junior!" says the midget. "He'll walk me and force in the tyin' run!" And he starts on up to the plate as cocky as if he was Willie Keeler.

I don't need to tell you Bethlehem broke loose on that there ball field. The fans got onto their hind legs, yellin' and whistlin', and everybody on the field begun wavin' their arms and hollerin' and shovin'. The plate umpire stalked over to Magrew like a traffic cop, waggin' his jaw and pointin' his finger, and the St. Louis manager kept yellin' like his house was on fire. When Pearl got up to the plate and stood there, the pitcher slammed his glove down onto the ground and started stompin' on it, and they ain't nobody can blame him. He's just walked two normal-sized human bein's, and now here's a guy up to the plate they ain't more'n twenty inches between his knees and his shoulders.

The plate umpire called in the field umpire, and they talked a while, like a couple doctors seein' the bucolic plague or somethin' for the first time. Then the plate umpire come over to Magrew with his arms folded acrost his chest, and he told him to go on and get a batter up, or he'd forfeit the game to St. Louis. He pulled out his watch, but somebody batted it outa his hand in the scuffin', and I thought there'd be a free-for-all, with everybody yellin' and shovin' except Pearl du Monville, who stood up at the plate with his little bat on his shoulder, not movin' a muscle.

Then Magrew played his ace. I seen him pull some papers outa his pocket and show 'em to the plate umpire. The umpire begun lookin' at 'em like they was bills for somethin' he not only never bought it, he never even heard of it. The other umpire studied 'em like they was a death warren, and all this time the St. Louis manager and the fans and the players is yellin' and hollerin'.

Well, sir, they fought about him bein' a midget, and they fought about him usin' a kid's bat, and they fought about where'd he been all season. They was eight or nine rule books brung out and everybody was thumbin' through 'em, tryin' to find out what it says about midgets, but it don't say nothin' about midgets, 'cause this was somethin' never'd come up in the history of the game before, and nobody'd ever dreamed about it, even when they has nightmares. Maybe you can't send no midgets in to bat nowadays, 'cause the old game's changed a lot, mostly for the worst, but you could then, it turned out.

The plate umpire finely decided the contrack papers was all legal and proper, like Magrew said, so he waved the St. Louis players back to their places and he pointed his finger at their manager and told him to quit hollerin' and get on back in the dugout. The manager says the game is percedin' under protest, and the umpire bawls, "Play ball!" over 'n' above the yellin' and booin', him havin' a voice like a hog-caller.

The St. Louis pitcher picked up his glove and beat at it with his fist six or eight times, and then got set on the mound and studied the situation. The fans realized he was really goin' to pitch to the midget, and they went crazy, hoopin' and hollerin' louder'n ever, and throwin' pop bottles and hats and cushions down onto the field. It took five, ten minutes to get the fans quieted down again, whilst our fellas that was on base set down on the bags and waited. And Pearl du Monville kept standin' up there with the bat on his shoulder, like he'd been told to.

So the pitcher starts studyin' the setup again, and you got to admit it was the strangest setup in a ball game since the players cut off their beards and begun wearin' gloves. I wisht I could call the pitcher's name — it wasn't old Barney Pelty nor Nig Jack Powell nor Harry Howell. He was a big right-hander, but I can't call his name. You could look it up. Even in a crotchin' position, the ketcher towers over the midget like the Washington Monument.

The plate umpire tries standin' on his tiptoes, then he tries crotchin' down, and he finely gets hisself into a stanch nobody'd ever seen on a ball field before, kinda squattin' down on his hanches.

Well, the pitcher is sore as a old buggy horse in fly time. He slams in the first pitch, hard and wild, and maybe two foot higher 'n the midget's head.

"Ball one!" hollers the umpire over 'n' above the racket, 'cause everybody is yellin' worsten ever.

The ketcher goes on out towards the mound and talks to the pitcher and hands him the ball. This time the big right-hander tries a under-shoot, and it comes in a little closer, maybe no higher'n a foot, foot and a half above Pearl's head. It would 'a' been a strike with a human bein' in there, but the umpire's got to call it, and he does.

"Ball two!" he bellers.

The ketcher walks on out to the mound again, and the whole infield comes over and gives advice to the pitcher about what they'd do in a case like this, with two balls and no strikes on a batter that oughta be in a bottle of alcohol 'stead of up there at the plate in a big-league game between the teams that is fightin' for first place.

For the third pitch, the pitcher stands there flat-footed and tosses up the ball like he's playin' ketch with a little girl.

Pearl stands there motionless as a hitchin' post, and the ball comes in big and slow and high — high for Pearl, that is, it bein' about on a level with his eyes, or a little higher'n a grown man's knees.

They ain't nothin' else for the umpire to do, so he calls, "Ball three!"

Everybody is onto their feet, hoopin' and hollerin', as the pitcher sets to throw ball four. The St. Louis manager is makin' signs and faces like he was a contorturer, and the infield is givin' the pitcher some more advice about what to do this time. Our boys who was on base stick right onto the bag, runnin' no risk of bein' nipped for the last out.

Well, the pitcher decides to give him a toss again, seein' he come closer with that than with a fast ball. They ain't nobody ever seen a slower ball throwed. It come in big as a balloon and slower'n any ball ever throwed before in the major leagues. It come right in over the plate in front of Pearl's chest, lookin' prob'ly big as a full moon to Pearl. They ain't never been a minute like the minute that followed since the United States was founded by the Pilgrim grandfathers.

Pearl du Monville took a cut at that ball, and he hit it! Magrew give a groan like a poleaxed steer as the ball rolls out in front a the plate into fair territory.

"Fair ball!" yells the umpire, and the midget starts runnin' for first, still carryin' that little bat, and makin' maybe ninety foot an hour. Bethlehem breaks loose on that ball field and in them stands. They ain't never been nothin' like it since creation was begun.

The ball's rollin' slow, on down towards third, goin' maybe eight, ten foot. The infield comes in fast and our boys break from their bases like hares in a brush fire. Everybody is standin' up, yellin' and hollerin', and Magrew is tearin' his hair outa his head, and the midget is scamperin' for first with all the speed of one of them little dashhounds carryin' a satchel in his mouth.

The ketcher gets to the ball first, but he boots it on out past the pitcher's box, the pitcher fallin' on his face tryin' to stop it, the shortstop sprawlin' after it full length and zaggin' it on over towards the second baseman, whilst Muller is scorin' with the tyin' run and Loesing is roundin' third with the winnin' run. Ty Cobb could 'a' made a three-bagger outa that bunt, with everybody fallin' over theirself tryin' to pick the ball up. But Pearl is still maybe fifteen, twenty feet from the bag, toddlin' like a baby and yeepin' like a trapped rabbit, when the second baseman finely gets a holt of that ball and slams it over to first. The first baseman ketches it and stomps on the bag, the base umpire waves Pearl out, and there goes your old ball game, the craziest ball game ever played in the history of the organized world.

Their players start runnin' in, and then I see Magrew. He starts after Pearl, runnin' faster'n any man ever run before. Pearl sees him comin' and runs behind the base umpire's legs and gets a holt onto 'em. Magrew comes up, pantin' and roarin', and him and the midget plays ring-around-a-rosy with the umpire, who keeps shovin' at Magrew with one hand and tryin' to slap the midget loose from his legs with the other.

Finely Magrew ketches the midget, who is still yeepin' like a stuck sheep. He gets holt of that little guy by both his ankles and starts whirlin' him round and round his head like Magrew was a hammer thrower and Pearl was the hammer. Nobody can stop him without gettin' their head knocked off, so everybody just stands there and yells. Then Magrew lets the midget fly. He flies on out towards second, high and fast, like a human home run, headed for the soap sign in center field.

Their shortstop tries to get to him, but he can't make it, and I knowed the little fella was goin' to bust to pieces like a dollar watch on a asphalt street when he hit the ground. But it so happens their center fielder is just crossin' second, and he starts runnin' back, tryin' to get under the midget, who had took to spiralin' like a football 'stead of turnin' head over foot, which give him more speed and more distance.

I know you never seen a midget ketched, and you prob'ly never even seen one throwed. To ketch a midget that's been throwed by a heavy-muscled man and is flyin' through the air, you got to run under him and with him and pull your hands and arms back and down when you ketch him, to break the compact of his body, or you'll bust him in two like a matchstick. I seen Bill Lange and Willie Keeler and Tris Speaker make some wonderful ketches in my day, but I never seen nothin' like that center fielder. He goes back and back and still further back and he pulls that midget down outa the air like he was liftin' a sleepin' baby from a cradle. They wasn't a bruise onto him, only his face was the color of cat's meat and he ain't got no air in his chest. In his excitement, the base umpire, who was runnin' back with the center fielder when he ketched Pearl, yells, "Out!" and that give hysteries to the Bethlehem which was ragin' like Niagry on that ball field.

Everybody was hoopin' and hollerin' and yellin' and runnin', with the fans swarmin' onto the field, and the cops tryin' to keep order, and some guys laughin' and some of the women fans cryin', and six or eight of us holdin' onto Magrew to keep him from gettin' at that midget and finishin' him off. Some of the fans picks up the St. Louis pitcher and the center fielder, and starts carryin' 'em around on their shoulders, and they was the craziest goin's-on knowed to the history of organized ball on this side of the 'Lantic Ocean.

I seen Pearl du Monville strugglin' in the arms of a lady fan with a ample bosom, who was laughin' and cryin' at the same time, and him beatin' at her with his little fists and bawlin' and yellin'. He clawed his way loose finely and disappeared in the forest of legs which made that ball field look like it was Coney Island on a hot summer's day.

That was the last I ever seen of Pearl du Monville. I never seen hide nor hair of him from that day to this, and neither did nobody else. He just vanished into the thin of the air, as the fella says. He was ketched for the final out of the ball game and that was the end of him, just like it was the end of the ball game, you might say, and also the end of our losin' streak, like I'm goin' to tell you.

That night we piled onto a train for Chicago, but we wasn't snarlin' and snappin' any more. No, sir, the ice was finely broke and a new spirit come into that ball club. The old zip come back with the disappearance of Pearl du Monville out back a second base. We got to laughin' and talkin' and kiddin' together, and 'fore long Magrew was laughin' with us. He got a human look onto his pan again, and he quit whinin' and complainin' and wishtin' he was in heaven with the angels.

Well, sir, we wiped up that Chicago series, winnin' all four games, and makin' seventeen hits in one of 'em. Funny thing was, St. Louis was so shook up by that last game with us, they never did hit their stride again. Their center fielder took to misjudgin' everything that come his way, and the rest a the fellas followed suit, the way a club'll do when one guy blows up.

'Fore we left Chicago, I and some of the fellas went out and bought a pair of them little baby shoes, which we had 'em golded over and give 'em to Magrew for a souvenir, and he took it all in good spirit. Whitey Cott and Billy Klinger made up and was fast friends again, and we hit our home lot like a ton of dynamite and they was nothin' could stop us from then on.

I don't recollect things as clear as I did thirty, forty year ago. I can't read no fine print no more, and the only person I got to check with on the golden days of the national pastime, as the fella says, is my friend, old Milt Kline, over in Springfield, and his mind ain't as strong as it once was.

He gets Rube Waddell mixed up with Rube Marquard, for one thing, and anybody does that oughta be put away where he won't bother nobody. So I can't tell you the exact margin we win the pennant by. Maybe it was two and a half games, or maybe it was three and a half. But it'll all be there in the newspapers and record books of thirty, thirty-one year ago and, like I was sayin', you could look it up.

TIME AND A HALF FOR A HERO

By Doug Welch

A THIN shrill cry of pain, a horrid screaming such as might have been wrested from a Crusader in his last torments upon the rack or from some hapless South Seas missionary about to become, with truffles, the thirty-five-cent blue *plat du jour,* rose and resounded in the city room of the Central City Daily Informer.

It was a primitive and blood-chilling cry, to be sure, but a familiar enough noise to the Informer's eighty-five editorial employees, and signified no more than that Mr. Robert ["Happy"] Digby had just reported for work and glanced over his forenoon assignment schedule. Mr. Digby, a photographer, was in no lower spirits than usual.

Indeed, Mr. Digby and the Informer's two other news photographers together not infrequently sounded like the whole second road company of Julius Caesar (the mob scene, Act III), playing a matinee at North Overshoes, Idaho, between trains and on empty stomachs. It was to the real credit of Mr. Digby that his voice invariably carried above the others.

"For crying out loud!" said Mr. Digby. "This ain't a newspaper, it's a rat race. What am I supposed to be, anyway? Superman? Today they only got me scheduled to be in about fourteen places at once. They think I'm riding around on a rocket or maybe a broom. Them boy scouts on the city desk ain't going to be satisfied until they can dream up some way to shoot photographers out of a cannon."

For the greater part of what might loosely be termed his adult life, Mr. Digby had been inveighing against desk men in terms which, among a more sensitive company, would long since have got him the finger. He was constantly amazed — and constantly and loudly voicing his amazement — by two phenomena: first, that with so many downright psychopathics among its editorial personnel, the Informer ever managed to get itself published, and, secondly, that people continued to buy it. It was Mr. Digby's considered opinion that the Informer was suitable only for wrapping fish and sitting upon at ball games.

Without admitting the allegation — or without denying it, either, for that matter — the Informer bore with Mr. Digby because he had more brass than a locomotive bell, more nerve than a male corset fitter, and was as efficient as he was dour. His superiors charitably ascribed his habitual belligerency to improper eating and artistic temperament, both of which are natural hazards of the publishing business. Just why the Informer should cherish brass, nerve and efficiency was something else again, apparent neither to Mr. Digby nor to any of his immediate associates.

In its younger, leaner days when Old Man Russell, the publisher, used to take his turn at the copy desk to make sure the stories and heads bristled with the proper amount of social significance, the Informer was a fighting sheet. Now, in comfortable middle age, its advertising revenues expanding in direct ratio with Mr. Russell's own waistline, the Informer wanted trouble with no one.

This editorial equanimity could be traced to a number of circumstances, among them the fact it was published largely by remote control — from Florida and California in the winter, from the Canadian north woods in the summer, and at other times from the reconditioning chambers of several Turkish baths around town. By the time the editors had submitted to Publisher Russell the prospectus of some lively campaign for the public good, and by the time he had become sufficiently dehydrated to consider it, the issue was as lively as a girl-scout cooky sale and as current as Whistler's Mother.

So, in the absence of more specific instructions, his editors played their cards close to their chests, and the Informer issued daily with glowing noncontroversial accounts of dogs which could count up to ten, cats with seven-toed paws, and persons who had grown potatoes or carrots faintly resembling either Mussolini or Charlie McCarthy.

"How do you like this?" exploded Mr. Digby. "I got to go clean out to West Park to grab off a shot of some broad which has a four-

teen-foot hollyhock in her back yard. We ain't got any other news
to run. Of course, the city council is all packing blackjacks, the
mayor comes down to work wearing a mask, the Colucci mob is
bombing laundries all over the joint, and they even got their slot machines in the day nurseries. But that ain't news. So we rush out of
here and make a hollyhock!"

His refrain carried throughout the city room, but his immediate
audience was Jimmy Ralston, a shy youth who had but recently been
promoted from office boy to cub reporter.

Young Ralston clucked sympathetically. "Well," he said, "I'm
ready to go if you are."

Mr. Digby stared at him in horror. "You don't mean," he said,
"that I got to take you along?"

The cub nodded unhappily.

"I ain't already got enough to do," said Mr. Digby, "so I got to run
a school of journalism on the side!"

"I'm sorry," the cub said, "but the desk wants me to pick up a
couple of stories to run with the pictures you make."

"All right," said Mr. Digby, "pull up your rompers and let's get out
of this squirrel cage before someone gets the bright idea to have me
run the elevator too."

"The desk," faltered the cub, "also wants you to take out some of
the pigeons today."

What then followed, as any one of the Informer's high-pressure re-
write men unhesitatingly would have phrased it, beggared description, staggered the imagination and caused reason itself to totter.
Mr. Digby had even a lower regard for his paper's current interest in
carrier pigeons than he had for desk men.

"I ain't going to do it," he told poor, patient Mr. Wood, the city
editor, when he had again become reasonably articulate.

"Why not?" said Mr. Wood.

"Because," said Mr. Digby, "I already got enough stuff to carry
around without packing no pigeons. You got me mixed up with a
moving van. Maybe you think I ought to let them pigeons fly around
loose in my car?"

Mr. Wood sighed and laid down his pencil. "Let's not be difficult about this, Happy," he said. "The other fellows have all done it, and now it's your turn. I'm not asking you to fly back any film. I'm only asking you to take out a few birds and release one each half hour, so we can check their time back into the loft from various parts of the city. All you've got to do is send along a little note where you released the bird and at what time. Now, that's not so tough, is it?"

"I got to walk into City Hall loaded like a pet store," said Mr. Digby. "I got to go into the mayor's office with a couple of pigeons hanging onto my collar, looking into my ears, and another one laying an egg on my hat. If pigeons is such a smart idea, why don't you send the pigeons out to make the pictures?"

"Sit down, Happy," said Mr. Wood. His manner was that of a man suddenly compelled to explain to a child of six why the square of the hypotenuse of a right-angle triangle is equivalent to the sum of the squares of the other two sides.

"Happy," he said, "there is something you should know. Whether you or I have any faith in this pigeon business doesn't really matter. Mr. Russell wants us to try pigeons, and Mr. Russell is publisher. It's not my paper, it's not your paper, it's not the managing editor's paper, but it very definitely is Mr. Russell's paper. As you probably already have heard, Mr. Russell has been sober for three weeks now, and almost anything can happen. Mr. Russell may have completely lost interest in pigeons by next week. But until he does, some photographer goes out of here every day with birds. As a matter of fact, pigeons have worked out rather well for the papers in Chicago and New York. I have here a letter from the Journal-American ——"

Mr. Digby's manner slowly and perceptibly changed, as if someone had pumped him full of a powerful narcotic. He was looking directly at Mr. Wood, and from time to time he nodded his head in silent affirmation, but the truth is, he was not listening to Mr. Wood at all. Mr. Wood never needed to speak more than twenty-five words to send Mr. Digby drifting dreamily away on a tide of his own thoughts. Ten years previous, in an inspired moment, Mr. Digby had decided that city editors never talk anything but nonsense.   And ever thereafter, upon the approach of a desk man, he had promptly closed a door at the front of his mind and swallowed the key.   This practice had perhaps earned him a reputation for being somewhat obtuse and a surface thinker, but it had also, he stoutly contended, prolonged his life by many years.   Mr. Digby had outworn three city editors.

There were, as a matter of fact, two problems of the most vital importance pulling at the stump of Mr. Digby's mind for solution. Mr. Digby, indeed, was in trouble neck-high to a giraffe.   He was in trouble with Mrs. Digby, and with a sad-eyed gentleman named Oscar Ketchum, who had, in an incautious moment, contracted to build for Mr. Digby a five-room house in the suburbs.   Of the two problems, that involving Mrs. Digby was the more pressing.

Mrs. Digby, a grim mountain of a woman, had, upon Mr. Digby's arrival home the night before, tossed his clothes out of a second-story window onto the front lawn — with appropriate sound effects — and had urged him to go far, far away.   While the neighbors applauded both the principals, Mr. Digby had gathered up his belongings and forced his way into the house through a pantry window.   Mrs. Digby had then locked herself into a bedroom, expecting in time to be wheedled out.   But Mr. Digby was in no mood for wheedling.   He considered himself the victim of a very bum rap.

At four o'clock that afternoon Mr. Digby had driven to the Clover Club to pick up a professional model whose picture he had been directed to make in Riverside Park for the fashion page.   To Mr. Digby she was no more than another chore, and he had noted with only passing interest that she was fried like a steak.   While they were waiting upon a traffic light, and at the precise moment Mrs. Digby emerged from a near-by market loaded down with a week's groceries, the young woman had succumbed to a sudden impulse and playfully tweaked Mr. Digby's ear.   Plunging through traffic, Mrs. Digby called loudly upon the heavens to witness what was going on behind her back.   Mr. Digby, appalled, and the young woman, vastly amused, had offered explanations.

The problem involving Mr. Ketchum, the builder, was somewhat less dramatic, but no less serious. Mr. Ketchum, with the low cunning bred of a college education, was building Mr. Digby a really excellent home, entirely according to the plans and specifications. He had, however, convicted himself of concealing something by using five and six syllable words in Mr. Digby's presence.

"I bet when he walks away from that joint," Mr. Digby had said, "the whole works will fall out into the street. He talks like a lawyer, and I got to watch him every minute."

Mr. Digby and Mr. Ketchum had most recently crossed invectives over a shower stall in the basement of the new house. Mr. Digby had made the delighted discovery that because of a heating conduit overhead he could not enter the shower while wearing his hat and shoes without stooping. Mr. Ketchum had replied, reasonably enough, that the occasions on which Mr. Digby might want to take a shower while wearing hat and shoes would be infrequent. The argument had not impressed Mr. Digby in the least.

"I got to hold up the house with one hand," he had countered, "while I wash myself with the other."

"And so," said Mr. Wood, concluding a fifteen-minute lecture, with gestures, on the care, feeding and commercial exploitation of the carrier pigeon, "you drive out to this fellow's place and pick up the birds."

"What birds?" said Mr. Digby, stirring slightly.

Mr. Wood turned wearily back to his work.

"You tell him, Ralston," he said. "I haven't the strength to go through it again. And don't forget to look for automobile accidents while you're out today. We've got to have another traffic-lesson picture in the sheet tomorrow for sure. . . . At least," he told his assistant, "that's one campaign the old man will let us carry on here."

He was mistaken. There was another. Ten minutes after Mr. Digby, still complaining bitterly, had departed, a message arrived from the unpredictable Mr. Russell.

OFFICE OF THE PUBLISHER

FROM: Mr. Russell
To: Mr. Wood
SUBJECT: Civic Betterment

I want a story tomorrow morning without fail tying up this Colucci gang with these recent laundry bombings. The story, of course, must be able to stand up in court, and should pass our attorneys first. Why haven't we had something on this in the past?

"It will take me at least a week, maybe two, to build up an airtight case against the Colucci mob," Mr. Wood told the managing editor. "For three years he's ignored this thing completely, and now he thinks he can order up an exposé like a ham on rye with mustard."

"In that case," said the managing editor, reaching for his hat, "there is only one thing we can do. We can go to the nearest bar and drink ourselves to death."

With a nice disregard for stop signs, restricted areas and safety zones, occasionally leaning out to exchange pleasantries with startled pedestrians, Mr. Digby raced his automobile toward the pigeon cote, young Ralston sitting beside him white-faced and silent.

At an intersection half a block ahead, a long gray sedan suddenly plunged into the thoroughfare with screaming brakes, swung unsteadily on two wheels in a wide circle, struck the curb and caromed into a steel light standard on the opposite side of the street. Three men alighted hurriedly, paused uncertainly beside it, then took to their heels.

At that exact moment Mr. Digby pressed the shutter release of the camera he was balancing on the left front window sill of his own car.

"Well," he said, "that takes care of the traffic-lesson picture. We can check one off the list." He put his car into gear.

"Hadn't we better stop and get the story?" said young Ralston doubtfully.

"What story?" said Mr. Digby. "A car just come around the curve too fast, that's all there was to it. You seen yourself that there didn't nobody get hurt. If you want to get some names, call up the police reporter in a couple of hours. I ain't got time to sit around here while you pick up a four-line item for only the first edition. I got to get them pigeons."

Neither he nor the reporter saw one of the trio, whose pictures, full face, he had made, turn in flight to note Mr. Digby's license number.

A few moments later, Mr. Digby was surveying the inside of a pigeon cote for the first time in his life, and doing it with an expression of extreme distaste.

"This one is Foo-Foo," said a busy young man. "And he's our star performer. Aren't you, Foo-Foo, old man? Foo-Foo flew the interstate races last month and placed second, coming up from Kansas City in three hours and two minutes. We're all pretty tickled with Foo-Foo. Of course, he had a tail wind all the way."

"Look," said Mr. Digby, "let's put them in the box and get going. I ain't got time to stand around and learn their names."

"If you haven't had birds out before," said the pigeon fancier, "you'll have to learn how to handle them. Particularly when you're going to have to take the capsules off their legs and send messages."

"I won't have no trouble," said Mr. Digby. "If I do, I will just shake them like I do canaries."

"You'll what?"

"I find out a long time ago," said Mr. Digby with pride, "that you don't never have trouble making a picture of a canary doing something if you first shake him a little, like a gin fizz. You give him a couple quick shakes like this, then you can stand him up anywhere, and he won't move for maybe five or ten minutes."

"By heaven," said the fancier, "if I ever catch you shaking one of my birds, I'll jolly well shake you!"

"He doesn't really hurt them," said young Ralston.

"I think it only makes them a little dizzy," said Mr. Digby, "and maybe sick to their stomach. I get a picture once of a couple canaries having tea at a doll's table. When the woman ain't looking, I shake them good. Picture went all over the country."

"Now see here!" exploded the pigeon fancier. "I'm not going to send my birds out with a man who —— "

"He's only kidding," said young Ralston hastily. "You know that the Informer is not going to let anyone mistreat your birds."

"I certainly hope not," said the fancier, "but I don't like this man's attitude a bit."

A little later Mr. Digby started his motor. "What are you trying to do?" he asked the reporter. "Queer me? Here I get this guy all worked up so he won't never let another pigeon out of the joint, and you got to put in the fix!"

"I think they're a good idea, that's why," said Ralston. "Someday you'll be going into the woods on a plane crash, and you'll be darn glad you've got a couple of birds along to fly out your film."

"Yeah," said Mr. Digby. "If I get hungry, I can always eat 'em."

He swung around a corner. The pigeons thrown off balance, pattered frantically in their large cardboard carton on the back seat.

"Listen to them stomping around with their big feet," cried Mr. Digby glumly. "Why don't the office get eagles? Then they can fly me in too."

"What's the next one on our list?" asked the cub.

"Eleven twenty-two Barstow Avenue. Kid locked hisself into the bathroom, and the fire department had to get him out. That's big stuff, ain't it? I ain't only made about four hundred shots just like it last week. In fact, we ain't had a picture in the paper of a kid locked in the bathroom since almost this morning." He drew up in front of a district firehouse.

"The kid isn't here, is he?" the cub asked.

"Look," said Mr. Digby, "you worry about the story and let me worry about the picture. I got to get a fireman's hat. When a kid gets hisself locked in a bathroom, you always got to make his picture wearing a fireman's hat. Just like when a kid gets lost and taken to the police station, you got to make him wearing a sergeant's hat and eating an ice-cream cone. If you make anything else, the desk screams their head off."

In the firehouse Mr. Digby paused at a telephone and dialed his home.

"Listen, honey," he said, "it's me; Bobby. Now don't go hanging up. I just want to say I'm —— Hello, hello!"

He returned the receiver savagely to its hook.

"I didn't have trouble enough already," he said, "so I had to run out and get myself married ten years ago!"

They turned north from the firehouse, and Ralston demurred. "This isn't the way to Barstow," he said. "You ought to go straight up the hill."

"I got to take a quick look at my new house," said Mr. Digby. "It ain't only but a couple of miles out of the way."

"What would the office say if they —— "

"How is the office going to find out," said Mr. Digby, "without you tell them?"

As he alighted in front of a small residence in the early stages of construction, a gentleman in overalls on a second-story scaffolding called inside, "Hey, Mike! Bill! The guy is here again!"

Carpenters, plumbers and brick masons poured expectantly out of the building, grinning broadly. Mr. Digby shouldered them aside.

"Where's that Ketchum?" he demanded.

"He's down in the basement," said a workman, "but I wouldn't bother him if I was you. On account of he said he was going to punch you right in the nose if you show up today."

Mr. Digby proceeded inside, closely followed by the group. To the straining ears of the reporter, seated in the photographer's car, there came presently the muffled sound of raised voices. Above the general uproar he could easily distinguish the high-pitched scream of Mr. Digby, a sort of aboriginal outpouring usually reserved for particularly distasteful assignments — dog shows, kiddies' parades and bathing girls perched on the hoods of new automobiles.

Mr. Digby emerged. "I tell him off," he said with satisfaction.

"Did he punch you in the nose?"

"I pick up a pipe wrench on the way down," said Mr. Digby, "and when I make out like I am going to use it, he is suddenly a very good dog."

"Before we leave here we've got to release one of the pigeons."

"You can do it," said Mr. Digby. "That don't come under the head of photography. It ain't in my line."

"The desk said you were to do it yourself," said the cub. "They want you to get the practice."

Mr. Digby slid his hand cautiously through the top of the carton.

"If I get bit," he said, "I'm going to have a pie tonight, and it won't be no steak-and-kidney pie, neither. I ain't taking nothing from no pigeon."

Somewhat to his disappointment, perhaps, Mr. Digby withdrew the bird without event, held it tightly against his stomach while the reporter detached and opened the capsule.

"I'll have to phony it up a little," Ralston said, "because we aren't supposed to be in this neighborhood, and the office might wonder. I'll make it that Barstow Street address."

In a minute or two, the thing was done, and the pigeon took off with a monstrous flapping. It spiraled briefly upward, then headed over the housetops in a direct line for its owner's cote.

"It's about six miles," said the reporter. "He ought to do it in at most fifteen minutes. Just think, in fifteen minutes the guy will be calling the office and reading our message."

"Yeah," said Mr. Digby, "if he don't meet some lady pigeon on the way." He brightened with a sudden thought. "Can you imagine," he said, "how the desk would scream their head off if the opposition starts sending up hawks?"

The youngster who had locked himself in the bathroom was napping when they arrived. They waited patiently while his mother dressed him. At the first sight of the fireman's helmet, the child burst into tears.

"Look," said Mr. Digby. "I'm a choo-choo train! Here I come! Toot-toot! Chug-a-chug, chug-a-chug! Toot! toot!"

"You're making him cry worse," said the reporter.

"Look," said Mr. Digby, mincing about on his tiptoes. "I'm an air-plane. B-r-r-r-r-r!"

"No good," said the reporter.

"All right," said Mr. Digby. "I'm a machine gun. Clack-clack-clack."

The youngster brightened.

"Can you imagine," said Mr. Digby, "a couple of grown-up men earning their living this way?"

Their next call was City Hall.

"We got to grab a shot," said Mr. Digby, "of the mayor shaking hands with the Queen of National Beautiful Teeth Week, and, for a gag, the office wants them both showing their choppers clean back to the molars. The desk thinks I got an X ray here."

They were forty-five minutes late for this one. Photographers and reporters from the opposition papers had long since departed, the mayor had gone into executive session with the council, but the queen had remained hopefully in his outer office.

"I'm sorry," the mayor's secretary purred, "but you should have been here when the others were making their pictures. The mayor is in conference now. You may have a long wait."

"You should live so long," said Mr. Digby. "Tell the guy if he wants to get that puss of his in the Informer tomorrow morning, he can come out now. I don't never wait for nobody."

The cub tugged at his sleeve in apprehension.

"Suppose she really tells him that?" he asked.

"Won't make no difference," said Mr. Digby. "The guy is a lens louse. You can't open up a box anywheres within a mile of him but what he's grinning right into it. He crawls out from under rocks."

"Well, well, gentlemen," said the mayor presently, "so you want to make my photograph with this charming young woman? It will be a pleasure. How do you want me?"

"To make it look natural," said Mr. Digby, "you might be snatching her purse."

"He's always kidding," his honor explained to the queen. "Happy Digby they call him. A character."

"The girl scouts," said Mr. Digby, screwing his camera on his tripod, "has a clubhouse out in my district, and they ain't been no slot machines moved in there yet. I wonder if maybe you can fix it."

"He insults everyone," said his honor. "Is one picture enough?"

"As far as I am concerned," said Mr. Digby, "one is too many."

Ralston and Digby separated at City Hall.

"I've just called the office," the reporter said, "and they want me to come in quick. There's a big story breaking. Somebody bombed the Elite Laundry about an hour ago and a couple of women were hurt. Give me the stuff you've made so far, and I'll take it in with me. And Wood says don't forget to turn those pigeons loose every half hour."

When he returned to his automobile parked outside the building, Mr. Digby was accosted by a stout middle-aged man, sucking on a toothpick.

"Say, chum," the latter hailed him, "you ain't by any chance Happy Digby, of the Informer, are you?"

"Yeah," said Mr. Digby. "What are you peddling?"

"I ain't peddling anything, chum," said the stranger, "but I might be in the market for a picture."

"Catch me sometime at the office," said Mr. Digby. "I ain't got time right now."

"This here is a pretty important matter to a couple buddies of mine," said the other.

"What picture you talking about?" said Mr. Digby.

"Well, it seems like you made a shot of an auto accident out in the West End this morning, and —— "

"How do you know I did?" said Mr. Digby.

"One of the boys in the wreck seen you make the shot," said the stranger, "and he got your license number. The Informer give us your schedule."

"How come you're so interested in the picture?" said Mr. Digby.

"Well, I'll tell you how it is, chum," said the other, lowering his voice. "A friend of mine is running around in his girl's car, see? So he has an accident, and if the picture comes out in the paper, his girl's husband is going to know all about it. Catch on? So we buy the negative off'n you, and she can tell her old man that she wrecked it herself. You know how that is, hey?" He nudged Mr. Digby familiarly.

"That's very interesting," said Mr. Digby. "Now tell me the real reason why you want it. What's the angle?"

"Look, chum," said the stranger. "I ain't got much time myself. You give me the negative and I'll slip you a hundred bucks, and that ain't peanuts."

"It ain't for sale," said Mr. Digby, neglecting to mention also that it was no longer in his possession anyway. In all due justice to Mr. Digby, he wouldn't have sold it if it had been. "If you got some good reason why you don't want it run, which I doubt," he added, "you can go up to the office and argue with the desk."

"I guess I ain't made myself clear, chum," said the other, his voice becoming hard. "You got your choice of handing over that film or taking on a load of trouble for yourself. See what I mean?"

He made a tentative grab for the photographer's plateholder bag. Acting with a precision born of long experience, Mr. Digby stepped nimbly back a pace, raised his heavy camera at arm's length, and brought it crashing down on the other's head. Exhaling noisily, the stranger sagged pleasantly to the sidewalk.

Mr. Digby examined the camera with disgust. The rack had been sprung and the front board had all but fallen out.

"They don't make these boxes so they stand up the way they used to," he said. "If I only had one of them old five-by-sevens, I could have knocked him right down into his shoes."

Mr. Digby got into his car and drove unconcernedly away, allowing himself to dwell for a moment or so with some amazement on the fact that any picture he had made for the Informer should have had a cash value of one hundred dollars, but beyond that his curiosity did not run. So many things went on about Mr. Digby in the course of his life for which he could perceive no immediate cause or reason that he had long since given up trying.

At two o'clock that afternoon, panting like a miler abreast of the tape, Mr. Digby drew up at the Lakeside Avenue clubhouse of the Daughters of the Glorious Union, a society assignment, and his next-to-last chore for the day. That done, there would remain only the woman who had grown the fourteen-foot hollyhock. After what had happened since his departure from City Hall, the hollyhock would distinctly be a pleasure.

Mr. Digby had filled six assignments, had called once again upon the embittered Mr. Ketchum, had twice tried to promote an honorable peace at home by telephone, had consumed a bowl of chili, a double chocolate malted milk and two stomach powders at a corner lunch, and had released five pigeons, one inadvertently. The bird had got away without a message while Mr. Digby was struggling to remove its capsule. After that Mr. Digby had wisely rolled up his windows, but a second bird had likewise slipped his grasp and led him a hectic chase. For three minutes, cursing mightily, he had crawled back and forth across the front seat, clutching at thin air. Mr. Digby, consequently, was in no mood for the good ladies of the program committee of the Daughters' annual founders'-day dinner.

The society editor of the Informer chided him gently for being late, and steered five generous ladies toward him out of the general confusion.

"For crying out loud!" said Mr. Digby. "I ain't got no wide-angle lens with me, you know."

"Sh-h-h-h!" said the society editor in a furious whisper. "They'll hear you."

"I thought the office wanted only a five-column spread," said Mr. Digby. "Are you kidding me? Each one of them babes is at least two columns wide herself. I ain't got a panorama camera here. In fact, I got to make the shot with a miniature, on account of I busted the other one. And, in order to get them all in, I will have to stand clear on the other side of town."

"I'll take them out on the back lawn," she said. "Under a tree, with their teacups."

"I'll catch them with the camera I've got out in the car," said Mr. Digby.

For perhaps fifteen minutes the ladies patiently awaited Mr. Digby. Then someone reported he had gone.

"Why, girls," she said, "he drove away with three other men. Mrs. Gildchrist was looking out the window."

"That's the last straw," said the society editor. "What I've put up with from that man! This time I'm going to tell the office!"

Mr. Digby turned to the gentleman beside him. "Where are you gorillas taking me?" he asked easily.

"Never mind, stupid," the gentleman replied. "You just drive where we tell you."

"I seen that ugly puss of yours somewhere before," said Mr. Digby. "I got it now — you run around with Joe Colucci!"

"Well, what do you know," said the gentleman.

"The guy is making a great mistake," said a second gentleman in the rear seat. "He ain't never seen you before. Maybe we better educate him a little before we take him to the boss."

"I guess maybe it ain't occurred to you," said Mr. Digby, "but the Informer ain't going to like this a little bit. It ain't healthy to go monkeying around with the press."

"You got me scared to death," said the first gentleman.

"I don't think he's got the right attitude," said the second gentleman. "Maybe we ought to go over him lightly like he done to Stinky this morning."

"Shut up, all you guys!" said the third gentleman.

Mr. Digby glanced at his watch. "Well," he said, "this is going to cost somebody a lot of dough. I been working overtime since ten minutes ago. I'm getting time and a half, so don't let's be in no hurry."

Their destination was a house and shed at the outer edge of town, bordering on the railway yards. Impatiently awaiting their arrival was a swarthy young man whom Mr. Digby at once recognized as Daddy-Boy Kelly, one of the ranking executives of the Colucci mob.

"Now, look," said Kelly, "we don't want no trouble with you or your paper, but you've got a picture we're going to have, and it's up to you whether we buy it or take it away from you. Make up your mind right now."

"We ain't allowed to sell pictures we make on the job," said Mr. Digby innocently. "There is a very strict rule. But if you go up to the office you might be able to talk them out of a print. Only it will cost you a buck."

"Take the guy and take all that stuff out of his car to the shed," directed the young man. "We'll get it the hard way."

In the shed Mr. Digby sat down on an apple box. "Nice place you got here," he said. "Next time there is a snatch in town I will know where to come."

"What you got in this box?" demanded the young man. "Chickens?"

"The film is all over here, boss," said one of the mobsters. "In this bag."

"All right," said the young man. "We'll send it in town and have it developed. . . . Now, look, pal, you're going to wait here a while, see? You ain't a bad guy, and if you just take it easy, you'll come out okay. Get me?"

They bolted the door behind them. Alone, Mr. Digby took off his coat and vest, wadded them into a pillow, and stretched lazily out on the floor.

"First chance I get today," he said, "to live like a white man."

From the cardboard carton came a soft cooing and a staccato pattering of feet. "When I don't send that pigeon in on time," he mused happily, "Wood will practically have a baby right there in the city room."

His eyes swept up the back wall of the shed to a four-inch gap at the eaves. Reluctantly he rose, fumbled in the carton and withdrew a bird. From his vest pocket he produced a cigarette paper and a blunt pencil.

"3.55 P.M.," he wrote. "Factory town." He hesitated. "I can't make D. G. U. and hollyhock," he added, "on account Colucci mob got me locked in shed near RR signal tower."

The pigeon, released, made unerringly for the gap. Mr. Digby opened the carton and released all the others as well.

"Now I don't have to think about nothing," he said, "except how them gorillas' faces are going to look when they see the tripe I shoot this afternoon." He paused. "They ain't going to be exactly pleased, neither," he decided. "In fact, I won't be surprised if they come back and try to muscle me around a little."

He prowled about the shed, thoughtfully hefted an old spade handle, then discarded it for his already-damaged camera.

"I only got to crack somebody with this box again," he said, "and I can put in with the insurance company for a complete new outfit."

Not one to cross a bridge until it slapped him in the face, Mr. Digby lay down again and gave himself up to a pleasant contemplation of his mounting overtime.

"Let's see," he said, "there's already an hour and ten minutes. I get a buck twenty-five an hour regular. One times a buck twenty-five is a buck twenty-five. Ten minutes is a sixth of an hour, and six goes into a buck twenty-five about twenty cents. That's a buck forty-five times once and a half. Let's see, a half of a buck forty-five is, two goes into fourteen ——— "

For fifteen minutes Mr. Digby wrestled with $1.45 times once and a half.

"For crying out loud!" he said. "I ain't already got enough to worry about, I also got to be a bookkeeper! I got to be an adding machine!"

He rose in anger and drew the apple box over to the front wall, mounted it and began to figure on a new pine board over the door. In his left hand he still clutched his camera, ready for any contingency.

"When I put in for this overtime," he said, "the office will scream their ears off. You will be able to hear them clear out here."

There was a sudden rush of feet outside, loud voices, a fumbling at the bolt.

"Well," said Mr. Digby, "I will get at least one of them hoods, and, if I am lucky, maybe two." And he brought his camera squarely down — upon the blue-cloth cap of a uniformed member of the Central City Police Department. A startled brother officer deftly laid his nightstick on Mr. Digby's skull.

Mr. Digby stirred slightly and opened his eyes. He appeared to be in a bed, attended by several dim shadows, one of which had the familiar heft and bulk of Mrs. Digby. From a great distance he heard the exultant voice of Mr. Wood.

"Take it easy, old man," said Mr. Wood. "You're all right. It was nothing but a little clout on the head. Just a mistake. The cops were coming to get you out."

Mr. Digby closed his eyes.

"Take it easy," said Mr. Wood. "It's the greatest scoop in years. That was smart thinking, Happy — sending that pigeon to let us know where you were. Old Man Russell is tickled to death. He's going to let you take full charge of the pigeons from here on in. And the picture was sensational. We're using it seven columns Page One. You can make out all their faces — Colucci, Little Joe and the mayor's nephew. They were getting away from that laundry job in a stolen car."

"Oh, Bobsy," sobbed Mrs. Digby, "they're going to give you a bonus. A hundred dollars! They have your picture being carried out of the shed on a stretcher. Everyone says you're a hero!"

Mr. Digby opened his eyes.

"He's going to say something," cried Mrs. Digby.

"I sure tell him off," said Mr. Digby feebly.

"Who, dear?" said Mrs. Digby.

"I sure tell off that Ketchum," said Mr. Digby. "I make him move that shower clean over to the other side of the basement."

SPITFIRE SQUADRON

By *Arch Whitehouse*

A SILKEN-PLUMAGED bantam cock bristles from the center of No. 4 Fighter Squadron's crest, embroidered on the left-hand coverall pocket of the R.A.F. Spitfire pilots who nightly risk The Notch. There's a garter below the crest bearing some Latin bother about "*gloria finis,*" which probably fits, everything considered.

The Notch is a narrow channel of terror charted anew each week and picketed on either side by unseen steel cables hung to slice through the dural wing of a fighter with the ease and hiss of a hot wire through butter. A number of bloated slugs, gorged with hydrogen, nestle down with their winches along the area bordered by Holland Park and Kensington Gardens. At night they wheeze, blubbery and limp, into the black sky and bear the weight of the cables that limit the width of The Notch. It is through this gangway to glory the night-flying pilots of No. 4 Squadron thunder to tackle Jerry.

It's quite a switch from a 1918 S.E.5 to a Spitfire fighter, as Pilot Officer H. V. March discovered after he had lied one letter from his name and eight years off his age. It's quite a jump from balloon shows behind St. Jean to risking The Notch at 367 m.p.h. in a Spitfire. March found that out in one show, and he'd been doing low-altitude interception for more than a week now. This was 1940 — September, 1940, and a blackened and scarred London lay below.

The darkness of the city took the form of a gray-blue velvet quilt through which subdued street glare and the glint of railway metal picked out a sequin design. There was a blackout somewhere below, but the A.R.P. couldn't douse all the light. There was the jetting flick of antiaircraft batteries and the reflection of searchlight beams that came up off the skylights and façades.

The Notch was ahead now. Yellow Flight had turned left over the unmuzzled glare of the coke works and was hurtling across North Kensington and Notting Hill.

"Tighten up, Yellow Flight," Ronny Crispin was saying into his flap mike. "Close formation and mind the kite strings."

March and Monty Jeys took up positions off the exhaust pennons flicking from Crispin's Merlin engine and moved in closer. Across the narrow stretch of slip-stream-charged blackness Monty Jeys was singing. Monty was always singing: "*H is for Heinkel. There's a dustbin gun on the Heinkel! . . . J is for Junkers. They can't fire below from the Junkers!*"

"Close it, Monty. You'll miss the turn," ranted Flight Lieutenant Crispin. "That only goes for the dive bomber. Where do you get such rot anyway?"

"Page Six, Figure Two, latest Identification of Enemy Aircraft Made Easy booklet, on sale at His Majesty's Stationery Office at the nominal price of sixpence — one small tanner. You sing and learn," explained Monty.

A bracket of shellfire coughed above the rage of their prop scream and the steely whine of superchargers. That would be the gunners in Kensington Park. They wouldn't be bunny-running the nurse-maids now.

"Cuddle in," warned Crispin. "Here we go!"

The three Spits seemed to hold their hot breaths. They huddled closer in the dull dural gleam of the night. A few more yards — seconds — and they would be safe and in the clear where they could square off and "have a go."

March trembled against the constriction of his loins. His hands were stiff and cold across the backs. There was no feel in his finger tips. He ruddered gently and managed to get the edge of his wind-screen frame on a bead with Crispin's port aileron slit. He took his thumb from his gun button because the safety was off. For the fiftieth time he wondered how you get out of a Spitfire — if you have to — if she suddenly breaks up while doing about three hundred.

"Stop thinking about it," he argued with himself. "It can't happen again in a dozen years."

A dozen years? It had happened twenty-two years ago, and twelve into twenty-two — one and ten to carry — and there were six hundred balloons up somewhere tonight.

"*We've got a navy, a fighting navy!*" That was Monty again. Monty loved all this. Big, bearish chap who played Rugby, and reveled in it. Big hands, big knees, and hair that stuck out. Monty gloried in the heat and excitement of all this.

March held his breath. There were Dorniers ahead somewhere. Slipped through the barrage somehow. They didn't seem to be afraid of the cables. Still, one or two a week got it. Marked up on the board to the credit of the Ack-Ack gunners.

The Spits were due for a scramble, and March knew it. He was certain his exhaust was sucked back into the manifolds when they cut between Holland Park and Kensington Gardens. There was perspiration in the hollows below his temples. He set the pivot in his upper jaw firmly on the cold filling of a lower molar and listened to Crispin report through to the air chief marshal of the Fighter Command, "Yellow Flight through The Notch. Yellow flight at three thousand, through The Notch. Give an area, please."

A group captain in the observer corps at Adastral House shot them the squares in a burry brogue. He added the altitude between munches on a Bath bun. It was repeated while Crispin stared about, and then the set retched off with an acidy discord. March glanced at the map strapped to his thigh and tried to figure it all out. Somehow, it had been easy at the advanced fighter school, but up here it was different. He always got the area squares mixed up with the altitude figures. That was when those eight years began to throw their weight about.

"*M is for Mess-up* —— I've forgotten the next line," cackled Monty.

"Stow it, Monty! We can tune in the B.B.C. if we want music! Take it in line astern!"

"All you'll get from the B.B.C. is Raymond Gram Swing — from

America," Monty answered in a high falsetto. "Mr. Swing says Italy is in the war. . . . Where's Italy, Ronny?"

The three Spitfires re-formed and March found himself behind Crispin's tabbed rudder. Queer that, being led by young Crispin. Crispin had two rings of braid on his sleeve. March and Monty had but one — a narrow one. Twenty-two years before, another Crispin had led him after that enemy balloon behind St. Jean. March had to think that; he couldn't say it. The flap mike picked up everything. No privacy of the heavenly sky in this war. You couldn't even die in privacy. They can hear you scream, and swear, back at Adastral House, when you stop a packet.

March didn't begrudge Crispin his rank or responsibility. The kid could really fly. All these youngsters could fly. Seemed born to Spits. Crispin got his Distinguished Flying Cross over Dunkirk and a bar to the ribbon ten days later, over the Estuary.

The three-winged projectiles were in the clear now and March exhaled deeply and took the clamps off his belly as they cut for the bend in the river. Limehouse was flaunting a gutting stomacher of fire — an expensive bauble for such a wench. The Embankment guns barked and rifled shells whelped the flame and splutter of burned amatol. Thunder and sheet-lightning effects by Messrs. Vickers and Kynochs provided the backdrop for this nocturnal extravaganza.

March shuddered against the impact of it all and recoiled with the realization that he should be part of it. The grim bulk of it all. The technical maze. That he should have been drawn into this when by rights he should have been viewing it abstractly from a splintered veneer seat of a picture house in far-off Guiana.

This was nothing like 1918. They were flying S.E.5's then. Hissos up front, a Vickers gun under the cowling and a shaky bracket for manning a Lewis gun on the top plane. They were heavy about the nose and you had to land them fast. With the flaps down you could bring the Spitfire in while you were loosening your chin strap and bellyband. There was 1030 h.p. in that Merlin, and eight guns in the wings.

March could never quite get over that. Eight guns in the wings. That was all an infantry battalion was allowed in 1916. But this was 1940 and he was still flying behind a guy named Crispin.

The lights stabbed out and exchanged parries like heavy broadswordsmen. Two as slim as rapiers lanced up from behind Woolwich and held a position. One began to cut its way across the sky like a silver scalpel slitting a gangrened wound. Crispin would get that signal. Leave it to the youngsters to get them. Crispin would make something of it. It meant something, that straight-up business. Too damned many things to remember in this war. Too many things to remember from the last. Overlapping wars. A man should never come back from his first war.

The earphones inside March's helmet jangled and he froze again. Crispin had spotted them. The devils were getting inside somehow. One had slapped a whistler into the Palace the other night. Another almost scraped his belly across Waterloo Bridge. Flinty Thompson had torched him, and the Jerry had stacked it all up in Victoria Station, just in front of the tearoom.

"Two bandits, half left," Crispin was saying. "Half left about five hundred below. Make sure of one first. Make sure of one. Archie is off."

He really meant they should not worry about the antiaircraft fire, but to concentrate on the leader and give him all they had. Get No. 1 and the other bloke is sure to do something silly.

Another scramble. Always a scramble too damn close to the roof tops. A stew of struts, chimney pots, wing tips and tracers being stirred with a hellish blinding blade of searchlight.

Young Crispin was already tackling the raiders. March could see his tracers crisscrossing over the intersection of Vauxhall Bridge Road and Warwick Street. Strange how he remembered places like that, and that one could spot them in the blackout.

Monty, squealing like a kid, was up on him now. His wing tip was almost clipping March's tail assembly.

"*B is for bandits! Bash the bloomin' bandits!*" he was singing into the flap mike. "Come on, March. Let Crispo have the leader bloke. We'll conk the other swine!"

Monty was raging over March's hatch cover before March could get his breath. Formation with six planes used to be less precarious than this. March drew in his breath again and saw a Nazi Dornier rip up to avoid Monty's charge. All March had to do was to keep straight on, depress the thumb button on the stick, and eight Brownings drilled their leaden hate into the Dornier.

It flamed at once. Wriggled in agony and belched a mushroom of scarlet-tinged smoke. It threw a motor away which fell off over Green Park. A section of wing fluttered down toward Birdcage Walk, and the Dornier rolled over on its back, spewing four men. A searchlight blade, flicking a smart riposte, caught the bomber just as it exploded amidships, illuminating the tangle for March to stare at as he slashed past.

There was no surging reaction of exultation. No blasphemy to punctuate the satisfaction. Just a cold hollow fear that set up a dull pain just behind the breastbone.

March turned, ran his eyes over the instruments, checked and called Crispin. He had to call Crispin. A natural reaction, because he was frightened. Terror gripped him and he floundered about wildly, trying to remember the limitations of their action area. Must keep this side of the river. Where was Crispin? Where was Monty? If Monty would only sing — just a bar or two.

He darted back and forth aimlessly, avoiding the shafts of light that seemed to be trying to trap him. He winced when his wing tip slipped through one and he half expected his main spar to foul and slice off against a balloon cable. "Crispin! Calling Yellow Flight! Crispin! March calling Crispin! Yellow Flight!"

Why did he have to click for Yellow Flight? Why couldn't they call them A, B and C Flights, as they did in the last war? Why Yellow Flight?

The earphones jangled again: "Come on down. Three hundred over the river at Shadwell. Who got that Dornier?" young Crispin was calling. Just like that. Who got the Dornier? Not interested in the possibility of someone stopping a packet from a Rheinmetall-Borsig gun in the dustbin of that Dornier.

"I fired it," admitted March. "Where's Monty?"

"Right behind you, ducky," came the voice. "You almost dropped him on my wing root. *D is for Dorniers. March diddled a Dornier!*"

They found Crispin as they crossed the river through a clear area near Poplar. There was a small fire spluttering near the West India Docks.

"What happened to your bloke, Crispo?" asked Monty.

"I gave him a burst. He somehow lost his tail assembly. Spun into the Embankment near the R. A. F. Memorial. Funny if he piled up on it, eh?"

"Funny? You'll be demoted to a second-class aircraftman and awarded a spanner," warned the Monty lad.

Ten minutes later they got the recall signal and turned for their area exit along Kingsland Road, followed the black gash of High Street and roared over Stamford Hill. Once clear of Tottenham, they turned west again and cut back for the aerodrome hidden away a bit north of Hendon.

They clumped into the briefing room and made a satisfactory gesture to the squadron leader. It's a compote of rubber-soled flying boots, phone jacks, map cases and a parachute pack smacking your rump with every stiff-legged step. All that, and a bantam cock on your breast pocket to add a bit of color. A cigarette and a batman who slops out a horrible concoction made of beef cubes, tinned biscuits and hot water. He always wants to know whether you are going out again tonight.

A squadron leader is a bloke who used to be called a major in the other war. Now he has three rings of braid on his sleeve and usually wishes he had but two. At any rate, that's what Vosper-the-Vesper Tempest wished. He really wished March could have his job. He was certain March was more than thirty-five. He was even more certain March had old Royal Flying Corps Castrol in his nostrils. He put it to him one day, but March tightened up the squint lines under his eyes and protested, "No, not me! I was in British Guiana during the last war. At school in Georgetown, as a matter of fact. Oh, we played at it, of course. Formed fours and dug trenches at the far end of the cricket pitch, but I was only a nipper then."

Somehow, the S. L. never bought that package.

"Everybody all right?" Tempest asked when he had jotted down the time brackets on the patrol report for the command.

"We're all back, but you've got to do something about Monty's singing," Crispin muttered, exposing a cigarette case half as big as a sandwich board. "He's doing nursery rhymes now. Clutters up the band."

Monty was flat on his back along an army bench set against the wall under the map. He was trying to make out a patrol report.

"That's your job, Crispin," the S. L. argued. "Ought to send him out to tail Red Flight. Give him his bellyful and let him sing himself out."

"That won't do. He likes to fly. He likes to go on patrol!"

"All right then; keep him off the next Yellow Flight show."

Crispin waged his head and lit a Gold Flake. "No, that won't do either. Know what he did the other night after we were washed out? The fool went as a gunner on a Blenheim bomber — with Number Fifty-nine to Cuxhaven. He likes to fly!"

"Stop that damn singing, Monty," the S. L. said tonelessly. "There's enough rot on the air as it is."

"Yes, sir!" Monty agreed, sucking the end of his pencil. "If you can't spell a word, can you draw it?"

The S. L. gave up and peered across at March.

"What did you give that Dornier, March? They have her — the wardens — in front of the Wellington Barracks. Tossed her port engine out. That right?"

"About right. She threw one away anyway."

"What did you spend on her?"

"Quite a long one, sir. Eight or ten seconds, I'd say. Afraid I froze on the button a bit, sir."

"Ah, well, you got him, at any rate. Nice work, March, old man."

"Put him in for a putty medal," suggested Monty from his sprawled position. "I had a go at the swine, but he nosed up and showed a full-plan target to March. Might as well have been shooting at a balloon!"

March didn't wince or make a false move. He didn't argue about it. He just sat there stiff, but the S. L. caught the look in his eyes.

Crispin stiffened too. He hated balloons, and London was full of them.

The S. L. went on jotting down the data: "Fired about a hundred and thirty rounds — eight-second burst." Then he added, over his double row of ribbons and wings, "Balloons aren't easy. They only look easy."

"Jerry's having a picnic with some of ours down the river."

"But they're not easy. You can never tell. Sometimes they flame with one burst, yes. But the next time you can pour in a whole belt and she still stays up."

"If you hit a bit of metal, a grommet along the rigging skirt," March broke in suddenly, "you sometimes make the right kind of a spark and —— "

Then he stopped, because the S. L. was studying him. Tempest's expression was blotched now, like the inside of a leg of mutton.

"Anyway, that's what they tell me. I don't really know," March floundered. "Maybe they're not easy. I wouldn't know."

Tempest agreed with himself that March really didn't look that old . . . but that grommet-and-rigging-skirt business, and he was always tugging at prop tips to feel for play in the shaft. All old 1918 stuff. He recalled March's explanation of his flying, which had sounded all right then: "I took my ticket out in Guiana. We had an old Ireland amphibian to fly up the river between the mines and Georgetown. Gold mine, you know. I just learned going back and forth with gear. No real training, of course. When this mess broke out, I just came home and — well, here I am. Had never flown anything that didn't have bilge drooling from the hull before."

That was March's pet joke and he had it in shreds within a week. But this balloon-grommet business. It brought back the first flick of an old scene — a scene flashed on quickly while a film was being threaded into an amateur projector.

Young Crispin was sitting on a bomb box, tearing his patrol-report form into one-inch strips.

Monty broke it up. "Of course, you can bash through them!" he boomed from the bench. "They say a Frenchman flew a Morane through a Zeppelin in the last war. That must have been funny! I'll bet he went straight through and then looked back to see if he'd left the outline of his bus through the bag. I can just see him. Boom! Bits of wire and sticking plaster on his wing tips and old Von Stickyback's hot-water bottle in his lap!"

"Oh, shut up, Monty," Crispin growled. "It wouldn't be that funny. There's nothing funny about balloons."

"All balloons are funny! Why do they sell them at the races and at Brighton and Blackpool? They have to be funny. I laugh like the devil at them on Christmas. Stick a fork in them and listen to them go pop. Upset the beer and the gravy and —— " Monty drooled off and rolled over on his back again.

A flight of Spitfires roared over the shed. The interruption gave young Crispin a chance to reshuffle his mind. He avoided the S. L.'s eyes and twirled his phone jack. But the balloons had him now. "There's nothing funny about balloons to me, Monty. My father went west trying to get a balloon in the other show."

Monty sat up suddenly, his pencil still in his mouth. He spat it out and kicked it away. "Sorry. Sorry, old boy! Let's bung off into the mess and down a double apiece. I can't write tonight. I can only draw things." He threw a crooked-fingered salute across the table. "I'll try to think up a good one in the morning, S. L. D'yer mind?"

Tempest did mind, but somehow he couldn't find the proper words to express his official attitude.

"Coming, March?" asked Monty. "Ought to wet your whistle for that Dornier you dropped into Wellington Barracks, you know. All the Guards will have souvenirs to send home in the morning. That will prove conclusively they are near the war and fighting bravely to keep the invaders from these shores. There's nothing like a bit of souvenir to pep up the troops."

"You are an ass, Monty," Crispin protested.

"You'd better let March bow out," the S. L. said. "I want to talk to him."

"Yes, I think I'd better wait," agreed March, his broad shoulders slumping in his coverall.

They waited until the footsteps of the youngsters died away. March's mouth was dry and parched. He knew now that the S. L. had him lined up. He wondered how bad it would be.

"Hard lines, March; you coming all the way from Guiana and running into this," the S. L. said as he packed his brier. "It never really dawned on me until you went into the detail about the balloon. Then it all came back."

March looked pitiful. "I never believed I'd get away with it for long, of course. After all, forty does something to you. You get in and out of the cockpit with a reasonable amount of care. You're settled, and you try to make out a reasonable patrol report. The kids, they just fill them out and vie with each other for brevity. Or is that real modesty?"

"Or they don't make them out at all, like Monty," the S. L. added, peering over the flame of his match. "That's why, after forty, chaps like you should have a squadron, three rings on your sleeve, and take things a bit easier."

"Easier? I don't think I'd like that, sir. I'm sure I wouldn't like sending men out there every night taking two chances."

"Two chances?"

"The Notch and Jerry."

The S. L. thumbed the bowl of his pipe reflectively. "Never thought of it that way, March. Is it that bad?"

"It's pretty narrow, sir. I'm surprised we don't come unstuck sometimes."

"Um — that can't be helped, of course. It's the field-siting system they use. If we put the balloons and cables up in a circle around the city, they'd hop over the barrier and get down low inside. This way we keep them worried. They never know where they are."

"But The Notch seems too narrow, sir. Look at it on your plotting map. If we get a sudden northeast wind, the cables of the bags up in Kensington Gardens are swung well out over Church Street, which leaves us only about a quarter of a mile clearance."

"It isn't much," the S. L. agreed. Was this funk or being forty? "The youngsters don't seem to notice it."

"These things never bother them. I don't suppose we did at that age, but we do now, sir."

"We've got to keep those balloons there, March. Keeps the devils up high where they belong."

That was the worst of being the S. L. You had to make excuses and provide justification for everything. You had to send these men off night after night to risk that lane of balloon cables less than half a mile wide. They had to fly that lane almost by guess, because of the blackout, and you, being the S. L., had to put their names down on the board in the briefing room.

"However," the S. L. heard himself saying, "I'll see what I can do for you, March. Might be something loose down at Halton."

"Halton, sir?"

"Boys' wing or school of technical training. You'd be all right there, you know. Administrative work."

"But you misunderstand me, sir. I'm not chucking this. Not because I'm, well, older than the others."

"I'm only trying to make it easier, March," the S. L. said to the double smoke ring before him. "You know, it's not just balloons or the Spits. It's not just The Notch and the northeast wind. That other balloon business will always be there. You can't adjust a throttle or dampen a flap and blank it out as you would a tricky gust near the ground. It will always be there, March."

"I — I don't quite understand, sir," lied the man in the wrinkled white coverall.

"You can change your age from forty-something to thirty-five,"

Temptest punctuated with his pipestem. "You can change the *s* in your name to *c* and make it March, but it's still Marsh. You may try to salve your conscience by coming back all the way from Guiana, but you'll always see that other chap tangled up in that balloon cable."

A blinding splatter of light, like the crash of a massive chandelier, drenched the man in the white coverall for three seconds. His new, small world tottered and crumbled.

"But I don't understand," March pleaded in a voice that had fallen to a whisper. He sat staring at Tempest. "How did you know? You weren't in our lot. I don't recall you, sir."

The S. L. waited and listened to the two Spitfires ramming in over the roof. He counted audibly and glared up at the flight board. There should have been three. "No," he said, fearing for No. 3 of Red Flight. "No. I was flying D. H.'s at Warloy then. Remember, you landed at Warloy after that balloon show."

March simply said, "I see. I came in there and wiped my under-carriage off. I was done in — all in."

"Rather!" agreed Tempest, listening again for No. 3 of the Red. "I remember it well. You were terribly upset about it. Argued it was all your own fault. It didn't seem very important to us — a chap going west."

"You didn't believe what I said, did you? You can't believe the babbling of a poor devil who had just crawled out of a crash?"

"No, I didn't then, but you were very convincing. I don't believe it now, but young Crispin might, you know."

"Crispin? You think he knows?"

"Some of it," the S. L. mumbled. "He told me the night he was awarded his D. F. C. We had a bit of a binge at the Savoy after the Palace business. Crispin had had a couple and began to get juicy. Got to talking about his father and the old days. Wanted to go home and put his medal on his father's photo. You know, showing his inner feelings sort of business."

"Telling the truth, like a man who crawls out of a crash, you mean."

There was no No. 3 of the Red Flight. The S. L. still listened for it, until March had to get to his feet and stride wide-legged up and down the room. There was a racket of some sort from the mess, the clangor of a radio set somewhere, doing a chorus from Gilbert and Sullivan.

"The situations are not the same, March," Tempest pointed out, gathering up some papers from his deal desk. "His was what I would call drunken drooling."

"What about me?"

"Whatever it was, yours keeps on. It brought you back here after more than twenty years. Either you have a conscience or you are being dramatic."

"You're wrong there, skipper. I didn't come back because of what I said that day. I came back to satisfy myself on one point."

"None of that, March! That's not playing the game. After all, hundreds of old-timers came back. You can't huddle behind patriotism — or whatever they call that business."

March took it all and steadied like a Quorn hound against a breast-high scent. His whole problem had been solved. "No, I'll play the game through, sir. Forget that Halton business, will you?"

"Of course. Buzz off, will you, March?"

"You don't think young Crispin has any idea, do you?"

"Of course not. He gives you the benefit of the eight years you tried to erase from the record. Now shove off. I have a plane missing from Red Flight."

They were still playing Gilbert and Sullivan on the five-valve set in the mess. Young Crispin was trying to think of the words of Pinafore. He still had a fairly full glass in his hand, and March figured it was his third.

The room was drab, with cheap stain and badly framed prints. The chairs creaked their age and weariness. Gray-eaved eyes of stuffing peered from the yawning seams of saddled cushions. Flight and The Aeroplane, tattered journals of the trade, littered the table.

"Good old March!" called Crispin. "Come on, March. A double on me. . . . March got a bandit tonight, you chaps!"

March muttered something inane and would have shoved off toward his cubicle, but a mess corporal in a white coat was demanding his order, holding Crispin's chit book at the alert position. "Mr. Crispin's treat, sir. Will it be a double brandy, sir? You could do with one, couldn't you, sir?"

"Not washed out, are we?" March asked dubiously. "Yellow Flight's not washed out yet, corporal? Only two of the Red came back."

The mess corporal ignored that and shuffled off, flipping Crispin's chit book on the bar.

"Yellow Flight!" spluttered young Crispin. "My lot, you chaps. Monty and old March in my flight. Good old Yellow Flight."

He hooked March's arm and dragged him into the group and then leaned heavily on him.

"Take it easy, Crispin," March said kindly. "It might be a long night yet."

"What of it? The more flights, the more bandits. Yellow Flight's got to get some Jerries. Monty's got to stop singing and get some Jerries."

"I'll sing 'em into a spin!" Monty argued, getting his right eye to focus. "*That's where the boys get around the girls — round the Marble Arch!*" he added with a throaty discord.

"Stop it, Monty!" Crispin remonstrated mechanically. "You stop singing, Monty, and I'll get you some Huns. I'll get you a D. F. C., Monty."

"Don't want a D. F. C. I want that girl who drives the A. C. M.'s car. Have you ever looked at her sideways, Crispo?"

"That's the only way you can look at them. They're always looking another way," Crispin replied in a discouraged tone.

The mess corporal brought the drink and March stared down into it, listening to the anatomical details of the girl who drove the air chief marshal's car.

"You ought to take it easy, you know, Crispin," he said. "We're not washed out yet, are we?"

Crispin declared they were never washed out.

Two more distinct figures thumped through the door and came up to the bar fluttering chit books.

"Where's the Beetle?"

"Down. Stopped a packet from a Junkers. The swine flamed him over E sector. Still, it might have been one of our gunners. They're damned careless in E sector."

"Did he get out?"

"No. No report yet. . . . Scotch and splash, corporal."

"Found a pub and probably flogged the silk in his parachute for a round of drinks," someone added. "They say barmaids make long-wearing drawers out of parachutes."

"You silly ass. It's past closing time."

"There should be a law for blokes who get skittled out of Spitfires after hours. You get bloody thirsty on the way down. I know. I stopped a packet out Finchley way. Had to drink milk."

"How did you know it was milk?"

"Comes under the head of intelligent guessing. I got that line from a journalist."

"If only Monty would stop singing," muttered Crispin.

March felt responsible for young Crispin now. It was that business about the balloons that had done this — this drinking between patrols.

Crispin's face jelled to a static mask amid the smoke over the bar, and March realized it was the same face — the same as the other Crispin. The same thin fold of wrinkle at the bridge of the nose. The same uneven distribution of frontal bone.

". . . but you needn't worry about me, March," Crispin was saying, poking home his words with a long forefinger. "You tail me and I'll bring you home."

"Of course you will. You always bring me home," placated March. "It's not that. I'd go anywhere with you, Crispin, but you ought to make sure we're washed out before you have any more."

"You're afraid of the balloons, March!" young Crispin said, selecting each word carefully. "You're afraid of them, March."

March stared into his drink again, hanging on gamely.

"You're afraid of balloons, March," persisted the young flight commander, "but you're not the only one. We're all afraid of them, but we're too damned stubborn to admit it."

"Of course not. Don't be silly," March said, and actually produced a smile.

"I'm silly, yes. You're not silly, March. You're afraid of the cables and you're not afraid to show it. Brave man. I'll give you my D. F. C. in the morning." Young Crispin gulped, drew himself up and considered all that again. "No, can't do that, March. Gave it to someone else." He waved a deprecatory hand and looked guilty.

"That's all right. I understand," March said before he took another sip.

Young Crispin swung around with an effort and snarled belligerently, "Of course you don't understand. How could you? You didn't know my father, did you? Can't understand, March."

March just nodded and the inter-squadron speaker over the bar retched. Everyone stared down at forty-five degrees and listened.

"Yellow Flight, all out! Yellow Flight, all out! Pilots of Yellow Flight! Green Flight stand by! Yellow Flight!"

"There you are," March growled, shoving his glass across the bar half emptied. "That's us, Crispin. Yellow Flight. Come on."

"Are we Yellow Flight?" young Crispin asked dumbly.

"Get your brolly, Crispo!" bellowed Monty. . . . "Snap his straps, March!"

The three Spitfires were trembling with restrained power on the cab rank, awaiting their pilots. The flight sergeants were clambering down from the cockpits after starting the engines. The glare from the gutting exhausts threw fringed shadows on the oil-spattered ground.

Dykes, the recording officer, was a heavy figure in his greatcoat, with a sheaf of papers fluttering in his hands. He snatched at Crispin as the flight lieutenant came up out of the darkness. "There's three more coming up the river. They must be getting through below Blackheath. Make The Notch at three thousand. Landing signal M. Get it, Crispin? Landing signal M."

Crispin saluted and said, "Landing signal M."

Dykes helped him with his gear, holding the papers between his teeth. He buttoned the top of Crispin's coverall and stuffed the papers in his greatcoat pocket. "Want my scarf, Crispin?"

But the flight lieutenant was climbing up without a word and palming his hatch cover back. He turned his head with a jerky gesture and peered out both sides. Then he spoke to March and Monty through his flap mike.

They were both ready and both were taking in another hole in their safety belts. Queer, how you can always take in another hole.

Crispin depressed one wheel brake, rammed the throttle knob up and snapped the Spitfire around hard and lurched away. A mobile floodlight thumped over the turf, took a position, and the long broad beam slapped down across the field. The driver leaped out and adjusted the shadow bar. The three Spitfires nosed into the thin blade of black and waited for the take-off signal from Dykes and his Aldis lamp.

"Steady, Yellow Flight," Crispin said thickly. "Check your temperatures."

He got affirmative replies from Monty and March, and the clearance flash from Dykes. The three fighters hoicked their tails up with a blast of prop pressure and began their canter down the shadow bar. They were off in seconds and screeching over the hooded light of the lorry. The flood snapped off and only a blackish stain marked their field.

"Through The Notch at three thousand," reported Crispin, who was suddenly very cold and none too sober. "There's three again, remember. Don't let a Jerry get away this time, Monty. He'll only come back."

"*I'll sing thee songs of Araby,*" tooted Monty from somewhere behind.

"Don't sing, Monty," pleaded Crispin. "Don't sing this time."

March took no notice of the chatter, but realized he was cold. The dash from the mess to the cab rank had not helped at all.

"Tight formation," Crispin was saying, "and keep it tight all the way. They may be well up the river."

Watling Street below. The old Watling Street that had seen

British traffic and trade since the days of the Romans. Brent Reservoir on the right and Cricklewood ahead. Farther on, the gray rectangle that was Hyde Park and the gleam from the Serpentine. Then suddenly the fencing blades of searchlight and the slap of antiaircraft shells against the mad midnight. Three sudden blotches of light down near the station — that would be Paddington Station.

"There they are," announced Monty. "Down low near Bayswater Road. Three of them! Junkers!"

March knew someone ought to say something. They ought to warn young Crispin, but you had to be careful what you said now — with Jerry there. Young Crispin was snapping orders again, and they were supposed to slip into line astern, but March knew that Crispin had forgotten The Notch. He was slamming down from a point directly above Lancaster Gate toward the Junkers, that were streaming away toward Kensington High Street. He was cutting directly across Kensington Gardens to head them off somewhere over Hammersmith way.

"Crispin!" March found himself calling. "Crispin! The Notch! Don't forget the cables, Crispin!"

But the young flight commander was in full cry now. Monty was yelling too. Yelling about The Notch. Monty was behind Crispin. He was out of it. It was up to March.

"Crispin!" March was yelling again as he rammed the throttle up the gate. "Sheer off, Crispin! You're right in the cables, man!"

Crispin was pressing his triggers to warm them. He took no notice of March and his flap-mike bellowing. He was after Junkers down inside.

It all came back again to March. That day in front of St. Jean when the other Crispin had flown into the balloon cable. He had done just what March knew he was going to do.

"Crispin! Crispin, man! Clear out, Crispin!"

But there was no other way now. March had to do it and take the chance. He gave the Merlin the last of the space left on the throttle gate and roared up to Crispin and edged in blindly. Anything to make him clear.

He could see the astounded face of young Crispin, high-lighted by the glare of exhaust. A searchlight below wagged frantically as a warning, but Crispin was still trying to understand this unbelievable disregard of orders — "line astern for flight attack."

Crispin yanked her over hard as the other Spitfire started to slither into him, its great wing slicing at him like a pike blade.

"March! Line astern!"

March had no chance to go into line astern. The balloon cable caught his leading edge just outside the prop arc and gave for a dozen yards or so. Then it twanged and the Spitfire spun hard and the cable slipped behind the prop and the tightening cord of doom drew March into its mesh.

The first shock yanked the tail assembly loose, and the stick went sour. March sat there and took it, waiting for his chance to get clear. He closed his eyes and fumbled for his safety latch.

"Did what I could, Crispin," he muttered into the flap mike. "Did what I could. You were slamming straight into the cables along The Notch."

The Spitfire went into a flat spin against the tug of the cable. The searchlights had caught it cold, and March knew that it was time to get clear.

"Did my best, Crispin," he tried to report again. "Hope you make it back, kid."

He reached up for the hatch-cover handle and then heard the rattle and snaky retching of the cable. He knew then what had happened. The quick-release snap of the balloon rigging above had parted and the whole length of cable was coiling down on the stalled Spitfire, trapping him inside the cockpit.

"Sorry, Crispin," he reported calmly. "Sorry to break up your flight, but I think I'm through. So long!"

He yanked his phone jack out, turned around and tried to wrench the hatch cover clear of the tangle of cable. He swore as he realized the guides had been fouled. The opening he had struggled with was not large enough for his shoulder. He jerked around with a moan, sat down and took it cold.

*   *   *

Young Crispin was bitter when they got in. Monty didn't sing either.

"Why does it always have to be balloons?" Crispin demanded of the squadron leader. "Poor old March smashed straight into it, and I'll bet he always figured he would."

"You can't help these things," the S. L. said. "That's what happens in a war like this."

"It happens in all wars," young Crispin argued. "I'll bet something like this happened in the Siege of Paris. I'll bet someone was killed as the result of that balloon."

"Balloons aren't funny," agreed the chastened Monty.

"Of course they're not! My father went west because of a balloon in France," Crispin was saying with bitterness. "He was flying with another chap who didn't figure the bellying out of the balloon cable." He was saying all this so word perfect now that the S. L. sensed he had said it many times before. "My father — so they say — saw what was happening and tried to head the other bird off. He saved him, but he hit the cable himself. No parachutes then, you know."

"I wonder why old March didn't take to the silk," Monty pondered, sucking on the tip of his pencil. "He just sat there, from what the balloon blokes say."

"I don't know, but I'll always feel that March saved me just as my father saved that other chap," Crispin stated, staring off into space above the time board. "I wonder whatever became of that other chap."